HADRIAN

LORD of HOPE

GRACE BURROWES

Hadrian Lord of Hope is Published by Grace Burrowes Publishing
21 Summit Avenue
Hagerstown, MD 21740
www.graceburrowes.com

DEDICATION

To the victims of crime—may they have the truth, safety, restitution, and a meaningful expression of remorse—and to the champions of restorative justice, now more than ever.

The Lonely Lords Series

Darius
Nicholas
Ethan
Beckman
Gabriel
Gareth
Andrew
Douglas
David
Trenton
Worth
Hadrian

CHAPTER ONE

"Must you be so gleeful about your departure?"

Hadrian Bothwell's question carried a hint of peevishness, because in addition to leaving behind the title, the wealth, and the status of Viscount Landover, Harold would also leave *him*, Hadrian, the only family Harold could claim for the past two decades.

"Yes, I must be so gleeful. I've waited years to be this gleeful, Hay." Harold rummaged inside the vast depths of the estate desk, then held up a piece of paper. "I knew it was in here!"

"What's that?"

"My Domesday list." Harold fairly bounced around the desk, bringing the paper to Hadrian. "These are all the petty instructions I'm afraid I'll forget. If you read them now, I can decipher them for you."

Hadrian set the paper aside rather than crumple it in his fist. "You really are leaving."

"God willing," Harold replied, his smile fading. "I pray you won't hate me for it."

Prayer. An interesting notion, considering Hadrian had left a vicar's calling in Yorkshire to heed Harold's summons.

"You'll come back and visit?"

"As often as you like, Hay. Give me time to dust off a convincing amount of Danish and settle myself among mama's cousins."

Sea voyages would lay between Hadrian and his brother, and sea voyages could be fatal. "You'll let me know if you don't end up in Denmark?"

Harold picked up his appropriately named list. "The address of my residence, the exact address, is right on this paper. Louise has been given the same information, in case you lose it, which you won't."

"I most assuredly will not be asking your... associate's wife where my brother has got off to."

"Associate." Harold leaned a hip on the desk and crossed his arms, the picture of typical Bothwell blond, blue-eyed good looks and country-squire health. Hadrian would look exactly like him in ten years.

"What do you call him?" The peevishness was back, closer to the surface, and Hadrian hated it. He also hated Harold's traveling companion, proof positive the Church of England was better off without Hadrian Bothwell in any pulpit.

"I call him Andy," Harold said, though they both knew he also referred to the man in far more intimate terms. "Or Finch, or sometimes, when he's being difficult, James Anderson Finch. If I want to twit him, I call him your lordship."

"Finch, then." A handsome blond fellow with sad blue eyes and a quiet laugh. Also—Hadrian could not fathom this—the father of two boys and a baby girl.

"Do you resent Andy because I'm going away with him, or resent him because he has the audacity to be close to your one and only brother, Hay?"

Close. The very word made Hadrian shudder. "Both, and because you are intent on traveling so far away."

Harold plucked a set of keys from the wax jack and tossed them aloft, catching them neatly. "Off I shall sail, leaving you orphaned amid all this wealth and comfort."

"I don't want the wealth and comfort." A vicar learned not to want them, but Hadrian hadn't missed them one bit during his sojourn with the church.

Up the keys went again, nearly to the cherubs cavorting about the molding.

"Yes, Hay, you do. You've always known you'd be my heir, always had the expectation of the titles, no matter you never traded on them. You'll be good at this."

All true enough, damn the man for his honesty. "I will do my duty. What makes you think I'm any more suited to marriage and procreation than you are?"

Harold's fine blond brows rose in consternation, and this time when he caught the keys, he kept hold of them. "*You?*"

"You assume because I was married to Rue I'm eager to trot up the church aisle and fill the nursery with my offspring."

"You were married to *Rue*," Harold said, firing the keys into a desk drawer and slamming it closed. "Meek, pretty, sweet Rue."

"You didn't like my wife?"

"She was lazy." Harold took a seat behind the desk, looking exactly appropriate there. "Ask your former parishioners if Vicar Bothwell's missus sat at many sickbeds or lying-ins. Ask them if she came to call as soon as condolences could be offered. Did she ever entertain a neighbor's children so the new mother could get off her feet?"

Hadrian perched a hip on the corner of the desk, because they were, after all, to have some difficult, plain speaking. "It's not like you to pillory Rue posthumously."

Though Hadrian would listen to Harold's criticism of Rue endlessly if it kept James Finch from the conversation.

Harold twiddled a white quill pen, a habit Hadrian had seen him indulge in since boyhood. "You do not approve of Andy; I was not pleased with your choice of spouse, either."

Finch was not Harold's spouse and never would be.

"You've had the good manners to keep this discontent to yourself," Hadrian surmised, "because Rue might have produced the Landover heir?"

Abetted by her husband, of course.

Harold brushed the quill across his chin. "You married her, and because she was part of your flirtation with the church, I preferred her company for you to that of some cavalry regiment's."

"Good of you." Hadrian shoved off the desk, because he, too, would have preferred marriage to a cavalry regiment for his only brother. This sailing trip fit somewhere far closer to the regiment than marriage. "Rue wasn't that bad."

Harold set the pen in its stand. "Neither is Andy. I will have this trip, Hay, whether you like him or not, so please like him."

"I'm trying," Hadrian replied, dredging up a smile for his brother. Though Hadrian was all but certain Harold and dear Andy were engaging in hanging felonies upon which the church frowned mightily.

And yet, who better than a former vicar to grasp the need for tolerance among frail and imperfect humans? Who better than a man with only one brother to call his own to admit the folly of casting aside that brother when Harold had all but raised Hadrian?

"Are you asking me to stay?" Harold pretended to study his list, but he was a considerate man, and he'd afford Hadrian what fig leaves he could. "You would still have the burden of the succession, and the Continent is a much more tolerant place for such as I."

What of Andy's lady wife, who had borne him three children—the requisite heir and spare among them? How was she to fare during this indefinite travel in search of tolerance and a fine command of Danish?

"I know you deserve to travel, after all these years of tending your acres, Hal, but I still feel as if I'm sending you away to war. I can't protect you when you're off across the water."

"Nor can I protect you," Harold pointed out, and as the elder by eight years,

Harold had protected Hadrian from much. "When's the last time you really needed a big brother, Hay? You've been all grown up for some time, and I think you turned out rather well."

If honesty was all that remained to them, then honesty they would have.

"I need you," Hadrian said, wandering over to the family Bible, which sat on a gate-legged table across from the hearth and by custom lay open to the Twenty-Third Psalm. Hadrian turned the page, to the Twenty-Seventh Psalm. *Hide not thy face far from me*, indeed.

"Maybe I don't need you the way I did as a youth," Hadrian went on, "but you are all the family I have, and when Rue died, nobody could have stepped in as you did."

"I'll still step in. The mails are more reliable than ever now that the Corsican isn't a threat."

"I've been thinking about that." Hadrian kept his voice even, lest he betray that he'd in truth been fretting endlessly, not merely thinking. "You should take some pigeons with you when you leave here."

"Pigeons?"

Hadrian flapped his hands. "The ones that fly *home?* Hazelton raises them over at Blessings. Wellington used them, and not much besides a bad storm can stop them."

"I hadn't considered them, that's all. It's a good idea, one of many you'll no doubt bring to Landover in the coming years."

Hadrian didn't bother parrying that thrust. He instead appropriated Harold's list, for the Viscount Landover had atrocious handwriting, and there would be no deciphering it in his absence.

"What's this? Aviary? Apiary?"

"Avie," Harold said. "Lady Avis Portmaine, Hazelton's sister, who yet resides at Blessings."

She also yet held Harold's affection—in some manner—for she figured near the top of his list.

"What of her?" Hadrian asked. "She's the lady of the manor now, isn't she? The other three siblings went south, or somewhere."

"She does run the place," Harold said, rising. "She and I are friends, and I regard it as a neighborly responsibility to keep an eye on her."

"She has to be quite of age, and she has two brothers." She also had more than her fair share of bad memories, though those memories would be more than a decade old by now. "What is this eye you want me to keep on her?"

"Avie's isolated over there, Hay," Harold said gently. "She remained cordial with me, because I am no threat to any lady, and she needs friends."

As if being no threat to a lady were an asset—though a vicar was also supposed to be no threat to a lady. "How does she know you're no threat?"

"Because I told her. She was relieved, and you're clergy, or you were, and that means you won't be a threat, either."

"Of course I won't be a threat," Hadrian muttered as he resumed his study of the infernal list. "What is this here? Looks like chocolate, or chandler, or God knows what."

They spent the rest of the morning deciphering Harold's penmanship, but each time Hadrian glanced up at the clock, try as he might to focus on the blighted list, all he could think was that they were closer and closer to Harold's departure date.

And while travel might be a rebirth for Hal, who'd struggled along with secretive half-measures for years as far as his Andy was concerned, for Hadrian the looming separation was yet another loss in a life that had become a long progression of sorrows and disappointments.

* * *

Since Hadrian had left his final church post weeks earlier, he'd wandered through his days with a sense of unreality. Harold's leaving was unreal, putting off the vestments and mannerisms of the clergy was unreal, and resuming life at Landover, where Hadrian hadn't spent any appreciable time for a dozen years, was particularly unreal.

Hadrian watched his brother preparing to leave and tried with limited success not to brood—or pout.

One tonic that effectively banished the dismals was a dose of Cumbrian morning air on a pretty spring day, particularly when enjoyed on the back of a fine, handsome steed. Hadrian ordered Caesar saddled—how long had it been since someone else had groomed and saddled his mount?—and prepared to seize the day.

The temperature was perfect, brisk at first, but suited to the exertion of riding. Caesar, well rested from his jaunt home from Yorkshire, was happy to canter along, soft spring grass under his hooves.

Hadrian had brought his mount down to the walk to cool out when Caesar's ears pricked up and his forward progress hesitated.

"Easy, lad." Hadrian stroked a gloved hand down the horse's crest, for he'd identified the sound his horse had reacted to.

A solo flute, rising up on the crisp country air, was incongruous, though it conjured the unbridled exuberance with which earth and spring reunited. Following the sound, Hadrian nudged Caesar up the track, higher, closer to the music. On and on the melody went, swooping, laughing, and caroling along, until Hadrian could see the musician through a thick stand of pine.

She sat on a rock like some kind of wood sprite, tootling away, no written music, just notes and skill and a flashing silver flute. She swayed minutely with her melodies, eyes closed, fingers slipping over the keys. Gradually the music changed, from vibrant rejoicing to a tender, lyrical, and not quite happy melody.

A cradle song, though the flutist rendered familiar melodies new and sweet. When she finished, she held still for a single moment, then slowly lowered the flute to her lap, eyes closed.

He ought to slip away, for he recognized the soloist now and he did not want to re-introduce himself to her up here, not far from the scene of her assault.

"Is somebody there?"

Lady Avis's voice was lower than Hadrian recalled. He swung off Caesar's back and led the beast from the concealing foliage, because her ladyship shouldn't have to endure the sense of unseen eyes spying on her.

"An appreciative audience," Hadrian said. "An impressed, appreciative audience."

"Sir, you have me at a—*Hadrian?*" Her expression, initially guarded, dissolved into consternation, then sheer joy. Why should she be happy to see him, of all people, and so willing—

She was in his arms, a solid female weight thumping into his chest, her flute set aside as she hugged him.

"Oh, you naughty, naughty man," she said, laughing, holding him at arm's length, then hugging him anew. "I have missed you so, and now here you are, and you look so bloomingly good, Hadrian Bothwell. You do. You caught me, just as you used to, skipping my lessons and playing truant."

She stepped back enough to hold him at arm's length again, leaned in and took a shameless sniff of Cumbrian morning air.

"You still wear a positively delicious scent. The wonderful impression you make on a lady's senses must have helped fill the pews on Sunday mornings."

More than a few of the ladies in the congregation had been damned nuisances, while Avis seemed so…normal. If anything, she'd grown more attractive—lovely dark hair, a fine figure, sparkling eyes. She accounted good looks an asset to a vicar, but would she view beauty as an asset in herself?

"And you," Hadrian heard himself say. "You still carry the scent of spring and meadow flowers." She still had that smile, a curving of her full lips that made a man think she knew wonderful, special secrets, secrets that gave her joy, very possibly secrets related to the fortunate object of her smile.

Though the secrets Hadrian shared with Lady Avis related to nothing worth smiling about.

"May I hope you were on your way to pay a call at Blessings?" she asked.

"You may," Hadrian replied, his vicar's skills allowing him to offer a kindly lie with deplorable smoothness. "Harold will leave on an extended sail later this spring, and I had hoped we could send some of your pigeons along with him."

"I've discussed this extended sail with Hal on many occasions." Avis's voice became censorious. "I trust you have too."

Harold had made up his mind, politely, of course, and the discussion had been quite limited. "I owe Hal much. If he wants a break from Landover, he's my only brother, and I'm his man."

She regarded him with a frankness not many women exhibited, and Hadrian was reminded of other qualities he'd forgotten—through significant effort—about Lady Avis Portmaine.

Her smile was only the start. He'd missed that smile, missed how it warmed his heart and had his own lips curving up. Avis was a bright woman, not only book smart—French, Latin, Greek, Italian, German book smart—and quick with facts and numbers, but also intuitive.

She was pretty too, though not in any conventional sense. Tallish for a woman—the Portmaines were all on the tall side—and dark-haired, as her full siblings were as well. On Avis, that hair carried red highlights, as if some lusty Norseman stalked her ancestry. This wasn't the pale beauty of the English rose, this was an older, more earthy and lasting sort of beauty, less apparent at first glance, and yet more capable of lingering in a man's memory.

"Harold is your only brother too," Avis observed as she deftly disassembled her flute and packed it in a velvet-lined case. "You have a life with the church, and Harold has no business calling you from the Lord's work to hold the reins at Landover while Harold larks about for a few months."

Of course she would think Hadrian was here only for the nonce. God willing, every gossip in the shire would see Hal's trip in exactly the same light, until the permanence of Hal's remove became quietly apparent.

"The Lord's work in Rosecroft village was not urgent," Hadrian answered truthfully. "Not to me and not to my parishioners."

"You had unhappy memories there." Avis draped a cloth over her flute and closed the case. "One can understand this."

She referred to Rue's death, and her solicitude left him feeling like a fraud. He fell back on small talk—a vicar's handiest weapon.

"I have happy memories too," he said. "But tell me how you go on, Lady Avis. Harold was a fine correspondent regarding crops yields and pounds of fleece, but not much for passing along the neighborhood news."

She slipped her arm through his, as if they hadn't walked home from church together for the last time more than twelve years ago.

"Harold was so happy when you took a post here in the North. It's all we heard about for months. He's very proud of you."

Which made one of them. "He's the best of brothers. Overlooking my flaws goes with the description."

Hadrian admonished himself to work on his sincerity. Hal *was* the best of brothers, regardless of his travel plans or preferred company, and Hadrian was nobody to judge him.

Hadrian was out of the judgment business, and glad of it.

"Will you join me for breakfast?" Avis asked as they made their way through the pines. "I rarely have company at Blessings, much less company I'm so glad to see."

"I would be pleased to join you." The church imbued a man with surpassing manners, though sooner or later, the past must intrude on Hadrian's dealings with Lady Avis. That moment would make all of his awkward discussions with Harold pale in comparison. "Riding in this air gives a man an appetite."

"You always could put away a decent meal, and your gelding looks like a horse who enjoys a good gallop."

"Caesar is a St. Just horse," Hadrian said, taking the reins in his free hand. "He's fit as the devil without being hot-tempered." Rather like Harold.

"And handsome," Avis added as they turned onto the track down the hill. "St. Just is the new Earl of Rosecroft?"

"He is," Hadrian replied, pushing a pine branch aside for her. "Former cavalry, as well as a friend."

"I'm glad you had some friends in Yorkshire. I imagine leading a flock can be a lonely business."

All manner of well-polished scriptural allusions begged to come bleating into the conversation. Hadrian pushed those aside too.

"Some flocks engender loneliness, for the congregation as well as its leader," Hadrian allowed, though it had taken him two years to put that label on the emotion his pastoral duties had inspired. "I hope that's not the case here?"

He was done with church business, utterly, absolutely, and that meant he didn't have to listen to griping about the vicar's sermons or the curate's inability to patch together a church without funds. Nonetheless, he hoped Avis found consolation in the company to be had at services.

"I do not attend," she said, dropping his arm.

Silence descended as they made their way down the hill, with Hadrian resenting the need to say something. He wasn't her spiritual authority, not her vicar, not even officially a fellow parishioner that she should burden him with this.

"I'm sorry," Avis said when they reached the bottom of the hill. "It will be like this for us, won't it? I'll understand if you want to decline breakfast, and you're welcome to as many pigeons as Harold can stow on his yacht."

They had been doing so well with the platitudes and small talk. Hadrian made a doomed attempt to regain that false, friendly footing. "Be like what?"

"We will try for cordiality and succeed swimmingly until something slips out amiss, and then all will be awkwardness until somebody tosses out another social nicety. While I cannot expect you to forget, I'm so very—"

She broke off and patted Caesar's neck.

"So very what, Lady Avis?"

She kept her back to him and leaned her forehead against Caesar's shaggy mane. "I used to be plain Avis to you, or even Avie, and now I'm this Lady Avis creature, whom I hardly know, and don't think I'd enjoy. I'll hush now and thank you for your escort."

She reached around him to retrieve her flute case from where he'd tied it to his saddle, but he reached it first, keeping possession.

Hadrian had left the clergy, and thus the only status remaining to him was that of gentleman. A gentleman would admit that his past with Lady Avis included far more than the scandal she'd endured.

"When a neighbor extends a hungry fellow an invitation to share a meal, that fellow does not expect the invitation to be retracted." He winged his arm at her and kept his smile genial.

Her expression went from puzzled to briefly mutinous, but she took his arm.

"Your gardens are impressive for so early in the season," Hadrian said as they approached the grounds behind Blessings. "You must tell me about them."

She accepted that challenge, pausing in her recitation only long enough for Hadrian to hand Caesar off to a groom. Then she fell silent, apparently content to stroll with him up to the stately expanse of the Blessings residence proper. The family seat was a huge old place, befitting a wealthy earldom, and yet to Hadrian, it had never seemed cold or lifeless, particularly not when the grounds were bursting with daffodils, tulips and all manner of flowering trees.

"Blessings looks to be thriving. Your landscaping is sumptuous."

"Winter is so long and cold here, I'm usually desperate for color and beauty by spring, and each year, I grow a little more ambitious."

These beautiful gardens were her passion, then, so he kept to that topic. "Those beds look similar to some we have at Landover. Did you do ours as well as your own?"

"I gave Harold my designs, because he complimented the patterns. Harold is the only man I know who isn't too proud to admire a pretty flower." She went on, describing what species went well together and why, while Hadrian was still trying to puzzle out their little exchange at the foot of the hill. He hadn't precisely been avoiding Blessings, but he had been reluctant to see Avis.

A bond still stretched between them, intimate, precious, and intensely private, but not altogether comfortable for either of them. Or maybe, he thought as she chattered on, there had been a bond, obliterated now, worn away by time, maturation, and the experiences that made up their separate lives.

"What is your favorite flower?" Hadrian asked, because he wasn't quite ready to closet himself with her over kedgeree and toast.

"I love them all," Avis said easily. "From the first crocus to the last chrysanthemum, and everything in between. What about you?"

"I like purple flowers. Purple and blue. Irises, pansies, bluebells, violets and so on. We can't quite replicate that palette of blues, lavenders, and purples God has given to the flowers, and I never tire of admiring it."

She plucked a pansy of a soft periwinkle shade and tucked it into the pin securing his cravat. "I wonder: Would the flowers appeal to us as strongly if the blooms never faded?"

Hadrian let her natter on and occasionally stop to pull off a spent bloom. The morning air was warming up, and wandering around her garden allowed him time to adjust.

This Avis Portmaine was pretty, vital, and confident. In some ways, Hadrian resented her, for she'd replaced a quiet, withdrawn young woman who'd needed him when he'd never been needed before. But that young woman hadn't entirely faded, either, for it had been she, the victim of an unspeakable crime, who'd made that comment about it being "like this" for them before she'd invited him to depart.

Hadrian was no longer eighteen and clueless about how to go on—a vicar also dealt with tragedy and ill fortune in quantity. Nor was he willing to give up a decent breakfast, when it would appease the convention that said he should call upon his closest neighbor now that he was home.

"Did you get my letter?" Avis asked.

Hadrian had to cast back to recover the sense of her words. "I did. Your condolences were much appreciated."

"You miss her?"

"I do," he said, because that was expected, then, "It's been two years, and one adjusts." Because that was honest.

"One does. I will miss Harold sorely; he's been a dear friend."

"Also a wonderful caretaker of our lands. He's leaving Landover in my hands when I've never had responsibility for more than a vegetable garden." The tending of which had been enjoyable only when compared to chairing pastoral committee meetings.

Another spike of gratuitous irritation shot through Hadrian's morning, along with a wave of weary bewilderment.

When would he *settle*? When would he let his old life go and come to terms with whatever this new life would be? When would he stop whining like a boy deprived of his sweet?

Lady Avis bent to snap off a daffodil gone brown and wrinkled. "Your brother loves Landover, so we must conclude he doesn't simply want to travel, he needs to."

Oh, delightful. Harold had not merely a friend in Lady Avis, but an advocate for his damned schemes. Hadrian trudged back into the conversation, trying not to let the effort of making idle talk show in his tone.

"What do you hear from your brothers?"

"Benjamin is in London, keeping a discreet eye on Alex, who has threatened to leave her post in Sussex. Wilhelm is off in Sweden, I think, or Norway by now, and will no doubt wander the north until the end of summer."

"What does he find to do up there?" What would Harold find to do in Denmark—other than make sheep's eyes at Finch?

"Who knows? It's time and past Vim took a wife and settled down, but we've Viking blood in our veins, and Vim must wander and call it trading in various goods."

Hadrian was perversely cheered to realize Avis had also been orphaned by excesses of familial *wanderlust*. "Lady Alexandra is in the south as well?"

Avis paused on the bottom step of a side entrance to the manor house, near a pot of roses still mostly leaves and thorns.

"Alexandra hides, Hadrian. She is an heiress and pretty, and yet she has wasted years governessing at some medieval hall on the southern coast. Her charge's mother has remarried, though, and this means Alex will soon be off again, like a tinker without a home or coin of her own."

The past abruptly swooped close to the conversation again, a raptor hungry to pounce on any stray comment, any veiled allusion.

"Lady Alexandra might enjoy being a governess." Though Hadrian couldn't reconcile that calling with the outspoken, bookish young lady he'd known.

Avis led the way into the house, which was cool and dark compared to the sunny outdoors. "Spare me your manners, Hadrian. Alex needs children of her own, a place to set down roots and to build a life." Hadrian followed her inside in silence, for Avis was likely the one hiding, the one lacking roots, the one…. Maybe she would not want children, would not be able to endure conceiving them.

"How does Hazelton stay out of trouble when he's not keeping an eye on Lady Alex?" The question seemed safe enough, though Hadrian's store of safe topics was running perilously low.

"Benjamin is close-mouthed about it. I suspect he's an expensive snooper."

"A what?"

She opened the door to a small parlor, one Hadrian didn't recall from his youth. The room was defined by the French doors running the length of its outside wall. Sunlight flooded in, bounced off pale hardwood floors, ricocheted into a long mirror on the opposite wall, and vaulted to the high arched ceiling. A half-dozen glazed crocks sported forced bulbs—lemony daffodils, periwinkle blue hyacinths, blushing pink tulips. The furniture was cozy and upholstered in pale colors, and the sense of the entire space was of warmth, light and comfort.

"Benjamin is an investigator for hire," Avis clarified. "You like my parlor?"

"I've never seen a room quite like it." Different wasn't the right word, wasn't a positive enough word.

"When I'm not designing my gardens, I'm turning my sights on the house itself. I spend many of my mornings here or out on the adjoining terrace."

"It's peaceful," Hadrian replied, but peaceful wasn't quite right, either. To step into this room was a relief. Darkness would find no purchase in such a chamber, neither would loneliness. Light poured in and came to stay, bringing with it warmth and cheer.

"The tea trolley should be along soon." Avis took a rocking chair, leaving Hadrian to choose an end of the cushioned sofa. "Tell me about leaving the church. Taking off your collar must be quite an adjustment."

"I haven't really left yet. I'm still nominally entangled with my last congregation." *Though why was that?*

"Over near York? St. Michael's of the Something."

"Sword, though nobody's quite sure where the appellation came from in a county of sheep farmers. The valley is pretty, not that different from our terrain here."

"Not as dramatic," Avis suggested. "The hills don't range quite as high, and they haven't the lakes."

She was reported to remain close to Blessings—very close. "Have you traveled over that way?"

"I have not, though Harold described it to me. He said it's lovely."

"The winters are no better than ours," Hadrian said, wishing the tea tray would arrive so he could dispense with his two polite cups, have a nibble of toast, then be done with this obligation. "The summers are quite fine."

"The summers are too short. You've avoided my question."

Apparently without success. "About?"

"Leaving the church, Hadrian. You've been ordained eight years, and now you must leave it behind."

Why was she the first person to ask him about this?

"I choose to leave it behind," Hadrian said, though it hadn't felt like much of a choice, not when Harold and his Finch had been growing desperate. "I'll miss some aspects of it."

"Such as?"

He was spared an immediate reply by the arrival of the tea trolley, and it was a trolley, of a size that tracks in the hallway wouldn't have been amiss.

"Shall we serve ourselves?" Avis asked, suiting actions to words. She passed Hadrian a cup of tea fixed with a healthy tot of cream and dash of sugar, as he'd always preferred it. "I'll smile graciously, while you make yourself up a plate and concoct a suitably polite, mendacious answer to my question."

The tea was ambrosially strong for even a spring morning in Cumberland could be brisk, while Avis's smile was more welcoming and mischievous than gracious. For the first time that morning, for the first time since coming home, Hadrian's smile was welcoming and mischievous too.

CHAPTER TWO

"What I miss about the church," Hadrian said, as if announcing a sermon topic. He chose a slice of buttered toast, a portion of omelet, a thick slice of ham, and—why the deuce not?—another slice of toast while arranging acceptable and honest thoughts into mental categories.

"I make mine into a sandwich," Avis said, as he assembled his meal. "We're not at table, so feel free to do the same."

Hadrian took a bite of his sandwich. "I haven't done this since university— it's a fine way to consume breakfast."

"We have plenty and you've been riding, so eat up." Avis took a nibble of her sandwich. "What do you miss?"

An astute, tenacious woman.

"A few people," Hadrian said, taking another bite of excellent fare. "Not many. I do miss the sense of rhythm about the life of a vicar."

"What sort of rhythm?"

"The days have a rhythm, as one prays at certain times, and visits, and has visitors, and works on the sermon, and prays some more." *Or one was supposed to.*

"Comfortable but boring?"

"At times, as with anything." How bored was Harold, watching the seasons change year after year at Landover, while feigning contentment? "The weeks have a rhythm, too, punctuated by the service on Sunday, then a day or two to regroup, and then the next service looms. The liturgical year has a rhythm, with high holy days, and conferences with the bishop and so forth at regular intervals. I could see my life unfolding in a certain sequence, and it wasn't unbearable."

Nor was it meaningful, though, and that—the sense of *empty* rhythm—had begun to wear on him.

"What did you do for enjoyment?" She passed him another sandwich, his first having somehow disappeared.

"I enjoyed…" He fell silent, staring at the second sandwich.

Another bog but less treacherous, for he'd had time to ponder this.

"I enjoyed the sense of being useful," Hadrian said. "Of offering some comfort and solace to those in greatest need, and of making remarkable some particular moments of joy."

"Weddings?" Avis guessed.

"And christenings. Those even more than weddings."

"I'd forgotten you'd be involved in those." Avis topped up their tea cups, but of course, babies might be something she'd want to forget. "Have some fruit."

Oranges sat in a blue crockery bowl along with hothouse strawberries.

Hadrian plucked a succulent red berry from the bowl. "You raise these?"

"I do. I've grown self-indulgent in many regards, Hadrian, the gardens and greenhouses being only one example."

Self-indulgent, and isolated. Though maybe an excess of privacy was another indulgence. "Your music being another?"

She grinned at him over her tea cup, and the grin lightened everything—the mood, her face, the room, *Hadrian's* mood.

"I love my music. I will also ask that you leave me at least three of those strawberries, though I've been enjoying them all week and likely will for another week at least."

"Three." Hadrian selected the largest trinity of berries and set them on her plate, then made free with the rest. "These are delicious. I haven't had any since last year."

"You didn't garden over in Yorkshire?"

"Not after the first couple of years." Hadrian paused in his consumption of the strawberries. "The congregants were an odd lot. It became apparent I was to buy my produce from them and use their choice of horse for my transportation, and their choice of housekeeper for my vicarage."

"This sounds more like being a child at the whim of the nursery staff than it does being the spiritual leader of a community."

She'd put words to something he'd avoided admitting even under the heading of honest thoughts.

"All clergy must resign themselves to a paradox," Hadrian said, eyeing a particularly large strawberry. "You are a leader, but in such way that nobody is offended, threatened, imposed upon, or otherwise inconvenienced. You effect this miracle not only because you are a shining example of diplomacy, humility, and self-sacrifice, but also because the folk you're leading stock your larder, shingle your roof and, if they've a mind to, write to your bishop."

"What would your bishop say, if this paradox chafed and the hypocrisy became too oppressive?"

"He'd say get the hell out of the church." Hadrian set the strawberry down. "I'm sorry, that was not well phrased." He rose, but caught the expression on his hostess's face.

Not shocked. Smiling, the minx.

"As a young man, you were intent on joining the military," she said. "You were intent on subduing the enemy and growing rich in foreign climes. Maybe you were the one who suffered the subduing."

"Suffered nominally, perhaps." Though others suffered far worse fates. "But subdued, apparently not."

A cheering thought, which had been in short supply lately.

"Good for you, Hay Bothwell." She smiled again, that soft, wonderful smile, and the word *alluring* popped into Hadrian's head. "Never admit defeat."

"Is that the Portmaine motto?"

"It's my motto," she said, getting to her feet and again slipping her arm through his. "Let's walk off a little of our meal, shall we?"

"If you like." He let her lead him from the bright little parlor, up to the Portmaine portrait gallery, which looked out over the sprawling back gardens.

"I do this with Harold," Hadrian said. "When I've been gone we spend a few minutes the next morning greeting the ancestors."

"A ritual. One with meaning."

"Yes." Her insight pleased him, tremendously, because so many of the supposedly holy rituals had felt devoid of meaning. Theatre conducted to facilitate a social gathering for the village, nothing more.

"Between ritual and routine lies a world of difference," Avis said, pausing before the first Viscount Hazelton. "Did you know he had twelve children and they all lived to adulthood?"

"He was lucky, or his children were." Hadrian would have missed her expression, except he turned his head to study the old fellow in his hose and collar.

Avis Portmaine did want children, desperately. Good God Almighty. The look in her eyes, the sorrow tracing her mouth, and the resolve in her spine all spoke of longing to the point of pain.

Hadrian strolled her past the viscount. "I've considered it fortunate that I did not have children with Rue. They would be struggling along with only me for a family, and any son would be burdened with expectation of Harold's title, and yet he'd be simply a clergyman's son, and that would be difficult."

"One could see it thus." Avis considered the next viscount's more austere countenance. Her gaze shifted then, brows knitting as she glanced out the window. "I wonder where Fen has been. He was supposed to meet with his shepherds this morning."

"Fen?"

"Ashton Fenwick, our steward. He's ridden out, perhaps enjoying the air as you did."

"But?"

"But the man is in the saddle more days than not. He has no need of an aimless ride, and as spring advances, we must organize."

As Hadrian needed to get organized. "For?"

"Lambing is almost done. Before we can drive the sheep up to summer pastures, we must get through shearing and dipping, and all that goes on while plowing and planting are tended to, and foaling, and calving, and we often work in concert with Landover's crews on such things, but Harold has been distracted this year."

"I am *not* distracted. I am, rather, terrified of the responsibility my brother is tossing onto my shoulders." The first time Hadrian had admitted as much, to himself or anyone else.

"Summer would have been a better time for Harold to travel, but fear not, we'll look after you."

They stood by the window, the morning light bringing out rich red highlights in Avis's hair, while down in the stable yard, her steward dismounted and handed his horse off. Hadrian could see the faintest of lines radiating from Avis's eyes, lines that would turn into laugh lines and crinkle with humor.

"I've a favor to ask," Hadrian said, because in some regard, he did need looking after—so did she. "Come to services with me this Sunday."

She moved away from the sunny window. "Hadrian, I do not enjoy attending."

"You think I will?" He tugged her down onto a cushioned window bench and kept her fingers laced with his lest she flee before he'd wheedled his boon from her.

She studied their hands. "You're a churchman, or the nearest thing to it, and Hal will go with you. If you're worried about forgetting names, or not recognizing—"

"I'm not a churchman," he said. "I'm not sure I ever was, and yet I'll be an object of interest, and the local vicar will be friendly but cautious, and then some some-damned-body will spout a piece of scripture, and someone else will reply with another little snippet, and all the while, they'll be watching me, to see how I manage, as if I'm the former but aging champion in an ecclesiastical game of battledore."

"You want me to be your decoy?"

"Not a decoy. Well, perhaps, or at least a distraction. Do you truly never attend?"

"I've been to some weddings. Occasionally I go at Yuletide to hear the children sing. I avoid Easter, though I often supply the flowers."

"I can make sure Hal comes along, and we'll have strength in numbers. You'll do it, then?"

He couldn't read what passed through her eyes, but she squeezed his fingers, then slipped her hand from his.

"Just this once Hay Bothwell, and you are not to let me out of your sight."

"Nor shall you take your gaze from my defenseless little self. Harold will be of no use whatsoever. He's too distracted with his upcoming travels."

They spent a few more minutes discussing the arrangements, and then Hadrian made his excuses, Lady Avis still on his arm as they approached the stables. She swung along beside him, matching his stride easily.

"Fen!" She dropped Hadrian's arm to hail a great brute of a fellow emerging from the stables. "Come meet Mr. Hadrian Bothwell. He'll manage Landover in Harold's absence."

"Mr. Bothwell." Fenwick barely inclined his head, as a dark eyebrow swooped upward. "You're the vicar, aren't you?"

"Former vicar. I'm also Harold's younger brother, and he's asked this of me. I will look forward to working with you this spring."

"Will you now?" The eyebrow lowered and humor flashed in dark, dark eyes. The buccaneering air was complemented by a substantial knife sheathed at his side and a certain slouching grace. "Can't say I've ever seen a vicar actually work."

"Recall your manners, or I'll turn you over my knee, Fen," Lady Avis scolded. "Hadrian is an old and very dear friend, as well as a neighbor. You're to treat him like family, and none of your nonsense."

Fenwick regarded the lady with a martyred air. "Lady Avis is forever threatening. I've yet to grace this knee of hers, not even once."

"Because you're all bluster, while I mean every word I say."

"Is this the vicar's beast?" Fenwick asked when Caesar was led from the stables.

I am not a vicar. "He is. I bought him from St. Just before leaving my last post."

Fenwick gave a low, appreciative whistle and ran a hand down the gelding's neck. "We're in the presence of royalty, Lady Avie. I'd heard St. Just moved up north, but I didn't know he had any stock with him."

"A few youngsters with more to follow this year," Hadrian said, willing to let his horse be admired by all comers. "You're welcome to take him out some day. He's a perfect gentleman."

"And up to my weight," Fenwick said, eyeing Caesar's muscular flanks. "Lady Avie, can you spare your vicar for a bit? I've a mind to try this beast. St. Just mounts are legendary."

"You were supposed to meet with the shepherds, Ashton."

"Already did, my lady." Fenwick hunkered and ran a caressing hand down Caesar's right foreleg. "You could come with us, keep an eye on me and make sure your vicar doesn't come to any harm."

He straightened and frankly leered at Avis, whose mouth thinned with impatience.

"So I can watch the two of you race neck or nothing over rabbit holes like a pair of heedless boys? Thank you, no. When will shearing start?"

They would have, too—raced over bad terrain for stupid, masculine reasons. Hadrian—Lady Avis's old and *very dear* friend—resisted the urge to stick his tongue out at Fenwick.

"Bothwell's herds spent more time on the hills than ours, so we should take off their wool first," Fen said, all business. "A couple more weeks to let the weather moderate and to finish up with the foaling, and we'll be ready to start, assuming his holiness, the vicar, agrees?"

"The former vicar," Hadrian said, *quite* pleasantly. "I'll likely agree once I've conferred with my brother on the matter. Is that your horse?"

A wizened groom led a big, raw-boned chestnut gelding from the stables.

Fen smiled at his horse the way some papas smiled at their firstborn sons. "You see before you Handsome Folly, also know as Handy, who, like his owner, is a fellow of hidden depths and unfaltering loyalties."

Oh, for pity's sake. In the next instant, an odd sort of pleasure welled, as Hadrian realized *he was no longer a vicar.* Truly, absolutely, in every fashion, he was free of his former vocation and could banter with this Fenwick fellow in any manner he pleased.

"He's as loyal to his bucket of oats as you are to your mug of ale," Avis scoffed. "Handy is less likely to be cutting up anyone's peace with his blather. Gentlemen, I'm off, for I never did finish my strawberries. Hadrian." She went up on her toes and kissed his cheek. "Lovely to have you home. I've missed you terribly, so call as often as you can. Fen, behave."

"Yes, yes." Fen waved his riding crop in circles. "Or over your dainty knee I will go. I'm trembling."

Avis snatched the riding crop from his hand, whacked him smartly on his backside, passed the crop to Hadrian and strode off.

"I adore that woman," Fen said, watching her retreat. "I do fear the sentiment is not mutual."

"If your adoration is always so respectfully expressed," Hadrian said dryly, "then one can hardly wonder why it would be." He passed over the crop, shifted to check Handy's girth, and put the stirrups up a hole, while Fenwick let Hadrian's leathers down a hole.

For all his banter and charm, Hadrian's first impression of Fenwick stuck with him: a big, dark brute.

Who called his employer Lady Avie and got his behind smacked for his cheek. That part, Hadrian had rather enjoyed.

Fen swung up and patted Caesar's neck. "Where shall we take them?"

"I haven't done much riding since coming back." Coming *home.* "If you don't mind spending time on Landover's side of the property line, there used to be a nice trail through the deer park."

"Lay on, Macduff." Fenwick gestured with his crop, then fell in beside Hadrian and Handy at the trot.

They rode along in silence, Hadrian using the time to explore Handy's responses. Handy was not as elegant as Caesar and could not boast youthful exuberance, or a perfect distribution of parts, but he was exquisitely trained.

"He'll do one-tempis, won't he?" Hadrian asked.

"When he's warmed up. How does a lowly vicar know of matters equestrian?"

Former vicar, thank the Deity. "I thought I would become a dragoon at one point. I spent all my summers tearing around the neighborhood on horseback. Harold always saw to it I had good horses, and what boy doesn't have at least a phase of horse madness?"

"What rich boy? How does one go from a horse-mad dragoon acolyte to a lowly vicar in the West Riding?"

"One grows up," Hadrian said shortly. "You've pranced around enough. Let's see what your boy can do between here and the property line." He touched his heels to Handy's sides, and the gelding gave a mighty, happy leap forward, followed by a flat-out, breakneck gallop over the relatively level ground before them.

Caesar put his heart into it and came level with Handy's shoulder, but the older horse was the more wily—knew how to conserve his energy, when to leap and when to swerve—and beat Caesar by half a neck when they flew over the stone wall separating Blessings and Landover.

"Good lad." Hadrian patted the horse soundly, and damned if the beast didn't break into a little display of *piaffe.* "Pay attention, Caesar, my boy. You want to grow up to be just like him."

"While I want to survive to tell of his victory," Fenwick groused, but he was patting his horse too. "Handy likes a good romp, and I tend to forget that."

"What about you? Do you share his fondness for a good romp?"

The humor in Fenwick's eyes took on an unfriendly gleam. "Will you counsel me to temperance, Vicar?"

"You are very familiar with your employer." Disrespectful of her, *almost.*

"So you'll join the pack of jackals hereabouts who attribute all manner of venery to her? I am disappointed, Vicar, as I did so like your horse." He was out of the saddle and putting the stirrups up a hole.

"How long have you known Lady Avis?" Hadrian asked, and what the hell was Fenwick nattering on about?

"Long enough to know your pontificating company is not fit to lick her boots," Fenwick said with a great pretense of pleasantness. "That woman has been through more misery than you can imagine, Bothwell, and she's weathered it—every bit of it—on her own. Her brothers are larking about all over creation while Avie tends the family seat, and her sister is too busy poaching other people's children to bother coming north for even a week or two. Get off my horse, now."

"So you can put out my lights?" Hadrian crossed his wrists over the pommel and regarded Fenwick from Handy's back. "I think not."

"I can drag you out of the saddle, but I'll withhold the beating you deserve because Avie would not appreciate the talk. Know this, though: When, like the rest of her neighbors, you don't come calling ever again, I will still be her friend and honored to serve her in any way I can."

Now this was interesting—also disturbing. "By finding me in a dark alley some night and beating me to a pulp?"

Fenwick gave Caesar a final, gentle pat. "If you're not off my horse in five seconds, then I'll swat this one on his handsome quarters and leave you to walk home."

Hadrian swung down. "I did not impugn the lady, not intentionally or otherwise, Fenwick. I asked a question, rather, pertaining to *you*, and here you are, spouting violence at me on Bothwell land."

Fenwick had made the mistake many men did, of assuming vicars sprang out of whole, pious cloth the day they took holy orders, no schoolboy scraps or university fisticuffs to hone their violent abilities.

"You asked if I enjoy a romp, your holiness. I am a healthy male without attachments. You may draw your own conclusions."

Fenwick snatched Handy's reins and would have swung up without bothering to let the stirrups down a hole, but Hadrian spoke slowly and distinctly, as if reciting a prayer.

"I was the one who found her."

Fenwick snorted. "Found her what? Languishing away here in Cumberland?"

"Twelve years ago," Hadrian said. "I was the one who found her, not two hundred yards over that rise, bruised, bleeding, half-naked and incoherent, her hands so cold they'd freeze your soul. If you trifle with Lady Avis, I shall kill you."

The words came out of Hadrian's own mouth, he heard them, and he meant them, but he had no idea where they'd come *from*.

Fenwick paused in his fussing with his stirrup leathers. "You mean this. You'd bloody kill me."

"In a heartbeat, and Hal would prime the gun for me."

Fenwick finished adjusting his equipment while Hadrian gloried, *gloried* in a purely violent impulse.

Fenwick swung into the saddle and for a moment simply sat on his unmoving horse. "Mount up, Saint Peter. We shouldn't let the horses stand around after they've had a good run."

They ambled along in the dappled sunshine of the Landover home wood, Hadrian's gratifying bout of temper cooling as the horses walked along.

"Avie doesn't talk about it," Fenwick said. "Her past is always there, in what she says, what she doesn't say, when the neighbors talk about her and in their silences."

Harold had called Avis retiring. "She's ostracized?"

"Of course. She allows it, as do those worthless brothers of hers."

Avie's brother were not worthless. They had very likely left her in peace at the family seat at her own insistence. "She was the victim of a heinous crime. Why on earth would she be castigated for that?"

"She was engaged to Collins at the time," Fenwick reminded him. "Some say Collins should not have been run out of the country simply for anticipating the vows. What could be more encouraging to a lusty young man than when a lady accepts his suit? She is regarded by some as a tease, a strumpet, a high-born lady who could not uphold the standards of conduct attendant to her birthright, and so forth."

Regarded by *some* was bad. A single dedicated gossip could ruin a woman's reputation, and "some" could ruin her life. "I had no idea."

"How could you? You were too busy ministering to the deserving faithful."

While Fenwick was becoming protective of his employer.

"Harold said nothing of this." Though, Hadrian hadn't exactly asked about Avis, had he?

"Harold is a title, and such an inherently good man, nobody thinks to include him in the gossip. Besides, he's known to be great friends with the Portmaine family, and his loyalties would not brook slander."

"Neither will mine. Does everybody regard Lady Avis in this unkind light?" Had Avis withstood this treatment for *twelve years*?

"Of course not. Though all it takes is one disdaining look, one little sniffy aside, and Avis retreats, until circumstances compel her to venture forth again."

Retreat was all bullies needed to inspire them to greater viciousness. This was true in the churchyard, the schoolyard, and everywhere in between. "Benjamin and Wilhelm tolerate this?"

"Benjamin and Vim are the highest-ranking title and deepest pockets in the shire, respectively," Fenwick said patiently. "Nobody would treat her amiss in their presence, and neither one of them will look beneath the surface where their sisters are concerned."

"Because their sisters have convinced the entire world they don't want anybody's probing."

"I can't speak for the governess. Avis is very clear her brothers are not to worry for her, so they've given up trying."

Caesar shuffled to a halt. "Good ehavens, what have I done?"

"Beat me on my own horse?"

Yes, handily. "Not that. I've coerced Lady Avis into attending services with me this Sunday, and the churchyard is the very last place she'll be comfortable."

Much like Hadrian himself, for different reasons.

Fenwick drew up at the edge of the deer park and regarded Hadrian in the brilliant morning sunshine. "Why'd you do it?"

"I thought I'd be doing her a good turn. Getting her off the property, out among the neighbors."

"Fair enough." Fenwick nudged his mount along the fork in the trail that turned toward Blessings. "But then we must ask ourselves, why did Lady Avis agree to go with you?"

* * *

Hadrian had seemed so lonely, so alone, holding Avis's hand in the cool morning sunshine of the portrait gallery, the Portmaine ancestors silently looking on. She should never have agreed to attend services with him, never fallen for his pretty words, or his charming smile, but the idea that she could do something for him—for *him*—had been irresistible.

He was irresistible, exactly as he had been twelve years earlier, a handsome youth on the cusp of truly attractive manhood. She'd adored him then, even before Hart Collins had assaulted her, and then after... Hay Bothwell had saved her life, her sanity, and her soul, just as he'd also broken her heart.

"You look preoccupied this morning." Lily Prentiss, Avis's companion, stood in the parlor doorway.

"The morning has been busy. Fenwick met with the shepherds and is off to confirm shearing plans with Landover, and I tarried too long on my constitutional and haven't started on the correspondence yet."

"It's a pretty day," Lily said, advancing into the room on a swish of pale blue skirts. She was blond, well formed, and less than a decade Avis's senior, and the blue looked good on her. "You can be forgiven for spending time out in the fresh air, though wandering on your own will never be a good idea."

"I didn't leave Blessings, and I stayed within shouting distance of the stables." *And you are not my gaoler.*

"If you say so." Lily's tone was diffident, not quite deferential, nor would Avis have wanted it to be.

"Are those menus?"

"I went ahead and brought them up." Lily passed along the papers in her hand. "It's Tuesday, and cook will be asking."

"I'd like to have the Bothwell brothers over for Sunday dinner." Avis leafed through the menus and shuffled Sunday's to the top.

"Brothers? Do you mean Landover and Lord James?"

"Lord James was Harold's guest," Avis explained. "Or he often has been, but no, not Lord James, but rather, Hadrian Bothwell."

Lily took a seat in one of the rockers. "I've been here nearly ten years, Avis, and I've never met Landover's brother. Let me guess, this brother has eight sons and that explains Harold's unwillingness to marry."

"No sons." Avis scratched notes on Sunday's menu to add two guests to the number expected. Lily had been with her only seven years, which somehow had started equating to a decade. "Hadrian Bothwell is ordained and a widower. Shall we have rice or potatoes?"

"Rice. More exotic than sorry old mashed potatoes."

"But potatoes lend themselves so nicely to cheese." This was what Avis's life had come down to: choosing vegetables and hoping her dinner invitation would not be politely refused.

"So it's the brother we must find a wife for?"

"Hadrian is quite capable of finding his own wife." As he had proven handily. Avis wrinkled her nose, second-guessing her selection. "Worthy vegetables are such a challenge this time of year."

"A viscountcy is flirting with escheat just across the property line, and you are worried about vegetables."

"Hadrian and Harold are both quite young enough to have large families yet. I hardly think ruin lurks around the corner."

The words were out of her mouth before Avis realized how they'd sound, and then they hung in the air, putting that awful, pitying look on Lily's pretty face.

"Ruin seldom announces its intent to call," Lily said quietly. "Much less its desire to become our nearest neighbor."

"Potatoes," Avis said. "Baked with our own cheddar and the earliest chives we can find."

Lily rose, rather than finish the sermon she was doubtless dying to deliver. "That sounds delicious. You'll bring those back to Cook?"

"When I'm done with them, and you will join us for luncheon on Sunday, Lily Prentiss. I won't be left to manage two hungry fellows on my own, much less three."

"Three?"

"Fen usually joins me on Sunday." Which Lily knew very well. "I do so enjoy tormenting him over his manners."

"Avis, have you considered that just possibly—"

Avis rose as well, abruptly tired to her bones with old arguments and old lectures that always rang loudly with "for your own good."

"Fen is my steward, and he's the next thing to family, and of course I will confer with him from time to time."

"But at table? He's too flirtatious by half, which only fuels the worst gossip."

"My own staff knows better than to gossip, or they had better. Fen flirts with everybody, so don't borrow trouble."

"No, Avis, he does not flirt with everybody." Lily let the implications sink in with a meaningful silence, then twitched her pretty skirts and left the parlor.

CHAPTER THREE

"Ashton Fenwick!" Harold rose from the estate desk and extended a hand. "When did you get back?"

"Several weeks ago," Fen said, returning the handshake. "Certain neighbors have been too preoccupied to bother noting my august presence."

"I'm noting it now. Winter in the south seems to have agreed with you."

"It usually does. Look what I found wandering the property line and in need of escort home."

"My errant baby brother." Harold grinned hugely, out of all proportion to the trite conversation. "He went missing from the breakfast table, and here I thought you'd gone back to bed, Hay."

"I took Caesar out. Fenwick wants to finalize his plans for the flocks, and I thought your imprimatur needed on such a serious undertaking." He took Caesar out almost daily, in sheer defense of his sanity, and also in hopes of hearing a certain flutist soloing among the pines.

"One hesitates to point it out, Bothwell," Fen said, "but aren't you the good shepherd in the family?"

One *delighted* in pointing it out.

"Stow it, Fen." The warning came from Harold, sparing Hadrian the effort. Fenwick rode like a demon, and he was protective of Avis, which ought to be marks in his favor, but Hadrian still felt a rankling unease around him.

Which was probably how Fenwick wanted it.

"I'm on my way to the kennels," Harold said. "Can we talk sheep over a morning visit to the hounds?"

"Avie said you were dispersing your pack," Fen replied as they moved off.

"What's afoot, Landover?"

Harold explained about crosses and traits and reasons why a man might want to start all over on his breeding program—tripe, the lot of it. Harold had found homes for his hounds because he didn't intend to come back. The knowledge made his eventual departure so much more real that Hadrian felt a pressing need to kick something.

"You're not inclined to stay your brother's hand in this?" Fenwick asked Hadrian. "He has the best pack this side of Ireland."

"I do not ride to hounds," Hadrian said, "and even were I inclined to start, I'll be so busy in Harold's absence, my first outing would have to wait until the hounds were ready to pounce on me rather than old Reynard."

"You'd make a meal," Fen allowed, "but surely, you'll not part with this handsome fellow?" Even from his considerable height, Fen didn't need to squat to pet the dog in question.

"Hamlet comes with me," Harold said, fondness in every syllable. "We'll visit his relations in Denmark, after all, or at least I hope to."

"Do they still have boar hunts there?" Fenwick asked. "I thought the Danes bred his kind for large game."

"The Danes, the Germans, and many noble courts throughout Europe," Harold said. "Also for companionship and protection, and just about every other fine quality in a fellow."

"Except fine fellows don't generally drool, chew up your best boots, and get hair all over the rugs and sofas." Fen offered that litany as he continued to pet the great beast, whose adoring gaze never left Harold.

Hadrian begrudgingly agreed with Fen, but promised himself he wouldn't make a habit of it. The dog, generally termed a Great Danish hound, was the most recent in a succession of his kind that Harold considered more pet than anything else.

Landover had sported dogs like Hamlet as far back as Hadrian could remember—stinking, drooling, and creating a great fuss when they decided to bark at some hapless rabbit.

God help him, was he jealous of even his brother's dog?

Harold paused some moments later in a litany of canine begats and out-ofs worthy of a book of the Old Testament.

"You're wool-gathering, Hay, though considering the topic, probably appropriate. We'll start shearing in a couple weeks' time, and you'll have to see it through, because I'll be leaving for Harwich."

Yes, and from thence to specific ports Hadrian was not yet privy to. "I thought I'd see you set sail."

"We can discuss that later. Fen, may we offer you sustenance before you leave us?"

"Perhaps something to drink and water for my horse."

"He's long since lost his saddle and bridle and found a pile of fodder," Harold assured him. "Hay, you'll join us?"

"No, thank you. I've some letters to write, and I've had my gallop for the morning. Fenwick, a pleasure."

He strode off, knowing his departure likely puzzled Harold, but seeing his brother in the role of hail-fellow-well-met bothered Hadrian. Harold was the best of men, but knowing what Hadrian did about his brother now, Hadrian's imagination wandered into nasty, dirty corners.

Did Fen suspect Harold could be attracted to him?

Did Harold watch Fen the way Fen had watched Avis's retreating backside? The way Hadrian had nearly done?

How in the bloody, benighted, stinking hell was Hadrian to tolerate months and months of this subterfuge of simple companionship with Finch? And when, please God when, would the jokes and innuendos about Hadrian's career in the church stop?

Hadrian's mood, not particularly sanguine at the start of the day, stumbled toward an irritable despondency. When his morning's post included a letter from Devlin St. Just, his spirits rose.

Before Hadrian had finished his reply to St. Just, Harold interrupted. He sprawled on the library sofa, his hound hitting the floor beside him.

"You're conscientious about your letters."

"With friends, of course. Staying in touch with St. Just takes no discipline."

"Nor will it take discipline for me to stay in touch with you, but leaving will be difficult."

Resentment flared—yet again. "You expect me to sympathize with this difficulty?"

"You need not." Harold scratched Hamlet's ears lazily. "I know this will be hard for you, which is why I'd rather you not accompany me to Harwich on Monday."

Hadrian cast sand on his unfinished letter, which he'd been filling with drivel about the beauty of spring and the pleasure of renewing old acquaintances.

"Monday is less than a week off."

"You've spent half this year scampering over the mountains and back on this bishop's or that friend's errand, and while I appreciate that you want to spend time with me, Hay, you're also putting off settling in here."

"I was raised here. I don't need a map to the breakfast parlor."

"You'll be Landover in all but name," Harold replied gently. "Your first priority is the estate, and spring is no time to be waving your handkerchief at your brother on the other side of England."

"If I'm to be Landover, then my first priority is the well-being of my family, and that would be you, you and only you."

"You can address that too." Harold left off petting his beast. "Take another wife, get you some babies. I'd adore my nieces and nephews, Hay. Spoil them rotten."

"And come visit them, bringing their Uncle Hal's dear friend James as well?"

"If he's welcome, then yes, occasionally."

The words were offered with a thread of steel, Harold rarely showed. Hadrian rose from the desk, needing to pace, or scream, or hit something, but preferably not his brother.

He hoped.

"James Finch will not be an uncle to my children," Hadrian said. "He cannot be, nor will I allow the fiction that he's some sort of informal cousin. His brother's the heir to a bloody marquessate, for God's sake."

Harold unfolded himself from the sofa and assessed Hadrian in silence while the dog rose as well.

"What?"

"Pitch all the tantrums you need to, Hay," Harold said. "I cannot stay here for another thirty-seven years, so that you can be a martyr to the church, and I can be a martyr to duty. If you're not happy, then you need to fix that. I can't fix it for you, though God knows I would if I could."

At least when Harold left, the dog would go with him. The sheer petulance of thought shamed Hadrian as fraternal lectures could not.

"When you announced your decision to join the church," Harold went on evenly, "my advice and outright bribery meant nothing to you."

Joining the Church of England hardly equated with sailing off to Denmark.

"I made the right decision at the time," Hadrian replied. "For me, at least. You would have immured me here as some kind of glorified steward, or bought me a seat in the Commons, and I've neither vocation."

"And your vocation for the church?"

How deftly Harold could twist a knife, and with what good intentions. "Was adequate for a time."

"That is horse shite," Harold retorted. "You were so damned rattled after the Portmaines' troubles that you scrambled into the arms of the church like a frightened boy, and you couldn't hear my suggestions that you consider other options or simply wait to take holy orders."

Something inside Hadrian snapped, something violent, and frighteningly appealing.

"You," he said in lethally soft tones, "wanted me to avoid the church, because it made your eventual plans for me and your choice of companions all that much more dangerous and uncomfortable. A brother in Parliament far to the south might overlook his rusticating elder's felonious eccentricities, but a man of the cloth could not."

Silence hung, while the dog looked back and forth between the two brothers, his expression worried.

Harold's hand dropped to the dog's ears. "You're missing St. Michael's, are you? Missing your pastoral committee's guidance, composing brilliant sermons in your head even as you ride the land here, pausing in your day to pray every few hours?"

Hadrian was silent, Harold's blows too well placed to parry.

"Come to Harwich if you like," Harold said. "That will leave Fen and Avis to see to Landover's shearing, to get our flocks up the hills, to make the decisions should the plowing and planting get behind schedule with rain or damage to the equipment or injury to the teams. I've done the same for Blessings, but if we say our good-byes here, Hay, we'll have privacy when we part."

Harold left the room, taking his idiot dog with him, while Hadrian resumed tending to his correspondence, and all the cheerful, false sentiments it contained.

* * *

"Master Hadrian." Tiny old Mrs. Carruthers beamed up at Hadrian, smaller and more wizened than any adult human had a right to be. "We are so happy to have you back among us. The Lord can wait His turn to get His hands on you, if you ask me. We've need of you here."

"I'm happy to be here." Hadrian had been spouting platitudes and civilities all morning, while that traitor, Lady Avis, had slipped away from him at the first opportunity. She was no doubt sitting in the coach right now, laughing heartily.

"Come on, Granna." Mrs. Carruthers's son, Young Deal, linked his arm through his mother's. The man was sixty if he was a day, but his father, Old Deal, had passed away only eight years ago. "You mustn't stand about in this breeze or you'll regret it tomorrow. Mr. Bothwell, we'll see you at shearing, if not before."

They left Hadrian an opening to depart for the safety of his equipage, and before any more neighbors, former retainers, local shopkeepers, or the tinkers coming up from the south could accost him, Hadrian made his escape. He was surprised Avis wasn't in the coach, but did find Lily Prentiss waiting patiently.

"Lady Avis isn't with you?" Hadrian asked.

"She is not," Lily said, tugging at pristine white gloves. "She gets out so seldom, and then has a hard time tearing herself away. She can't help it. Her nature is friendly, but not everyone understands that."

An odd observation—Avis was not a garrulous girl at her first assembly. Hadrian attributed Lily's worry to the protectiveness of a longtime employee toward her employer.

"I'll find her." Hadrian withdrew from the coach and closed the door. His height gave him an advantage, but he did not see his quarry among the faithful gossiping in the churchyard.

"In the graveyard, most like," said Mr. Chadwick, at Hadrian's elbow. With sandy hair starting to thin, a liberal complement of freckles, and friendly blue eyes, Chadwick was the picture of the country vicar. The *contented* country vicar.

"Chadwick." Hadrian extended a hand. "Excellent sermon." Though Hadrian could not recall a word of it.

Chadwick smiled the perfect, complaisant smile appropriate to post-service pleasantries. "Had I some warning you'd join us, I'd have got out some of my heavy artillery, but we're all so glad to see winter retreating, weighty thoughts of any kind are an effort."

"Don't waste your powder on my account. One of the aspects of your position I do not miss is the need to be either witty or profound for twenty minutes every week." Preferably both.

"Witty generally garners more listeners than weighty," Chadwick said. "If you ever want to talk about what else you don't miss, or even some of the things you do, you know you're welcome at the vicarage."

"You must call on us at Landover," Hadrian said, trying to mean it, though who was *us*? "Did you suggest Lady Avis is in the graveyard?"

"I saw her slip off that way. I've invited her to services more times than I can count, but she rarely comes, and when she does, it's like this. The last hymn concludes, and she vanishes."

"Shall we walk?"

Chadwick had the instincts of a churchman, and he no doubt sensed the flock circling closer the longer he and Hadrian chatted.

"Lovely morning for a stroll," Chadwick said, moving off with Hadrian. "The children you sent us continue to thrive."

"They're well and happy, then?"

"There," Chadwick said quietly. "The boy patting your off-side wheeler."

"That's a Carruthers, isn't it?"

"Deal's youngest grandchild. They tried and tried, and the Lord didn't bless them with a baby. It's a wonder the lad learned to walk, so constantly did his parents hug and fuss him."

"And the girl?"

"Her parents have three boys. The last lying-in didn't go well, and they're not to have more. The girl was explained as a cousin's child, and too many at the cousin's table. She is well loved and well protected."

"Happy endings, then," Hadrian said. He'd underestimated Chadwick.

"Will we be a party to any more such happy endings?"

"I cannot say. Foundlings have a way of turning up when they're least expected, and I'd hope my successor at Rosecroft would feel free to call on us if the need arose."

Chadwick let Hadrian precede him through the lych-gate. "If that should be the case, there are more families here who would open their hearts to a child."

"Good to know," Hadrian murmured, as he spotted Lady Avis on a bench at the far side of the graveyard.

"I'll leave you," Chadwick said, touching Hadrian's arm, as if Hadrian sought to commune with the dead rather than one pretty lady. "Please let Lady Avis know how happy we are to have her company."

"I'll do that." Why wouldn't Chadwick extend his welcome in person? He was the vicar, the moral compass of the community and leader of the faithful.

Who doubtless had his own pastoral committee to placate.

Hadrian ambled across the graveyard where he'd played as a child and attended a few burials as he'd matured. He trespassed on long association and took a seat beside the lady uninvited.

"Visiting the departed?"

"Hiding from those yet to depart."

"You abandoned me, Avis Portmaine. I suffered all manner of fawning, cooing, and teasing."

"Teasing?"

"Wandering back into the fold. Napping through the sermon for a change, the usual lame jokes."

"They are coping too, Hadrian."

"With?"

"Harold is a good neighbor to one and all. Anybody in need could prevail on him, and he'd lend a hand. Your neighbors are worried you'll not continue that tradition and with reason, when times have been difficult."

"I wasn't off in Peru. I know what the past few winters have been like. I know how many widows the Corsican's armies created. I read the *Times*, the same as Harold no doubt does."

Why was it every bench in every churchyard had the same hard, damp, chilly, uncomfortable quality?

"You've been gone for twelve years," Avis said. "People change."

"People also run off and leave unsuspecting friends at the mercy of Gran Carruthers. That woman has claws, so tightly did she pinch my forearm."

Avis rose, all unassisted. "She cut a dash, back in the day. You mustn't begrudge her a moment on the arm of a handsome fellow."

"Back in German George's day."

"Is there any part of you that's glad to be back, Hadrian?"

He was about to say no. He felt that out of sorts, and that honest, but Avis was regarding him with such patience, such concern, he surprised himself.

"I am glad to see you again. Glad to see that you are thriving and your life has meaning, and you still have the kindest smile a man ever beheld."

"You say that so seriously." That smile he'd mentioned graced her features, conjured by his compliment, and inside him, something eased. He could still make a solitary lady smile.

Hadrian winged his arm. "Your companion awaits us in the coach. If we make a dash for it, we might elude capture by the enemy."

"Or we could take the path around the outer hedge, then there'd be no dashing needed."

Hadrian acceded to that suggestion because it would give them more privacy, and Avis apparently craved solitude, despite Lily Prentiss's comments to the contrary.

"When did you acquire Miss Prentiss's services?"

"She was Vim's idea, seven years ago or so, when it became clear my future lay at Blessings. She's mostly my companion and a little bit my secretary, and eyes and ears belowstairs. Her papa was a churchman, who, like you, stepped down from his pulpit, though I'm not entirely sure of the circumstances."

"Lily's your curate." A thankless post and a handy ecclesiastical cupboard for storing unmarried clergy. "I never had a curate. The livings I took were too humble."

Hadrian had surprised her. His determination to minister without a curate had surprised him too.

"Your brother holds an old title, you've family wealth, and you're astute. Why the modest livings, Hadrian?"

Rue had asked the same thing, repeatedly, suggesting she'd aspired to be the wife of a bishop, not a garden variety rural vicar.

"I had no need of coin, and the church is full of worthy men dependent on their flocks. Those fellows were motivated to take on the more ambitious parishes, and then too, Rue wanted to remain close to her sisters."

They reached the coach, sparing Hadrian further interrogation. Lily Prentiss's relief was palpable, though Hadrian was forced to leave the ladies to pry Harold away from a discussion with one of the local squires.

"He wanted Hamlet." Harold settled in beside Hadrian on the backward-facing seat. "Can you believe such nonsense?"

"What could he have been thinking?" Hadrian did not roll his eyes, while Avis took an inordinate time to adjust her skirts.

"Exactly." Harold thumped his cane on the roof, and the coach moved off. "That dog hasn't left my care since he was a pup, and God willing, I'll be the one to plant him. Did Chadwick grill you terribly?"

"He's a smart fellow. He has the vocation." A relief, that. To find a true churchman contentedly ministering to the flock in Hadrian's back yard.

"Chadwick knows the only good sermon is a short sermon," Harold said. "Miss Prentiss, you are blessed with a particularly pretty soprano."

The rest of the journey to Blessings continued in that vein, while Hadrian watched the greening countryside go by and wondered if next Sunday, he could skip services without causing a storm of gossip.

Though—novel thought—what would the gossip matter when Hadrian was no longer a vicar?

Lunch was a pleasant meal, which Fenwick joined. He queried Harold regarding plans for plowing and planting, the progress made thus far with foaling, lambing and calving, and Harold's schedule for the rest of the spring and summer.

Hadrian listened with half an ear, until Fenwick rose. "I'm for a stroll, and you, Landover, have an appointment in the stables. The lads want to make their farewells to you."

"Fair enough." Harold got to his feet. "I'm in need of some movement as well."

Fenwick turned his smile on his hostess. "Avie, dearest, you'll grace my arm?"

"If I must."

"I was such a good boy at table, I think I deserve better than that."

"You were a hungry boy," Avis countered, as she took Fenwick's arm with easy familiarity.

"Miss Prentiss." Hadrian held the lady's chair, bowing to the inevitable. "Will you oblige me with your company?"

"I'd be delighted, particularly if we maintain enough distance from Mr. Fenwick that we needn't overhear his efforts at conversation."

"I heard that, Lilith," Fenwick called as he held the door for Avis. "Your scorn maketh my manly confidence to wither."

Lily treated Fen to a scolding silence, and Hadrian to a long-suffering sigh.

"He means no harm," Hadrian observed as they gained the back terrace.

"Men never do, then some unsuspecting young lady can't distinguish between teasing and worse, and disaster strikes."

"You refer to any lady in particular?" A good dozen yards ahead, Fenwick bent close to Avis, all but kissing her cheek.

Miss Prentiss nodded at the other couple. "You see? He might be stealing a kiss, but Lady Avis won't realize he's up to no good until it's too late."

"A kiss stolen under these circumstances is little more than joking between familiars. Do you have an interest in gardening, Miss Prentiss?"

For she certainly had an interest in digging about in the dirt.

"The gardens are Lady Avis's domain, and she does a wonderful job with them." Miss Prentiss offered this as if she were a mother complimenting a child's hobby.

"You have other pastimes, I take it?"

"I am but a companion, Mr. Bothwell. A friend as well, I hope, but my time is not my own." Her tone reminded Hadrian of his late wife, and the comparison flattered no one. Rue had tried her best.

"Shall we enjoy the walk through the birches?" Or perhaps stroll over a bed of hot coals?

"I'd really rather keep Lady Avis in sight, in case she has need of me."

"The daffodils, then." Hadrian couldn't criticize devotion to duty, even if Avis was unlikely to recall Miss Prentiss trailed along behind her.

"How long do you think Lord Landover will be traveling, Mr. Bothwell?"

"There's no telling. Harold has been chained to his oar at Landover since early manhood, and he deserves time to ramble and roam." Nothing less than the truth, damn it.

The daffodils were in their glory, sending a sweet, sunny scent aloft on the afternoon breeze. Despite the company, the scent soothed Hadrian's mood.

"What of you, Mr. Bothwell? Lady Avis says you went from university to your first church post and haven't taken a holiday since. You could hire a steward and go with your brother."

"If the boat were to sink," Hadrian pointed out, "thus endeth the house of Bothwell." Then too, Hadrian had not been invited to join his brother, and the notion of sharing a yacht with Harold and Finch held no appeal anyway.

"My goodness. I suppose you'll be looking for a wife sooner rather than later."

She was still nosing about, however delicately. Maybe, to the daughter of a minister, life would ever be one great churchyard.

"If I were looking for a wife, the last thing I'd do is announce my task." Hadrian winked to suggest camaraderie rather than rebuke, but this bantering small talk was tedious and tiring.

Just what did Fenwick discuss so intently with Avis?

"I assume you've already familiarized yourself with the local ladies?"

Lily Prentiss was damnably persistent. "I grew up here, Miss Prentiss. I consider many of the ladies cordial acquaintances, but none are under consideration in any other capacity."

"They can be very intolerant." Intolerance was apparently a deadly sin in Miss Prentiss's opinion. "Lady Avis was sorely tried in her youth, though you may not know the details. The upshot was a broken engagement, and many of the ladies have never forgiven her for that."

"I was at university when Lady Avis came of age," Hadrian said, because something in Lily Prentiss's words again rankled—but then, everything rankled of late. "That was a long time ago. How does Lady Avis get her daffodils to grow so large?"

"Fenwick would tell you it's a matter of fertilizer, and enjoy conveying the information in as indelicate a manner as possible."

"You don't approve of him?"

"I don't approve of any man who thinks Avis Portmaine is available for a flirtation. Ashton Fenwick does not know his place."

Hadrian was coming to like that about him. "Isn't it for Lady Avis to say what his place is?"

"My regard for Lady Avis is without limit, Mr. Bothwell, but her judgment has been faulty in the past. I will not share details, though you may trust that I have only her best interests at heart when I regard Mr. Fenwick's attentions with skepticism."

Oh, for mercy's sake. Avis was not some blushing seventeen-year-old fluttering around London in anticipation of her first season.

"In the next few weeks, Mr. Fenwick will be kept so busy, you won't have to worry about him attending to anything but woolly sheep and bleating lambs."

Thankfully, they'd come full circuit on the tiled slate walkway. Fenwick bowed over Lady Avis's hand, and Hadrian made a correspondingly appropriate fuss over Lily Prentiss.

"I'm off to the stables to say my good-byes to Harold," Avis said. "He'll try to slip away without any scenes, but the lads have their orders."

"I'll leave you then," Miss Prentiss said. "Mr. Bothwell, my thanks for your escort." She left in a swirl of skirts, her curtsy to Hadrian as deferential as her rudeness to Fenwick was blatant.

"I don't think she cares for you, Fenwick." Which was puzzling.

"She doesn't care for anybody or anything that comes between her and Avis," Fenwick said. "Much less my dirty, disreputable self."

"You're reasonably well turned out. Any steward will work up a sweat if he's earning his salt." Today Fen was without his sizeable knife, though even in Sunday finery, he bore a piratical air.

"You don't know, do you, Bothwell?"

"What don't I know?" Hadrian fell in step beside him as they trailed Avis to the stables.

"My mother was the daughter of an Irish earl," Fenwick said. "My father was a younger son of an impoverished Highland title, and a rascal. He eventually married my mother, though by then I was a busy little fellow with two younger sisters. As it happens, my younger brother might well inherit that Highland title, and so I keep my distance here for the nonce."

"You had a mother and a father." Hadrian slapped his riding gloves against his palm, wondering if he'd ever escape small-minded rural communities. "The same can be said for each of us."

"My parents were hardly respectable, Bothwell. Not according to any customs recognized in civilized society."

Hence Fen's swagger and flirtatiousness, in aid of living down to the family tradition of disgrace.

"I've often wondered if Cain and Abel were legitimate," Hadrian mused. "Who cried the banns and in what church? How did they know what vows to say? Heaven help us, none of Adam and Eve's offspring could have been baptized, for the custom of dashing cold water at squalling infants hadn't yet originated. I must conclude that by the lights of Genesis, we are all illegitimate in our antecedents."

"Some vicar you are. Did you dazzle the bishops with that thinking?" Despite his flippant tone, Fenwick's expression was considering—respectfully so.

"Dazzling bishops should not rank high on any Christian's list of priorities. Is Miss Prentiss a lady fallen on hard times, that she must be in service here at Blessings?"

Hadrian asked, because something about the name Prentiss rang a vague, churchly, bell.

Fenwick slowed his march as they drew near the stable. "The fair Lily is one of Vim's brilliant ideas. She's the daughter of some clergyman who put off his collar, though nobody seems to have any details beyond that. Avie had no females about, and Vim was trying to salve his conscience for leaving his sister alone for months on end."

"Lady Avis does seem to appreciate the company."

Fenwick came to a halt as Avis disappeared into the stables. "You've heard the expression, the girls all get prettier when you're drunk and the pub is closing?"

"Well, no, not exactly." Not for twelve years or so.

"Lady Avis has no other source of female companionship. *Of course* she would appreciate Lily Prentiss."

He stalked off, yelling at the lads to fetch the Bothwell coach, while Hadrian wondered how, exactly, an earl's daughter had become so smitten with a laird's rascally son that she'd tossed propriety to the winds, three times over, before solemnizing their union.

Ashton Fenwick certainly came from passionate, if not exactly respectable, stock.

CHAPTER FOUR

"You'll use those pigeons?" Avis asked Harold as Hadrian watched them emerge from the stables.

"I promise I will." Harold patted the hand she'd wrapped over his forearm. "I will write frequently and send back whatever fantastical treasures I find that might appeal to you."

"You don't need to send gifts, Harold. Just be safe and happy, and let us know how you go on. I'll miss you."

"None of this sentiment, Avie Portmaine," Harold replied, wrapping her in his embrace. "You'll have need of my handkerchief, and then I'll have to borrow Hay's when we get into the coach." He held her, his chin resting on her temple, while Hadrian considered riding back to Yorkshire for the sheer, predictable hell of it. "You'll remember what we talked about?"

She nodded and stayed right where she was, the sight of her clinging to Harold twisting Hadrian's heart most disagreeably.

"I hate good-byes," she said. "You've been such a good friend, and I will miss you." She dissolved into open weeping, while Harold shot a chagrined look over her shoulder at Hadrian.

"We'll miss him together," Hadrian reminded her, tucking his handkerchief into her hand. "At least Harold's departure means you and I might renew our acquaintance, and I flatter myself that's a good thing."

A good thing years overdue, in fact.

"It is," Avis agreed, stepping back. "A very good thing, and I know Harold won't take any silly chances, and he won't leave port unless the sea is as calm as glass, and he'll be sure to write, and to be careful, and to send us a pigeon every so often."

"Two pigeons," Harold agreed, kissing her cheek. "Now I really must go, lest I embarrass us all by canceling my travel plans because I miss my neighbors before I even set sail."

He kissed her cheek again and then let Hadrian bundle him into the coach.

Harold slumped against the squabs before the horses were moving. "Ye merciful gods. I've been so focused on the practicalities of leaving, and the thought of leaving you, I didn't see that coming."

The coach clattered out of the stable yard, while Avis stood curiously alone, waving Hadrian's handkerchief.

"That?"

Harold flourished his handkerchief out the window, then folded up his linen and tucked it away. "I'm a decade Avis's senior, and she and her sister are the closest thing I will have to daughters or younger sisters. I shall miss Avis sorely and worry for her endlessly."

"You love her." Hadrian said the words slowly, tasting them for signs of insult and finding none. Harold loved Avis, while Hadrian…probably loved her too, in a fraternal fashion.

"I do love Lady Avis, enough that I keep an eye on Hart Collins and pass along all I learn regarding his whereabouts to Benjamin and Vim."

Somebody should certainly remain apprised of Collins's movements. "I'm surprised Collins still draws breath. He's an offense against the natural order and stupid to boot."

A vicar could not have been so honest.

"Coming from you that is harsh, though I have to agree. Collins has been forced to eke out an existence on the Continent for most of the past decade, but he periodically slips back to England. He holds the barony now and is owed the occasional coin as a result."

Wilhelm Carpentier, Avis's older half-brother—Vim to his familiars—was likely responsible for ensuring Collins kept his distance from Cumberland. "Have you been tempted to challenge Collins?"

While Harold considered his answer, the coach topped the rise that separated Blessings from Landover.

"Vim asked me not to call Collins out. Said it wasn't my place and my contribution was looking after the girls as they convalesced. I was to leave Collins's comeuppance to Vim and Benjamin."

Hadrian braced his boot on the facing bench as the coach headed down the declivity toward home. "It's been twelve years, Hal. Avie lives at Blessings like a hermit, and Collins has not been brought to account by her brothers."

"She's content, Hay."

"She doesn't have any choice," Hadrian said, thinking of Fenwick's reasoning regarding Lily Prentiss. "This life is all she can imagine, but she deserves more."

"So show her more."

"Hal, if you think—"

Harold waved a dismissive hand. "You're a man of the church, full of principle, a gentleman, and not subject to the same base urges as the rest of us. Avie's a woman grown, she never took holy orders, and you are likely one of few who might be able to pierce her armor."

The Landover succession needed an heir, in other words. "Spring is upon us, and you're off on romantic idyll. Spare me your innuendo, Harold."

And of course, Harold's smile turned appallingly sweet. "I *am* off on a romantic idyll. I've waited years and years for this, Hay, and I have you to thank for allowing me this freedom."

As if Hadrian had had a choice.

"You will send pigeons," Hadrian said in his most stern tones. "You will write. You will not set sail unless the sea is calm as glass. You will not take chances, nor drink too much with Swedes and Danes who are even bigger than you are, and you will come back to us, when you can, in great good health and better spirits."

"I won't let you down, Hay." Harold's expression was utterly serious. "Not even about the Danes and Swedes."

"Lest your Finch fly away. I suppose the man has his uses after all."

The next morning, Hadrian couldn't think of one positive thing to say regarding James Anderson Finch, except perhaps—just perhaps—Finch loved Harold, made him happy, and gave him the courage to dream.

Three things, then, but only three. Finch was also tolerant of large, slobbering hounds, which added a foot note to the short list of his virtues.

"I'll write," Harold recited as he and Hadrian stood alone at the mounting block. "I'll sail only calm waters, I'll send pigeons, I'll come back to visit often and I will be fine."

"One has no choice but to trust you on this," Hadrian said, as the dog bounded along the fence row.

"I trust you as well," Harold replied, tugging on his horse's girth.

"Trust me?"

"You'll do right by Landover," Harold said, gazing across the empty saddle at the cavorting hound. "You'll do right by your legacy, but I think Landover will also do right by you, if you allow it."

"You're waxing cryptic in your dotage."

"I'm nearly eight-and-thirty years old, Hay, and I feel like a boy going up to Town for the first time."

"You look like a boy too. Eager, happy, and ready to take on life. You will enjoy this excursion or I'll know the reason why."

Harold pulled Hadrian in to a fierce hug and held on, and for the first time in their relationship, Hadrian had the sense of being the elder, the one who brought more wisdom to a situation.

"Finch is your choice, Hal," Hadrian said softly, "but you're also his. You're leaving behind land and a title, but he's leaving his entire family, because he can't bear to live without you any longer, because you make him a better man. Trust that."

Harold stepped back, surprised and beamish. "You understand."

"In my better moments." In his best moments, perhaps. "They never last long where hanging felonies and sinful abominations are concerned. You think you'll miss me and Landover, and you will, but by the time you're at the foot of the drive, you'll be thinking of the future, not the past. By the time you're off our land, you'll be so eager to get to Harwich, you'll barely keep your horse from a flat-out gallop."

"I never said those things to you," Harold mused. "All the times you went off to school, up to Town, I never knew what to say."

"You say good-bye." Hadrian initiated this hug. "Godspeed and safe journey."

Harold took a long slow inhale in his brother's arms then stepped back.

"Good-bye, Hay. God love you, and I will never, ever cease being grateful that you're allowing me this."

"On the horse, Hal, now. Your future awaits."

Hal swung up, whistled for his dog, and cantered off.

And because Hadrian *was* more experienced than his brother when it came to partings, he called for his own horse and rode not down the driveway after Harold, but rather, up into the hills, into the brisk morning air, into the brilliant light of the rising sun, into the breathtaking views of...all Hadrian was now responsible for.

* * *

"When Lily comes down," Avis said, "tell her not to wait breakfast on me."

"Very good, my lady." The footman held the door for her, and Avis was out into the lovely morning air, ready to begin another week of managing her brother's estate. With that responsibility in mind, she would pay a call on a neighbor, the first such call in five years.

Getting to Landover took longer than it should have because Avis made a habit out of avoiding the most direct path. She instead trotted into the Landover home wood, the trees above her only beginning to leaf out.

And then, that sensation prickled at her nape, the feeling she dreaded most, of being tracked like prey.

"Who's there?"

The trees were tall enough to weaken the early morning sunlight, and patches of mist still clung to the ground. The forest should have been otherworldly, a fairy glen of old, but instead, Avis's surroundings felt alien and unsafe.

"Avis?" Hadrian Bothwell emerged from the bend in the bridle path, his blond hair windblown, his cheeks ruddy.

Relief coursed through her, and a pleasure beyond simple relief. "Good morning, Hadrian. You've seen Harold off?"

"At very first light." Hadrian drew his chestnut up beside her black. "Shall we walk? Caesar needs to cool out."

"You were galloping off the dismals?"

"I'm fine, thank you, and you?" He smiled self-consciously, and Avis let him have a little silence, a little dignity. "I've always been the one striking out into the world while Hal stayed here, tending the flock, so to speak."

"You tended different flocks. Brothers grow up."

"We at least grow older, though Hal never once complained, never shirked, never implied by word or deed that raising his little brother was an imposition." Harold had been, in short, a good shepherd.

Avis nudged her horse forward down the path, Hadrian doing likewise. "Your brother has a strong parental streak. I've understood why Harold might not want to marry, but I've always thought he'd make a wonderful papa."

"Why wouldn't he want to marry?"

What did Hadrian know, and what would he be comfortable discussing? "Not everyone feels the need to marry. Harold has the gift of appearing content, and he's been patient enough not to settle. He could well meet somebody on these travels who strikes his fancy."

"I doubt he'll marry," Hadrian said. Carefully.

What was a former vicar to do with a beloved older brother bent on thwarting society's most prosaic conventions?

Avis patted her horse's neck and searched for safe conversational ground. "I expect marriage can be as much a prison for men as it is for women, at least once the children start coming."

"Prison? I hope my late wife didn't see it as such."

"I think you'd know if she had, and you'd certainly know if you did."

"One forgets," Hadrian said slowly, "how insightful you can be."

Or maybe one forgot how little tolerance she had for small talk. "One forgets how hard you'll work to dodge a moment of sentiment, Hadrian Bothwell. You love your brother, and you'll miss him terribly."

Beside her, Hadrian let his horse amble along on a loose rein. Fenwick had sung rhapsodies about that horse, and Hadrian looked entirely comfortable with the beast.

"Are you in love with Harold, Avie?"

Hadrian's company was not exactly restful. Avis had forgotten that, too, though not even Fenwick called her Avie in that exact, familiar tone of voice.

"I love your brother, of course, and I owe him much, but he never showed more than a brotherly or avuncular interest in me, and for that, I am grateful."

Birds flitted from branch to branch, the soft green leaves stirred in a mild breeze, and the forest was once again pretty rather than sinister. Nonetheless, the past abruptly yawned before Avis, a conversational quagmire in the middle of an otherwise lovely morning.

"I didn't mean—" Avis began. "Well, maybe I did mean... Were Harold interested in me in that way, it would have been awkward. I thought for a while he'd offer me a white marriage, but was relieved when he didn't."

"A white marriage might have solved some problems," Hadrian said in that same neutral voice. "For him."

"Relieved him of the perennially hunting mamas and widows?" Avis suggested. "They were no real problem for him. He smiled, flirted, and escorted them on the dance floor, and they made no progress."

"What about you?" Hadrian stretched up in the stirrups then settled back into the saddle. For a man of the church, he was quite at home on a horse. "Would a white marriage have solved problems for you?"

"You're brave, Hadrian." He was also still her friend, to ask such a question, and friends were honest with each other. "I would have wanted children, you see, and Harold would have tried to accommodate me, and our white marriage would have awkwardly become something much less than the friendship we shared instead."

"Or maybe something more?"

"We'll never know. I attribute that to your brother's great and often underestimated perceptivity. What of you? Have you thought to remarry?"

He scowled at the bracken bordering the path. "I was not a very good husband."

He'd not been a happy husband, then. "Tell me about your wife."

Avis didn't want to listen, not to this, but twelve years ago Hadrian had listened to her, listened, and listened, and listened, no matter how sordid and unbecoming the tale, and she owed him the same courtesy.

"Her name was Rue. She was the daughter of a clergyman and seemed suited to the life I envisioned. Harold didn't like her."

Had Hadrian liked her? "Harold once said she had her eye on Landover, not you. That observation was a rare breach of manners for him, so I recall it clearly."

"Harold likely had the right of it. I wanted children, though once the marriage had settled, Rue wanted to wait. For what, I don't know." He rode a length ahead and held a branch back so Avis's horse could pass.

"Was your wife waiting for a better position?"

"I provided from my own funds, not from the livings I held. We never wanted for much, though a vicar doesn't exactly seek an image of idle luxury."

"You had servants?" Avis was no pattern card of Christian virtue, to be relieved that the memory of Hadrian's late wife did not cause him raging grief.

"We had at least a maid of all work and a man of all work," Hadrian said. "We had a conveyance to use, more than tallow and rushlights. I didn't feel material want, but a woman needs a few simple comforts."

"She had you," Avis said, wanting to throttle this Rue person who'd put such doubt in a good man's eyes. "You're much more than a simple comfort."

He straightened in the saddle and took up the reins. "Generous words, coming from you."

"I speak the truth, Hadrian Bothwell," she said sternly. "Perhaps your wife failed to appreciate the wealth she had because she was too busy anticipating the wealth to come."

"One doesn't want to speak ill of the dead."

Oh, yes, one did. The vicar was already losing his hold of the man, which was doubtless what Harold had hoped would happen.

"There's something you're not telling me," Avis said. "Something that doesn't speak well of your former spouse."

"Late spouse."

The last of the mists dissipated around them, while Avis waited, as Hadrian had so often waited for her to find words.

"There were letters," he admitted some distance later. "She wrote to her sisters of her discontent. Upon her death they gave me the letters, likely not recalling their exact contents."

"The lot of them sound in want of loving kindness." Or plain common sense.

"Death doesn't always make us think more clearly or carefully," Hadrian said, as they emerged from the trees. "When Rue died, I stopped thinking for a time. I stopped nearly every mental function, while the body soldiered on, like a ghost ship without rudder or crew."

"But you watched yourself soldiering on, like reading a book about the life and times of one Hay Bothwell, a tale neither boring nor amusing, but simply…a tale."

He drew his horse up, the morning sun showing both the fatigue in his eyes and the sheer male attractiveness of his features.

"Is it still like that for you, Avie? You're observing as somebody resembling you lives your life?" His voice and his gaze held such concern, she looked away, across the dewy loveliness of the deer park.

Avis seldom rode this close to the mares' pasture, though it was fitting Hadrian be the one to accompany her. "Usually, I am content, Hadrian, and I can take pride in running Blessings; nonetheless, I'm having the dower house refurbished."

The admission felt like a confession, a sin of which she should repent.

"The dower house?"

"I'll be thirty in less than two years, Hadrian."

"You said you'd want children."

He had wanted children, too. "What one wants and what one gets are not always the same," Avis said, addressing herself to a space above and between her horse's ears. "One sometimes has to send a brother in his fourth decade off on a quest across the water."

"Not a quest, but rather, a contented retirement."

"Or stepping aside, because he thinks it's best for you. He has often said your children will inherit Landover so you must have the reins."

"You talked with Harold a lot, didn't you?"

She had *listened* to Harold a lot; she'd talked with Hadrian, years ago, and made idle conversation with most people since.

"He missed you terribly, Hadrian, and he fretted over you. Because I had occasion to share some of those sentiments, yes, he talked to me." She sent her horse out into the morning sun, because those words had been incautious— another unexpected confession.

"You fretted over me this morning."

"It's a pretty morning for a ride." She kept her gaze ahead, lest Hadrian see the trepidation beneath that lie. She seldom left Blessings land any more, much less on cool spring mornings, much less to ride in the direction of Landover.

"You rode out without a groom, Avie."

She let her horse walk on, knowing damned good and well the point Hadrian made, but being him, and fearless, he had to put it into words.

And call her Avie.

"You left your grooms at home," he went on, "in case you found me in an embarrassing state, having parted from Harold this morning. You were protecting my dignity at the cost of your safety and peace of mind."

She turned her horse to walk off at a slight angle to his.

"Avie?"

Just her name, spoken gently, and a lump rose in her throat. She brought her horse to a halt, lest he come after her. *It's me, Avie, Hay Bothwell. We danced a ländler. You're scaring a fellow here...*

"Thank you."

Avie heard him over the clamoring of the voices in her memory, though he spoke quietly. She nodded, then turned her gelding, to head back to Blessings. Hadrian kept pace beside her to the property line then he let her go on alone. He remained on the rise, watching until she descended the slope to the stable yard, where she could again be certain of her safety.

* * *

"Mr. Bothwell, you are quite the topic of conversation among the shearing crews."

Lily Prentiss scolded Hadrian, all smiles and patient condescension as she wielded her verbal birch rod. The damned woman should have been married to a bishop.

Damned woman. Shame on him, though Hadrian relished every curse and profanity that tripped through his head.

In the past week, there had been more than a few. Shearing had put calluses on his calluses, seen him kicked in unmentionable places, and sent him naked into the frigid waters of the quarry pond and grateful for the cold. The gathering of neighbors marking the end of shearing was simply a social endurance test on top of the physical trials.

Now he was to put up with a gratuitous scolding. A quote from the book of Job sniffed at the edge of the conversation.

"I insist we talk of something other than shearing, Miss Prentiss," Hadrian said, his best churchyard smile nailed into place. "Not sheep, not wool, not crews, nor shears, nor lambs even. Let us talk, say, of desserts. Which among these do you recommend?"

"Every one is good," she replied, as they neared a long trestle table laden with sweet bounty. "I'd leave the strawberries and cream for those who haven't access to the hothouses, and suggest the éclairs."

"Excellent choice. May I fetch you an éclair on a plate?"

Hadrian kept up the polite chatter and stayed by the lady's side while she nibbled her way through a treat that wanted devouring. Perhaps a week among the shearing crews had taken a toll on his manners, but then he overheard Avis, laughing with Fenwick and his crew chiefs by the barrel of ale.

"She doesn't understand how that looks," Lily Prentiss said in low, unhappy tones. "Swilling ale and laughing with them like that."

"I believe she's serving the ale," Hadrian replied. "If you're concerned about the appearances, I'll intervene and the gentlemen can serve themselves."

He was off, happy to seize any pretext to leave Miss Prentiss to her fretting and nibbling, and more than ready to pry Avis from Ashton Fenwick's side. The week had been grueling, exhausting, and satisfying in some way, but in other regards, the work hadn't been nearly exhausting enough.

"Lady Avis." Hadrian held up an empty mug. "When the server is so pretty, the ale must taste ambrosial."

Fenwick thumped him on the back. "Well said, Bothwell. I suppose now you'll ask her to dance?"

Avis took Hadrian's mug and held it under the barrel's tap, though Hadrian had had enough ale in the past week to float the Danish navy. "For shame, Fen. Hadrian can hardly move thanks to your slave-driving, much less dance."

Hoots and catcalls greeted her taunt, and Hadrian set his full mug aside untasted.

"You really ought not to have said that, Lady Avis." He winged his brutally sore arm. "After the week we've put in, you have to know I won't back down from a challenge."

"Challenge me, Lady Avis," one fellow called.

"You're challenged simply to remain upright," Fenwick countered to his fellow. "Go ahead and dance with young Bothwell, my lady. We'll guard the ale in your absence."

"I'm not that sore," Hadrian lied as he and Avis moved in the direction of the temporary dance floor.

"I'm not that inclined to dance, but thank you for retrieving me from the tap. The men were getting boisterous."

"Lily Prentiss put me up to it. She's protective of you."

"Sometimes too much so. She means well. Where are we going?"

The road to hell was where well-meaning people belonged. "We're off to enjoy your gardens by evening, if we're not to dance."

Hadrian dearly hoped they would not attempt the makeshift dance floor, lest he fall on his tired, aching arse before Avis, the tenants, neighbors, and local gentry. Avis let him lead her way from the noise and exuberance of the assembled crowd, around to the back of the house, where the soft light of gloaming spread over the gardens.

"When was the last time you danced, Avie?"

"Not recently. I don't miss it." Her tone was clipped, almost afraid.

"You loved to dance."

Hadrian enjoyed it too, which was one of the reasons he'd never been drawn to highly visible, politically important church posts. He liked to dance, to consume good liquor, to play cards, and otherwise flirt with the behaviors the strictest churchmen frowned upon.

He also, lately, liked to air his naughtier vocabulary.

"Dancing is for girls and their swains," Avis said tiredly.

"Shall we tell that to Gran Carruthers?"

"She was dancing?"

"She danced Young Deal under the table. It's often that way, at the weddings, anyway. The grannies can dance all the callow swains under the table."

While the old men were too wise to enter the affray.

"The grannies can hold their liquor, maybe."

"Dance with me, Avie."

"Hadrian, you needn't."

"Wrong," he countered, stopping their progress near the back terrace. "If I sit, I'll seize up like a plough horse after Sunday rations. Take pity on an aging swain, Avie, and dance with me. Nobody has been willing to approach Mr. Bothwell to allow him such a plebian pleasure at even a simple shearing party."

Hadrian sensed both longing and sadness in her gaze, but no relenting.

"Please." He held up his hand, escort fashion, and waited, and waited, until her bare fingers slipped over his knuckles.

"I would be honored," she murmured when he'd led her to the terrace. As the makeshift orchestra gave the introduction to a slow, triple meter, he bowed, she dipped, and they took up positions appropriate to a *ländler*.

In silence they stepped through the dance, a partner dance related to the waltz, but older, more gracious and less vigorous. Hadrian was drawn back, across years and years, to the last time he'd danced this dance with her—with anybody.

She'd been barely seventeen, and gloriously blooming with newfound womanhood. She'd been innocent and so in a sense had he, and that innocence had been taken from them both.

He stepped closer and she looked away as the dance prescribed, but when the music died, and he lifted her from her final curtsy, he didn't step back, but rather, dipped his head and brushed a kiss to her mouth.

She might have hurried off, but instead, she leaned in, and Hadrian took the opportunity to put his arms around her.

Just to hold her.

"Thank you," he said, "Anything more vigorous, and I'd have been unable to creak my way through it."

"Hush." She stayed tucked against him, and he shut up, concentrating instead on the feel of her, warm, soft and yielding in his embrace. His hands relearned the elegant, sturdy contour of her back, and inside him, something finally, finally came to rest. Exhaustion hadn't done it, cold plunges hadn't done it, swilling whiskey with Fen hadn't done it, but holding Avis, simply holding her, brought him peace.

"Thank you for the dance," Hadrian said, stepping back to consider her. "Though the sun is fast waning, and I don't want you to take a chill." He had his coat off and snugged around her shoulders in a moment, then slid an arm around her waist as they turned back toward the gardens. "What are you thinking?"

"You are so kind."

"To inveigle you into dancing? To dragoon you away from your guests and steal you a while all to myself?"

She shook her head.

"What then?"

"Nobody touches me, Hadrian."

Well, of course. Old people could touch others, probably had to, when their spouses were gone and their children were grown. Gran Carruthers was a clutchy little thing, but one expected that. As a widower, Hadrian knew what it was to be beyond the limit of human touch, to drift along in the bubble of his own skin, lonely in ways the mute beasts never had to suffer in their barns and byres. He already knew that kind of isolation well, though he'd lost Rue only a couple of years past, while for more than a decade Avis...

He settled his arm around her shoulders and walked with her along the pathway.

"The lack of familiarity from your servants and neighbors is out of respect," he suggested.

"Not respect. I'm contaminated by my unfortunate past, and you need not pretend otherwise."

"If you're lonely," he said slowly, "why not get out more, call upon the occasional neighbor, attend services?"

"Don't be an idiot."

He puzzled over that as they wandered past the daffodils, though the flowers were spent, with only the occasional late bloomer still bobbing over its fallen comrades.

"I'm an idiot to suggest you socialize?"

"I've tried socializing, Hadrian." She pulled his coat more closely around her. "I've hauled Lily around the parish to every neighbor and tenant in the shire, and it's always the same. Some might be willing to overlook my past, but others will not, and I come home feeling more angry and—why are we talking about this?"

"Angry and what?"

She paused amid the forlorn beds. "Crazy," she said very softly. "As if I'm turning invisible, my skin becoming transparent, or I've magically leapt over what remains of my youth, to be an old woman in a young woman's body."

"You are not old, you are not invisible, you are not crazy, and neither am I."

He kissed her again, not a gracious gesture offered at the end of a gracious dance. He tasted her, the soft, sensitive fullness of her lips, the intriguing corner of her mouth with that small, barely noticeable scar. When she only burrowed closer and threaded her fingers into his hair, he seamed her lips with his tongue, slowly, exploring contour and response, until she opened for him and he had to pause.

"Assure me, please," he said, resting his forehead against hers, "that I do not take advantage. I could not live with myself—"

She fused her mouth to his, and Hadrian's gentlemanly restraint went creaking off into the undergrowth at the feel of her lush breasts against his chest and deft feminine fingers tracing his ears.

"Again." She breathed her command against his mouth, her tongue seeking his, and Hadrian fell into the kiss like the starving man he'd become. He tucked her against the crook of his shoulder, bracing her for a kiss that became voracious and mutually exuberant.

"Avie." He drew back long moments later. "We have to stop." He was supposed to say that—he'd panted it, in truth—though his mind was stingy with the reasons.

"More." She rose up on her toes and moved her mouth over his jaw, his cheeks, the sides of his neck. "Hadrian, I want—"

"Hush, love," he chided, for a reason had kicked him hard in the shins. "Anybody could come along here, Avie, and neither one of us wants that."

The eager, happy light in her eyes died, and she tried to move away, but Hadrian prevented it, taking her by one slender wrist and tugging her to a bench.

"That isn't what I meant." He sat and settled her beside him, still holding her hand.

"You can't be seen kissing me," she agreed all too crisply. "You'll need to marry, and dallying with me won't help toward that end."

"Avie, I'll not be marrying anybody for some while. I'm only two years past Rue's death, and I've much to learn about Landover before I can consider a bride."

She nodded, the movement jerky, brittle, and very much at odds with the lyrical, joyous feel of her in his arms moments before.

"I'd feel better if you slapped me," he said. "Do you suppose you could oblige?"

Her lips quirked, apparently despite her mood. "I might kiss my brothers, or Lily, or Harold's puppies, or my horse, but nobody kisses me, Hadrian— nobody. Do you think I'll slap you for being the first to even try?"

"We ventured a bit past trying, Avie." He was supposed to sound displeased with himself, but he simply could not. He and Avie had shared one glorious hell of a kiss, not like the kisses he'd shared with Rue, and as for the other women in his bed, well, they hadn't been the kind who appreciated much kissing.

Avis wrinkled her nose. "A pity kiss. That's worse than being ostracized."

He sat beside her in the soft, slanting evening light and felt something shift at her words. He'd left behind friends, familiars and church and thrown himself into Harold's scheme, as if someday, Landover and its title might truly be his responsibility. He wasn't the same old Hadrian, and for the first time, he didn't want to be.

The old Hadrian would have reasoned with her, offered philosophy and platitudes.

This Hadrian slid her hand down to his falls. "That was not a pity kiss, dear heart."

Rather than pull her hand away in horror, she shaped the length of him, closing her eyes and leaning her head back. "This is not pity."

"You mustn't be too offended." Hadrian moved her hand, capturing it in both of his lest that hand get to wandering on its own. "I've had limited congress with women since taking holy orders, and unlike those with a true vocation, I do not view the bodily urges as welcome opportunities for restraint."

"Put away your book of sermons, Hadrian. What does that mean?"

"I enjoy satisfying my lust with willing parties," he said, impressing himself with his directness. "Since Rue died, I haven't been entirely a saint, Avie. I can't be a saint where you're concerned, and you deserve saintly behavior."

She wrenched her hand from his, though—mercy and disappointment, both—she did not resume caressing his cock.

"I'm not some virgin martyr, Hadrian Bothwell. I'm a grown woman, with the same bodily urges you allude to, but alone of all God's creatures, I'm not supposed to acknowledge them, not ever."

Society's fictions to the contrary, women did experience lust. Hadrian had presided over enough hasty weddings and christenings of "early" babies to know this truth.

"You're lonely," he suggested, then winced, as her fingers glossed over his falls again, once.

"Lonely. Right."

They sat side by side, Hadrian wishing for and dreading another adventurous touch from her, when Avis seemed to come to some decision.

"We should be getting back."

Bloody damned sensible of her. "We should."

"Shall I leave you here to compose yourself?" She was trying not to smile, but Hadrian had to like her for her sense of humor, among other things.

He rose and offered his arm. "I am sufficiently composed that I should be presentable, provided we discuss only sheep, wool, and the quarry pond as we approach civilization, but I want you know something."

"Yes?"

"I haven't kissed anybody else like that, Avie Portmaine, not my wife, not my passing fancies at university, not my horse."

"If that's a warning, it isn't having the intended effect."

Must she sound so amused? "You are the last woman I want to disrespect."

She faced him squarely amid beds of roses about to bloom. "I've learned a painful lesson, Hadrian. One I hope no other woman has to learn as I did." He had no idea what was coming, but she had taken his hand and the amusement had fled her eyes. "I've learned that passion can be used to express the depths of disrespect, to degrade, and violate and hurt, intimately."

"It can," he agreed, heart breaking for her.

"I want to believe it can be used for the opposite as well, to express caring, and tenderness, to cherish and savor, not destroy."

He drew her to him, feeling such a wave of protectiveness that words were difficult.

"It should be," he said finally. "Even a casual encounter should convey some hint of those finer sentiments."

"So you meant no disrespect by your kiss, nor I with mine."

He kissed her cheek, absolved by her words, because she had the right of it. Still, offering her his arm and returning her to the safety of the crowd took effort, when he wanted to remain in the garden shadows, holding her close and cherishing her with yet more kisses.

CHAPTER FIVE

"Dance with me, Avie love." Fenwick's voice crooned low in Avis's ear, startling her with his proximity.

"How many times have I asked you to not to sneak up on me like that, Ashton Fenwick?"

"I wasn't sneaking," he said, looking genuinely contrite. "You were so distracted watching yonder vicar prancing about with Miss Primness, you didn't hear me."

"They are a handsome couple." Both Lily and Hadrian sported the blond, blue-eyed coloring and lean grace of the British aristocrat.

"You and I are a handsome couple too, and Bothwell's back is shot, so he's moving poorly."

"Your back is in fine fettle?"

Fenwick bowed with a flourish. "With you in my arms, I have the back of a mere lad." He tugged her onto the dance floor when the music ended, while Hadrian accompanied Lily to the punch bowl.

The Almighty was punishing her for kissing Hadrian, surely. "Had I known it was a waltz, Fen, I would have fled to York."

"Had I known it was a waltz,"—Fenwick positioned her in his arms—"I would have bribed old Sully to make it a half hour long."

"You'll be asleep on your feet before too much longer." God willing.

She and Fenwick had never danced the waltz before. He was surprisingly graceful and had the knack of being a secure partner without hauling her around the floor like a sack of wheat.

"You hush, Avie Portmaine." He drew her closer, to within an inch of what propriety forbid. "Let me lead for once and just enjoy yourself."

Having small-talked herself out for the evening, Avis did as he suggested, enjoying the music and her partner's skill. Fen smelled good, of something meadowy and fresh, and he exuded a bodily competence borne of both his size and his strength.

And yet, he wasn't Hadrian.

When Hadrian had tucked his jacket around her, she'd had an abrupt, intense sense of *déjà vu*. Once before, his citrus and clove scent had enveloped her. Once before he'd offered his coat warm from his body to keep the chill away. Once before his voice had found her when she'd been trapped in her own thoughts.

Hadrian was kind, and he was braver than most, for all his manners and warnings.

"You've gone away," Fenwick observed as the music slowed. "I feel like I'm holding air, Avie."

"You told me to enjoy myself. The silence was lovely."

"I saw you giving old Bothwell back his jacket." Fenwick kept his voice down.

"I suppose Lily will lecture me on that tomorrow at breakfast, and Hadrian might be no older than you, Ashton."

"Bugger Lily," Fenwick muttered. "You listen to me, Avie. If Bothwell casts lures, and you're inclined, you give the man a chance."

"I beg your pardon?"

"Bothwell is a thoroughgoing gentleman. I know you consider him a friend, but Bothwell is both gentleman and man."

"The two are often found in conjunction."

"No, my lady, they are not," Fenwick replied too softly to be overheard. "You've rusticated for too long here at Blessings without any flirting or courting, and it's time you rejoined the living."

"You're presuming a great deal here, Mr. Fenwick," Avis said, her tone as chilly as she could make it, but predictably, her scold had no effect on her steward.

"I know all about your unfortunate past, Avie. That was twelve years ago, and you're too lovely a woman to go to waste here when there's a worthy fellow whom you could put to the plough with a little effort."

"Put to the *plough?*"

"I can be more graphic. I am not a gentleman." A circumstance Fen delighted in. "What would Vim and Benjamin think of you for encouraging me to further ruin?" Avis asked in an outraged whisper.

"Vim and Ben would double my salary were I to report that you'd discreetly allowed Bothwell some liberties. Me, Bothwell, Young Deal, just about anybody you took a fancy to, and they'd be happy for you."

"*You?*"

"You've spent too much time around Miss Prejudice," Fenwick said as he led Avis through a slow turn. "Of course *me*, though I know you'd never trifle with the help."

"Now you're the help?"

"I can be whatever you need me to be, my lady, but the sparks aren't there between us, and you know it."

"Ashton, when did you become so ungallantly blunt?" Though when Hadrian had been blunt, she'd liked him for it.

"When did you become blind to the way a handsome man looks at you?"

"You consider yourself handsome?"

"In the eyes of some, yes," he countered with an odd gravity. "I was referring to Bothwell, Avie. Bothwell, who stole you off to the gardens for a protracted stroll; Bothwell, whose jacket appeared around your shoulders that he might show off his manly physique in waistcoat and shirt-sleeves. Bothwell, who's probably cozening your secrets out of Lily Prunish even as we speak."

"Prunish?"

"I knew I could get you to smile."

He was worse than both of her brothers put together. "You can, though my situation is complicated, Ashton, and while I know you mean well, there are facets of it you can't understand."

"I understand being lonely, Avie, and having needs that go unmet for too long and for no good reason."

The music came to a close, so Avis stopped casting around for a flippant reply, went up on her toes, and kissed Fen's cheek. "You are a good friend, Ashton Fenwick."

"And a better steward," he rejoined, leading her off the dance floor. "You'll think about what I said?"

"Not the prunish part," she said airily, "but the rest of it…"

"Hadrian Bothwell is good folk, Avie, and he'll treat you well."

Hadrian Bothwell kissed divinely. "He'd castigate you sorely for attempting to cause this mischief."

"For form's sake, he might," Fenwick allowed as Gran Carruthers bore down on him. "But only for form's sake."

* * *

"One forgets the blessed quiet in the wake of shearing," Lily remarked at breakfast.

"I get so I don't even hear the bleating," Avis replied, passing the teapot down the table. "After handling all the lambs, at least one's hands are soft."

"And reeking." Lily—who had handled not one single lamb—wrinkled her nose.

"At least we don't have to wrestle the grown beasts about. I'm not sure Sully will be willing to heft the shears next year."

Lily poured herself a cup of tea rather than reply, and Avis knew the same sinking sensation she felt every time she casually offended her companion's sensibilities. The situation would have been unbearable, except Lily was devoted to smoothing off Avis's rough edges, and incorrigible in her hope that Avis's past could someday be overcome.

"I shouldn't have said that," Avis said on a sigh. "But Sully dropped like a stone when he was kicked in the—when he was kicked, and for once, the other fellows weren't laughing."

"You shouldn't have seen that." Lily set her tea cup down silently. "You should have been with the other ladies, dandling their babies, asking after their daughters, and pouring cold tea."

Lily hadn't dandled any babies. Avis kept that observation to herself, just as she didn't point out that many of the ladies could deliver a social blow as stout as what Sully had endured.

"I did not remark what happened to Sully anywhere, save at my own breakfast table, but you're right. The subject is indelicate. Will you join me when the mercer comes by later today?"

Lily gamely launched into a monologue about the fabrics best suited to drapery in the dower house. Her sermon regarding velvet's tendency to fade was interrupted by a footman bearing a salver with a very small folded document on it.

"Good morning, my lady, miss. A birdie has come, but the note is addressed to Master Hay—to Mr. Bothwell, over to Landover."

"Thank you, Denver. We'll see he gets it." Avis took the note and slipped it into a pocket. "I'll tend to this message, Lily, and join you in the dower house by eleven."

Avis left the manor house with a sense of relief. The milestones in the agricultural year—lambing, shearing, planting, haying, grain harvest, apple harvest and so on—left her exhausted and pleased, but cast down as well. The earth was fruitful, the horses, geese, cows, and goats, and God knew the sheep were fruitful.

But not Avis Portmaine.

Each season, each accomplishment for the estate of Blessings, was a reminder that Avis was denied children, and a family, and the life she'd been raised to want.

"Bad thoughts," she muttered to herself. "No more bad thoughts, Avis, my girl." The morning was lovely, and Hadrian would be pleased to have word from Harold.

Assuming this was word from Harold.

Avis waved off the grooms and climbed aboard her horse. The message might be from Benjamin or Vim, or some mercantile connection they'd made. Both men took a goodly number of birds off with them when they departed Blessings after periodic visits.

Forty-five minutes later, Avis was shown into the Landover library, a masculine preserve saved from somberness by a row of tall windows, and by paintings of gamboling puppies and wide-eyed foals.

Everywhere, new life, but not for Avis Portmaine.

Another bad thought.

"Lady Avis." Hadrian rose from his desk, shirt-sleeves turned back. "A very great pleasure and a lovely start to my otherwise boring day." He didn't merely bow, he kissed her cheek, which had Avis's insides lifting happily.

"I hope I come bearing good news. Fenwick worked you nigh to death, didn't he?"

"I worked myself." He seemed happy about that. "Shall I ring for tea?"

"Please." She pulled off her gloves and withdrew the message from her pocket. "This came for you this morning."

He took the paper from her, carefully, as if it might bite him. "Do you mind if I read it?"

"Of course not." She busied herself at the door, requesting tea and some sustenance from a footman, and when she turned back to Hadrian, he was already refolding the message.

"Harold took on some cargo in Calais, dropped off some last-minute passengers in Amsterdam, and is probably making landfall at Copenhagen as we speak."

"Isn't that like him? A recitation of facts, but no real information."

"He says the sailing is wonderful, and he can't recall when he enjoyed himself so much."

"Then your sacrifice is worthwhile?"

Hadrian's answer mattered, because nothing stood in the way of him hiring a senior steward and taking himself off to London or back to Yorkshire, or even to Copenhagen, for that matter.

In which case Avis would miss him. All over again, worse than ever, she'd miss him. She excelled at missing people she cared for.

"I'm no longer convinced it's a sacrifice," Hadrian said. "The weather is turning beautiful, the company is delightful, and the work gratifying."

"Is that why your hands look like Gran Carruthers's this morning?" Avis had watched his hands as he'd folded the note. They were heavily blistered across his palms, the right worse than the left.

Hadrian frowned at his paws as if he hadn't a clue what had befallen them.

"Using the shears is so repetitive, one blisters even through the gloves."

"Does one? And yet, here you are, without gloves, probably scratching away at some correspondence rather than giving your hands a chance to heal."

Hadrian stuffed his hands into his pockets, like a schoolboy. "I neglected my ledgers and letters while I played at shearing."

He'd worked as hard as Fen, which was very hard. "Are you pleased to hear from Harold?" Avis asked.

"Am I over my pout, do you mean?" His tone confirmed he wasn't quite, but his smile suggested progress.

"You judge yourself too harshly, Hadrian. Harold is sailing the waves, and you're here,"—she took his hands—"ignoring your blisters."

He led her to a long comfortably worn sofa that faced a set of sparkling windows. "Do you know how long it has been since I've had blisters?"

Did he know how long it had been since Avis had taken a man's hands in hers? "I do not."

"When I was a boy, learning to ride," he said, seating her in the middle and coming down beside her. "I acquired those calluses caused by contact with the reins. I was proud of them."

"These." Avis touched his hand with her index finger, gliding over the calluses he referred to.

"You have them too," Hadrian observed, tracing the side of her fourth finger and leaving tendrils of pleasure in his wake.

So wicked of her. "Calluses are only one of my many infractions against the code of ladylike behavior."

He drew back, and Avis waited for the moment to degenerate into awkwardness, but Hadrian simply rose and admitted two footmen, each bearing a tray.

"First, tea, then we see to your hands, Hadrian."

He gave the appropriate direction to his staff and submitted with good grace, seeming to welcome both the company and the chance to take a break from his desk work. Avis forced a pair of buttered scones on him, and then set her teacup aside.

"Rue used to scold me for forgetting to eat," Hadrian said as Avis unscrewed a jar of comfrey salve. "I'd get to toiling away on a sermon, or looking up this or that text, and next thing I knew, she'd be standing over me, demanding my presence in the kitchen."

"You miss her." Avis put his left hand on her thigh, the better to wrap a strip of linen around an abused index finger.

"I miss the company, but there are times, too, when I can't clearly recall her features."

He sounded bewildered by that, by not knowing whether to be grateful or upset by the fading of memory.

"Forgetting can be a mercy," Avis said, smoothing unguent over his palm. "Though you need somebody to scold you if this is how you treat yourself. I imagine Fenwick is in the same condition."

"Probably not quite as bad. He had less to prove than I did."

Avis spread salve over his knuckles. "You were being men."

"Guilty as charged," Hadrian said, sounding smug. "Though on that topic, I am particularly glad to see you."

"Other hand," Avis said, giving back the left and reaching for the right.

"I am glad to see you," Hadrian said, his voice dropping into a register that had Avis's insides fluttering happily again. "Because I wanted very much to be assured that my conduct in the garden did not, upon sober reflection, offend you."

She went to work on his right hand, taking particular care, for he'd wrecked it thoroughly. "Offend me?"

"I took liberties, Avie."

"Then I took them too," she replied over the butterfly wings beating in her belly. "I threw myself at a sober, upright man, a man good enough for the church, one who couldn't possibly withstand the wicked advances of a woman like me."

"You're so wicked."

"Are you laughing at me?"

"I am laughing at your perceptions of our respective wickedness," Hadrian said, his hand still curled in hers. "Do you know, Avis, I am on a first-name basis with at least three soiled doves in the city of York?"

"You're a man."

"A grown man, and you're a grown woman. I kissed you, Avis. You didn't jump out of the bushes, beat me over the head, and then have your wicked way with me as I lay half-insensate among the flowers."

She liked that image, of having her wicked way with him among the bobbing tulips. Roses would be a bit tricky, but oh, the fragrance.

"It's different for women. You didn't get to know those ladies in York while Rue was alive."

"I did not. Nor did I engage in any great, salacious adventure, Avis. It was simple pleasure, offered for simple coin. At university, I consumed such pleasure on at least four occasions that I can recall."

How did he hold the two parts of himself, the human and saintly, in such easy balance? "We should not discuss this."

"Shouldn't a useless concept when we're already discussing it. One of them was Mavis, another Elfrida, and the third—"

"So we'll change the subject," she suggested, but at some point, Hadrian had started rubbing his thumb over her palm, a slow, sweet slide made more sensuous by the salve and the fresh, grassy scent of comfrey.

He kissed her cheek, lingering for a moment, his nose near her temple. "There was only the one. I forget her name. I think she had red hair, or possibly a mousy brown. She called me Henry."

Avis didn't know whether to strike him or kiss him back. "Wretch. What was that kiss for?"

His smile was crooked when he drew away. "Courage, I suppose. I am glad to see you, Avie, and I'll not be going back to York."

He wasn't ashamed of that trip to York, but it had proved whatever he'd needed it to prove.

Henry, indeed.

"I'm glad you've heard from Harold," she said, slipping her fingers from his. "I must leave you, though. I've an appointment with the mercer in the dower house, and Lily will be disappointed if I am late."

"You're truly set on removing from the manor proper?"

"It's time," she said, rising. Hadrian was on his feet as well, putting her hand on his arm as he escorted her to the door.

"Has somebody signed a writ of ejectment, that you must remove from the only home you've known?"

"Benjamin needs to take a bride," Avis said. "His countess will have an easier time settling in if I'm not underfoot, ordering the servants about, reviewing menus, and getting in the way."

"Oh, right. Leave the poor dear to stumble around, with Benjamin's tender guidance to see her through—Benjamin, who forgets that butter goes with scones, if I recall aright. You're running away from home, Avis."

There it was, the pity Avis detested more than she detested the scorn that had come her way—though Hadrian served up pity with an edge of challenge.

"I'm running to a home, or as close to my own home as I'm likely to find in this life. Besides, Lily and I are having great fun refurbishing the place."

Lily was having great fun.

"You look like a lady anticipating great fun," Hadrian countered dryly. "About like I'd look, if you told me we had five more days of shearing."

"It will be fun," Avis said as they arrived to the front door.

Hadrian glanced around, though his staff was nowhere in evidence.

"This is fun." He kissed her on the mouth, lingeringly, his fingers trailing over her cheek, but not the lavish undertaking of the previous night.

"Shame on you." Avis stepped back—when she was sure he had finished.

"You have the right of it, Avis. Shame on me, not on you. I kissed you—again."

"So you did." She couldn't help but smile.

"And I enjoyed it again," he whispered, leaning closer, "and I will enjoy it next time too, and the time after that, and the time after that, and the time after—"

"Good-bye, Henry."

She swept out the door, knowing that however much fun it might be to select drapery fabric with Lily and the mercer, flirting with Hadrian had been more fun still.

Much more fun.

* * *

"Read this."

Harold passed Hadrian's first letter to Finch, then handed over his reading spectacles. He and Finch lounged on deck chairs at their berth in the Copenhagen harbor, and though they were on the lee side of the yacht, a cool breeze stirred the air.

Finch squinted against the brilliant sunshine bouncing off the water. "Your vicar brother misses you. This surprises you?"

"It does not. Now read this." Harold passed along the second letter, for both had been waiting for him when they'd docked.

Finch scanned the letter, his eyebrows—blonder than they'd been upon leaving England—rising.

"You introduced me to this Lady Avis. She was pretty, quick, and going to waste in the wilds of Cumberland every bit as much as you were."

"She has an unfortunate past." A pair of gulls wheeled overhead, the sun sparkled on the water, and old scandals in Cumberland seemed lifetimes away.

"A failed elopement? A child out of wedlock?"

"A rape," Harold said flatly. "She was engaged to Hart Collins, but at the point of breaking things off, and Collins decided if he forced matters, crying off would be removed from consideration, for no one else would have her."

Finch stretched out long legs encased in the loose white trousers sailors favored. His feet were bare, and for the twentieth time, Harold fell in love with the look of him, lounging in the Danish sun.

"Rape isn't something anybody forgets," Finch said. "Would the malefactor be the Baron Collins?"

"One and the same."

"Hence your inquiries in Amsterdam and Calais. This misbehavior had to be some time ago. The man hasn't set foot in England for years."

Finch was a treasure trove of gossip, one of his many endearing traits.

"Collins slips in, harasses his solicitors for money, then slips out. Vim and Ben promised him a slow, painful death if they caught him underfoot." As had Harold.

"Why not provide him a quick, painful death over pistols or swords?"

Finch also had a protective streak Harold quite simply adored.

"Avis begged them not to make a greater scandal." Harold fell silent a moment as the gulls rose higher on the brisk shore breeze. "Her brothers felt guilty enough without putting her through the ordeal of a duel."

Finch propped his bare feet on the railing, the way Harold often propped his feet on the corner of his desk. "There's another daughter, isn't there?"

"You do keep up, don't you?"

"Not any more, love."

"The younger sister, Lady Alexandra, was riding with Avis when Collins and his merry men accosted them. Alex won free and jumped on the first horse she could reach. She wasn't used to riding astride, her feet didn't quite reach the stirrups, and she was dumped, dragged, and nearly lost the ability to walk."

"The brothers didn't tie Collins behind a horse for similar treatment?"

Harold resisted the urge to kiss Finch's imaginative cheek. "Collins decamped post-haste when I paid a call on him the same day." The gulls flew directly toward the sun, forcing Harold to drop his gaze.

"I hope you at least beat him within an inch of his life."

Harold remained silent. He'd beat Collins within half an inch of his life, and it hadn't been enough.

"You did, didn't you?"

"Something like it. The young ladies were at Landover, with no one but Hadrian to see to them, so I couldn't protract the exercise as much as circumstances deserved."

"Hadrian took the ladies in hand? He had to be just a stripling."

"He was eighteen and every bit as tall as he is now, though not as muscled. He was the one who came upon Avis first, and for a week at least, she wouldn't let him out of her sight." How awkward that had been, and how proud Harold had been of Hadrian for his patience with young and distraught Lady Avis.

Finch tapped the letter against slightly sunburned lips. "I'll bet that caused some talk."

"Not as much as you'd think. Landover's staff is both loyal and discreet."

"That they are," Finch agreed, lashes lowering, "thank ye gods. But what eighteen-year-old is equipped to deal with a woman who's been through that kind of ordeal?"

"I was ready to pounce," Harold said. "Ready to step in and start giving orders, though what I would have ordered, besides tea and sympathy, I know not."

Hadrian had known what to do, though, had known when to remain silent, when to tease, when to hug.

"Hadrian was unbelievably patient with her." Harold gently removed the spectacles from Finch's patrician nose, which was also unfashionably sunburned.

"They went for long walks, he read to her, they planted flowers, he found her a flute and some lesson books. I'm not sure what all they got up to, but gradually, Avis came back to us."

"You're not sure what all they got up to?" Finch lifted a perfectly arched blond eyebrow. "He wasn't a vicar at eighteen, Hal. Nobody is."

"She was hurt. Hadrian would not have taken advantage."

Finch passed the second letter back over. "Not then, but what about now?"

Harold folded the letter. "Now, it's twelve years later, and Hay is damaged goods too, as we all are, after a time."

Though Harold was feeling his own damage less and less.

"I dearly hope our Hadrian hasn't been raped."

Hadrian would faint at the least to know Finch considered him "our Hadrian." "Hay was taken advantage of by that woman he married, though he won't admit it."

"Many people would say I took advantage of Louise," Finch said quietly. "They wouldn't be wrong."

"You gave her a lifetime of security, three wonderful children, and a choice, Andy." They would go over this ground as often as necessary, for Andy and Louise had been married by parental arrangement, and she'd loved another even while reciting her vows. "She chose her freedom, and you chose me."

"I did. I have no regrets, and Louise assured me she hadn't any, either, but I think you do."

For a moment, Harold let jealousy tear at him. Louise and Finch had made children together, they'd endured an arranged match together, and planned their respective escapes from it—together. Such closeness had a lasting, unassailable quality that Harold envied.

Then he saw how the breeze snatched at Andy's hair, and let the jealousy flutter away on the morning sunbeams.

"I have no regrets," Harold said. "Hadrian would no more approach Avis while I was on hand than you'd approach me with him looking on."

"I love being able to approach you," Finch said, covering Hal's hand with his own. "I love not having to lock doors and wait for the servants to go to sleep, or having always to make certain I'm back in my own rooms before the chambermaids stir."

"I can't believe it's real," Harold said, closing his fingers around Finch's.

Finch smiled the smile of a beloved conspirator. "It's real, but you're worried for your brother."

"No, actually." Harold had to look away from that smile, much as he'd had to look away from gulls wheeling in the direct path of the sun. "I was worried, when he went haring back to university, no longer set on a cavalry commission, but spouting fancies about the church."

"One can see how that might cause you to worry."

"Not for me." The gulls were back, flapping to a landing on the gunwale, then folding their wings as if settling in for a listen. "I was worried for Hay. He's too genuine for the church, too uncomplicated, unsubtle, and yet he's smart enough to put those qualities on for a time, as needs must."

Finch kissed Harold's knuckles. "Nobody gets through life without a little dissembling."

"A little, maybe, but we both know what a steady diet of pretending to be something you're not does to a person's soul."

Finch studied their joined hands. "We do."

"I thought Hadrian would offer for Avie before he went back to finish his studies, but something happened, I know not what, and they parted company."

"Sometimes it's life happening." Finch closed his eyes and lifted his face to the sun. "I shall become as sunburned and wind-chapped as all these Danish sailors, and swill good beer, and sing like they do."

"You'll get wrinkles." Harold would adore those wrinkles too.

"Character lines." Finch opened his eyes and grinned. "They're good-looking fellows, those sailors."

"Tramp." Harold couldn't keep the affection from his voice.

"Just making an observation." Finch closed his eyes again. "What will your vicar do?"

"What he'll probably do is be a perfect gentleman. I raised him to be a perfect gentleman."

"Probably?"

"What he ought to do is dally with a willing lady, assuming Avie has as much sense as I think she does, and see where matters go."

"He might hurt her. Badly."

"He might get hurt, badly, and he might not. Avis can tell him she's not interested, and then he can do that perfect-gentleman business."

"So write to him, Harold. You warned him about Collins, now write him something to remind him his big brother is still on the job."

"Write him about the dallying?"

"Romance, my love, is romance, and loneliness is loneliness, and sex is sex. He's your brother, your only family, and he's asking for your guidance."

"I suppose he is. Fancy that."

"The vicar is trying to stray." Finch crossed his arms and settled back against his chaise. "You've given him a clear and worthy example—once again."

CHAPTER SIX

Fenwick glared from the back of his unprepossessing horse. "It's your fault my hands have been smelling like bloody damask roses and comfrey these three days and more. I hope you're pleased with yourself, Bothwell."

"My fault?"

"Avis and her salves and liniments and whatnots." Fenwick's mount stomped a back hoof, as if in sympathy with his owner. "Next she'll have me carrying a fan."

"She sent some salve over to Landover," Hadrian countered, while Caesar stood like a perfect gentleman. "Considerate of her." Though who was considerate of Avie, besides Fenwick in his backhanded way?

"She's kind. But roses, Bothwell? You might have kept your gloves on when she came calling and spared us both."

"She likes roses, and writing letters while wearing gloves is awkward." Caressing a woman's cheek while wearing gloves would be awkward too.

"She likes you, and fussing."

Avis probably liked Fenwick too—as did Hadrian. "Let her fuss. I've something to discuss with you."

"My petty complaints and indignities can be cast to the wind while I await your every word, fairly panting to know what I might do for you."

Nobody talked to their vicar that way, more's the pity.

"As you should be," Hadrian rejoined, "*humbly* awaiting. I wish I did not have to raise this topic, for your complaints are always at least colorful, but the discussion is necessary."

The bantering light died from Fen's dark eyes, and he nudged his horse forward. "Say on."

Hadrian let Caesar fall in step beside Handy. "My brother has made inquiries on his journey regarding Hart Collins."

"The sodding bastard who raped Lady Avie?"

Blunt masculine speech was also something Hadrian hadn't heard much of while tending to the Lord's flock. He hadn't realized until that moment how much he'd missed it.

"That would be he. Collins decamped to the Continent on the end of Harold's boot twelve years ago, though Harold never said as much, but the baron slinks back occasionally, or so Harold says."

"Harold has kept track of Collins all these years?"

"He has, or he, Benjamin, and Vim have between them and their various correspondents. According to Harold, Collins is pockets to let and reported to be on his way back into the country."

"This is good news," Fenwick said, sitting up straighter in the saddle. "Now we can kill him."

How refreshing. "As simple as that?"

"Among some indigenous peoples, when a woman is violated, her community considers itself violated, and the entire village is justified in seeking revenge. A quaint concept, but it effectively discourages that particular trespass against women."

"Alas, there's that bit about thou shallt not kill among my people—another quaint concept. Even if the Almighty didn't take a dim view of murder, Avie would hear of it, and if one of us stood trial for it, she'd suffer."

Fenwick shifted his gaze to the heavens as if praying for patience. "There you go again, thinking things through when what's wanted is a little spontaneous violence."

"Spontaneous violence is how Avie was hurt in the first place."

Fenwick drew his horse up. "Choir Boy, you are in error. She was hurt as a result of premeditated violence, planned, complete with accomplices, and executed in cold, if semi-inebriated, blood."

Fen's characterization was accurate. "She's spoken to you about it?"

"Never once, and yet it's present at many points in our conversations."

From what Hadrian had observed, the past loomed over Avie's every waking moment, and probably her sleeping moments too.

That was untenable, and yet, Avie could not remedy matters on her own.

Fenwick went ahead where the path narrowed, held a branch back, then let go so it smacked Hadrian in the chest. "She danced with me at the shearing party."

"One noticed this. You dance well."

"For a lumbering ox? A person can't survive in the Scottish Highlands making a racket the game will hear a hundred yards off. But yes, I danced with her. Did you notice how all eyes followed us and how that Prentiss creature fretted?"

"I did. You and Avis are a handsome couple and Avis is the lady of the manor." Hadrian wasn't entirely sure what Lily Prentiss's function was.

"We're handsome *friends*," Fenwick said, allowing Hadrian to take a turn going first. "That one dance will cost her months, possibly years of gossip."

"Because she danced with somebody who works for her family?"

"Because she danced *at all*. She deserves to dance as much as you, me, Gran Carruthers, or old Sully, but she hasn't, not a waltz, not since I've known her. The Prentiss woman can dance with you all night, and she's simply being gracious to a widower, but if Avie dances, she's thrown herself at her partner, shown a lack of restraint, and flirted with ruin all over again."

Placed as he was, above the menials, below the best society, Fen would hear the talk, and his words confirmed Hadrian's sense of the situation.

Hadrian held a branch back for Fen, and did not let it go until Handy had passed before it.

"The small-minded few will always find someone to prey on with their gossip," Hadrian said. "I am more concerned with the threat from Collins, should he decide to destroy Avie's peace." Hadrian was concerned about Avie's reputation and her safety, in truth, and the solution to those problems lay within his grasp.

"Collins won't show his face around here."

"His seat is not five miles distant, Fenwick." More significantly, if Harold had charged Hadrian specifically with protecting Avie from this threat, then the threat was real. "You are not to do anything rash without a choir boy at your side."

"What would the bishop say?"

"He'd say, 'Pray devoutly, but hammer stoutly.'"

"Smart fellows, those old bishops."

"Some of them, at least when sober. I haven't joined you on your morning ride for the sheer pleasure of your company, Fenwick."

Fenwick batted his lashes. "How you do flatter a fellow. I take it you're on your way to call on Avie?"

"I am." Despite the knowledge that while Avie had danced a *ländler* with Hadrian, she'd danced the waltz far more publicly with Ashton Fenwick—who viewed avenging her honor with reckless glee.

Fenwick gave his horse a loud, whacking pat. "About time you showed the colors, Choir Boy. I've told Avie my money is on you. You'll do her a power of good, if she allows it."

Hadrian certainly hoped so. "You aren't concerned about gossip, old scandal or worse?"

"You'll be discreet or I'll cut your balls off," Fenwick said easily. "Word of friendly warning, though?"

"That wasn't a warning?"

Fenwick's smile was sweet, though Hadrian had reason to know the knife ever present at his side was lethally sharp. "That was a promise, love. The fair Lily will cut your balls off even if you are discreet, should she learn you intend to build on your friendship with Avie."

"Harsh." But friendly enough on this lovely morning. "Lily seems devoted to Avie, and the perfect lady's companion." If a bit fretful.

They turned onto the trail that led to the Blessings stable yard. "You're not after ladylike behavior from our Avie, are you?"

"One doesn't admit such a thing. I'd have Avie decide what she wants and doesn't want."

"This time, you mean. That's the entire point of the exercise, isn't it?"

Hadrian added penetrating insight to Fenwick's short list of good qualities, rare bouts of penetrating insight.

"May I ask why you haven't given Avie the opportunity to choose, Fenwick?"

"What makes you think I haven't?" Fenwick's sleepy, sensuous, satisfied smile made Hadrian's fingers itch to hold a sharp knife against certain parts of Fenwick's anatomy.

Which impulse deserved consideration, because in several years of marriage, Hadrian could never once recall being jealous of Rue.

"You haven't made Avie any offers," Hadrian said. "She would not be as relaxed and trusting of you if you had." Would never have danced with him in public, either.

"She doesn't view me as anything other than an unruly brother, and she's needed that more than a doting swain, at least up to this point."

Fenwick's explanation made sense, though it felt incomplete. He'd been on the property for years, which could make dallying convenient, but also, when one wanted privacy, solitude, or an end to the dallying, mortally inconvenient.

"You're making it too complicated," Fenwick said as they turned into the Blessings stable yard. "I'm Avie's friend and her steward, and I'll be her henchman should Collins show his ugly, evil face, but she's weighed me in the scales and found me wanting, Bothwell. Not so, you."

A fine speech—complete with a reference to the book of Daniel, chapter five, verse 27—though fundamentally mendacious.

"You've weighed yourself in the scales and come up with the idea you're wanting," Hadrian said, "but there's more to this situation than you can perceive, and discretion forbids that I share it with you."

"Have to get you drunk then, for the tale wants telling, and I'd take it with me to my grave." He winked at Hadrian, then hopped off his horse, landing as softly as a kitten.

* * *

Hadrian decided on a sneak attack and went around to the back of the Blessings manor house, thinking to use an entrance other than the front door. He came upon Avie denuding a bed of pansies of its fallen soldiers, a tartan blanket spread beneath her knees.

He dropped beside her and pulled off a dead blossom. "You should be wearing a hat, shouldn't you?"

Avie smiled over at him, momentarily disorienting him, for her eyes held a shy greeting and maybe a hint of challenge. "Shouldn't you as well?"

He pulled off his riding gloves.

"I've taken to not wearing a hat when I ride out," Hadrian said, plucking off a blue and yellow bloom that was nowhere near wilted. "I lose it when Caesar stretches his legs, and then I have to hunt it up, lest my staff be wroth with me." He tucked the flower behind her ear and sat back to survey the results. "How are you, Avie?"

"Well, thank you, and you?"

"Better now," he said, moving the flower to her other ear. "Why are there no green flowers?"

"Grass flowers are green," she said, setting her shears and his gloves in a wicker basket. "Let me see your hands."

Hadrian held out his left hand. She took it in both of hers and examined the healing blisters and nicks.

"Improving," she allowed. "You're likely riding every day, and scribbling away for hours on estate correspondence, and otherwise not allowing your hands to idle."

He gave her his right, for holding hands with her made a pretty day even more agreeable. "Surely you'll want to inspect both?"

"You're as bad as Ashton Fenwick. This hand has not healed as well."

"I use it more, and shearing left it in worse condition. You should kiss it better."

Her lashes lowered, and he thought she would deliver him some sermon about Fenwick being a sorry influence—which he was, thank ye gods—or perhaps get to her feet and put some distance between them, which she should.

She smoothed her fingers over his knuckles, then turned his hand over and laid her cheek against his palm.

And holy *God*, if the entire household of servants were not likely glued to the windows watching their every move, Hadrian would have pressed her back, down onto the blanket, and started in kissing her right then and there.

Spring in Cumberland was a force to be reckoned with.

Avie saved him from hopeless folly by giving him back his hand and picking up her shears.

"It's good of you to call, Hadrian." Her tone was friendly, dismissively so.

"Bother that. You show me a little affection, then retreat to the Highlands, Avie. I've come to issue an invitation."

"I'm quite busy," she said, snipping off one spent bloom after another.

"You're quite worried somebody saw us touching, but I do enjoy your touch, Avie Portmaine, any place, any time, anywhere on my person. You aren't the only one who feels a little isolated."

She kept to her task, but her very focus confirmed she was listening to him. "A little?"

"That woman in York was a damned desperate measure for a man still wearing a collar. Pathetically desperate."

"Not pathetic," she said between snips. "You're a man."

Must she make his very gender synonymous with a class of felon?

"Guilty as charged, but I proposed not only to the two women in Rosecroft village least likely to have me, I proposed to one of them twice. That's three failed proposals within a couple of years of Rue's death."

She paused in her pruning to regard him in puzzlement. "Three, Hadrian?"

What fiend had claimed confession was good for the soul?

"The one lady went on to marry a man I consider a friend, and that made for no little awkwardness."

"You asked her twice?" He could see Avie trying to picture it, the choir boy and the reluctant damsel, and he hoped it gave her some indication of how far gone he'd been.

The memory troubled his dignity sorely, though it troubled his heart not at all.

"I would have accepted marriage, dallying, anything she'd give me." Hadrian pinched off a wilted bloom and tossed it over his shoulder. "The lady allowed me exactly two kisses, then turned around and plighted her troth with St. Just. I'm convinced he allowed me to buy Caesar as a consolation for my failed suit. The horse is the finest quality, and yet, the pity was quite lowering."

"Oh, Hadrian." Avie's tone conveyed understanding, and a touch of humor, precisely the reception this tale deserved. "What a busy place, little Rosecroft village."

"What a frustrating, lonely place." Hadrian pinched off another bloom and tossed that one aside too. "So come on a picnic with me." He'd pondered late into the night on how best to begin his siege, and the out of doors had struck him as offering the most privacy.

"A picnic?"

"Up at the old slate quarry. The pond is lovely and not too far on foot."

Avis snipped away with her shears, a sound that reminded Hadrian of bleating sheep and cool ale. "Not far at all. Today is warm."

"While you've been gardening half the morning. I'm asking, Avie. I'll beg or bribe, if I must. With Harold gone, I rattle around Landover, trying to give the servants enough to do, and waiting for Fen to tell me haying has arrived so I can wreck my hands all over again, just to have you kiss them better."

Avis snatched off a blossom that looked quite healthy. "Hush that talk."

"You want to go on this picnic. I'll read you poetry."

Her smile was back, and how he rejoiced to see it. "You hated reading me poetry."

"I'm older and wiser now. I know more poetry." He knew some naughty poetry now, too, in English, French and even Latin.

"Dignity, Mr. Bothwell," she chided. "Come for me at one of the clock, and I will have selected the most vapid, sleep-inducing poetry ever written."

Victory, of a sort. Hadrian retrieved his gloves, rose and drew her to her feet. "Walk me to my horse and prepare to waste an afternoon with me."

"You can find your horse on your own. You've distracted me from my task long enough, and if I'm to waste an hour with you later today, I'd best be productive now."

Two hours, at least.

"So pragmatic." Hadrian kissed her cheek—Fenwick would have expected at least that of him. "I will see you later, and we can walk up to the quarry."

"Shall I pack the hamper?"

"You shall not. I will tend to the details. You will wear a comfortable old dress and shoes you can take off when you want to dip your toes in the water."

She looked interested in that, so he stole another kiss and went on his way, swaggering a bit for the benefit of the gaze he hoped she had clapped on his backside.

* * *

Avis had no business wasting even an hour with Hadrian Bothwell. The dower house hadn't had residents since Avis's great-grandmother's day and had become a glorified storage facility in the intervening generations. For five years, Avis had promised herself she'd weed out the gold from the dross, but with her twenty-eighth birthday behind her, the task felt abruptly urgent.

"Have you considered how you'll landscape the dower house?" Lily asked as Avis arranged a bowl of pansies on the sideboard in her personal sitting room.

"I have not," Avis replied, shifting a certain blue and yellow bloom a half inch. "I can tend to that when I've moved in and have a better sense of the place."

When she knew she could tolerate living there, in much closer quarters with Lily.

"I'm still not sure setting up your own household is the best idea, Avis." Lily frowned at the pansies, and Avis knew, she just knew, Lily wanted to move the blue and yellow specimen back where it had been.

"The dower house won't be my own household. It will be a private part of this household, and you'll be with me."

"There will be talk," Lily said hesitantly.

"There is always talk, but living in the dower house should send a signal that the talk can die down. By moving there, I officially acknowledge my spinsterhood."

For all that such a notion ought to hold relief, Avis also admitted to resentment. Most women her age had several children, some ladies had even been widowed and remarried.

"You're young yet, not even thirty. You danced with Fenwick, and everybody saw you. Spinsters don't waltz with handsome single men."

Lily had conveniently forgotten her own dance with Hadrian. "You think Ashton is handsome?"

Lily peered into the bowl of pansies, as if ensuring Avis had given them water. "He has a certain animal appeal, and as steward he has privileges others do not. Privileges he abuses."

Perhaps he did. Lily enjoyed a few privileges herself. Rearranging Avis's flowers was not among them.

"I could have refused his invitation to dance. Ashton was being Ashton, and I enjoyed the dance." Avis had enjoyed the dance with Hadrian far more. Thank goodness Lily couldn't get her sermonizing teeth into that topic.

Something approaching exasperation flashed in Lily's eyes, and Avis resisted the impulse to hurl the bowl of flowers through the window.

Avis planted her fists on her hips. "Just say it, Lily. I should not have danced with one of few men I can honestly call a friend, or if I had to dance with him, I should not have enjoyed it. Better yet, if I had to dance with him, *and* I enjoyed the experience, I should dissemble, and carry on, as if spending a few minutes in a simple social pastime was a great imposition, as if I could not wait to escape Ashton's company."

This small display of temper felt daring, and altogether too good.

"Avis, he held you too closely, he whispered in your ear as he led you about, and he met the eye of anybody who thought to gape at the spectacle the two of you created. I say these things so you'll be honest with yourself. I hope you did enjoy the dance, because you'll pay a price for your pleasure, one I do not wish to see extracted from you merely so Fenwick can crow that he danced the pretty with a titled lady."

Lily shifted the pansy, and that she even touched the flower Hadrian had tucked behind Avis's ear was blasphemous.

"I hurt for you," Lily went on. "I know you should be able to dance with anybody you choose, to call on anyone you choose, to live wherever you choose, but we are ladies, and such freedoms are beyond us if we're to be regarded as worthy of our station."

The patience in Lily's tone, the implied condescension, and the *pity* sliced at Avis today more sharply than ever. Lily was doing her job, serving as a companion and guide, as a friend, regarding matters with which Avis lacked both experience and confidence.

And friends were honest with each other.

"These flowers will be happier on the table in the servants' parlor." Where they'd be safe from Lily's meddling. Avis picked up the bowl and shifted the pansy back where it belonged. "What time will the glazier come?"

"You'd have to ask Fenwick. Will I see you at luncheon?"

"You will not. I'd best be on my way if I'm to catch Fen before he's off to parts unknown."

"Haven't you heard a word I've said? Send the man a note."

"He's my steward," Avis rejoined, the words coming out more abruptly than she'd intended. "I will not disrespect him by communicating exclusively in notes and imperatives, Lily."

"Of course not," Lily said, though her gaze held reproach. "I know you respect his work, and I meant nothing to the contrary."

Avis took her leave, the bowl of pansies in her hands. Lily *did* mean to disrespect Ashton Fenwick. The woman flat disapproved of him and always had, and worse, the feeling appeared to be mutual.

Walking up to the quarry pond with Hadrian would be a relief, Avis decided as she changed into half-boots. Lily would likely have a scold to deliver at tea time, but that was hours hence, and sufficient unto the moment, or so it felt to Avis, were the remonstrations thereof.

* * *

When Hadrian came ambling around the side of the house, Avis made sure to again be in the garden, lest Lily become aware of their plans and invite herself along as chaperone.

"You're still ordained, aren't you?" Avis asked him.

"I am," Hadrian replied, helping her to her feet, "but retired, more or less."

"You'll hear my confession then."

"I will not." He seemed amused, not affronted.

"I want to strangle dear Lily."

Hadrian slipped her arm through his. "You and Fen both." He seemed to sense Avis wasn't entirely jesting, which in itself lightened Avis's spirits.

"Are we to dine on fresh air and sunshine, Hadrian?"

"I've already taken our hamper up to the quarry. Why are you contemplating murder?"

Torture and murder, in fact. "Lily is a good person, the daughter of clergy and an example of ladylike deportment. I am not a good person. She doesn't mean to be a walking reproach to me, but she is. She simply is, and I suspect that's why Benjamin and Wilhelm hired her."

"They hired her because they've abandoned you up here," Hadrian said, and though his tone was mild, his words held a gratifying hint of accusation. "Miss Prentiss is a sop to their consciences, but Avie, if she isn't congenial company, then write her a character and tell her to find another position."

"I can't do that." Though a part of her wanted to do exactly that, which was different. Very different. "Where will she go? I can't bear to think of her having to listen to some crotchety dowager carping for her dish of tea, or having to take the dowager's crotchety little dog walking every hour in all kinds of weather."

"You're too kind, Avis. Lily might end up as a finishing governess if she's really so intent on the social niceties, or a companion to a widow who likes to travel, but it's up to Lily to find a position she can enjoy. Give her plenty of severance and send her on her way."

"With what excuse?" Avis wailed softly. "That I want to be alone, rattling around Blessings without benefit of any female companionship whatsoever? Do you know how that would look?"

Hadrian stopped walking and put his arms around her. Avis should have protested, though they'd passed from the view of the house, and his embrace was exactly, perfectly right.

"I'm a ninnyhammer," Avis mumbled against his throat. Worse, she was a ninnyhammer who knew better than to pass up the chance to be held, simply held, in the arms of a friend. She'd pushed him away earlier in the day, figuratively, because this need for physical comfort was growing with time, not diminishing.

"You're a ninnyhammer who's sensitive to the needs of others, perhaps at the expense of your own. Mayhap you have a calling in the church, though of course, one would never mistake you for a good person."

"A nunnery, Hadrian?" She stepped back, lest she spend the entire afternoon in his embrace. "Had I been allowed to retreat to a nunnery, much awkwardness might have been avoided."

While Avis regretted alluding to the past, Hadrian slid an arm around her shoulders and resumed their walk. "Besides being a theological impossibility for a devout member of the Church of England, you'd go mad at a nunnery within a week."

"Mad?" Part of her was going mad at her family home.

"The church comprises all manner of people, Avie. Most of them good folk, some of them very good, but a liberal portion of the not-good-at-all also gravitate to the church. Because they're masquerading as holy, they can be very bad, indeed. I have friends among the Papists and Dissenters, and know of what I speak. No nunneries for you, my lady."

"So another option is precluded by common sense. Why haven't I a greater capacity for dishonesty? Why can't I simper and smile and be as I'm supposed to be?"

The questions were old, and overlaid a fundamental bewilderment: Why couldn't *her life* be as it was supposed to be?

"What has provoked this spate of self-castigation? Did you whistle for your horse, or come to breakfast in your dressing gown?"

"I danced with Fenwick, or worse, I waltzed with him, and most heinous of all, I was seen to *enjoy* my wickedness."

"So you did and so you were. You made a very fetching couple, too."

"Fen dances well, particularly for such a large fellow."

"And you trust him, so you thought you could have a few minutes of what everybody else has at social gatherings."

Hadrian was not upset with her, which was a comfort—but couldn't he have been the smallest bit jealous of Fen?

"I had my waltz, but then Lily must pounce, days later, just when I think I've escaped notice for my folly."

She stopped, for they'd reached the quarry pond, and there, beneath the gauzy green of the leafing-out trees, Hadrian had spread three thicknesses of tartan wool blanket and positioned a hamper at two of the blankets' corners. A bottle of wine chilled in a bucket of ice, and another blanket had been folded on the rocks to afford a comfortable bench for dangling one's feet in the water.

"My lady, your banquet awaits."

"I am impressed." Avis strolled over to the blankets and dropped to her knees. She was moved nearly to tears, and by a simple picnic. "Won't you join me?"

For the next half hour, they merely chatted. Avis had confessed, and Hadrian had neither taken Lily's part nor condemned her, as Fen might have. The cold chicken, buttered bread, strawberries, and tea cakes were wonderful, and Hadrian distracted Avis by feeding her a nibble of this, or a nibble of that, then insisting she do likewise.

Avis passed Hadrian a perfectly ripe strawberry. "Lily would not approve of this."

He munched his fruit, then leaned back against a sturdy rowan trunk and patted the blanket beside him.

"Lily is not here, for which God be thanked. I'm lonely, Avie. Won't you lie down beside me?"

Abruptly, Avis's mouth, which had been full of succulent berry moments before, went dry as a pressed rose.

"Now, don't poker up. I'm good old Hay Bothwell, with a full stomach and empty arms, and a pretty lady to share a pleasant day with. We've things to discuss, Avie, and now is the time."

Now was the time to move to the dower house. "Now?"

"We have privacy and leisure. Quit stalling and cuddle up."

She knee-walked across the blanket and sat a few inches from him. This cuddling up he proposed sounded both lovely and frustrating, because the more Avis had of Hadrian's affections, the more she craved.

"Better," he pronounced and hauled her against his side. She scooted around, until her head rested on his shoulder.

"You mustn't doze off," Hadrian said, though his hand wandered up and down her arm and practically commanded her to close her eyes. "This is serious, Avie."

"I'm listening." Mostly, though, she was reveling in the solid warmth of Hadrian Bothwell, in the pleasant citrus and clove scent of him, and in a sense of freedom that had only partly to do with fresh air and sunshine.

Hadrian took her hand and folded his fingers around hers. "Hart Collins is headed for England, and we're trying to ascertain what his specific destination might be."

Avis heard the words and understood them on one level. Her body understood them on an altogether different level, as heat, cold, panic, and a curious detachment assailed her in turn.

"Who are *we* doing this ascertaining?" And would Hadrian please keep his arms around her for the next twelve years at least?

"Harold and myself. I'll notify Benjamin if I can locate him, and Fenwick knows."

She nodded, but her ears were buzzing and her chest felt tight.

Hadrian's arms settled around her more closely. "He won't come within five miles of you. If I have to shoot him in the back, he won't."

"You told Fen?"

"I did."

"He'd spare you the felony hanging."

"Why not lay information against Collins?"

Hadrian held her snugly, and Avis turned her face into his shoulder, for she'd asked herself the same question many, many times. "You know why not, and it has been twelve years. Isn't there a statute of limitations?"

"For many felonies, it's twenty-one years, love." Hadrian's hand stroked her hair now, slowly, gently. "Kidnapping, rape, assault, false imprisonment, take your pick. Your sister is an adult now, and so are you."

"We were on our own land."

"But you were taken off your land, onto Harold's property. Harold would jaunt home for the trial. He's promised."

The Bothwell brothers had corresponded about this. Avis was both touched and panicked. "You really have considered my situation, haven't you?"

"At great length," Hadrian replied, and Avis was pressed so close to him, she could feel his voice rumbling through his chest. "And not only recently."

"I was whining because Lily is an irritation." Avis told herself to ease her grip on the solid, muscular man holding her so carefully. "This news of yours surpasses mere irritation handily."

"Lily is an irritation for all she means well, but Collins could be a menace of a different sort. I thought you'd want to know what's afoot."

And in that, in his consideration for what *Avis* wanted, Hadrian was different from all the other men professing to care for her, except perhaps Fen on his good days.

"My brothers would not have told me," Avis said, rubbing her nose along his collarbone. "Collins was back a few years ago when his papa died, and I had to hear about it from Lily."

"What did you do?"

She'd panicked, of course. Had reverted to a girl terrified of her own shadow, unable to eat, unable to sleep. Worse, she'd had no Hay Bothwell at hand to reassure and distract her.

"I remained indoors for the ten days he was at his seat. He made some pretense of traveling in disguise. He'd grown a beard and darkened his hair, but he was easily recognized."

"Lily warned you?"

Were those Hadrian's lips grazing her ear? "Lily socializes more than I do, with the housekeepers and other companions or governesses in the area. She's well informed as a result, and so, thank God, was I."

"I don't doubt Lily's loyalty," Hadrian murmured against her hair. "Only Collins's sense."

"You can't call him out, Hadrian." Avis did ease away, far enough to meet Hadrian's gaze. "Promise me." Did ordination preclude a man from dueling? Did *anything* preclude a man from dueling?

"I won't call him out, but you will not stop me from thrashing him soundly, very soundly, should our paths cross."

Hadrian—lovely fellow—had the height and reach to thrash a man within an inch of the pearly gates.

"Don't let your path cross his, Hadrian." Avis leaned against him, which felt all too right and comfortable. "He's a devil and he won't fight fair. He'll stab you in the back and laugh while he does it."

"You are not to distress yourself over this," Hadrian rejoined, his hand resuming its rhythm on her hair. "I will tell you everything I learn about his whereabouts, and you will tell me or Fen if you see or sense anything suspicious."

"I will. You may depend on that."

"Good." Hadrian's voice sounded very near her ear, pleasantly so, which was incongruous given the topic. "I want you to consider something else, Avie."

"This sounds serious."

"It needn't be." Hadrian eased her back and shifted so she was not merely in his arms, but lying against him. "I didn't want this business with Collins to force the next topic onto the table, but it rather has."

"What is this next topic?"

"Marriage," Hadrian said, and Avis felt that hot and cold sensation again, but in a different way, and in different and private parts of her body.

"Between?"

"You and me."

CHAPTER SEVEN

Avie hadn't flounced off and she hadn't laughed. On the strength of those encouraging facts, Hadrian laced his fingers with hers and brought her knuckles to his lips for a lingering kiss.

"You should at least consider becoming engaged to me." Not the bended knee and tender sentiments she deserved, but if Hadrian attempted those, she'd likely toss him in the pond.

"I've been engaged before," Avie said, making it sound as if she'd taken a turn in the stocks. "I didn't care for it."

Hadrian's grasp on her fingers firmed, because he could feel the urge to flee building in her. "You were engaged to Collins, and your common sense was about to assert itself and retrace that misguided step."

"I'm not still engaged to him, am I?"

Had she haunted herself with that fear for *twelve years*?

"You are not. Harold had Benjamin write and officially break the engagement on your behalf. The letter was witnessed, and the copies were as well."

"Thank heavens."

Her brothers should have told her this, but Hadrian understood their reticence. Any mention of the past was avoided when that past was miserable, violent, and traumatic.

"You are free to give your hand where you choose, Avie. I hope you will consider my suit for two reasons." He'd also prayed about it, oddly enough, a different sort of prayer than he'd undertaken when vicaring.

"You're lonely," Avis suggested, "and prone to proposing where you know you'll be refused."

She was not entirely wrong.

"Bother you." He kissed her temple. "I'm mending my ways. If Collins does come sniffing about, I want the right as your fiancé to protect you, and I want him to know you're absolutely, unequivocally spoken for. You deserve that protection, Avie."

She deserved more than simple safety, though. A dash of joy, some love, a future that did not consist of choosing curtains for a dower house and biting her tongue in the face of Lily Prentiss's scolds.

"My tenants and my staff will protect me," Avis said, sounding more hopeful than confident.

"They won't take on a titled neighbor with Collins's reputation for viciousness."

She fell silent, while out in the pond, a fish jumped. Hadrian considered hunting down Hart Collins and taking a knife to his delicate parts. Fenwick would assist—cheerfully—and Harold would applaud.

"If I put it about that I'm marrying you, there will be talk, Hadrian."

The eleventh biblical plague, though no mention of it appeared in the book of Exodus. "There will always be *talk*. We are discussing your safety, and my ability to protect you."

"I could summon Benjamin home."

A fine idea, except she'd had twelve years to demand that her brothers share a roof with her, and both of them kept their distance, thinking she wanted privacy.

"Benjamin would take at least a week to wrap up his affairs, more likely two if he's larking about the Home Counties on some project or other, and then he'd have to make the journey north. Collins could be here by then. Besides, I have another motive in offering for you."

"I'm not sure I want to hear this."

"Listen anyway." He shifted again and fitted her arm across his middle, trying to convey that she could hold on to him, even as he held on to her. "You're lonely, Avie, and I can help with that."

"Like you're helping now?"

"I don't see you hopping up and bolting off in a fit of the vapors." Gratifying, that.

"I haven't had the vapors in twelve years."

"You haven't had fun in twelve years, either," Hadrian countered, though what he meant was that she hadn't had *pleasure*. Hadn't had close friends, shared tears, hearty laughs, or a real future. "You dance with Fen, then collapse into paroxysms of guilt and resentment. If you were engaged, you could dance all you pleased and nobody would comment."

Nobody would dare comment if Hadrian smiled indulgently at Avie's every waltz and flirtation. A tree root prodded him in the middle of his back, but he did not shift a single inch.

"I could dance with you, Hadrian."

"With anybody," Hadrian corrected her. "As long as I don't take umbrage, nobody will remark it." A woman on her way to the altar was considered brought to heel and allowed a certain paradoxical freedom, particularly with her fiancé at hand.

"When I've waltzed and cavorted with all the local swains, then what?"

That she would ask was further encouragement. "You face the same choice as any engaged lady. You can marry me or change your mind."

"And be a jilt as well as a Jezebel?" Her capacity for self-criticism was daunting. Why hadn't Lily Prentiss addressed this tendency, when it was entirely unwarranted?

"My challenge will be to inspire you to become a wife, instead." *His* wife.

Now, she tried to sit up, which flight Hadrian gently thwarted.

"Hadrian, I can't let you do this."

Very different from *I do not want to be engaged to you.*

"You can't stop me." This was the part that had kept him up past midnight, not clarifying his intentions, but puzzling out their implementation.

"I will call upon you," he said, "making sure Lily chaperones us. I will ride out with you when your grooms are in attendance. I will escort you to and from services. I will stand up with you at the local assemblies and make sheep's eyes at you when all the other couples announce their engagements. I will compose sonnets to you and offer them to the patrons of the local watering hole when I've overimbibed. I will—what?"

She was laughing silently against his side. "You would be a callow swain?"

"The most callow, while anybody was looking."

"And when they weren't?" Her laughter died, no doubt because his answer could hurt her badly.

"I would be a devoted suitor, Avie." He hugged her, a *friendly*, devoted suitor. "If you wanted to anticipate the intimacies of marriage, I would do my best to make them pleasurable for you."

This was the aspect of his offer that had occurred to him only as sunlight had inched across his bed. The intimate, feminine confidence Collins had taken from Avie must be restored, and an engagement would allow Hadrian to offer that to her.

"You'd anticipate vows I had no intention of taking?"

He would, because in a convoluted sense, he owed her that, but his answer had to be more honest than a simple yes.

"I want this to be a real engagement. I'm a man grown, Avie. I've seen all manner of heartache, mischief and loss among my flock and in my life. I don't expect you to buy a saddle horse without trying him over a few fences."

The analogy was borrowed from Colonel Devlin St. Just, a devotee of all things equestrian, and of his countess, to whom Hadrian had twice proposed.

In Hadrian's arms, Avie seemed to grow smaller. "You mean, you can't marry without being sure your wife can tolerate the steps necessary to conceive Harold's heir?"

She'd tried to keep the bitterness from her voice, without success. More honesty was called for, lest she cultivate this wrong-headed notion.

"You doubt you can tolerate joining with me, Avie?"

"Any sane person would doubt that, Hadrian, given my past."

"I know your past better than anybody," Hadrian said, glad for a chance to remind her of the signal honor she'd bestowed on him twelve years earlier. "I know you can enjoy pleasure, as well or better than most."

She buried her face against his throat. The heat in her cheeks suggested mortification, and that was the last sentiment Hadrian wanted to provoke.

"Shall I remind you, Avie?" He shifted her again, bringing her over him as he lay on his back, then scooting down, so the tree root no longer plagued him. He reached to the edge of the blanket, retrieved his jacket, and wadded it up under his head.

"We shouldn't do this."

"We should have done this more than once, twelve years ago. Kiss me, Avie, and I'll remind you of the pleasure you've denied yourself while hiding alone at Blessings."

* * *

Avis straddled Hadrian, skirts bunched, a thousand conflicting feelings fluttering about inside her, but acutely aware that beneath her, right beneath her, lay a man bent on seduction, and not just any man.

This was Hadrian, who had kept her confidences for twelve years, whom she'd sent away when she should not have let him from her sight. That was a lament for a different day, because his hand had found its way to her nape, urging her down over him.

"Kiss me, love, please." He closed his eyes, as if to better absorb the feel of her under his fingers, or perhaps to give her privacy. Hadrian Bothwell was that perceptive.

Despite a welter of sensations and emotions, Avis wanted to kiss him. She'd enjoyed every kiss they'd shared. Every single one, back for twelve years. She started by kissing his cheek, and even that took courage.

Hadrian turned his head as if seeking light or warmth and pressed his lips to her cheek as well. By degrees, they teased their way to each other's mouths, and then Avis let herself sink into him, into his mouth, his body, his warmth and strength, his scent.

Him.

Her body came alive over his, until the hard ridge of his arousal felt good, pressing against her sex. Even through their clothes, even knowing such intimacy was naughty, Hadrian felt good to her, and when he arched up against her, he felt even better.

"Kiss, Avie," he reminded her when she merely hung over him, focusing on the place where their bodies met. When his mouth found hers again, he became ravenous, and she gloried in his passion. His tongue invaded, his lips and teeth consumed, and yet she wanted to be closer. When his hand closed carefully over her breast, she pushed against his palm, beseechingly, shamelessly.

Memories of Hart Collins's assault slunk at the edges of her awareness, bringing with them echoes of pain, humiliation, shock, and grief. Avis beat the memories away with a cudgel of pure, keen rage. For twelve years, she'd managed, coped, and compensated in isolation. For twelve years, she'd allowed herself no intimacy with anybody, shared no confidences, indulged in no affection.

Damn Hart Collins to the coldest circle of hell for all the ways he'd ruined her life. Avis would not allow a selfish, violent, puerile thief to steal the beauty from what Hadrian offered now.

"Easy, love," Hadrian whispered against her throat. "You can stop me, Avie. Any time. You say so, and I'll stop, but I won't want to. Ever."

He nuzzled her breast, and frustration had Avis growling. And then, blessedly, his hand on her thigh shifted her skirts away, so she could be closer still.

"Hadrian, *please.*"

"No begging," he said, undoing the drawstring and bows that held her bodice together. "You may command me all you please, but no begging."

Hadrian's hands were not the elegant, pale appendages of a pampered gentleman. Shearing had taken a toll, the bright sunshine of approaching summer had too. His knuckles had been scraped, and a blister was healing between his right thumb and forefinger.

As he unlaced her bodice, then set to work on her jumps, his hands were beautiful.

"I want to hurry," Avis said, both because she might lose her nerve, but also because Hadrian had bestowed upon her the great gift of honest arousal.

"I want to savor the unveiling of your treasures, my lady. We'll hurry soon."

Good God, how did a woman endure such consideration? Beneath Avis's dress and jumps lay her chemise, and that too sported a plethora of tidy bows.

When all those bows, hundreds of them surely, had been patiently untied, Hadrian lay back and didn't so much as push her clothing aside.

"More kisses," he said, his hand drifting along Avis's thigh. "As many kisses as there are leaves on the budding rowans. Kiss me as deep as that endless, bottomless pond, as hot as the summer sun on your bare neck at mid-day, as passionately—"

Avis kissed him, lest he prose on for the length of a Sunday sermon. Still, he teased her, with his tongue and lips, and so enthralling were his kisses that Avis took long moments to notice that his hand was stealing along her leg, frothing up her skirts.

"Patience is not always a virtue, Hadrian Bothwell." Avis tugged on his hair even as she settled right on his falls and tried to find relief in simple pressure.

He might have laughed, or groaned, she didn't care which. She took his free hand and pressed it over her bare breast.

And that was an entire universe of fascinating sensations.

Heat—Hadrian's hands were warm—and tactile impressions. His calloused palm cupping the tender underside of Avis's breast, then gentle, knowing fingers teasing at her nipple. If Hadrian's palm was warm, his fingers were lit spills, igniting glory across the night sky inside her. Avis's breathing deepened as Hadrian's hand rode the rise and fall of her chest.

"Tell me what you need, Avie."

He kissed the slope of her breast, a sweet, lazy tease for which she would get even, some fine day when her reasoning powers had been restored. Avis bent forward and took her weight on one hand so she could lever up enough to give him room to touch her.

Touch…her…right…*there*.

Bless him, he understood what she sought and brushed his thumb through her curls—more damnable deliberateness, but in a promising location, at least. In the last functioning quadrant of her rational mind, Avis grasped that Hadrian was being patient and considerate, giving her time to panic, to change her mind, to reconsider.

She nearly hated him for his kindness, and then the pad of his thumb grazed over that particular spot she'd never had the nerve to explore on her own, and the intensity of the resulting sensation nearly struck her dumb.

"Again." Avis anchored her free arm around Hadrian's shoulders and held on, as that wonderful touch glided across her slick flesh again and again, the pressure minutely increasing each time.

She remembered not to beg, but twelve years ago, Hadrian had made sure she at least knew the pleasure her body was capable of.

A breeze stirred the green canopy overhead, and dappled shadows shook and danced on the blankets, as desire shook and danced through Avis. The sun was a perfect benevolence, the scent of new grass and wildflowers a delicate fragrance. For a moment, Avis savored the sheer perfection of the setting

Hadrian had chosen, for here in a high, secluded glen, she could be free of past and future, and give herself up to the joy of his skilled loving.

She soared, free of all save the pleasure Hadrian lavished on her with such tender determination. When she thought his touch would leave her, he merely slowed his caresses, letting sensation thicken and redouble as it reverberated through her anew.

She had missed this transcendent affirmation of the goodness of life, missed it badly, doubted it even existed but for the one experience of it so long ago.

Avis would have hung over her lover, panting, except he urged her down onto his chest, and she went gratefully. She even slept, though she would have sworn Hadrian had kept up slow, easy caresses on her back, neck and hair the entire time.

"You've undone me, Hadrian Bothwell." She'd desperately needed undoing and hadn't dared admit that to herself.

"Simply arguing my point."

"Your point?"

"Will you marry me?"

What came out of her mouth was not an argument, but a fear. "I'm a shameless wanton." Shameless, at any rate. Two lapses in twelve years probably did not amount to wantonness.

"I'll take that for a yes, because I am a shameless wanton too, and wantonness is a challenge better tackled with a partner."

How articulate he was, and—despite his casual humor—how aroused. The arousal ought to disquiet her, but this was Hadrian.

The best she could do was to sit up, straddling him. "I cannot marry you."

"Not yet," he said, so agreeably. "You'll consider my suit?"

He might have offered her another tea cake in the same tone. "My judgment is not sound in these matters, Hadrian." Particularly not when she was distracted by the evidence of his unsatisfied arousal.

He smiled, a universe of male wickedness and even a touch of smugness in the curve of his mouth and the light in his blue eyes.

"There's nothing wrong with any part of you, Avie."

"God help me." She looked down at his long male fingers so competently setting to rights the clothing she'd forgotten was askew, giving him a fine view of her breasts.

"All I ask for is an engagement, Avie." He left a few buttons undone, which was well advised, because Avie was quite warm. "One that serves several purposes and can be put aside when you please. You've sent me packing before, and I went then."

"You finished university then. You'll be on the neighboring estate this time." She was delighted this was so, also worried, for she knew well the path to his door.

"You have many neighbors you do not see," Hadrian reminded her. "I can join their number, but I won't like it."

"You won't be humiliated when I reject you?"

"I make it a policy to be fast friends with all the ladies who reject my suit." Hadrian petted her breast through her clothes. "I come with references in this regard. An appalling number of them."

"Two is not appalling."

"Neither is deciding we do not suit when we've hardly had a chance to know each other for twelve years, but Avie?"

"Stop that." She covered his hand with her own and pressed it closer to her breast.

"I will leave the field, so to speak, when you command it, provided you are safe, but we're friends, aren't we?"

"We're something." She climbed off him, because the discussion wanted rational thought, which was in short supply when she roosted upon her suitor. He let her get only as far as his side, where he bundled her against him with gentle insistence.

"We're friends," Hadrian reiterated. "We have a past, a present, and a future, and a little thing like a failed engagement would not cost you my friendship."

"Until you take a wife."

"That wife could be you, though I'm in no hurry to remarry, and being engaged to you will keep the local predators at bay."

"Is this your plan? To flaunt me in church and send the hopefuls packing?" Hadrian would never be so cavalier, least of all in the churchyard.

"Believe it is my plan if that soothes your nerves," he said, a touch of coolness in his tone. "I'm offering for you because I want to marry you."

He meant it, the demented man.

"Because I'm lonely."

"Because I am lonely. Now hush, so you might rest after your exertions, and cease arguing with someone who means you only the best."

She let him tuck her face against his shoulder and for once, did exactly as she was told.

* * *

As Avis dozed in Hadrian's arms, her thoughts went winging back twelve years, to the first and only other time she'd found intimate pleasure with a man—with Hadrian. They'd been on that dangerous cusp of inexperience and bravado. She'd been seventeen to his eighteen and had only recently realized Alexandra didn't want her sister hovering in the invalid's room, a *walking* reminder of the worst day of both of their lives. With silent, furious determination, Alex had started getting around on crutches. Less than week after that development,

Aunt Beulah had returned to the north, and arrangements had been made for the Portmaine sisters to leave Landover and return to their brothers' care at Blessings.

Hadrian would soon travel south for his final Michaelmas term at university. Hadrian, who had become Avis's devoted shadow in the weeks since she'd been assaulted. He'd walked with her all over the rugged countryside, inspiring her to a physical vigor she'd not known before. He'd shown her how to defend herself from such as Hart Collins, and that more than anything had renewed a kind of confidence she'd taken for granted as a girl.

He'd argued with her over all manner of topics worthy of debate by university scholars and shown her that her intellect was the equal of anyone's. He'd started her reading novels for her enjoyment and found her a copy of the *Scots Musical Museum*, because even earthy, unpretentious songs of love, loss, nature, and rural life gave her something to focus on.

He kissed her—playfully, true, like a cousin, or a particularly nice brother, but Avis knew exactly what he was about. He would push, pull, drag or flirt her back onto her emotional feet, and she'd been grateful.

Not until separation had loomed had Avis found the nerve to trust Hadrian with a question that had plagued her every waking moment.

"Why do women have relations with men?"

On his side of their picnic blanket, Hadrian paused in his reading of *The Lay of the Last Minstrel*. He did not immediately look over at Avis, but she had learned him well in the long weeks of summer.

He was no longer reading.

"Not to have children," Avis went on. "Having children is dangerous and occasionally fatal. Allowing a man intimate congress can't be to entice him into marriage, because marriage will simply mean more of same. Who would want to marry a fellow who comes to the altar panting from his naughty exertions?"

A yellow rowan leaf came twirling down, though the sunshine was at its late summer most benevolent.

"You really want me to answer that question?" Hadrian turned a page of his poem, quite the scholar. "The entire business is something your husband will explain to you."

She wanted the answer to one question, not an entire business. "I won't have a husband, Hadrian. I wouldn't want one, and none will offer for me. We know this."

"We don't know it," Hadrian rejoined, setting his poem aside and rolling to his back. "Only you have the power to refuse all comers, Avie, and you're barely seventeen. You'll get offers."

His casual confidence both pleased and perturbed her. Must he be such a relentlessly good friend?

"I haven't received a single invitation all summer, Hay." She flopped down beside him on the blanket; they were that at ease with each other. "Who wants to endure all that socializing if the result is supposed to be marriage proposals and what follows?"

"You won't always feel this way. The right man will earn your trust and show you what pleasure a husband can offer you."

The only man to earn her trust was soon to depart for points south, to resume drinking, wenching, arguing, and—coincidentally—studying with his peers.

"The right man, a decent, proper fellow who esteems decent, proper women, won't have me, even if I'd have him. You show me, Hay."

The idea had come to her weeks earlier, when she'd overheard Harold and Benjamin heartily assure each other Alexandra would someday "get back on the horse." What was Avis to do, for heaven's sake? Many proper ladies never graced the back of a horse, but only that pathetic creature, the spinster, avoided intimate congress with a man.

Hadrian bolted to sitting as if the blanket were on fire. "For God's sake. You are the victim of a crime, Avie. Would you be the victim of a seduction as well?"

"Better a seduction than ignorance," she shot back. "You kiss me, Hadrian, and I like that. I never thought I would, but I do."

"On the cheek!" He ran a hand through his hair, which he'd kept long in some young male bid for individuality. "On the hand, on the temple. I don't kiss your mouth, much as I might want to."

He sounded nearly angry, but not necessarily with her. "Why don't you?"

"Because it would be wrong. Because I would not want to stop there, and that would be beyond wrong."

"You've seen me," she said slowly. "Half-naked, bruised, beaten, stupid with shock, and crying, and yet you want me?"

Hadrian rose in one lithe movement and paced off the blanket. "That day, that day was one very bad moment, Avie, a nightmare moment in your life, and mine, but the fault for it lies exclusively at Hart Collins's feet. That was one awful day, which does not define you, nor does it limit my admiration for you."

She watched his restless movement, liking the way muscle moved beneath his doeskin breeches, not liking at all that he'd left their blanket.

"At best, I'm a victim. More likely, I'm stupid, shallow, conniving, and got exactly what I deserved."

Sunday mornings came around regularly, and the churchyard gossips made sure she did penance every week.

"You are not, and you did not." He dropped back down to the blanket and took her by the shoulders. He'd knelt in the same posture when he'd found her sitting on the steps outside that wretched little cottage.

She met his gaze, willing him to see her acquiescence. No, not acquiescence, not capitulation, her *hope*. She wanted his kiss, wanted his hands on her, wanted things from him she couldn't even name.

Did he but know it, those very wantings had been responsible for her decision to end her engagement with Hart Collins.

"Damn us both for this," Hadrian whispered, then pressed his mouth to hers.

Even in Avis's ignorance, wonder, and rejoicing, she grasped that Hadrian Bothwell was a skilled, even talented kisser. She'd endured her share of furtive, slobbery attempts from the local fellows, but this was lush, lovely, tender beyond imagining.

With only his mouth on hers, Hadrian brought Avis to life in a way she'd known he could, and the change felt *wonderful*. If her soul was a house, Hadrian's kisses were light pouring in the windows, fresh air wafting through her hallways, and music ringing from the rafters.

She pulled him over her, so she was on her back and he was the sun above her, and still they kissed. Avis kissed him with weeks of frustrated curiosity and passion, weeks of avoiding this moment, and weeks of trying to imagine it into being.

Hadrian took his mouth from hers, and she wanted to weep.

"Avie, we have to stop." His hair had come loose from its queue, and she speared her fingers through it and brought his face back to hers.

"Don't you dare stop. I want you to show me."

He dropped his forehead to her shoulder. "I will not despoil you, not even if you hate me for my refusal."

"Then just kiss me." And so it went, with him kissing her within an inch of her sanity, while she'd demanded, pleaded, and begged him to make love to her, and he refused, and kissed her some more. She went so far as to put his hand on her breast, knowing that if it was forbidden, it must have something to do with what she craved.

And, ah, God, his touch was beyond description. Careful, reverent, and both pleasure and torment. She only begged harder, until Hadrian hung over her, lungs heaving.

Another yellow leaf came spinning down through the sunshine to land on his shoulder. "Stop your infernal wheedling, Avis. Please."

She brushed the leaf away and cupped his cheek against her palm. He shaved now, something else he'd learned among the scholars far to the south.

"I will miss you to the bottom of my soul, Hadrian, and there's nobody else I can ask. If you deny me, I'll never know."

Hadrian trapped her hand in his own and kissed her knuckles, then shifted to brace on his forearms, so his weight pressed Avis into the blanket. "I will regret this all my days. Even if you don't hate me for it, I'll hate myself."

Capitulation. Had he not pinned her to the earth, Avie might have floated with a combination of trepidation and glee.

"Shall we undress?" For she wanted Hadrian to assure her that no trace of her ordeal was visible on her person.

And she wanted to see him, only him.

He'd shifted to his side, close, but not as close as she wanted him. "We shall not, lest I lose my last pretensions to honor. Close your eyes, Avie, and hold on to me."

A few more moments of attention to her breasts, a few more of those shockingly pleasurable kisses, and a deft, determined exploration of what lay under her skirts, and Hadrian sent Avis's world spinning.

All without removing a stitch of his own clothes and without letting her do more than kiss him.

When Hadrian rolled to his back, Avis tucked herself against his side. An echo of the dazed, detached, feeling she'd experienced right after her assault crept up on her, but the sunshine was warm, *Hadrian* held her, his scent enveloped her, his heartbeat thundered right beneath her ear.

Oh, God. God in heaven.

"I hope you comprehend now," he said, "why a woman might allow a man, the right man, intimate liberties."

He spoke so sternly, so disapprovingly, that the lovely haze of newfound knowledge thinned.

"You did find pleasure, didn't you?" He might have been a schoolmaster scolding an unruly little scholar.

"I did."

"Thank God for that."

He was relieved, while Avis had, for a few lovely moments, been pleased—so pleased.

While Hadrian was disgusted? Or worse, disappointed—in her? The last of the warm, happy sense of well-being left on a spate of exasperation. *What had she done?*

Hadrian withdrew his arm and sat up. "We'd best be on our way. The clouds are gathering."

"Hadrian?"

He busied himself finding his boots and passed her hers as well. Sometimes, he put them on her, but not today. Not ever again, most likely. With his face set in such harsh lines, he looked more handsome than ever, but also different. Not her Hadrian, but some angry angel, forced to sin.

"I'm not sorry," she'd said, pulling on her boots.

"This wasn't well done of me, or of you. I wanted—"

"I know what you wanted," she interrupted, yanking on the second boot. "You wanted me to live the rest of my life in complete ignorance, with memories of Hart Collins all I had to sustain my interest in the opposite sex. You were very clear on that."

"Avie, no."

She glimpsed shame in his eyes, heard it in his tone, the one thing she'd never wanted to bring down on her only friend. Avie got up, shook out her skirts, and made him a stupid little curtsy.

"Good day, Hadrian. I wish you every success when you return to school."

She'd flounced off, making it to the safety of the trees and their horses before she heard him behind her. Silently, he boosted her to her mount, and just as silently, he escorted her back to her own stable yard. Angry, disappointed, or even hating her, Hadrian would not let her come to harm.

"We have to talk, Avie," he said before she dismounted. "Things today did not go as they should have."

"No. They did not." Though what had she expected? That Hadrian would tolerate her wanton inquiries without thinking less of her? Did he think less of himself?

He helped her to dismount, and she stood beside the horse, her hands on his muscular arms, just as she had many, many times before. His blue eyes held concern now, and Avis knew—she just knew—he was about to apologize for giving her the single glimmer of hope she'd found in an entire summer of lonely self-doubt.

Pride had her whirling away when what she wanted was to fall weeping against his chest. She'd done that before too, too many times to count, and her tattered dignity came to her rescue.

Off she stomped, refusing to be home to him for the next three days, and then he departed to Oxford a week early. When Harold told her a month later that Hadrian was studying for the church, she'd nearly spilled her tea.

And now, twelve years later, Hadrian was no longer a churchman, he was no longer a young man shatteringly disappointed in a friend, he was offering instead to be a fiancé.

"You're awake." His arms stayed around her, and his lips brushed her brow. "Have I learned anything worth knowing in twelve years?"

"Will you use my answer as a pretext to disappear for the next twelve years?" A significant part of her feared he would.

"I will not." He spoke easily and steadily, and this time he kissed her ear.

Avis nuzzled his collarbone. "Then I'd say you are more knowledgeable than ever."

Hadrian gathered her closer without her having to ask. "Go back to sleep. We'll talk when you've rested."

CHAPTER EIGHT

They would talk, Hadrian silently promised Avie, when his raging case of frustrated lust subsided yet further, for Avie was apparently no more knowledgeable regarding male erotic functioning than either of them had been twelve years earlier.

What a scene that had been. Him, thinking on the strength of his strutting college boy's experiences, he could pleasure a woman, and her, not even realizing what she'd asked of him. He'd ached badly that day and not only in the physical sense. He'd wanted to propose to her, but kept hearing her contempt for marriage at every turn.

Avis had wanted him for a lover but not for a husband. His overblown eighteen-year-old sense of honor and his delicate young man's pride hadn't been sophisticated enough to understand the time and trust she needed.

Still needed.

Thank God for the passage of the years.

The prayer was sincere, one of his first sincere prayers in weeks.

"I can't sleep," Avis said on a yawn. "Not any more. Neither am I in a hurry to scurry back to the dower house and oversee the work of the glaziers."

"Harlan Danvers has been glazing windows since he was in short coats. He'll manage. Would you like some wine?"

"I would, but I don't want to move."

"Alas, we did not learn when studying scripture how to make wine bottles levitate." When she pushed off him and sat up, Hadrian got to his feet, discreetly adjusting his clothes while she fussed with her hair.

He kissed her shoulder, happy in the knowledge that he had more sense than he'd had at eighteen—he wanted to linger and cherish, not bolt off to commit the sin of Onan. "Leave that, Avie. I'll see to your braid, but first, your libation."

He retrieved the wine, poured her a glass, and then took up a position behind her on the blanket, his fingers tugging pins from her hair.

She plucked a clover flower from the grass. "I'm glad you're not angry with me this time."

Hadrian paused in his leisurely quest for hairpins. "I beg your pardon?"

"Twelve years ago. You were so wroth with me, I thought you would hurl thunderbolts because I'd importuned you, and you were such a decent young man."

Hadrian hugged her from behind and dredged up the courage that was supposed to come with maturity. "Twelve years ago I was sexually frustrated, disappointed in myself, and hurt that you wanted me for a lover but nothing more. I was not angry with you, though I was an utter buffoon."

Not the last instance of buffoonery on his part, but confessing to Avie eased his heart.

She shredded the clover, dusted her hands, then plucked another victim. "When you called the next day, you weren't seeking me out to scold me and heap scorn on my head?"

Her question made his heart ache all over again. "I sought you out to propose, but with you, I didn't even get as far as a rejection. I suppose you were my first, best failed proposal."

Why hadn't he seen that earlier?

She leaned back against his chest. "My poor Hadrian. I'm sorry."

"I assumed you were wroth with me, thinking I'd used the same tactic as Collins had, or a version of it."

"What on earth do you mean?"

Truly, this was a conversation they should have had years ago.

"He thought by despoiling you, you'd be forced to keep your engagement to him," Hadrian said, drawing her hair over her shoulders. "I was determined to offer for you, but then realized you'd feel just as trapped, just as manipulated, and I wanted you to know, before I left for school, that I'd wait."

Perhaps he was waiting still. Interesting notion.

"Then I didn't receive you. What a tangled web."

A tangled web that had led them back here, to a blanket shared amid the fresh air and sunshine of the Cumbrian countryside.

"Have you a pocket comb?" He drew his hands through the silky glory of her unbound hair again while his cock, which had been obediently subsiding, stirred back to life.

Exactly as if he were still eighteen.

She passed a small comb over her shoulder, and Hadrian focused on his task, despite having a few questions of his own.

"I wrote to you, my first term back at Oxford and then again in the spring."

"I was off at Aunt Beulah's in Scotland. Hers was not the most organized household, and the letters might not have received the attention they deserved. I could not write to you. Aunt would have forbidden such an impropriety."

"I didn't expect a reply," Hadrian said, but he had hoped for one. He'd spent months hoping. "I wrote to you again before I married Rue."

"How long ago?"

"Years." He thought back, even as he drew the comb through her hair, something he'd never done for his wife. "Not quite six."

"I should have received it, but the king's mail is not as reliable as we're supposed to believe. That feels good."

"Better than good." He swept her hair aside, to kiss her nape and turn the conversation from that long ago letter. His last epistle had been the most pathetic, baring his soul, begging, pleading, and promising with all the frustration and passion in him. What a mercy, in some sense, that the missive had gone astray.

"I wrote to you," Avis said. "When Rue died."

"I received that letter," he replied, running his tongue over the top of her spine. She tasted of lavender soap with a touch of lemon. "Your kindness was a consolation, but this is a pleasure." One that abetted his unruly manhood, so he forced himself to get back to work on her hair.

"What was your Rue like?"

A question to bring a fellow's parts to heel.

"She was my escape route out of the frustrated ranks of young curates, and I was her escape from her father's parsonage. She was the youngest of several sisters and at risk for being the one left behind to look after her aging parents."

"The plain girl. I've envied a few plain girls. At least they have parents to love."

Hadrian leaned in closer. "If you marry me, you can have babies to love, Avie. I'd thrive on giving you babies. Rejoice in it, exuberantly."

"And you were being so good. I can accept the advisability of being courted by you to appearances, Hadrian, at least until we know what Collins is up to, but I doubt you'll embark on the business strictly for show."

"No, I will not. A vicar has ample opportunity to observe his flock making sheep's eyes, Avie, particularly during his sermons. All and sundry will remark my callowness."

"I don't want to give you false hope."

She was so good, so decent. "What happened on this blanket didn't give you some real hope?"

"You gave me real pleasure."

"That, my love, is a start."

* * *

Never had a bridle sported such a shiny bit, never had the leather been so thoroughly cleaned and oiled. Fen was about to unbuckle the entire business and start back at the beginning when his favorite Choir Boy came sauntering into the stable yard.

His holiness had been getting some sun lately. Maybe a few kisses, too, judging from the state of his hair and neckcloth.

"Well, if it isn't Bothwell the Younger, come to interrupt my work."

"Fenwick." Bothwell slid onto the bench beside him. "Haven't you a pasture full of sheep to visit or some hay to scythe?"

"Give the hay another few days." Bothwell bore more than a hint of Avie's rose scent, too. "Soon we'll scythe until we have blisters on our blisters. We'll get through one more rainy patch, according to Sully's lumbago, and then the sun will be out for a solid week."

"Somewhere, maybe. Not here in Cumberland."

"I listen to whatever guidance I can get when it comes to haying." Fenwick set his bridle aside and resisted the urge to get off a bench that had grown uncomfortable an hour ago. "How did your discussion go with Lady Avis?"

Bothwell had warned Fen that the quarry pond was unavailable to staff, stewards, and meddling companions until further notice.

"I informed Lady Avis of Collins's possible plans to turn up locally and offered her the protection of both my stout right arm and my name, should it come to that."

"Fast work there, Bothwell. How did she respond?" Fen sustained a dart of jealously, followed by an equally sharp shaft of admiration. Bothwell grasped the magnitude of Avis's problem and didn't hesitate to take responsibility for its solution.

"Her ladyship tried to reject my suit out of hand, but has too much sense not to see the wisdom of it." Bothwell shifted, crossing his legs at the ankle. "Why is it I can comfortably occupy a blanket on the hard, unforgiving ground of a Cumbrian hillside for better than an hour, but five minutes on a bench next to you and my backside protests?"

"Because you've a skinny arse." And because Avie had occupied that blanket—those blankets—with him. "You're rich as a nabob, already broken to the marital bridle, good-looking, pious to all appearances, and in line for a title. Poor Avie Portmaine will be reduced to becoming your viscountess."

Bothwell let the pious-to-all-appearances jab pass, such were the reviving effects of time spent on blankets in the Cumbrian hills.

"Fenwick, you will not lecture her, you will not exhort her, and you will not offer her an alternative."

Avie's choir boy was turning up both possessive and protective.

"She hasn't any alternatives," Fen said, fingering the stout, dark leather of the curb reins, "unless she wants to summer down in London with Benjamin, and nobody in their right mind wants to do that."

"You've spent summers in Town?"

He'd endured London, as young men from good families were supposed to. "I've spent time in London in spring, before the members of Parliament abandon weighty matters of state to shoot at hapless grouse with greater focus than they ever bring to affairs of state. I found the capital a pestilentially miserable experience."

"One does recall the stench, even years later."

"She'll have you, Bothwell." Fenwick looped the reins up through the headstall, the first step in tying up the bridle.

"Yes, I hope she does, but will she marry me thereafter?"

Bothwell rose and disappeared into the shadows of the stable, while Fen finished seeing to his bridle, then took out his knife, and once again polished the gleaming blade.

* * *

"I thought nothing could equal the ache resulting from shearing, but haying is an altogether hotter, itchier torment," Hadrian said as he pulled on his second boot and straightened—carefully. The bank of the pond held lovely memories for him, but now it also qualified as the place where he'd nearly toppled into the water, so stiff was his back.

"Haying smells better than shearing," Fenwick remarked philosophically as he slicked back his wet hair. "Haying doesn't involve all that damned bleating and wailing for mama the livelong week. Then too, the quarry pond isn't quite so frigid come haying."

The pond was cold as the ninth circle of hell, which probably accounted for why Hadrian was still awake.

"I'm cleaner than I've been in two days. All I want now is my dinner." Hadrian had left his shirt partly unbuttoned, his waistcoat as well, as had Fen. Their progress down the hillside was as slow as a pair of old veterans heading from the alehouse on a moonless night, but as they approached the stables, Lily Prentiss caught sight of them, her lips turning down at the corners as she veered off toward the dower house.

"We've been found wanting," Fenwick noted, alluding to a verse from the book of Daniel he'd cited on other occasions. "That woman could teach raisins to wrinkle."

"She's pleasant enough. Perhaps you'd like to teach her something?"

"How to decamp for distant parts," Fenwick muttered. "She's a blight on the landscape, and you would do well to watch your back around her."

Lily Prentiss was also loyal to Avis and her only female friend, as Fen well knew.

"Fenwick, the woman has been nothing but pleasant to me, and she's a spinster, for pity's sake. Do you expect all women to embrace your flirting and irreverence?"

"If they won't embrace me, then my larking about is harmless fun, so yes, I do."

Damnably logical. In addition to the ache in Hadrian's back and the misery that was his hands, his head also throbbed from too much sun, or perhaps too much of Fen's company. "Will we have another party after the haying?"

"There is no life after haying," Fenwick said as they thumped onto his back porch. "Haying goes on for two weeks at least, if the damned rain doesn't spoil the crop. Then you're too tired to sport about between the keg and the dance floor."

"A party then." Inevitable, much like village assemblies had been back at Rosecroft. "I am too old for the demands of country living."

More and more, Hadrian understood why Harold, living alone at Landover year after year, had sought an escape.

"We'll toughen you up, Choir Boy. The biggest celebration comes after harvest, but we do a sort of midsummer bonfire after haying. The solstice generally arrives as we're putting up our hay forks."

Pleasant memories rose from Hadrian's distant youth as Fen led the way to the kitchen. "Naughty old solstice. Do the young people still sneak off after dark to make free with the ancient traditions?"

"Make free with each other, you mean? Oh, of course."

Fenwick's house smelled good, of dried herbs and—truly, Hadrian had gone for a country squire—hay.

"You're plotting the downfall of Lady Avis, aren't you? Do you church fellows make a ritual of even your swiving?"

"For the last bleating time, I am not a churchman. I am a damned tired, hungry neighbor, who dreads the thought of lifting a rake tomorrow or ever again." Though Hadrian also looked forward to it far more than he'd ever looked forward to delivering a sermon.

"At least Avie can't scold you for wrecking your hands."

"Perhaps not." Hadrian looked at his paws, which he'd kept conscientiously gloved the livelong day, and which had developed a complement of calluses in any case. "My back is about ninety-four years old, though, and my arms are ready to fall off."

"I've some horse liniment that will do wonders."

"While leaving me noisome in the extreme?" Fen would pull such a maneuver, too, in retaliation for the rose and comfrey salve, and for the sheer hell of it.

"If you start attracting all the fillies, you can blame me."

"Let's eat outside," Hadrian suggested, wondering where Fen found the energy for his humor. "There's a breeze and the night should be clear."

"Your flowing tresses will dry more quickly."

Fen's dark hair was nearly as long.

"I could use a trim, but when I was at university, I let it grow past my shoulders."

"A Viking vicar?" Fen disappeared into the pantry and emerged bearing their trays. "I'll bet the bishops had something to say about that."

"I cut it before I was ordained," Hadrian said, fingering his hair. Avie had loved playing with his longer hair.

"Like a sheep, shorn before being turned out to fatten in high pasture." Fen handed him a tray. "Stop complaining and start eating."

They sat on Fen's porch and demolished substantial trays as the sun faded to pink, then orange, then blue and indigo.

"You asleep?" Fenwick asked when they'd been sitting in silence for some time.

"Almost. Lest I stiffen up and be mistaken for a handsome corpse, I'll take a short constitutional."

"Bang the door on your way in, else I'll fret you've been set upon by highwaymen." Fenwick gave Hadrian's arm a gentle avuncular pat, stacked their trays, and disappeared into the house.

Fenwick's company was by turns gruff, merry, insightful, taciturn, protective, and irreverent, but he was ferociously competent at his job, and a good friend. Hadrian had learned much from him and hoped Fen derived some benefit from their association as well.

It had been a year for friendships, Hadrian reflected as he made his way to the back gardens. Harold had become more of a friend and less of an older brother, Devlin St. Just had become a friend, and Hadrian had renewed his friendship with Avis.

St. Just had threatened by letter to come for a visit, and Emmie would want her husband kept busy before the baby came. The thought was purely sweet, and a bit surprising, given that Hadrian had at one time envisioned himself as the father of Emmie Farnum St. Just's babies.

He chose a bench bordered by blooming honeysuckle from which to watch the rising moon, though he'd no sooner taken his seat than a shadow detached itself from the house. A woman, based on the white shawl visible in the gloom, and not in any hurry.

He hoped it was Avis, but the gait was off as she came down the path, and she wasn't tall enough.

"Good evening, Miss Prentiss." Though if Hadrian had foiled a tryst between Miss Prentiss and, say, Ashton Fenwick, she might not regard it as a good evening after all.

"Mr. Bothwell!" The lady's hand went to her throat. "You startled me, sir."

"My apologies." Hadrian ambled toward her. "It's a pretty night, though, isn't it?"

She took a step back, as if Hadrian might intend something other than an exchange of pleasantries.

Which, in a sense, he did.

"The evening is pleasant enough," she said. "You're taking the air?"

"As are you." He offered his arm, curious to see what reasons Miss Prentiss might give for her nocturnal constitutional. "The moon will be up soon. Shall we keep each other company?"

Her hand on his arm communicated caution, but she fell in step beside him, suggesting the oh-so-proper Lily Prentiss could wander off the path of propriety in the company of a chance-met former vicar.

"I suppose haying makes a lot of work for the house staff?"

"Oh, my goodness, yes," Lily replied, apparently relieved to have a safe topic. "The kitchens are going round the clock, and Cook gets quite short-tempered if I don't have the menus to her almost before the ink is dry. Then too, the laundresses have extra duty. Haying is untidy business, and the laundresses require careful direction lest they get to squabbling over their beer.

"The footmen and maids are stepping and fetching for the kitchens the whole day and half the night, and that must be kept organized," Lily went on, as if this household bustle were the very lifeblood of the realm, "and the stables are busy, for every plough horse and mule on the property must be pressed into use. But you know all of this."

"I do not," Hadrian assured her. "As a child, haying meant riding around in the wagons, or on the backs of the plough horses, sneaking lemonade or cider or ale, and so on. I didn't pay attention to the work involved."

"Children have that luxury. We adults must see to our appointed tasks and hope the yield is adequate."

"We're lucky so far this year. The crop is good, and hasn't been rained on," Hadrian replied, but something in Lily's recitation struck him as off. She was the lady's companion, and none of the tasks she'd listed fell into her ambit. The work she'd described was for Avis to direct and the staff to carry out. From what Hadrian had observed, Avis saw to the lot cheerfully and competently.

But, then, Avis would likely delegate to any willing underling, and Lily was that.

"Do you enjoy the midsummer celebration to follow the haying?" he asked.

"I most assuredly do not. Not after Vicar Chadwick has blessed the crop, at least."

Hadrian had blessed the crops, the hounds, the occasional tartan, and more than a few ailing beasts. "A prudent man then, who knows how to blend the old ways with the new. I'm rather looking forward to a little relaxation."

She was silent, her disapproval as tangible as the scent of honeysuckle on the evening air.

"Miss Prentiss, you don't truly begrudge the local folk their gatherings, do you?"

"Of course not, but these gatherings you refer to include not only the help, but their betters as well."

"You refer to your employer, Lady Avis?"

"I do, and I consider her not my employer, for her brother is that, but my charge, and it is trying in the extreme to stand by while she struggles with these social occasions."

Hadrian borrowed a tactic from his church days and held his peace. Silence could encourage confidences more than sermons or small talk would, and pointing out to Lily that Avis was less than ten years her junior—and by no means her *charge*—was not Hadrian's place.

"She means well," Lily went on, her tone earnest, "and for a while I thought she was getting better, but lately, Lady Avis has forgotten her place."

Wonderfully so. "In what regard?"

"She doesn't understand how she'll be perceived," Lily expostulated. "She smiles at all the young fellows, and this is seen as flirting. She danced with Mr. Fenwick, who is not a gentleman, not by any lights. She serves ale in public and lets old Sully share her mug and sits on the same blanket with Young Deal, and it's all very improper, but she forgets her upbringing when the men are around."

Lily was fairly charging down the path, so impassioned was she. "I know she misses her brothers, Mr. Bothwell, but others aren't so charitable. The neighbors have long memories and will not forget the unfortunate missteps of her youth. I hope you will be charitable toward her, sir. You are her neighbor, too."

"I am," Hadrian said mildly, though Miss Prentiss's hope had the quality of a scold. "I am also her friend."

"As I am," Lily said, her pace moderating. "As her friend, I have to tell you that little picnics by the pond will not aid her reputation one bit."

Lily Prentiss enjoyed absolute certainty about her conclusions "She told you about that?"

"We have no secrets. She trusts me implicitly, as she should."

"Then you know that was a simple meal in the fresh air and my effort to see that Lady Avis has some enjoyment in her day, nothing more."

"Of course it wasn't meant to be anything more, and you can trust my discretion, Mr. Bothwell. I know a man of the church would be inclined to kindness and generosity with his company, but you must have a care for the lady's well-being."

"The very point of the outing," Hadrian murmured. Was this how his more admonitory sermons had come off, as so much bleating and condescension?

Lily patted his arm. "You mean well, but the subtleties often elude you fellows. I'm glad we've cleared the air, though, and I thank you for your escort. I would have missed the moonrise had you not been willing to share the night air with me."

"May I leave you with a question, Miss Prentiss?" He dropped her arm and regarded the pale sphere ascending into the night sky.

"Of course."

"How is it a picnic in the broad light of day between people who've known each other their entire lives is somehow the very essence of inchoate scandal, but strolling alone in the moonlight with a man you hardly know is not?"

He bowed and took his leave, lest his question give her grist for another half-hour of lecturing and instructing. Miss Prentiss took her position seriously, which was a fine quality, except she did not, apparently, have a firm grasp of what that position was.

Her charge, indeed.

Hadrian understood protectiveness, though, and thus, when he returned to Fenwick's little house, he banged the back door loudly before he sought his bed.

* * *

Haying, by its nature, best happened when the sun was at its strongest, the days longest, unlike shearing or the grain, vegetable, or fruit harvests. For that reason, Avis had always found a grueling aspect to haying, a brutish, dragging interminability and a burning exhaustion.

And an urgency, for a passing shower could ruin an entire winter's fodder. If the rain hit before the scything, then the crop grew coarse and overripe and lost much of its nutritional value. If the rain hit when the fodder was scythed and drying on the ground, then the entire field had to be raked over, or tedded, to spend more days drying. If the rain came as the crop was brought in, then the risk of fire from moldy hay in the barn increased dramatically.

Make hay while the sun shines.

Avis arched her back against an ache that had deepened as the week progressed. Arching one's back was not ladylike. Thank heavens Lily hadn't set foot out of the house since mid-day, or Avis might have had some unladylike words to go with her sore back.

She hefted one of the few remaining full small kegs stacked at the back of a donkey cart, but had to set the barrel back down on the ground, for the effort nearly overbalanced her.

"Give me that." Hadrian Bothwell snatched up the keg as if it were so much laundry and set it on the cart. "I cannot believe you were left to pack up the ale on your own. Where is Young Deal when there's manual labor to be done?"

"He took the last load to the tithe barn," Avis said, for finally, finally, the haying was over for another year.

Hadrian had worn a straw hat when working in the fields, its distinctive floppy shape making him easier for Avis to keep track of. His hat was off now, and his complexion had a ruddy quality suggesting he'd taken some sun.

"Thank you," Avis said, as Hadrian tossed another keg into the cart. She perched her backside on the tailgate of the cart, took out her much abused handkerchief and patted her temples and throat.

"You look pale, my lady. Fenwick and I will finish loading this wagon while you sit."

"Best heed him, Lady Avie," Fenwick advised, striding up the hedgerow. "Man has a stubborn streak."

One of Hadrian's many fine qualities, else he would have faded with the heat of the day, as Lily had.

As Avis should have. She was sticky, hot, dirty, and probably sporting more than a few bits of hay on her person. That Hadrian should see her thus—

"What are you thinking?" Hadrian asked, as he passed Fenwick another keg.

She was thinking she'd liked the look of him, wielding his rake, cantering from one field to the next, sleeves turned back, collar open, not so much the proper gentleman.

"I'm glad this is over for another year and glad the crop is in."

He passed her a flask, which turned out to contain sweet, tepid tea.

"Fen, can you drive the cart in? I'll walk her ladyship up to the house."

Fen climbed onto the cart and unwrapped the reins. "I get the donkey. You get the lovely filly."

Hadrian pulled Avis to her feet, which was fortunate, or she would have taken her first ride in the back of a donkey cart—she was that tired.

"You will accept my escort, madam, and we will embark on a stately turn toward the house."

"Slow it shall be. Gran Carruthers could beat me in a foot-race about now."

"She had the sense to quit after nooning. Where is your companion?"

Right where she should be—anywhere else. "Lily's fair coloring doesn't tolerate the heat well." Lily had convenient, if hidden, reserves of intolerance for all manner of trials.

"So she should wear a hat rather than leave you to suffer by yourself."

"I had help."

"Which you shooed away at every opportunity."

"Don't fuss at me, Hadrian." They were making slow progress, in part because Hadrian led her around the edge of the garden, keeping to the shaded paths. "It's late enough you don't have to keep me from the sun."

"I'm keeping you from the house," Hadrian said, turning her up the hill.

"You expect me to climb the hill to view the sunset with you? I'll fall asleep before we reach the top."

"We're going only as far as the pond, and I'll carry you if I have to."

She was too tired to argue with him, though the idea of him carrying her was appealing. "You probably could too. I saw you without your shirt, Hadrian Bothwell."

"Then you saw Fen and every man under fifty in the same state. How did I measure up?"

Avis had stared until Gran Carruthers had caught her at it. Gran, oddly enough, hadn't made a single teasing remark, but had muttered something wistful about youth being wasted on the young.

"You're beautiful. So is Fen, of course. Young Deal cuts quite a figure for a man of his mature years."

"Oh, of course."

"And the two of you together make a nice contrast." Fen, for example, was probably at the stables by now, while Hadrian had taken Avis's hand to help her up the hill. "Are you as relieved as I am to get the haying over with?"

"I am. I never realized what a chancy business it is, deciding when to cut, whether and when to sheave, whether to send the first or the last wagons to the tithe barn. When I wore a collar, I watched it all progress and saw the relief on the small holders' faces when it was done, and the strain when it had gone badly."

Was that what leading a flock had been to him? A collar? "In either case, you prayed?"

"I did, either in thanksgiving or for fortitude. A winter without a full hay barn is a frightening prospect."

"Much like spring without new life," Avis said as the pond came into view.

Now that she'd made the climb, the expanse of cool water beckoned, and she would have commenced stripping off her half-boots and stockings, at least, but Hadrian had gone still beside her.

He'd also kept his fingers laced with hers.

"I wanted children too, Avie. That was part of what motivated me to marry."

"Children?" New life—of course he would not miss that reference.

"Yes, children. Messy, disruptive little beasts who make noise and break things by accident, and sometimes on purpose. I never considered that my wife wouldn't share that objective."

He seldom referred to the lady by name, but Avis wondered if Rue Bothwell was ever far from his thoughts.

"She didn't want children?"

"She wanted something." He took off his jacket, which at one time might have been a fine piece of apparel, and spread it on the ground. The green slopes rose around them, while the pond was a flat mirror of the evening sky. "She perceived more clearly than I that Harold wouldn't have sons. I suppose she wanted Landover."

"Did she say as much?" For Hadrian's sake, Avis hoped his wife had at least been tactful about her ambitions. He deserved that much kindness. "Maybe her mother had a hard time in childbed, and she was anxious."

Hadrian handed Avis down onto his jacket, then joined her, carefully, slowly.

"Her mother produced several healthy daughters in rapid succession. They fascinated me, with their looks, indecipherable asides, and exclusionary airs." His tone said he wasn't pleased with his easily fascinated younger self.

"Exclusionary?"

He took Avis's hand, though his had to be sore. "A sibling group of sisters, no brothers, and their dear papa was devoted to the Lord's work in sheer self-defense. They were a mystery to me, a sweet-smelling, coy, teasing, unknowable mystery."

"So you married to unwrap the mystery?" He'd had no sister, not even a mother for most of his boyhood. Avis would not have blamed him for marrying to unwrap the mystery of femininity.

"I married in part because they decided their baby sister would have me, and into parson's mousetrap I went."

He was trying to lighten the moment, and yet his grip on her hand had tightened.

"You went willingly." Or had he sought marriage because for one summer, Avis and Alex had sheltered under Landover's roof, and Hadrian had liked that?

"We were both willing, at the time. We weren't miserable."

"Not miserable." Avis said the words as one might have said "slightly putrid" or "a little fatal," for Hadrian had clearly been something worse than miserable. He'd been resigned.

Out in the pond, a fish leapt. How did fish find their way into a hillside pond?

He untangled his hand from Avis's grasp. "Not miserable is better than my parents had. Perhaps we should remove to a blanket?"

"Somebody has been making regular visits," Avis said, for an oilskin covered a hamper under a particular rowan tree, and the edge of a tartan blanket peeked out from under the wicker lid.

"Fen and I have taken to bathing up here. We keep soap, towels, blankets, and if I'm not mistaken, a bottle in there."

"A bottle? What resourceful fellows." And how easily Hadrian made a friend of the steward Avis had taken several years to turn into an ally.

"The bottle was my idea," Hadrian said, rising and opening the basket. "If

Fen asks me to help him build a tree-fort, I'll be tempted."

"Would you play castaways too?" The notion appealed to Avis. Haying had made her daft.

"Only if Fen is the loyal companion, and I get to be head of the expedition," Hadrian said, moving things around in the hamper.

"The Cumbrian countryside can be a lonely place to grow up." Avis pushed to her feet, because clearly, Hadrian was intent on some objective. "I had Alex, until she went a-governessing."

Hadrian stopped plundering the basket's stores long enough to let Avis have a look. "Is that when Miss Prentiss joined the household?"

"More or less." Avis extracted a corked bottle—haying was thirsty business. "Shall we?"

"Certainly." Hadrian spread the oilskin then laid a blanket over it and retrieved his jacket from the bank of the pond. "We can celebrate the end of haying, and your return to besieging the dower house with Miss Prentiss."

Daunting thought.

"The dower house needs besieging." Avis took a seat on the blankets, uncorked the bottle and cautiously sampled of the contents, finding them a blend of fruit and fire. "What on earth is this?"

"Peach brandy." Hadrian settled cross-legged beside her. "Fenwick came across it on his travels in the south. Imbibe carefully; it packs a devil of a kick."

"It's different, like a cordial, but fiery." Peach brandy put her in mind of Hadrian's kisses.

He appropriated the bottle. "If you don't exercise moderation, you'll regret it in the morning, as much as you were in the heat today."

"I should be ordering myself a bath right this minute." Avis passed him the cork. "Except the house staff is run ragged along with the rest of us." So she'd soak her feet in the pond and enjoy the peace and quiet of the hillside.

Hadrian pulled off a boot. "I don't know about you, but I'm not inclined to wait for my bath."

Another boot came off. Hadrian pitched both to the side of the blanket, and abruptly, Avis's fatigue had also been tossed aside.

"Hadrian Bothwell, what are you about? It's broad daylight, and you are not alone."

"A lady is present," he allowed, as his stockings came off. "A very hot, tired and, dare we say it, unrefreshed lady, one who could join me in yonder water and feel much better in short order."

Unrefreshed. A telling summary of the past twelve years. "I haven't been swimming for years. That water must be freezing."

"Two months ago, it was freezing." Hadrian's shirt went over his head. "Now it's pleasantly brisk." He stood and began to unbutton his falls.

CHAPTER NINE

"Hadrian. This is not a good idea." Though Avis would not object if his fingers worked more quickly.

"I have to agree," he said as his breeches and drawers came off together. "It's a *wonderful* idea." Naked as God made him, he moved around behind her and hunkered to unfasten her dress. "The sun is dropping, the moon will be nearly full, and we can watch it rise together, but mind you, don't be telling your duenna about this."

"My who?"

A soft, warm sensation on her nape informed her Hadrian was sneaking kisses. "You're unbuttoned, my lady. You can extract yourself from there, but please do not offend your Creator or present company by leaving your shift on. If you're willing to celebrate Beltane, then celebrate Beltane."

Beltane had come and gone. Avis was more interested in celebrating *him*.

Which was bad of her. Very bad. "Hadrian, I should not." Though, why not? What had twelve years of careful propriety earned her but a loneliness as deep as the quarry pond and twice as cold?

"We're almost engaged," Hadrian whispered, nuzzling her shoulder, "and it's only me, Avie."

"Only you." She leaned back against the hands he'd rested on her shoulders. "Stark, stitchless naked."

"And it feels wonderful, so stop stalling. I want to see you."

"You must have what you want," she murmured, and before her courage could desert her, she drew her dress up and over her head.

She was glad to be rid of it, for even an old, soft, summer walking dress was a weight, and for once, Avis wanted to be weightless.

"The shift, love." Hadrian came around and held out a hand to her, drawing her to her feet.

"How can you strut about, unclothed and unconcerned?"

"Do you like what you see?" He stepped back and spread his arms. "If you like the view, I'm happy not to cover it up. I'm also in need of a liberal dose of soap and water and getting clean will feel nearly as wonderful as, say, kissing you."

"How do you have the energy for this?" She turned her face away and let him untie the bows of her jumps and shift.

"How do you have the energy to resist?"

Avis shimmied out of her stays; Hadrian drew her shift over her head, and there she stood, naked, but for boots and stockings.

"I feel silly." Also chilly.

"You're overdressed," Hadrian said, going down on his knees to roll down her stockings and unlace her boots. He also managed to work in a goodly number of little touches and caresses to her feet, ankles, and calves.

He hadn't learned this masculine competence, with her clothing, with her body, in vicar school, and he hadn't learned it from his ambitious, un-maternal wife. He'd had it before, during their one shared summer.

Avis had thanked God for it then; she nearly worshipped Hadrian for it now.

"You are lovely." Hadrian rose when Avis had stepped out of her boots. "You honor me with your trust, and I shall perish of my own stickiness if we don't get in the water immediately." He set towels and soap on the bank, while Avis dashed past him, lest she expire from a combination of mortification, curiosity, and desire.

She came up sputtering, the cold reverberating through her bones. "Ye gods, Hadrian!"

He stood on the bank, a grinning pagan god. "You'll adjust, just don't stop moving."

"It's refreshing. Shockingly so."

"I generally bathe first," Hadrian said, balancing atop a rock that jutted out over the water, "in case my resolve fails, or winter comes early."

He executed a graceful arc, knifing into the water with barely a splash.

Avis was standing in water up to her neck—the cold had become nearly bearable—when Hadrian approached her with the soap.

"You're interested in using the soap, Mr. Bothwell?"

"On you."

He didn't give her a chance to argue—she'd meant to argue—he simply scrubbed up a lather and applied his wet, slippery hands to her neck, making a slow, massaging job of her ablutions. He washed every inch of skin, behind her ears, around to her throat and over her shoulders.

And merciful days, his attentions were pleasure itself. "I should not let you do this."

"Not in water this deep," Hadrian replied, tugging her a few steps closer to the bank. "Hold still."

When she was submerged only up to her thighs, he resumed bathing her. He worked his way over her belly and ribs, up and down her arms, and finally, when her eyes were closed, and she was resting against him, to her breasts.

"I shall be quite clean," she sighed, not opening her eyes. "Cleaner than I can recall ever being."

"The cold water has you in a state."

"The cold water does not have me in a state."

He brushed a slick thumb over each ruched nipple in slow, repeated caresses, while a hard, warm, column of male flesh prodded Avis's hip.

"You're in a state, sir." The sight of which might have disturbed her, but this was Hadrian.

"Rather." He cupped water in his hands to rinse off her breasts, his smile distracted. "I was relying on the cold water to assist with my self-restraint. Turn."

She obliged, for it was safer when he wasn't in her line of sight.

"You get to bathe me next," he informed her, "and I want a deal of washing."

Generous man. In contrast to his brisk pronouncements, his hands were the embodiment of gentleness on her backside. "We might be up here until moonrise, Hadrian."

"We might at that. You have dimples in an interesting location." His hands slid to the base of her spine. "Be warned: Your dimples are of the kissable variety, and this part,"—his hands slipped lower—"is entirely enticing."

That part of her was enthralled. He soaped her thoroughly, gently kneaded each buttock—how was it even her backside could be tired?—then rinsed her lovingly and knelt behind her in the water to rest his cheek on the slope of one curve.

"Hadrian?"

"Recovering from my labors. If you swim off, I'll likely drown."

"Avoiding your bath?"

He kissed her on the swell of her fundament, nuzzled her dimples, and stood. "Quite the opposite. I'm anticipating it."

* * *

Avie's revenge was thorough, and more skilled than Hadrian had thought her capable of. She got him clean, but it was a process of *nearly* touching his cock, *glancingly* caressing his fundament, *almost* gliding a hand over his nipples. She'd press her body fleetingly against his—ostensibly to reach around him—and let her hip nudge at his cockstand—purely by accident.

The only thought giving him a measure of control was that this was the closest they'd come to reciprocal intimate play, and for Avie, that was likely as important as the actual joining.

And important to him. Who would have thought?

He'd reassured himself in York that he was still a man, still had functional organs unique to men, but he'd yet to reassure himself he was a *lover*. With Avis, only a lover would do.

"You're quiet," Avis remarked, tossing the soap onto the bank.

"Rendered speechless by your tender ministrations."

"This is eloquent." She sleeved his erect cock with cool fingers, then her hand was gone.

"You are more than welcome to touch me," he managed. She rinsed the soap from her hands under the pond's surface. Was she rinsing off the feel of him too? He tried again, more honestly. "I'd love for you to touch me."

His nymph of the hillside pond regarded him curiously. "We're such different creatures."

Not repulsed, then, but in want of confidence.

"Delightfully so. I certainly explored your treasures when you gave me leave to do so."

Birds had begun their evening chorus as the sun dipped, though despite the brisk temperature of the water and the cooling air—also despite two weeks of relentless physical labor, bone-deep exhaustion, and a bit too much summer ale—Hadrian's arousal was unabated.

"You honestly don't mind?"

She had twelve years of wondering, waiting and wishing to make up for, and she'd chosen to cover that precious ground with him.

"At this moment, your touch on my intimate parts would be my fondest dream." Fondest, most desperate, passionate, wildest... Even if it killed him.

She tugged him by the hand toward the bank and toward a fate he could not have anticipated when he'd given his last sermon over in Rosecroft village.

Hadrian lowered himself to the blankets and passed her his shirt. "It's clean enough. I had it off for much of the day."

He didn't want her taking a chill, and his self-restraint would benefit from a sop to her modesty. The daft woman didn't button the shirt closed, though, but merely drew the sides together, leaving all manner of curves and shadows to tantalize his fevered brain.

Hadrian lay back, his head pillowed on his jacket, and let his hands fall to his sides.

"Do with me what you will, Avie love." Such a pronouncement should have felt silly, to use her word, and yet, putting control of their intimacy into her hands was the only gift he had to offer her.

Avie sat beside him and swaddled herself in a length of toweling. He hadn't kissed her enough lately, but as she settled cross-legged at his hip, he kept his gaze on the darkening sky. Watching her mouth had his mouth aching. His mouth, *aching*. His tongue, his hands, his chest…

God in heaven.

Then he had to close his eyes, as a fleeting brush of Avie's index finger circled the crown of his cock.

"That spot," he rasped. "That…right *there*. You could bring me off in a minute flat, less than a—God, Avie."

She desisted, only to caress his balls, and when Hadrian might have been shivering in the cooling air, he was burning.

"These are odd bits."

"Odd, and vulnerable."

"They don't look vulnerable. Does this hurt?" She closed her hand around him and tugged his stones gently away from his body.

"Not hurt. It doesn't exactly soothe, either." Nothing involving her hands and his breeding organs would soothe.

"Shall I do it again?"

"You shall do as you please, Avie. Whatever you please, for as long as you please." For the next twelve years, and for the next eternity.

"But you'll want to…" She hadn't the words for that they embarked on now. Hadrian would give her those too.

"I'll want to spend. I already do, but that's of no moment. A man learns to deal with his urges, or he's not worth the name."

She drew his cock straight up, perpendicular to his body, then let it bounce back up against his belly, and even that—

"I got you into this state," Avis mused. "Some say a man's bodily urges should never be thwarted."

Oh, for God's sake. "A man, particularly a young man, gets into this state frequently. That doesn't create responsibility in any handy female, Avie. The high street of the smallest village wouldn't be safe if it did."

"I'm not done with you."

He closed his eyes again, knowing that in short order, he'd be *done*, one way or another. He was only human, all his honorable blather notwithstanding, and the past twelve years had been long for him too.

Also lonely.

"Holy hallelujahs."

She'd leaned in and licked the head of his cock. "Is that your seed?"

"Just a drop," he whispered. "Touch me like that again and I will spend, Avie. It isn't tidy."

"I want to do it again."

Hadrian prayed, earnestly and sincerely, for strength, then realized what she was asking. His role was not to withstand or endure what she offered, but to surrender to it—to her.

"You must do as you please, Avie. Whatever you please."

"You care for me." She came to this conclusion while beaming at his rigid cock, having hopscotched intuitively from one sort of intimacy to another.

"I do." Could not recall a time when he hadn't cared for her, hadn't included her in his prayers, hadn't known on some level that coming home to Landover would also be coming home to her.

She leaned forward, and while he watched, drew her tongue up the length of him. "I care for you too."

"One has hoped—*singing saints*, that feels—" She did it again, and he couldn't get the words out. His brain shut down, save for the ability to recognize and rejoice in the pleasure she brought him.

She got comfortable, resting her head on his belly, and Hadrian had to touch her, had to be connected to her through more than his straining cock. He tangled his grasp in her damp hair and wished he hadn't offered her his shirt. His fingers and palms yearned for the glory of her bare skin.

"How does one do this?" She licked up his length, as if he were a sweet on a stick, and he fought to recover his command of English.

"You take your time, and you satisfy your most prurient curiosity," he said, and that was a prayer too.

"Honestly?" She twisted to glance up at him, her expression so full of devilment Hadrian felt an honest frisson of anxiety.

"Honestly."

She said nothing more for a quite a while, but tasted every inch of him, nuzzled his balls, and drove him beyond reason with her tongue. His hips lifted, despite all his intentions, resolutions and prayers to the contrary.

"You're allowed to move," Avis said. Then she plunged her mouth down on him and drew on him in a slow, relentless rhythm, even as her wet hand worked the base of his shaft.

"Avie—"

"Hush."

She teased, tormented, nibbled, licked and experimented until Hadrian was moving mindlessly to her rhythm. She was proving something to herself, asserting dominion over him, and over some aspect of her adult femaleness Hadrian didn't comprehend.

He should finish in his hand, the blankets, or some-damned-where besides her mouth, but Avie wasn't leaving him an instant to figure out how to manage—

Abruptly, satisfaction welled. "Avie, I'm about to—"

Hadrian dropped his hand from her hair, lest he force her to keep him in her mouth, but she didn't leave him, she drove him with that mouth beyond sanity, beyond earthly experience, into the most glorious, intense, *unbearable* experience of protracted bodily delight he'd ever endured.

Had he been capable of using words, the term transcendent would have accurately applied.

"Avie." Some creature dwelling in dark bliss had rasped her name, not Hadrian Bothwell. His body sang fading hosannas as the sky welcomed the night, and Avie subsided onto his belly. "For God's sake, love, hold me."

She obligingly shifted over him and wrapped her arms around his shoulders, then buried her face in his neck.

As he tried to recover his breath—his wits were a hopeless cause—she said something against his throat. Asked a question. He wasn't sure what. He closed his arms around her in answer.

Precious, was all he could think. The experience was precious, yes, but more than that, the woman was precious. He'd teased her, telling her he was lonely and needed relief from matchmaking mamas. He'd also told her he wanted to keep her safe, but his words had not been honest.

He was beyond lonely, *for her*. Had been for years, and he didn't want to keep her safe, he *needed* to, more than he needed to breathe air.

"You didn't answer, Hadrian."

"I couldn't hear the question for all the bells ringing in my ears."

She tucked her face against him again, but Hadrian was focused now, and he heard her.

"Did I do it right?"

"Well, to be honest, no." He kissed her chin, feeling her brace herself for his judgment. "Not quite, though it wasn't a bad effort, and one appreciates your enthusiasm. With my selfless and generous cooperation, if you practice diligently at *every* opportunity and apply yourself assiduously and *very* frequently to the—"

She hit his shoulder, and then they were laughing and rolling in a tangle of naked, happy limbs, until he rose above her and kissed the stuffing out of her.

"If I live to be older than Gran Carruthers," Hadrian said, "I will never forget the pleasure and trust you've given me this evening, Avis Portmaine. You showed me nothing less than heaven on earth, and I will treasure you always for your generosity and courage."

He nearly told her they'd shared some sort of baptism of the heart on this outing, but her brows were drawn down.

"I managed well enough?"

He kissed her cheek and lowered himself to wrap his arms around her. "No other lady has shown me such consideration. You have ruined me, and I am pleased to be your wreckage."

She stroked his hair. "We're both ruined, then."

He angled back up. "You cannot be ruined. You're to marry me, or have you forgotten?"

"I haven't forgotten," Avie said, though clearly, Hadrian had spoiled the moment. "But I've yet to accept you, or had you forgotten?"

"Apparently that detail slipped from what passes for my brain." Hadrian pushed over to lie at her side lest his unruly parts become inspired. "Trifling with me and tossing me over won't be well done of you, Lady Avis."

"Shame on you, Hadrian." She rolled away from him, clearly unappreciative of his attempt at humor—if that's what it had been.

He spooned himself around her and threaded his arm under her neck so she might use his biceps for a pillow, then drew half the blanket up over them. "I truly want to marry you. Please say yes."

"You're not thinking clearly."

She was right—and she wasn't.

Hadrian kissed her shoulder. "About this, I am thinking very clearly. I won't argue with you now. I'm too happy."

"You're sated," she said, pleased with herself, *as well she should be.* Every kiss and caress, every inch of bared flesh they shared was a powerful light banishing the shadows left by her past.

"I'm plotting revenge, silly wench." He fell asleep, wondering if she'd let him use his mouth on her. That delight had been denied him by his wife, and now he was glad of it. With Rue, such an adventure would have been the result of curiosity and boredom.

With Avie, his intimate attentions were driven by the need to protect, to treasure, and to love.

* * *

"Going somewhere, Lily my love?" Fenwick's question had the intended result of freezing Lily Prentiss in her tracks.

"I am not your love," she hissed, "and I have never given you leave to use my name, nor will I."

"Alas for me." Fen ambled out of the shadows on Blessings's back terrace, because he intended to detain his prey. "Care to join me for a moonlit stroll in the gardens?"

"Do you never listen, Mr. Fenwick? Your company is not agreeable to me."

"I listen." Though he often regretted what he overheard. "I look too, and I see a lady out by herself after dark. Clearly, you're bent on mischief."

Lily drew herself up, sails filling with a purpose Fen was determined to thwart.

"I am bent on finding Lady Avie. She hasn't come in yet, and the evening grows both chilly and dark."

Chilly indeed. "After remaining behind to tidy up the ale station, Lady Avis accepted Mr. Bothwell's escort. You may toddle back to your needlepoint, assured our mutual employer will come to no harm."

Lily's gaze darted up the shadowed slope, confirming that she'd been spying on Avis—again.

"She'll need her shawl." Lily started toward the trees. "She worked too long in the sun today. She'll take sick—"

Fen plucked the shawl from Lily's hands.

"I'm sure Bothwell will lend her his jacket, gentleman that he is. I'll hang on to this so you don't have to loiter here in the night air, waiting for your employer."

"She's not my—" But Lily wasn't entirely foolish. She and Fen were at best equals, and forcing Avis to choose between them was not prudent—not with Bothwell taking Lady Avis for moonlit strolls.

"You are insufferable, Mr. Fenwick, but what else should I expect from a half-savage heathen like you?"

"I believe you've commented similarly before." Fenwick let his eyelids droop, as if she'd offered a flirtatious innuendo. "We heathen have our endearing attributes. Was that why you came out here searching for me?"

"I hate you," Lily said through gritted teeth. "You are the furthest thing from a gentleman, and you do not deserve to walk the same ground as Avis Portmaine, much less interfere with my protection of her."

"Dearest Lily," Fenwick drawled, "it's time you accepted that Avie can look after herself, and took your interfering self off to bed. Shall I escort you?"

She slapped him, a good hard smack, much as he'd suffered from her on previous occasions.

He touched his cheek, then his heart, the better to aggravate the silly bitch. "A parting token of your esteem. Good night, sweet Lily. Pleasant dreams."

He held his ground, and Lily had the sense to retreat into the house. If she dealt him a blow every so often, it took the edge off her ire. Fen didn't exactly like being slapped, but violence from her was proof of something besides the towering disdain she affected.

Some fellow had probably dealt a figurative death blow to her feminine confidence ages ago, but even that thought didn't stir in him one ounce of pity for her.

* * *

"We should be getting back." Avis rubbed her cheek against Hadrian's arm, reveling in the warmth and utter relaxation she'd found in his embrace.

"You're awake then."

"You were the one who dropped off, Mr. Bothwell. Exhausted from your labors."

From his passion, which had been beautiful, peculiar, intimate and precious. Avis took risks with Hadrian, not risks to her reputation, but risks to her heart. If at any point she faltered or failed in these intimate endeavors, she had twelve years of self-doubt waiting to collapse on her like a muddy hillside.

And only Hadrian's regard to shelter her from harm. That troubled her, for if she became engaged to him, any ill will directed at her could spread to him, and in twelve years, she'd endured ill will aplenty.

"Making hay is hard work." Hadrian kissed her ear, and she heard the smile in his voice, the smile she'd put there. His hand slid down her spine to knead her backside. Thank heaven he couldn't see the idiot grin his caresses provoked.

"The stars are coming out. Somebody will miss me." Somebody named Lily, who would be rousing a searching party and rehearsing a grand scold.

"Fen knows where we are," Hadrian murmured against her nape. "Stop looking for excuses to abandon me."

"Are you too weak to give chase?"

"And cease gloating." Hadrian bit her earlobe, and Avis knew she would indeed gloat, wallow, *and* glory in her ability to give him pleasure.

"You've created a monster," she assured him, pressing her lips to the muscular forearm he'd laced over her collarbone.

"We need to talk before you drag me down the mountain by my hair, my love."

"It's only a hill, and your hair isn't quite as long as I'd like it."

"I've received another letter from Harold, Avie."

"He's well?"

"He's disgustingly well, but his factors have been watching Collins, and the baron has taken ship for Portsmouth."

"In the south?"

Hadrian's body remained relaxed and warm behind her, but Avie felt as if she'd spotted the tail of a serpent slithering into the undergrowth of the first paradise she'd known in years.

Hadrian gathered her closer. "Collins will land as far south from here as an English port can be, but he may be in England even as we speak, or finding a packet to get him to Liverpool from London."

Hadrian could think, while Avis could only dread—and regret. "What could he be about?"

"If he's intent on money, then he'll have to meet with his solicitors, and they're in London." Hadrian traced a pattern on her back now—the Tree of Life?—so he had to feel the tension his words caused her.

"If he's intent on something else?"

"You're safe, Avie. You'd be safer married to me and ensconced as my lady at Landover."

Hadrian was sweet, dear and wonderful—also ruthless and not in command of as many facts as he believed himself to be. "Then you would not be safe."

"From Collins?"

"From him too," Avis said, "but from the gossip mostly." Surely a former vicar had a proper respect for the damage gossip could do?

"I care naught for gossip, particularly when compared with your safety."

His response was gratifyingly swift, also unacceptable.

"You say that now. When nobody meets your eye at church, when nobody stands up with you at the assemblies, when nobody comes to call even at the holidays, then you'll begin to understand. I gave my promise to wed to an eligible young man, then refused him the intimacies that usually follow such an agreement. I'm a jilt and a tease, and Collins doubtless made sure I was called every vile name attendant there to."

Hadrian didn't argue, for which Avis was grateful. She'd been so pleased with herself, pleased to bring him pleasure, pleased that not every intimate form of sharing had been taken from her twelve years ago.

This discussion reminded her that such pleasure was stolen, illicit, and only fleetingly hers.

"I got a letter too," she ventured, hoping to turn the subject.

"From?"

"Alex. She's traveling to some earl's seat in Kent. She describes it as a revolving house party. The earl and his new countess entertain incessantly, but then she's off to seek another post."

"She'll stay in the south?"

"To be near Benjamin, yes."

"And away from you?"

Avis felt the blessed protectiveness of Hadrian's embrace, and even that didn't obliterate the ache that missing her sister had become.

"We are sad reminders to each other of unhappy times, Hadrian. So yes, away from me."

Hadrian withdrew his arm and shifted her, so he was still on his side, but Avis faced him, her leg hiked across his hips, her cheek pillowed against his shoulder.

"From a different perspective,"—Hadrian spoke with his lips against her temple—"you and Alexandra are reminders to each other of not only your assault, but also of how you've both put your lives back together thereafter, and made something meaningful of yourselves."

"She has meaning of a sort. Raising other people's children. I know she loves both little Priscilla and the girl's mother."

"Running Blessings isn't meaningful?"

Something about nudity must engender honesty, for Avis could offer Hadrian only the truth.

"Fen runs Blessings. Fen and Vim and, from his post in the south, Benjamin. I am merely ornamental, a poor relation."

"You're the lady of the manor. The place would have no heart but for you."

"Heart is not accounted very useful, compared to wool, crops, livestock and coin."

"None of that other means anything without heart. I have wool, crops, livestock and coin at Landover, but I'd gladly go back to driving a sway-backed gelding in the wilds of Yorkshire if you'd go with me."

What was he going on about?

"As inappropriate as I'd be as mistress of Landover, I'd be an outright scandal as a clergyman's wife."

He kissed her forehead. "You most assuredly would not, though I'm no longer fit for the church myself. Are you getting cold?"

"No." Cuddled up with him, naked under the blanket, watching the stars come out, was the closest she'd known to utter contentment.

"You fit perfectly in my arms, Avie love." He fell silent, and she was grateful he wasn't haranguing her. Not haranguing her to marry him, or to allow him carnal liberties, or to move her exhausted limbs.

Tomorrow evening would be the midsummer celebration, the most difficult milestone of Avis's year. The village maidens would disappear with their lads, the maids with the footmen and grooms, the wives with their husbands. A child conceived at midsummer arrived in spring, and by May many little babies would be brought to services in their baskets as reminders of last year's celebration.

She could not bring herself to reject Hadrian's proposal of marriage outright. For his sake, she should, but—

A shaft of insight penetrated her honorable fit of moroseness: She'd be condemned for marrying Hadrian, for tainting a good man with her scandalous past.

She would *also* be condemned for turning him away, if anybody got wind he'd offered.

"You shivered, my love. Much as I wish it weren't so, we must return from the land of Nod, lest you catch your death."

"I'm not cold, but if we stay up here much longer, you'll be compromised, and then we'll be dragooned into parson's mousetrap."

"Do you think so?"

"Don't sound so hopeful." She rolled from his embrace, and he let her go— which was for the best. "Your shirt is here somewhere."

"Shall I rebraid your hair?"

"I can do it when I find my bed. My heavens, you're—"

"Aroused." He lay on his back, a pagan happy to bathe in moonlight. "Again. I like holding you, Avie, and I love cuddling with you."

"You're in want of something more than cuddling." Avis wanted more too, but how could she possibly turn her back on his proposal if they shared marital intimacies?

"Fret not." He thumbed his erection down and watched it bob back up. "This will subside somewhat as we dress and turn our thoughts to mundane matters. You'll go to the gathering tomorrow?"

She gathered her clothes, though the way he *handled* himself was— "I'd rather not attend, though it's less formal than an assembly. I preside every year."

He passed her a half-boot. "To prove what?"

"That the old biddies and small-minded menfolk in this shire haven't made me a complete prisoner in a tower." She wadded up his shirt and tossed it over to him, then his boots.

He didn't seem in any hurry to dress, but indulged in a leisurely sip of the peach brandy. Avis paused with half the bows on her chemise still undone, while Hadrian sat two feet away, a god of the deepening night.

"I enjoyed this, Hadrian." More than enjoyed it, for Hadrian's intimate company put something right for her.

"You like conquering me." He offered her the bottle, but she could not risk the maids sniffing spirits on her breath.

"No, thank you. You didn't put up a great fuss about being conquered."

"You'll never know what a fuss I put up." He corked the bottle, a little smile teasing the corners of his sinful mouth.

"Will you put it up again for me sometime?"

CHAPTER TEN

"I do believe,"—Hadrian got his arms into his shirt-sleeves—"you made a naughty play on words. I am proud of you."

"You're trying to corrupt me." Avis went back to her bows when she wanted to see to Hadrian's buttons, mostly as an excuse to touch him. "That has already been seen to. This is yours." She tossed his cravat at him, considerably wrinkled. He folded it up and stuffed it in a jacket pocket.

"You are not corrupted," Hadrian admonished her as he rooted around on hands and knees for his breeches. "But to answer your question, yes, you may conquer me as often as it takes for me to win your hand."

She sat back, her dress frothing loosely around her. "I should not marry you, Hadrian Bothwell. I like you too much for that."

"You care for me," he reminded her. "You don't simply like me. Like is such an insipid word. Have you seen my stockings?"

"Inside your boots."

"So they are." He crawled over to kneel behind her. "I'll get your hooks." His fingers were deft, and she was soon done up, though her hair was a fright, and exhaustion was reminding her of the week she'd put in. Hadrian's arms came around her shoulders, and she leaned back into him, closing her eyes.

"I wish I could stay here with you on these blankets forever." She sighed the words, more dream than wish. He was above and behind her, and the warmth and strength of him were more seductive than all his erotic folly combined.

"Landover could be our blanket. Harold has given us his blessing, you know."

"Harold?" She pulled away, because Harold's regard would mean something to the community.

Something, not enough.

"Lord Landover himself." Hadrian stood to pull on his breeches. "Said he thought we'd have plighted our troth years past, so there. He's about as un-matrimonially minded as a man can be, and he sees we should be together."

"Hadrian, cut line. Even if I did accept your proposal, it would only be to allow you a better vantage for running off Hart Collins."

This reasoning was as seductive as Hadrian's kisses, because Collins was mean to the bone and a real threat to Avis's well-being.

"Avie, I won't run the bastard off, I'll run him through, or blow a hole in him. Why Harold didn't see to it years ago, I'll never know."

"I asked him not to," Avis said, because Hadrian now put her in mind of his eighteen-year-old self, all confidence, honor and determination. "In the first place, it was for Benjamin and Vim to see to my safety, and we imposed on you and your brother far beyond the dictates of neighborly courtesy. In the second place, Alex and I were of the same mind on this and wanted no more talk, no more scandal, and we certainly didn't want Hart Collins's blood on our hands."

Not figuratively, not literally.

"Avie, the man has to answer for his actions," Hadrian said, yanking on his boots. "Has it occurred to you that putting period to his existence could be exactly what is needed to stop all the talk you're so infernally plagued by?"

Yes, it had, because Collins might be physically absent, but he could maintain voluminous correspondence with the neighbors, he could spread talk, he could drop the occasional word in the wrong ear in his London clubs.

"Murder doesn't stop talk," she shot back. "It stops a life, and what about that commandment, Hadrian?"

"Thou shalt not kill?" Hadrian shrugged into his waistcoat but didn't button it. "Tadpole vicars love to debate that one, particularly when their next option after the church is usually the military. We concluded on many occasions that it meant one mustn't take a life by stealth and dishonor. A duel gives a man a fair chance and isn't murder."

"The law says it is." Avis shoved a loose strand of hair out of her eyes. "I say it is. Promise me, Hadrian."

"You made Harold promise too, didn't you?" He didn't sound sweet or loverlike now. He sounded shrewd and dangerous. "I will not call Hart Collins out, but if he threatens you, Avis, he will not survive to regret it."

"Hart Collins has cost me my family, unless you count the few winter months when Vim trades off with Fen for the pleasure of keeping me company. I could not abide it if that man costs me you, all over again."

"All over again?"

"It's getting late," she said, focusing on the laces of her boots. "Tomorrow will be another long day, and I don't want to spoil a lovely evening with more argument."

Hadrian ducked when she flung his coat at him. "You'll dance with me?"

"Do you never give up? I don't dance, Hadrian. One waltz with Fen at the shearing party—with Fen, who has danced with Gran Carruthers and old Maudie—and there was talk enough. I cannot bring attention to myself that way without shaming my family."

"The shame lies with those who begrudge you the right to any pleasure." He stood and helped her to her feet, kissed her nose, then bent to retrieve the blanket. They shook it out and folded it, stashed the towels, soap, and liquor, then shook out and folded the oilskin on top of the hamper.

"I will never see this pond with quite the same eyes." Hadrian slung his coat over his shoulder, his shirt gaping open in the moonlight. "I understand better now why the Romans had sacred groves and grottoes."

"You blaspheme," Avis responded, lacing her fingers with his.

"I do not," he countered, taking a firm hold of her hand. "You've damned near enshrined Hart Collins's disrespect of you, Avie. Allow me to do the same with a much happier memory."

His words hurt, in part because they had the ring of truth, but also because they identified with ruthless clarity the distance between Avis and Hadrian. She had been the victim, he had not. She was the object of pity at best, scorn more often, and he was a favored local son, returning to take his proper place among the best families in the shire.

Avis forgot Collins's disrespect at her peril. Many others were all too happy to remind her of it, and of her responsibility for what had happened that day.

"I should not have said that." Hadrian's voice in the darkness was laden with regret. "I speak out of frustration on your behalf."

"You speak out of frustration with me." While Avis was frustrated with her entire life.

"We're exhausted," he said, "and I am not entirely comfortable with allowing you to pleasure me, when I made no effort to see to your needs."

"You've seen to my needs." Needs she'd tried to ignore—for affection, companionship, and much more.

"Twice in twelve years, Avie? I deserve to have my proposal turned down if I regard that as adequate."

"You deserve to be happy." She needed for him to be happy, in fact. Also safe.

He brought her fingers to his lips. "Then you do not reject me. You merely play out the line."

"You're not a trout."

"I rather felt like one." His gaze on their joined hands was soft. "Dazed, gasping for breath, hopelessly undone."

"Hush," she chided, for they would soon be out of the trees, and his pleased expression was a scandal in itself. "Did Harold say anything else in his letter?"

"He said he loves Denmark and he's already spent time with our second cousins, renewing old acquaintances. They assure him the winters there aren't that bad."

Hadrian drew her into his arms at the edge of the trees, then pressed his mouth to hers. "I haven't kissed you enough."

She leaned into him. "We kiss and my wits fail."

So, of course, she kissed him and kissed him and kissed him.

* * *

"Do you know," Fenwick said, as the crowd on Blessings's back terrace shifted to create room for dancing, "some thieving miscreant has raided our stash by the pond?"

"Do tell." Hadrian's gaze was on Avie, who was demurely attired in a pale green frock with a raised waistline. The dress accentuated her willowy lines and made him long to smooth his hands down her curves. She could be in sackcloth, though, and he'd suffer the same impulse.

"Bothwell, you are in danger of becoming pathetic."

Hadrian hoped he was in danger of becoming remarried. "I drank the damned brandy. Avie had a sip too."

"Doubtless she was inebriated on your charms," Fen murmured. "Have a care that Miss Prentiss doesn't track you to your trysts and idylls. She was ready to trudge up that hill on the pretext that Avis needed her shawl."

The last thing Avis Portmaine needed was a shawl. She needed fun, and freedom, and respect, and a husband who could ensure she had them in abundance.

"Thank you for dissuading dear Lily from her quest." Where had Lily been when the ale station had needed packing up? "Just how bad is the gossip?"

They stood at the edge of the terrace, which had been pressed into service as a makeshift dance floor, while the gardens were full of picnic blankets for those who'd enjoyed the buffet. The fragrance of summer flowers mingled with the scent of a crowd enjoying its exertions, creating a uniquely bucolic, happy perfume.

Had these voluble, carefree people begrudged Avis Portmaine the joys they themselves indulged in without limit?

"I'm not the best person to ask about the gossip surrounding your lady." Fen sipped his ale and tapped his toe the same as every other yeoman in attendance, but his gaze was keen, as if he contemplated mischief, and though the occasion was social, his knife was tucked into its sheath at his side.

"People have learned to watch what they say around me," Fen went on, "and some of the talk is sympathetic. Most of it is judgmental. Avis pretends to virtue no longer hers, she puts on false airs of respectability, she's after every man under the age of eighty, and so on. Avis is friendly and approachable to those beneath her station, and some see that as providing a basis in truth for the gossip."

Fen was likely being diplomatic.

"She does nothing to earn such viciousness," Hadrian said. "I don't understand it."

Gran Carruthers went skipping by in the arms of a ploughman who had to be less than a third her age. Who was leading whom seemed up for debate.

"What don't you understand, Bothwell?"

"I grew up here," Hadrian said. "These are not cruel people. They help each other, they work their land, tend their shops, and try not to offend God or neighbor with their failings. They take in foundlings. Hart Collins was a scourge as a young man, sent down from one school after another, the stories increasingly bad. At the time of the incident, I'm certain nobody of any standing blamed Avis for what happened to her."

Though he couldn't know that for a fact, because he'd spent the rest of summer affixed to Avie's side. Then he'd gone haring south to be a scholar.

A randy scholar.

"She was engaged to Collins," Fen pointed out. "She was the most envied young woman in the shire—a lady by birth, well dowered, and pretty, with a titled husband in her future. That alone would have made her a target for envy."

Envy was a fleeting, unchristian thought, a remark one was ashamed of in hindsight. Envy should not be the ruin of a blameless woman's happiness.

An older couple came spinning past, the male half of which looked none too steady on his pins. He swung his lady too vigorously, so Fen had to scoot back while Hadrian caught the lady, righted her, and spun her back to her fellow.

"Collins had family in the area, and they must have blamed Avis," Fen said when the dancers went reeling on their way. "His mother still dwells at the family seat, and mothers can be blind to their children's failings."

"Collins's parents were the ones sending him to disreputable boarding schools. He made it impossible for them to keep help when he was home."

Or that had been the rumor before Hadrian had gone off to university.

Fen discreetly poured half his ale into the roses. "He was the heir, and Avis likely had high spirits, and no mama to show her how to go on. I'd guess breaking her engagement with Collins wasn't her first misstep. Vim had already started to travel, and Benjamin would have been enjoying the fleshpots of London."

Avie had been high-spirited, also strong-willed. Hadrian had adored that about her, and still did.

The musicians switched to a lively strathspey, and a whoop of approval went up from the dancers.

"I feel the urge to cut a dash," Fenwick said. "And I see Miss Prentiss succumbing to the same impulse, though her partner is Sir Walter Monteith's darling boy."

Fen passed Hadrian the remains of his drink and had old Maudie on his arm an instant later, as if by prearrangement. He lurked with her in the shadows until the lines formed, then joined the far end when the introduction sounded. Sure enough, when the figures changed and Lily saw who her next partner would be, her dismay was plain on her pretty face.

Hadrian set Fen's drink down and ambled away, rather than watch Fen at his games. The moon was up, the party gathering momentum, and all Hadrian wanted was to find Avie and walk with her up to the pond.

Which, of course, in present company, would be remarked by all and sundry.

He took a bench between the roses and the privet hedge and contented himself with admiring the scent of the garden by moonlight. He'd just closed his eyes when his peace was cut up by voices from beyond the privet hedge.

"No better than she should be, as usual." The words carried the buoyant malice of a woman intent on a good gossip.

"She's the hostess, Hortensia, nominally," a second voice reasoned. "She has to be in evidence and ordering the footmen about."

"But patting them on the arm?" Hortensia verbally shuddered. "And that Mr. Fenwick thinks he can stand up with whomever he pleases, now that she's let him waltz her."

Shock held Hadrian still, for it appeared Avis was, indeed, crucified for imaginary transgressions, just as she'd told him she would be.

"Maudie is the one who stands up with anybody." The second woman's voice held humor. "Fen's being gallant."

"He's Lady Avis's lover," Hortensia retorted. "They say his brother's in line for an earldom, but Fenwick hangs about here because Lady Avis has bewitched him."

Like the worst gossip, that sentiment had elements of truth—Fen's brother was an earl's heir, and Fen was loyal to Avis.

"For pity's sake," the second woman said. "Fen stays here because he's well paid and good at his job. I think you have your eye on Mr. Fenwick."

"That great, hulking brute?" Hortensia's footsteps scraped to a halt mere yards from Hadrian's secluded bench. "Knowing he's dallied with a slut like Avis Portmaine makes him beneath my notice, yours too."

"Where do you hear these things, Hortensia? You never used to be so spiteful."

"Not spite—truth. I speak from the *best* authority, Delia. My lady's maid is friends with the governess at Holderness, and she knows everything from Lady Holderness's abigail, who goes with her ladyship everywhere."

"Avis is only a couple of years older than we are," the second woman chided. "She was in our catechism classes. We sang in the choir with her and feared for her when her engagement to Collins was announced. Doesn't she deserve a little peace?"

A *lot* of peace, for God's sake?

"She led the poor boy on, enticed him, then tossed him over," Hortensia retorted. "He'd be taking his proper place as baron if she hadn't treated him so ill. All these years he's been kept from his birthright by her vindictiveness. No wonder she hasn't had a single offer from a proper gentleman, despite her title and wealth."

Hadrian rose, though what would it serve for him to storm around the hedge and deliver Hortensia Dillington a rousing scold? He'd wanted to know what was said about Avis, and what he heard rendered him motionless and silent in the shadows.

"Do you really think, Hortensia, that the shire would be a better place were Hart Collins dancing up on the terrace tonight?"

"He's not married yet."

"I beg your pardon?"

"Hart Collins is not married," Hortensia insisted in an excited whisper. "Reformed rakes make the best husbands. His staff is preparing his rooms, and it's said he's soon to visit his seat."

"He wasn't a rake," her companion said. "He was an out out-and-out bully, and I for one think Avis Portmaine paid much too high a price for her brothers' willingness to betroth her to the man. Now come along, or the men will have eaten all the best desserts."

They moved back toward the terrace, while Hadrian wrestled a seething urge to kill, to wring the necks of all who had nothing better to do than condemn Avis for Collins's crimes. He wanted to wring Vim's and Benjamin's necks too, for betrothing Avie to the monster in the first place, and he wanted to wring Hortensia Dillington's gossiping neck for good measure.

As the evening wore on, Hadrian caught other snippets of talk, mostly among the women, regarding Avis and her every gesture and glance. The sheer maliciousness left him hurting for her, and disappointed in his neighbors.

Though he was also puzzled.

As a former vicar, Hadrian knew well, too damned well, how powerfully the gossip mill could churn in any community. People would talk, as surely as they would sin and grow gardens and fornicate. Nonetheless, they'd seldom spend twelve years talking about the same old scandals. New gossip was much more entertaining than the old tales, and his own arrival back at Landover was fresher grist than Avie's wicked past.

No one talked about him; no one talked about Harold's extended absence. No one talked much about the haying, the Regent's extravagances or even the weather.

Interesting.

What could a man intent on protecting Avis Portmaine's well-being give his neighbors to talk about that would end their spiteful gossip regarding the woman he dearly hoped to marry?

* * *

"Dance with me."

Hadrian's voice came from the shadows to Avis's left, and she wasn't sure he was even speaking to her. The evening had been long, but busy enough that she hadn't had to think much—to *feel* much.

"In the garden shadows?" Avis replied when Hadrian stepped closer. "Enough people are strolling that we'd be recognized." Enough people had also stolen off into the garden to engage in behaviors Avis could only envy.

"Dance with me here, on the terrace, in full view of our neighbors." Hadrian ambled forward, and by torchlight his blond features had a resolute, Viking quality.

"I have much to do, Hadrian," she replied, rearranging empty glasses on the punch table. "If I tarry on the dance floor, it will cause talk, and ensure the help has to stay up that much later."

"The help,"—Hadrian took her hand in his—"is hanging back, lest they get in your way as you make excuses to avoid mingling and enjoying yourself."

Avis was so shocked at that bluntness she let Hadrian tug her from behind the punch table while—blast and damnation—several footmen and two maids hovered nearby, apparently waiting for her to take herself elsewhere.

"I'm right," Hadrian went on, "and you haven't danced once this evening."

"Because the last time I did dance, Fenwick heard endless sermons about getting above his station." While Avis had heard a few from Lily about not knowing hers.

"I'm your almost-fiancé," Hadrian said as the little orchestra tuned up. "You belong in my arms, at my side, and not among the servants, longing for this night to be over."

She'd been praying for that, between aiming false smiles in no particular direction and ignoring Lily's anxious surveillance between every dance.

"Hadrian, I know you mean well—"

She allowed him to arrange her in waltz position—the last dance of the evening would be a waltz—because she could not dissuade him without creating a scene for which she would be more than lectured.

He held her a hair closer than he should, and she submitted to this presumption because it wasn't nearly as close as she wanted to hold him. The music was slow, lilting and sweet, and perfect for ending a summer night's revelry.

"You have to be exhausted," Hadrian said near her ear. "You're letting me lead."

"You're more subtle about it than Fen," Avis said, stifling a yawn. "I fit you better."

"You fit me perfectly." He fell silent, as if expecting her to argue, but she let him pull her particularly near on a turn. For the duration of this dance, she was best served by not making a fuss, and if she enjoyed not making a fuss, well, the dance would soon be over.

"People are staring," Hadrian noted moments later. "Do you ever get used to it?"

"I haven't, though it's gone on for years."

"Do you recall when it started?"

"Started?"

"I can't believe anybody would say or do anything to insult Benjamin and Vim's sister. While you and Alex recuperated at Landover, Harold would have beaten to a pulp any man who tried."

"The men aren't the problem," Avis said, sad—and relieved—that Hadrian was seeing the truth of her situation. "The rutting goats among them insult all women, fallen, ruined, virtuous, what have you. The decent men keep their mouths shut."

While they drank her ladyship's ale, ate her food, and avoided her company.

"Thus, you avoid the women?"

"If I avoid them, I am haughty; if I make overtures, I am presumptuous. Once tarred with the brush of scandal, one has few good options except to grow indifferent."

Which Avis had never quite managed.

"Was it always so bad?"

"I don't know, Hadrian." She wanted, more than anything, to lay her head on his shoulder and dance off into the darkness with him. The conversation was difficult but necessary, and dragging Hadrian into the shadows was the worst mistake she could make—for her, but for him as well. "When Alex was on hand and Benjamin was about, I don't recall it being so bad, but maybe that's because people truly could not blame her for what happened."

"She still limps?"

"Not badly. Benjamin says it shows only when she's tired or the terrain is uneven, but she hardly goes out of doors, which confirms that the injury still pains her in some way."

"While you hardly leave Blessings. This has gone on long enough, Avis."

Not Avie, and Hadrian's voice held a thread of anger she didn't often hear from him.

"It isn't your problem, Hadrian," she said as quietly as she could without whispering. Whispering would cause talk, leaning up to speak softly to him would cause talk, dashing off the dance floor would cause more talk.

"It damned well needs to be somebody's problem." He'd spoken in normal tones, and she shuddered to think who overheard him. "You shall have the respect you deserve, even if it arrives to you twelve years overdue."

She danced in his arms silently, wishing the music would end, wishing it would go on forever. Hadrian was a good man, and his anger on her behalf was a reminder of Avis's own frustration. She'd been frustrated for years, but somewhere along the way, the frustration had faded to anxious, weary bewilderment, leaving only a need for peace.

Peace and quiet.

The music ended, and when she would have stepped back to offer the requisite curtsy, Hadrian trapped her hand in his.

"Hadrian?"

"Come along. You can break something over my head tomorrow, but tonight, we're taking action."

Foreboding welled as Hadrian towed her up the few steps to the first tier of the terrace, where the musicians were returning violins and guitars to their cases.

"Friends, neighbors!" Hadrian called out. "If I might have your attention for one moment before you seek your beds?"

A good-natured smattering of response came, mostly from the men about seeking something other than their beds.

"I recall that it's tradition at our assemblies to announce betrothals, and in that spirit, I'd like you all to know I've put the marital question to Lady Avis. You will end our evening on the best note by offering your congratulations now."

A cheer went up over the roaring in Avis's ears.

God help her, God help them both. When she would have raised her voice to make a jest of Hadrian's announcement, he sealed his mouth over hers, and the cheering grew louder.

"Don't fuss," he murmured against her lips. "You can jilt me tomorrow."

He ended the kiss and held Avie's hand up over his head, as if she were the successful contender at a bare-knuckle match. Unable to stand the scrutiny of her neighbors, Avis merely turned into Hadrian's body and forced him to shield her from the grinning, cheering fools around them.

She endured a few more toasts and good wishes, and then let Hadrian haul her into the house. He didn't stop until they reached her private parlor, where, thank a merciful Deity, some servant had drawn the blinds, giving them privacy.

"I cannot believe you did that," she fumed as he lit a single candle from the coals in the hearth. "I simply cannot believe—Hadrian, what were you thinking? My life was ruined when I jilted one fiancé, and now you—*what were you thinking?*"

"I was thinking you'd make a fuss if I told you my plans. Shall I stir up the fire?"

He'd already stirred up one fire.

"Please." Avis was cold, though the room wasn't chilly. Mostly, she wanted to keep Hadrian near until she'd set this folly to rights. "I know you meant well, Hadrian, but this dramatic gesture,"—she flopped down on her sofa, feeling centuries old—"it won't help."

"Ignoring cruel gossip wasn't helping, either."

Hadrian rose from the hearth, the fireplace giving off a deceptively cheery blaze. By firelight, *he* did not look cheery. He looked big, grim, and diabolically determined.

"Ignoring the talk helps me endure my life."

"Endure." Hadrian spat the word. "Do you endure my attentions, Avis?"

She could not fathom his point, though he would doubtless elaborate upon it. "I very much enjoy your attentions."

"Then why not very much enjoy your life?" He angled his long frame so he could prop an elbow on the mantel when Avis would have liked him better within hand-holding range. "Why not look forward to seeing friends at church, why not have the occasional guest at luncheon, why not exchange a few smiles and greetings when you shop in the village?"

"Because I *can't*," she cried. "Because those activities require the felicity of the people in one's community, something I have lacked for years."

"Well, I haven't," Hadrian shot back. "I was a damned vicar, and I can be so bloody pleasant our neighbors will wish Harold had left years ago."

"A damned vicar?" Avis was amused, despite the gravity of the situation, despite Hadrian's wrong-headedness.

"And bloody pleasant." He nodded, clearly proud of his foul language. "I heard talk about you tonight."

Well, of course. "So you must gallop to the rescue."

He settled beside her. "Either that or I must break some heads. What has become of Hortensia Dillington?"

She'd become quite stout. Avis kept that unkind thought to herself.

"Hortensia Cuthbert now. She married the miller's second son, who has a tidy small holding of his own, but Hortensia had no other offers and thus feels her lot sorely."

"She's jealous, then."

"Jealous?"

"She married out of expedience, while you have wealth, doting if distant brothers, freedom, and authority. Of course she's jealous."

Hadrian was very sure of his conclusions, and yet Avis resisted the impulse to take his hand. She was simply too tired—exhausted in body and soul—to disabuse him of his addled notions.

To protect him—though she would.

Somehow, she'd preserve him from the folly he'd wrought in the last five minutes, even if it meant she became the first woman in the history of the shire to jilt not one but two eligible bachelors.

Who could possibly be jealous of her for that?

CHAPTER ELEVEN

Of all the gifts Hadrian wanted to restore to his intended—for Avie was his intended—her capacity for anger ranked at the top of the list. He wanted every form of ire put back in her hands—fury, simple testiness, irritability, fuming—for if she could locate her indignation, perhaps her courage might be returned to her too.

"I hadn't thought any lady could be jealous of my situation," she said. "But what does that matter? I now have you for my fiancé, Hadrian, and without having accepted your suit. Not well done of you."

Not well done of you. He usurped her future, albeit with the best intentions, and that was the scolding he received?

"You want to marry me, you just can't admit it, and I'm damned sure I want to marry you." His assurances sounded more pugnacious than he'd intended.

"Of course I want to marry you." Now, when Hadrian would have taken her hand, Avie rose and made a production of poking at the already blazing fire. "You're toothsome, wealthy, and my friend."

Though not quite her lover. Not yet.

"And you care for me," he reminded her, "and you've seen me as God made me." She'd done considerably more than that—and enjoyed herself thoroughly.

As had he.

"Hadrian, you're newly free of the church, at loose ends, mindful of the need for heirs, and I'm a familiar old friend. You're at sixes and sevens, and I'm—"

She was daft, also exhausted, and too willing to cope with any and all challenges on her own.

"Am I familiar to you, Avis?"

She settled on the low table facing him, an indication of how badly he'd rattled her. Miss Prentiss would have been scandalized by such abuse of good furniture.

"You are wonderfully familiar to me, Hadrian Bothwell, and yet you are also wonderfully new."

"Stop flittering around, Avie." He took her hand and tugged. "I could not stand to hear your name bandied about among the gossips when you've done not one thing to merit their contumely. We can have a long engagement, a year if you want, but let me give you this much protection, and you can see if you like it."

"Oh, I'll like it," she said, letting him pull her to his side. "Though you have to promise me two things."

"I'm listening." Listening, but he wasn't promising blindly. He'd learned a few things in his years as a husband.

"First, you cannot use your appeal to coerce me to the altar."

"Love, you'll have to translate that. If you think this will be a chaste engagement—" In Hadrian's experience, a chaste engagement was a rare beast, unless a fellow had proposed to a clergyman's youngest daughter.

"I don't want a chaste engagement."

Bless her and the fresh Cumbrian country air. "Well, then—"

"Promise you won't withhold your favors to inspire me to accept your proposal."

"You think I could withhold my favors, so to speak, and render you biddable?" She had a poor grasp of her effect on him if that was the case.

"Wretch." She took a leaf from his book and bit his earlobe. "You could. I am that lost to propriety. That wanton."

The urge to wring Hortensia's neck rose anew—and Hart Collins's as well. Avis was entitled to be wroth with her petty, judgmental neighbors, but she had instead accepted a load of shame and uncertainty that was not hers to bear.

"You are not wanton," Hadrian said, looping his arm across her shoulders, lest she hare away to arrange flowers—or cry into her pillow. "You are curious. Your curiosity is part of what endears you to me." Along with her sheer dauntlessness, which he knew better than to mention now. "You've asked for two promises, the first relating to my intimate availability, do I have that right?"

"You do."

"You shall have me, Avis, exclusively, and absolutely." He hoped she'd have him often and always too. "What is your second demand?"

She gazed at the fire, her expression so sad Hadrian might be the one crying into his pillow. "You must be honest with yourself, Hadrian."

"About?"

"When the shopkeepers won't put coin in your gloved hand, but only set it on the counter, when nobody tips his hat to me, when you aren't invited anywhere, when nobody calls, even to congratulate you on our betrothal."

She had kept this litany of miseries to herself rather than share it with her brothers, and they had likely been loath to pry.

To hell with such consideration, if it consigned Avis to more lonely misery.

Hadrian traced the shell of her ear with a single finger. "You want me to report these supposed slights to you?"

"I want you to report them to yourself. I want you to acknowledge that the good opinion of your neighbors is valuable, and marriage to me will jeopardize that asset. Then I want you to multiply the loss of that good opinion by the decades you hope to be married to me, and ask yourself honestly if you can bear that cost."

She was ignoring his caresses, so he didn't tell her his calculations went in a different direction: All the slights and indignities Avie had endured times the number of years she'd born them. That was the sum of the smiles he'd give her in the first year of their marriage.

"You have my promise, Avie. I will assess the impact of marriage to you on all facets of my happiness." He kissed her brow to reward himself for his honesty.

"Do we tell Benjamin or Vim about this engagement?"

"Vim being whereabouts unknown," Hadrian said, "I'll send the requisite flowery epistle to Benjamin, provided we can determine his location. My inquiries have resulted in a note from his solicitors that he's on business outside London."

"He'd be relieved to see me safely wed."

"He'd be happy," Hadrian countered evenly. "For you. You should write to your sister of this development."

"I should not." Her tone said she *would* not. "I haven't accepted your suit, Hadrian, no matter you are determined on this course, and no matter an engagement will send a message to Collins. Alex will be hurt to think I've found a mate, while she contents herself to raise other people's children."

Hadrian kissed her temple, as a reward for not bellowing. "Now it's Alex for whom you must sacrifice your happiness?"

"She very nearly sacrificed her ability to walk for me."

Hadrian could not allow that flight of martyrdom to go unchallenged.

"Did you sacrifice *your* happiness to keep Alexandra safe? Collins had both of you in that cottage and could easily have finished with you then moved on to her but for your distracting him."

Avis hunched forward, out from under Hadrian's arm. "She was fourteen, Hadrian. How could she have prevented what happened?"

"She left you," Hadrian said. "Left you to face that brute alone and failed to get help in time. I assure you, your sister carries tremendous guilt for leaving you to Collins's dubious handling."

The word *rape* echoed in the shadows flickering across the hearth rug.

"My poor Alex."

"And her poor Avie. Rather than talk about this with each other, you've put a realm between you and lost what ease you might have had years ago."

Much as Hadrian had gone pelting into the arms of the church and kept the West Riding between him and his older brother.

"I didn't want Alex to go south. We fought about that, but we should have been fighting about this other."

"This rape?"

"Assault."

Avis hadn't discussed the details of the incident itself in all the weeks Hadrian had been home. Surely, it needed discussing, when Avis was ready. Not before that.

Hadrian urged Avis to resume her place cuddled against him.

"As vicar, one is called upon to resolve differences between neighbors. I was often amazed how different people's perceptions could be of the same incident, even an incident I had observed myself and would not have described as any of the disputants did."

"I can't go south uninvited," Avis said. "Alex and I both have to be willing to have this discussion."

"If we're married," Hadrian said, pressing a kiss to her cheek, "I can escort you south, merely to see the capital, or to avoid the damned northern winter."

"You have property in the south?"

"We have a farm in Kent, close enough to Town to be convenient. Harold also has a house in Mayfair, because he occasionally voted his seat and did the pretty." And likely kept company with Finch, about which Hadrian had ceased to care much at all.

"You haven't promised me you'll be honest about the gossip."

"I'll be honest. You must be honest too, Avis."

"About?"

"About how much joy you find in the thought of being my wife, having our children, and availing yourself of my charms."

"I'll jilt you," she warned. "I'll avail myself from one end of the shire to the other, then toss you over."

"Of course you will." Hadrian kissed her again, because she was trying too hard to look after him. "You're wicked Avis Portmaine, scheming seducer and despoiler of innocent lambs like myself. Shall you start availing yourself now? I'm in serious want of despoiling."

And had been for years.

She yawned. "For pity's sake, Hadrian. Not here, not now, and possibly not ever. We're both exhausted, and the night has been quite exciting enough."

When a lady yawned in the face of an offer of seduction, even a lamb in need of despoiling made a strategic retreat.

"You'll make me work for it, then. Excellent tactic. I adore a challenge."

"Well, challenge yourself to go to bed. We've been closeted in here too long as it is."

Not nearly long enough.

"Tomorrow's Sunday," Hadrian said, rising and helping Avis to her feet. "Will you come to services with me?"

"Again?"

"I'll probably ask next week too and the week after that."

"Are you having the banns cried?"

He smiled in contemplation of that step. "Suppose I shall."

"Don't you dare," Avis hissed. "No special licenses, either."

"Stubborn." Hadrian kissed her *again*, a consolation kiss, because even the summer nights in Cumbria could be chilly.

"I'm also exhausted, so away with you."

Hadrian jammed his hands into his pockets, a desperate schoolboy tactic for dealing with the results of too many kisses. "Good night, my love. Until tomorrow."

* * *

"Can this be the newly engaged Mr. Bothwell?" Fen drawled from the darkness of his back porch steps. "Is there trouble in paradise, Choir Boy? Did the lady disdain your impromptu wooing? Or perhaps she needed to ring a peal over your handsome, impetuous head before sending you to my cold, hard guest bed?"

Though Bothwell had probably chosen his moment after a lengthy consideration of strategy.

"Lady Avis is worried about you." Bothwell took a stair below Fen. "Lily Prentiss was glaring such daggers at you, surely you must have given her the French compliment."

Miss Prentiss deserved such a fate, though Fen wouldn't be the one to bestow it on her.

"Some are prone to smiling, some are prone to glaring." Fen passed a bottle. "It's *uisge beatha*. Be careful."

Bothwell took a casual pull of libation no decent vicar should have managed so easily. "You're swearing off the peach brew?"

"I like variety in my pleasures." Fen accepted the bottle back. "All that dancing worked up a thirst." And, predictably, all that dancing worked up a sorry case of longing for home.

"Avie isn't happy with me."

Choir boys must be allowed their confessions. "Dramatic tactics, old man. Did something inspire your declaration?"

"Hortensia Cuthbert." Bothwell appropriated the bottle again. "Elmira Woodman, Josephina Dandridge."

"The harpies were in full force tonight," Fen allowed. "You asked me how bad the gossip is regarding Avie, and I said it comes and goes, but it's as bad now as I've ever heard it." The meanness of the talk had an edge that two generations ago might have turned to mutterings about stillborn babies and the devil's handmaiden.

"Maybe now you're listening for it. I know I am."

In truth, Fen had been trying desperately to ignore the gossip. "Will she marry you?"

"Maybe." The doubt was making Bothwell miserable, but the man wouldn't lie—not even to himself. "I desperately hope so, or I'll have to swear off proposing."

"Practice makes perfect." Fen shifted so he sat on the same step as Bothwell. "You mean well." He took another drink from the bottle. What did it say about Fen's courage, that he'd never proposed to any of the several women to catch his fancy?

"I do not *mean well*. I mean to marry the woman, and I mean to have the privilege of threatening death to any man who thinks to harm her. Avie merely wants to be left alone, and is likely weighing the burden of having me for a husband against the benefit of taking me on as her devoted watchdog."

Sometimes, a fellow could be too honest.

"Was Lady Avis leaving you alone up at the pond last night?"

Bothwell's posture didn't shift, but in his very stillness, Fen perceived menace. "Did you spy on us, Fenwick?"

"I don't have to spy to know you're turning her head, Vicar, and it's about time somebody did. She might just give up and marry you." If Avie had appointed Bothwell her champion, then Fen could make a visit to the north, because summer was the only time such a journey made sense.

"She might give up what?"

The moon rose higher, the night birds went hunting, and Fen fashioned his thoughts into a parable, because Bothwell would grasp a parable most easily.

"Have you ever put a wounded creature in a cage, to help it heal?"

"I have not."

"In the Highlands, as a boy, I came across all manner of creatures in distress. It seemed my special gift, in fact. I found the stags who'd lost the mating matches, horns bloodied, noses bloodied. I found the fledglings who fell from the nest too soon. I found the rabbits caught in some crofter's snare. My grandfather told me I wasn't supposed to heal the beasts. I was to end their misery and gratefully commend them to the stewpot, but I didn't listen."

Fen was still in the business of finding wounded creatures, apparently, or perhaps he'd joined their number.

"I found one of those rabbits," Fen went on, though he hadn't thought of this particular beast in years. "Its hind foot was neatly cut, but the wound was clean, and I thought I'd give the creature a chance to heal. By spring it would be hopping about, nibbling clover, making little bunnies, and proving my grandfather wrong."

Always a pleasure to prove Grandpapa wrong.

"Your rabbit didn't survive?"

"She healed up well enough, but the day came for me to open the door to the cage and let her bound forth. She cowered in the back corner, unable to move, as if by opening that door I'd served her a dire betrayal."

Grandfather had extricated the rabbit from her captivity anyway, for which Fen had been grateful.

"Your point?"

"Avie knows how to be a strong victim, of Collins's attack, of gossip, or of her family's benign neglect. You want her to give up that cage and be Landover's viscountess. She might not have the courage for it, Bothwell. She's coped so long in her cage, she might not even know how to want something else."

"As you've coped in yours?"

Not exactly, for in some ways, Fen shared captivity with Lady Avis, did she but know it. "We all cope, Vicar. You're staying here tonight?"

"I am." He leaned back and rested his elbows on the stair above. "I'll have to pop over to Landover in the morning to roust my coachman. I'm escorting Avie to services."

Fenwick doubted Avie had been apprised of that development. "After last night's announcement, it will be expected. Shall I come along?"

"Of course. Avie deserves all the support she can get."

"And I need to prove old Maudie didn't dance me off my feet." Fen fished the cork from his pocket and stoppered the bottle rather than give in to the temptation to remain under the stars until it was empty. "You've put in a bloody awful week with the crews, Bothwell. Then to take on Avie's situation… You deserve some support too, if not a keeper."

And yet, the man's own brother had sailed off to parts distant.

"Avie is trying to ignore the fact that Collins is somewhere in England. I'm merely providing her a distraction."

"Right." Fen stretched his back, which had also put in a bloody awful week. "Marriage is one hell of a distraction. You'll wake me in the morning if I'm still at my slumbers?"

"At first light." Bothwell followed Fen into the house and took himself down the hall to the guest room.

Avie would be an idiot to refuse Bothwell's suit, and Scotland was lovely in summer. On that thought, Fen took the bottle back outside, saluted the full moon, and headed for the trees.

* * *

"Last night, I forgot to tell you something," Fenwick said as he and Hadrian cleared the trees on the Landover side of the property line.

Ashton Fenwick did not *forget*. He likely didn't forgive much, either. "Something important?"

Fenwick drew rein such that a sunbeam slashed across his face, and in the dappled morning light, he looked nearly haggard. "You have a guest at Landover."

"A guest?" Hadrian's first thought was that Finch had journeyed back from Denmark to report that misfortune had befallen Harold, but Finch had pigeons to convey all but the worst news.

"Devlin St. Just, Earl of Rosecroft," Fenwick replied. "He arrived late yesterday afternoon, and your staff sent word to my house. St. Just's note said not to disturb you needlessly."

"So when I was busy proposing before God and man to Avie, my houseguest was rattling around Landover without a host?"

"I expect he was sleeping. Traveling overland from Yorkshire is devilish tiring. I meant to tell you, but then you proposed and I decided it would wait until morning."

Hadrian urged his horse forward, because Fen was embarrassed to have taken steps to assure a friend a good night's sleep.

"Then I must thank you. I was barely on my feet by the time I found my bed. St. Just doesn't stand on ceremony. Come along and I'll introduce you, assuming he's kept to his usual habit of rising with the sun."

Fenwick's gaze traveled back in the direction of Blessings. "He's an earl. You can introduce us at church after I've had a decent breakfast and donned my Sunday best."

"You'll hide," Hadrian countered. For God's sake, Fenwick's uncle was an earl. "You want to meet him just so you can ask him about how he trains horses."

"I do?"

He did, and they both knew it. They were dismounting in the Landover stable yard when a voice sang out from the barn.

"Where have you been, Hadrian Bothwell, that you come stumbling home, peaked and wan at the crack of doom? If this is country living in Cumberland,

I'll have to visit more often."

"St. Just, welcome to Landover." Hadrian extended a hand to a dark-haired, green-eyed broadsword of a man, only to be pulled into a rough embrace.

"Emmie sends her love," St. Just growled, walloping Hadrian between the shoulder blades. "As does Winnie, to you and to Caesar. She says Scout sends his love too."

The chestnut horse pricked his ears at the sound of his name, and St. Just turned to inspect the beast—while Fenwick took a small eternity to run his stirrups up their leathers.

"Caesar's in good shape," St. Just said. "You've kept the muscle on him, and his coat is blooming too. Well done, Bothwell, and who is this sturdy fellow?"

Fenwick declined to capitalize on the opening, so Hadrian answered St. Just's question.

"Handy belongs to Mr. Ashton Fenwick, steward over at Blessings and my host for the past week's haying."

"Haying." St. Just grimaced. "Makes me itch in unmentionable places just to hear the word. Fenwick, Devlin St. Just, at your service—or Rosecroft if we're doing the pretty. This one has an Iberian ancestor grazing on the family tree, doesn't he? Maybe by way of the Dutch trotters."

As they walked toward the house, Fenwick almost shyly joined the discussion of horses, but was soon trading opinions with St. Just on the merits of shallow versus deep shoulder angles.

"Have you broken your fast, St. Just? Fenwick and I are off to services when we've eaten and seen me put to rights."

"You've put on muscle," St. Just said as they crossed the Landover terrace. "Fenwick must be hitching you to the plough, and your staff is seeing to your victualing."

"He puts his own shoulder to the plough," Fenwick volunteered. "You'd think the church would spoil a man for hard work, but this one doesn't know when to quit."

St. Just slung an arm over Hadrian's shoulders, the gesture surprisingly endearing, considering all present were sober. "You aren't pining for your congregation over in Rosecroft village?"

"I am not." Not in the smallest degree, not a one of them. Hadrian wasn't even missing Harold too terribly much. "How is your countess?"

"Emmie is doing splendidly, which leaves an expectant father rather without dragons to slay. She shooed me off, claiming I scowl too much, and our first born will pick up the habit from me prior to birth."

Their first born would likely canter out of the womb. "Feeling *de trop*?"

"Abysmally." St. Just's smile was lopsided. "Emmie needs to have Winnie all to herself for a bit before the baby comes, and they've been patient with me.

You are the first stop on a jaunt south."

"Their Graces need to see you?" For St. Just was the oldest of a ducal brood of ten, and illegitimacy meant, if anything, St. Just endured an extra helping of fretting from the duke and duchess.

"I need to see my parents, and my brothers and sisters, and I've nephews and nieces to spoil. Life has become complicated."

Fen remained silent throughout this exchange and nearly so at breakfast, though the earl ambushed him nonetheless between sips of tea.

"Mr. Fenwick, you do not appear cheered by the prospect of morning services."

Something about Ashton Fenwick was never entirely cheerful, but Fen had waited up for Hadrian the previous night and looked like his slumbers had not been peaceful.

"If you'd rather retire from the field, Fen, St. Just is a newly minted earl. We can tuck Avie's hand on his arm and make a point quite nicely."

"I was trying to think of a way to suggest you put his lordship to that very use," Fen replied, "without revealing my appalling lack of Christian virtue."

"Avie would be Lady Avis Portmaine, of hallowed fame in Bothwell's letters?"

Hallowed fame was better than some of the characterizations St. Just might have trotted out.

Fen smeared half the jam pot onto his buttered toast. "Been writing the lady's praises, Vicar?"

"I will resort to violence if you insist on addressing me thus much longer." Hadrian topped off tea cups all round, though in the space of a glance, an alliance formed between Fen and St. Just that promised much misery for Hadrian's dignity.

"I don't use the title," St. Just said, "except on rare occasions, such as the need to impress Bothwell's neighbors. If I'm off to curvet about the churchyard, I'm faced with a dilemma. My horse can't be left to idle all day, or he'll stiffen up. After our jaunt through the hills, somebody who's up to his weight has to at least hack him out, or I'll be a week working out the kinks."

And so the mighty Fenwick was reduced to the status of excited new recruit given his first battle mount. "Think you can handle a St. Just horse, Fen?"

Fen drained his tea cup with unceremonious haste. "If he's anything like Bothwell's chestnut, then I'm your man."

St. Just picked up Fenwick's half-eaten toast. "Another sinner gallops astray. Apologies to your Maker, Bothwell."

"Apologize to your own Maker," Hadrian rejoined. "Give me a few minutes to get into decent linen, and I'll meet you out front."

"I'll be in the stables, introducing Mr. Fenwick to Apollo. Ethelred came with us on a leading line, but he's a less steady fellow altogether."

"Fen, to my friends," Fenwick said as he got to his feet. "You will please tell me about this Apollo beast, lest I disgrace myself before we're beyond the stable yard."

They disappeared, both lost in a discussion of stiffness to the left and a tendency to drag on the reins when bored, while Hadrian considered that he was having his first house guest, and St. Just was somebody he truly welcomed as a friend.

At least, when Hadrian had proposed to Emmie, the lasting effect on his relationship with St. Just had been the winner's sympathy and respect for the loser. And how fortunate that Hadrian *had* lost. Emmie was deliriously happy with her growling earl, and Hadrian intended to be just as blissful with his Avie.

Provided she accepted his proposal.

* * *

Emmie St. Just, though far gone with child, had practically led Apollo out and boosted her husband into the saddle, so insistent had she been that St. Just make his bow before Their Graces and look in on their dear friend Mr. Bothwell.

St. Just had battled old feelings, of being the odd man out, the marginalized sibling who'd joined the family late and awkwardly, until he'd confided these sentiments to his wife and been roundly—affectionately—scolded for "goose-ishness."

Emmie and Winnie had been right: Somebody had to look in on Bothwell and ensure that having mustered out of the clergy, he was bearing up under the strain of life as a civilian sinner.

Now that Fenwick was off on his pony ride and the coach rolling toward Blessings, St. Just expected a report, for Emmie would expect a report, and little Winnie would too.

"You wrote that Lady Avis was the victim of an assault," St. Just said, "but that happened years ago, before you even finished at university."

Bothwell made a study of the lovely Cumbrian countryside, and a small part of St. Just was relieved that Emmie wasn't there to admire their friend in his Sunday finest. He'd not only put on muscle, he'd also put something *off* too—something churchy and foreign to Bothwell's true nature.

"Lady Avis was brutally attacked by the fiancé she was intent on jilting," Bothwell said. "Some in the shire took the position Collins was merely anticipating vows and Avis put a vile name on his attentions to see him run off in disgrace."

"A costly tactic on her part, when sending a note would have sufficed, or sending a brother or two."

"You're right. If she wanted to break things off, she had better options. I'm the one who found her, St. Just, after she was raped."

St. Just had seen rape aplenty in the wake of broken sieges. The screams of the violated were in some ways more traumatizing than the screams of the dying, and nothing in the theological curriculum at Oxford would have prepared Bothwell for either.

"What else can you tell me that you didn't put in your dispatches?"

"Collins is somewhere on English soil, though we're fairly certain he disembarked in Portsmouth."

"Fairly certain?"

"He's evil," Bothwell said, resuming his study of the green, rolling landscape. "I went into the church knowing evil exists mostly because of Hart Collins. He sensed Avie was having second thoughts about marrying him, knew his future was slipping away, and did what he expected would guarantee him her settlements, regardless of the cost to her. As young as she was, if he'd turned up sweet, brought her some damned flowers, promised to honeymoon in the south, she would likely have come to heel."

"Evil, ruthless and stupid. Not a good combination. The lady welcomes your suit?"

Now Bothwell fussed at the lace of his cravat—a wardrobe affectation St. Just recalled seeing on him in Rosecroft village. "She does not welcome my suit, though she's receptive to my company under some circumstances."

"Bothwell." St. Just kept his tone gentle, for rejected proposals were a sorry habit in this otherwise intelligent man. "Not again?"

"Fenwick says practice makes perfect."

Confession might be good for the sinner's soul, but the unburdening was hell on the confessor.

"Emmie worries about you, and thus I must trouble myself with your welfare as well—you have no say in the matter. Have you been indiscriminately offering your hand to the fair damsels of the shire?"

"Before offering for Emmie either time, there was Rue's older sister," Bothwell said, and he was not proud of his recitation. "I tried walking out with Mary, but she laughed at my proposal and informed me I would do for her younger sister, who was admittedly pretty and agreeable. I had little say in that matter, either."

"Bad things come in threes," St. Just muttered, though failed proposals qualified as something more than bad luck. "Will your Lady Avis have you?'

"Have me, yes. As for marrying me—I'm permitted to offer her arguments on the merits of my suit." The coach bumped and swayed along the rutted country lane while Bothwell aimed a fatuous smile at his boots.

"Arguments? Am I to conclude you offered these *arguments* to my countess?"

"You are not. Emmie never saw me as a man, St. Just. I was only a means of ensuring she and Winnie did not part, and a way for her to deny you what you needed."

"Needed?'

"You needed Emmie and she needed you, and all's well."

A report after a fashion, and St. Just was pleased with Bothwell's summary—also with that love-drunk smile. "Does Lady Avis need you?"

"Not for the right reasons. Maybe need is too strong a word."

St. Just had several younger brothers—also half a regiment of younger sisters and female cousins.

"Bothwell, if Lady Avis needs you in any capacity, you make do, and improvise, and adjust—you *argue*, if need be. Faint heart never won fair maid, and neither did sitting on your arse waiting for perfect conditions before you join battle."

"Marriage has turned you up romantic, St. Just."

Marriage had made him happy. "Who's the English rose?"

Bothwell peered out St. Just's side of the coach as a tidy blond woman disappeared back into the house, leaving a pretty dark-haired lady standing on the Blessings front porch.

"The blonde is Lily Prentiss," Bothwell said, his tone unenthusiastic. "Lady's companion and general conscience. She hates Fen and is mightily loyal to Avie."

"Avie?"

"Lady Avis. We've known each other since childhood, and one develops a certain informality."

A certain tendency to smile at one's boots, too.

"Don't poker up. Am I to charm the companion or put her in her place?" Though what sort of companion abandoned her employer right as guests arrived?

"If your lordship charms her, she will be put in her place."

"My lordship," St. Just muttered. "Famous. Your saint-ship can see to it we're not invited anywhere after services, because my lordship's arse is tired from my journey."

Then too, St. Just did not want to be hurried from the company of the woman who had inspired Hadrian Bothwell, former Kissing Vicar of Rosecroft village, not only to propose—Bothwell excelled at offers of marriage—but also to offer the lady his heart.

CHAPTER TWELVE

St. Just was in grand good looks and nattily turned out in his country gentleman's Sunday best. Hadrian tended to the introductions when Lily emerged from the house with a shawl over her arm. The coach was cozy, with two long-legged men on the backward-facing seat and Lily nearly cooing to be introduced to an earl, while Avis was oddly quiet.

St. Just was charming, but then the man had five sisters, a wife, a step-mother, and a step-daughter, and female cousins. Hadrian knew there was more to Devlin St. Just than the battle-scarred former cavalry officer.

"We've lost our host to woolgathering," St. Just remarked as the carriage rolled onto the village square. "Bothwell, you haven't added your opinion. At what age should I permit Winnie to waltz?"

"It isn't an age," Hadrian replied. "It's with whom. She can waltz with her Uncle Valentine now, provided somebody else supplies the music, but certain other fellows you'd not want her waltzing with when she's seen her threescore and ten."

"Precisely," Lily jumped in. "I remarked much the same thing to Lady Avis over breakfast."

Which probably explained Avie's subdued demeanor. Hadrian stuck close to her when they arrived at church, making sure she was seated between him and St. Just, with Lily on St. Just's other side. After church, St. Just took Avis's arm and kept her near him to make introductions, leaving Hadrian to escort Lily among the tombstones.

"So you and Lady Avis were discussing waltzes over breakfast," Hadrian remarked. "A pleasant topic."

"We weren't discussing waltzes, per se," Lily replied, her tone repressive, "but rather, propriety."

"Do I take it you disapprove of our engagement?"

Lily paused before the oldest gravestone in the entire plot, though nobody knew exactly how old, or who was interred beneath it. Engraved letters had faded into obscurity centuries ago, so all that remained was a lichen-encrusted block of granite.

"I do not disapprove, but I worry, for her, and also for you, Mr. Bothwell."

No, she did not. Hadrian had associated at close quarters with many a worried Christian of the earnest variety. Lily worried for Avis's *reputation*, rather than for Avis.

"Marriage is always a chancy proposition. I will take the best possible care of Lady Avis. You needn't worry on that score." Avis would take care of Hadrian too, which thought pleased him enormously.

"You'll try," Lily said, brushing a fallen twig from the top of the stone. "Lady Avis grew up without a mother's guiding hand, though, and that has created a certain lack she can't help. I speak only out of concern for her welfare when I say she is destined to misstep if you expect her to assume the role of mistress of Landover."

Please, let her misstep enthusiastically and often in the vicinity of Hadrian's bed.

"We all misstep," Hadrian said, leading Lily away from the gravestone.

"But she suffers so when she does," Lily protested. "Every time she falters and crosses the boundaries of good behavior, she feels again the burden of her youthful misfortunes. She blames herself for what she cannot help, and in her misery often missteps again. I would spare her this, and if you truly care for her, you won't ask it of her."

Hadrian studied the newer gravestones off to their left. His parents lay there, an infant brother with them, along with grandparents and ancestors beyond antiquity. Someday, he'd be laid to rest with them, and in due time, Avie and their children would find an eternal home in that same churchyard.

On this, he was determined.

"Miss Prentiss, if you love Lady Avis, you will not stand between her and what and who she wants."

"You are wrong." Lily dropped his arm, her tone despairing. "I saw my father hounded from his calling by nothing more substantial than gossip and innuendo. Somebody needs to stand between Lady Avis and her impulsive desires, or she'll not even be welcome in this tolerant atmosphere on the arm of an earl."

She stalked away, skirts twitching, and Hadrian let her go when he wanted to throttle her. Lily Prentiss was perceptive in at least two regards.

First, Avie hadn't had a mother's guiding hand. Governesses, nannies and older brothers didn't compensate for that lack. Second, Avie did torment herself, ceaselessly, as if every mistake, whether real or simply attributed to her, reawakened her guilt over Hart Collins's attack years ago.

But Lily's insight ended there. Everybody misstepped, everybody.

When the coach returned to Blessings, Hadrian exchanged a look with St. Just, who'd dumped entire hogsheads of charm over the ladies and the good Christians of the parish.

"Miss Prentiss," the earl said as he handed her out of the coach, "could I trouble you to escort me through the stables? I'm always curious regarding the keeping of horses, and Blessings seems to be a well-run place."

Lily allowed the earl to keep her hand in his. "Lady Avis? You'll manage?"

As if Avie might become lost between the stables and the house?

"Of course. Hadrian and I can take a turn about the garden."

Lily looked unconvinced, but when St. Just tucked her hand onto his arm, she let him lead her away.

"She'll dine out on this for weeks," Hadrian remarked quietly.

"A handsome earl is worth crowing over, though he seems friendly."

"St. Just is illegitimate," Hadrian said, his voice pitched not to carry. "The earldom was a sop thrown to his father the duke, though bravery in battle made a creditable pretext for bestowing a bankrupt title."

"He loves his wife," Avis said, as they drew even with the rose bushes, "and that child."

Could she hear the longing in her own words?

"Bronwyn. A terror only this high." Hadrian held his hand at waist level. "I gather Lily terrorized you at breakfast?"

"Just doing her job, reminding me that engagements are when we test the decision to remain married forever and always to one person, when a lady can change her mind, and so forth."

While Lily referred to it as a discussion of propriety. "I got much the same lecture from her. She does not see you clearly, Avie."

"She doesn't?"

Hadrian paused, because the scent of the roses was soothing, and because Avie's pace suggested she sought the sanctuary of the house after a trying morning.

In Hadrian's company.

"Lily thinks you're fragile and confused, lacking proper social instincts. She sees you as you might have been for a short time at age seventeen. I see you as my viscountess."

Avis resumed walking toward the house. "Then you don't see me clearly, either, do you?"

How easily Lily's admonitions stole Avie's courage, though the morning's sermon had been a good-natured exploration of the Lord's instructions regarding rest and renewal.

"I'm sorry for haranguing you." Hadrian caught up to her and slid his arm across her shoulders, relieved when she didn't resist. "Now that haying is done, what will occupy your time?"

"The dower house," she said, apparently willing to change the subject. "Summer is fleeting. We must work like demons while the light lasts."

"You must take the sermon's sentiments to heart and rest," Hadrian rejoined. "You worked like a demon all last week and you have staff. Let them use the light while you put the bloom back in your cheeks."

"I like to be busy. Lord Rosecroft has finished with his tour."

"He's given us as much privacy as he thinks we want," Hadrian said, though not as much as they needed. Perhaps Lily's charms had paled that quickly. "I wish I could cuddle up with you this afternoon. Rub your back, brush your hair, read to you."

She studied a cheerful border of pansies, as if puzzled by this impulse, and Hadrian was hard put not to express his exasperation.

"I'm not a strutting tom cat, Avie."

"I never said you were. The heat will soon kill these pansies, though they've held up longer than they often do."

Hang the bloody pansies. Hadrian laced his fingers through Avie's.

"Love, you offered me no insult. It's yourself upon whom you cast aspersion."

He drew her into his arms, knowing St. Just, Lily, the stable hands, and likely half the house servants were looking on. She dropped her head to his shoulder, a small triumph that she'd permit affection like this before others, that she'd let him hold her.

"Will you ride out with us tomorrow morning?" he asked.

"Us?"

"St. Just, myself, Fenwick too, if we can get him past his shyness."

"Fen is shy? I must see this."

"He's in awe of St. Just's horsemanship." Hadrian tucked a curl behind her ear. "It's sweet."

"I thought Fen was to join us at services today."

"He cadged a ride on St. Just's current mount. He was like a boy with a new puppy."

"Well, then, yes, I'll ride out with you tomorrow, weather permitting, but then you must join us for breakfast thereafter."

Hadrian hesitated, for he'd been intent on having her break bread under his roof; but, then, he also wanted to rub Lily Prentiss's face in this engagement, wanted to give Avis the chance to be the gracious hostess, the lady who knew exactly how to go on in a social situation.

"Ride first, then feast," he agreed. "We'll join you an hour after first light."

"Until then." She went up on her toes and pressed her mouth to his, and that simple, relatively bland kiss was enough to put a smile on Hadrian's face all the way back to Landover.

* * *

Avis was accustomed to Lily's lectures, could recite them almost word for word, complete with gestures and weighty sighs. She had not anticipated Fenwick pulling her aside after yesterday's morning ride and warning her not to lead Mr. Bothwell a dance he'd done nothing to deserve.

Fen had overstepped egregiously, but he'd also made a valid point: Avie should not remain engaged to a man she had no intention of marrying. It was as if Fen had divined the exact course of her thoughts.

Hadrian's return to Landover had shifted the balance between Avis's courage and her fear, a balance that had grown increasingly burdensome over the past twelve years. She had dallied with Hadrian, true, and had the sense if she refused the pleasure he offered, that balance would revert to its previous, miserable stance.

She had even been tempted to consider his proposal in truth.

Then she'd returned from church and realized she could not ask that of him.

With Hadrian's complicity, she could, however, deal one last, telling blow to Hart Collins and the influence he continued to exert over her life. Hadrian was a lovely, decent, good man. Sooner or later, he'd find the right wife—he'd deserve at least that after Avis was through with him.

"You're early," Avis said as Hadrian strode up the hill to their preferred picnic spot, for here was where she'd face the demons Hart Collins had turned loose in her life.

"Would you believe I'm hungry?"

He was gorgeous, his blond hair sun-kissed and windblown, his riding attire showing his muscular physique to excellent advantage.

"For food?"

"That too. But Avie…" He kept his pace steady as he ambled toward her blanket, as if he were closing in on an objective. "You asked me to join you for an outdoor repast where we'd be assured of privacy. Why now?"

Hadrian had never suffered from excesses of delicacy. He could be kind, considerate, and exquisitely polite, but he'd never lacked for the courage to face an issue.

Avis was relieved that he understood her agenda for inviting him to another al fresco meal. She was not relieved to see him shrugging out of his jacket and tugging off his boots and stockings.

"Now we're engaged," she said. "If not now, when?"

He lowered himself to the blankets spread beneath the tree. "You want to get this over with?" His tone was curious rather than angry.

"Will you run screaming down the hill if I say yes, a little, I do want to get this over with?" A lot, she wanted to put this encounter behind her.

Hadrian tossed his stockings over the tops of his boots. "What's the worst that could happen?"

"I could be unable." And ashamed all over again, because this time, not even hope would survive the encounter.

His cuff-links came next, and those he slipped into a pocket. "Unable to what?"

"I might be unable to join with you."

"You're able," he said, sounding reassuringly testy.

"You're certain of this."

He went after his cravat, demolishing the elegant knot without getting it undone. "Sexual congress need not be demanding for a woman." Sexual congress. His term was neither vulgar nor sentimental.

"What does that mean?"

"It means you could probably lie there, eyes closed, sighing occasionally, and I'd be overjoyed to have that much of a response from you."

She pushed his hands away from his neckcloth. "What are you going on about? Lie there and sigh? Surely there's more to it than that." She hoped there was more to it than that.

He lifted his chin so she could divest him of his cravat, staring over her shoulder as she undid his linen. "You've experienced sexual pleasure, Avie."

"With you, I have." With Collins she wasn't sure what she'd experienced, but it had hurt in more ways than the physical. She folded the linen and tucked it into the pocket of his jacket. "I liked what I've shared with you, though it's overwhelming. I'm not sure I should like it." Though Gran Carruthers and some of the other older women talked as if marital intimacies were among their fondest recollections.

"Many women go their whole lives without experiencing the pleasure that befell you with me," he said, still staring at a point beyond her shoulder. "They don't care to be overwhelmed in such an intimate manner. My wife was such a one."

"Her again." Avis had tried not to think too much about Hadrian's sainted wife.

"Yes, *her*. She tolerated marital intimacies as a matter of duty."

"*Tolerated?* Tolerated *you?* I do not comprehend this."

Hadrian was not a spotty, pudgy boy with clammy hands and foul breath. He was in every regard a man of worth, and desirable. That his wife of all people should fail to appreciate him—

Abruptly, Avis became determined that their encounter be *mutually* pleasurable, and felt the first stirrings of confidence that she could make it thus.

"Hadrian, I am so sorry." This wife had *hurt* him, for which Avis wanted to lecture her sternly and at length.

"We had relations infrequently, in the dark, under the covers, as she all but pretended to sleep. I learned not to miss what I would not ever share with my devoted helpmeet."

A breeze sprang up and fanned ripples across the quiet surface of the pond, while Avis struggled with bottomless consternation. "In the dark? Under the covers?"

"Infrequently."

His complete lack of expression confirmed that the memories were painful still, and that Hadrian had not found a way to make sense of a woman who promised to love, honor and obey, and then delivered an intimate rejection instead.

Not so very different form Hart Collins, pledging his lifelong companionship, respect and affection, then delivering violation and betrayal in their place. At least Hart Collins had done his damage then decamped for the Continent.

"Were her marital duties painful for her?"

"Physically? I can assure you I took every measure to guarantee they were not, and she never accused me of hurting her."

"Not in words."

"You begin to grasp an element of the marital dynamic I found baffling for the entire length of our union. If the woman didn't want to be my wife in the most basic sense, then why marry me?"

My poor Hadrian. Rue had married the handsome Mr. Bothwell for the same reason Avis had at least temporarily accepted Hart Collins's suit.

"Rue accepted your suit because a woman must marry or she's an object of pity and derision. Her sisters chose you for her, and you had a viscount's title in your future."

"Why are we speaking of this?" He began unbuttoning his waistcoat, a blue paisley silk that did marvelous things for his eyes. "The day is spectacularly lovely. I'm in the best company, and we're alone for as long as we please." He cupped the curve of Avis's jaw, his hand callused and warm against her cheek.

He was more than half-undressed, while Avis needed time to adjust to his disclosures. Her ordeal with Collins had been painful and scandalous, but over in minutes. Hadrian's marriage had lasted several years.

"Shall we eat?"

He dropped his hand. "Maybe. You will make me a promise first, though."

"You would ask me for vows, Hadrian? I'm surprised you'd trust another woman to keep her word." Surprised he'd consider marriage ever again under any circumstances.

"You'll make this promise or I will set off down the hill at a dead run. You must assure me, Avie, that if you're at all uncomfortable, physically or otherwise, you'll stop me."

What was he asking? "I'm uncomfortable now."

"Painfully uncomfortable," he clarified. "A certain anxiety is to be expected, on both of our parts, for I am at something of a loss myself. If I exercise excessive control, you'll have time to fret and worry and think yourself out of your pleasures. If my attentions become too precipitous, you might be reminded of Collins."

Hart Collins was never very far from Avis's awareness, which was in some ways his greatest transgression. Avis decided, between one breeze and the next, that Collins would have no part of what transpired between her and Hadrian on that blanket.

And yet, what about Hadrian's past, which he'd born with the polite, mendacious good cheer of a rural vicar? "Tell me about Rue."

He sat a foot away from Avis, his waistcoat gaping open. "I already did. We were married and we learned to be content."

"You learned to cope. One does."

He and Avis had been coping separately, but with at least some of the same demons. Avis pushed Hadrian's waistcoat off his shoulders.

"One did," he said. "I'm here now with you, and for that I am grateful."

"As am I. Profoundly grateful." Not the dutiful, pious, Christian sort of gratitude, but—despite all manner of looming difficulties and impossible choices—a wild, joyous, incredulous gratitude that needed the endless blue of the Cumbrian summer sky to encompass it.

Hadrian shifted so his back was to the tree shading their blanket and patted the place beside him. "Then stop being so skittish, my love, and cuddle up. Shall I tell you what I'm planning for you?"

* * *

"Merciful days, Hadrian. You shall not deliver a sermon on the topic of my pleasures." Despite her scolding tone, Avie took the place beside Hadrian, her knees drawn up under her chin.

Hadrian settled a hand on the back of her neck, such a vulnerable, pretty neck, and mustered not a sermon but rather an ode.

"I'll start with the little touches, for they calm something that clamors inside me when I'm near you. I think,"—he traced the curve of her ear—"this is what fatuous young men mean when they say, 'She completes me.' To touch you in any way is soothing and compelling at once."

He watched her for a reaction, and perhaps, just perhaps, her head dropped forward an inch in relaxation.

"Touching you makes me want to kiss you," Hadrian went on, his tone steadier than his nerves. "I want to kiss you all over, your hair, your face, your hands, your luscious breasts, your *everything*. I want my mouth on you everywhere, learning the taste of you, the scent of you, and that, of course, makes me want your mouth on me."

He scooted, so he could start on the hooks of her dress. She held quite, quite still for that, too.

"When my mouth,"—he leaned in for a kiss to her nape—"and my hands are on you, I want to be inside you. I want to feel your passion as we join, and give you pleasure upon pleasure upon pleasure." He paused to slip his hands around, slowly, slowly, and rest them on her waist.

"I want to take pleasure from you too," he admitted, brushing his palms over her breasts as he returned to the endless—endless!—procession of hooks down her back. "I want to feel you writhing beneath me, eager for what I can give you, demanding it. I want those lover sounds pouring from you in a desperate torrent. I want your nails,"—he brought her hand to his mouth and sucked on an index finger—"scoring my back in mindless abandon and sinking into my—"

"Stop."

He fell silent, almost glad for the freedom to focus on disrobing her.

"I didn't mean you must cease speaking." She peered at him over her shoulder, her gaze a bit dazed. "I can get this dress off now."

"I'll get the dress off you." Hadrian slid his hands forward again, under yards and billows of fabric. "Soon."

"Now," she said, her voice taking on a new, stubborn edge.

"Very well." Hadrian moved around to face her on the blanket. "Now I really must kiss you."

He'd found his rhythm, no doubt a little faster than she wanted, a lot slower than he wanted, but it was working. Avis's gaze was softening, and her mind was easing into the tempo of passion. He brushed his lips over her eyelids, and a happy, sweet sigh breezed past his ear.

"Hadrian Chastain Bothwell…"

He went on a kissing tour of her features, tending to her eyebrows, her jaw, her cheek, her forehead, and finding the place just above her collarbone that provoked a sigh slightly more ragged and needy than its predecessors.

She turned her face, seeking his mouth, and Hadrian sat back.

"Help me with my shirt, Avie."

She hauled him forward by grabbing a fistful of that shirt, and Hadrian fell into the role of kissee rather than kisser. Avie undid the buttons of his shirt, then stroked her hands over his chest as if she'd been expiring for the feel of his bare skin beneath her palms.

He should have kept his shirt on, literally, for the desire to ruck up her skirts and start rutting kicked hard at his self-control.

No rucking, old boy.

Collins had no doubt done some rucking and worse, and the thought was enough to jerk hard on the reins of Hadrian's arousal. He settled for pulling the shirt over his head, the better to oblige Avie's curiosity.

She dropped her forehead to his bare shoulder, and God help him, she tasted him, a tentative flick of her tongue that had heat arcing through him, into his bones, and down.

"Hadrian, you must kiss me." A little breathless, but a command rather than a request.

Bless the woman. Commandments were something he understood.

"I assuredly must kiss you." He nuzzled at her throat, pressing her back, until she lay flat, her dress loose. He brushed her hair off her forehead, giving himself a moment to steady his galloping impulses, and then stretched out beside her. "Or you could kiss me."

That she launched herself at him like a female variant of the Congreve rocket suggested she liked the idea.

"I want to gobble you up," she said, rolling up on her side and using that infernal tongue of hers to taste his chest. "In little bites, slowly, and thoroughly."

"I'm willing to be gobbled." He was only human, though, so he had to touch her while she tortured him. He sank his hands into her hair and wondered fleetingly if she'd rather have it loose, and then his fingers were searching out the pins, because *he'd* rather have it undone, brushing across his chest, fanning his belly, spilling around them in soft, fragrant abundance.

He teased the neckline of her dress down, and she smiled more radiantly.

"I'm glad we're outside," she said, then pressed her face to his shoulder. "It's better, like this."

He cradled the back of her head against his palm, respect for her courage washing through him and gentling the lust. *Better* was her euphemism for unashamed. Not in some musty little cottage, not furtive or dark or under the covers. Better, gloriously better.

She put them both out of their misery and brought her mouth to his at the same moment Hadrian drew the last pin from her hair. As she shifted over him, her mouth still joined to his, her hair tumbled down in silky, shimmering waves.

Hadrian gathered up her tresses, glorying in their warmth and abundance. She paused in her plundering of his mouth to shake her head, the better to spill her hair over them both.

"Kiss me, Avie, or I'll start howling and panting, my eyes will cross and my—"

She sighed into his mouth. Precious, her life's breath, tasting of peppermint tea and sweetness. She was tentative, seaming his lips, tracing his teeth, then gradually, going deeper.

She touched him too, making the newly created *no rucking* commandment a sore trial. Her fingers traced Hadrian's jaw, his hairline, his ear, and on down his neck, to his throat, his collarbone—she was particularly interested in that, or in driving him mad pausing there—and then to his chest.

He trapped her hand in his and brought it to his falls, and when she startled above him, he cursed himself for being too headlong, too greedy.

No rucking, and now, *no rushing*.

Then she shaped him through his breeches, and he couldn't ruck, or rush, or think, because her touch was too *wonderful*.

"Easy, love." He kissed her around the words, arching up when what he wanted to do was thrust hard into that curious hand. "Perhaps you could get me out of my breeches?"

"While I'm still dressed?"

"You're only somewhat dressed." He lay beneath her, nearly panting with the need to be naked.

And when, he wondered vaguely, had he developed such wanton inclinations?

And why had he waited so long to indulge them?

"Buttons, Avie. Please."

She smiled a secret, smug smile—he'd have to remember to beg more often—and her deft fingers were soon undoing his breeches, thank ye gods. When she had his falls open, she sat back, a prizefighter regaining her wind between rounds, then went exploring among the folds and tucks of his clothing, gently extracting the treasure she found.

"Oh, my."

"Avie, dearest, if you keep looking at me like that, I will surely disgrace myself." Though what a pleasurable disgrace it would be.

She scooted back and leaned down to swipe her tongue up the length of him, lingering for a swirl right up under the tip, where his best intentions had never resided.

He stroked his hand over the back of her head. "Love, if you don't get on your pony this instant, he'll gallop off without you."

"Bad pony, to leave a lady stranded," she said, letting her hands fall away from Hadrian's cock. "How does one do this?"

"Two do it. Straddle me," he said, keeping his tone brisk, for the moment was critical given the doubt in her eyes. "Then you owe me some proper kissing."

"Improper kissing," she corrected, but she gave him room to peel out of his breeches and then took a moment to survey his naked body, slowly, from head to toe, and back up.

"What a magnificent man-beast you are."

Eve might have said those very words in the Garden of Paradise.

"You can stare at me all you like." Hadrian made a show of folding his arms behind his head. "Or you can stop dithering."

CHAPTER THIRTEEN

"You're nicely put together."

And dear Avie was still dithering. "The part you're staring at is in proportion to the rest of me, and you're stalling."

"Admiring, not staring at."

"Stalling." He hoisted her over him, and she went unresisting to her fate. "That wasn't so difficult. Now hush and kiss me, lest I run screaming after all."

She looked like she wanted to argue, so he settled his hands on her shoulders and urged her down within kissing range. She seemed to appreciate his initiative. Her tongue was soon back in his mouth, boldly tangling with his own.

"Hadrian, when do we—"

He didn't let her finish the question, but gave her breast a gentle squeeze— no stays!—thus reminding her that her dress had been pushed off her shoulders by some mysterious force of nature.

"Let me get my arms—" She pulled free of the sleeves and fell upon his mouth again, which suited Hadrian's plans delightfully. While she pillaged his lips and teeth and mouth and tongue, he slid both hands up over the graceful planes of her back, through her hair, and down her arms.

"Hadrian, when—?"

"Soon." He had to work to get his hand up under her skirts, but he wasn't about to let matters progress without assuring himself she was ready. Kisses were one thing, but female bodies didn't lie in the most intimate regards, and so he manually tunneled, dug, slipped and slid through billows of soft fabric until his palm met smooth, firm thigh.

She cradled his head with both hands and held him immobile for kisses that were growing voracious, then went still when he cupped his hand around her derrière.

He sucked on her bottom lip, a suggestion that she was to kiss him, and she gave him another sigh. For long moments he was content to stroke her backside, which relaxed her, turning her to a boneless heap of fragrant, kissing, warm female over him.

"You like that, Avie?"

She broke off kissing and rested her cheek against his shoulder. "Naughty."

He patted her bottom. "I'll show you what's closer to naughty." He worked his hand around under all the infernal fabric of her dress and found the seat of her pleasure, giving it a glancing caress with his thumb.

"Don't tease, Hadrian."

"Teasing is fun," he countered, sifting his fingers through her curls. "A little teasing. You've been teasing me."

"I have, haven't I?" God bless her, she sounded saucy, probably for the first time in twelve years.

"Unmercifully. You're damp, Avie."

"Is that bad?"

"Is my being hard with wanting you bad?"

"It is not."

"Then this,"—he eased a finger shallowly into her depths—"is not bad. It's luscious, lovely, dear, and arousing." Painfully arousing.

"It's time now, isn't it?"

"If you like."

He stilled his hand when what he wanted was to touch and taste and explore until his ears rang.

"Tell me how to do this, Hadrian."

He did not ask if she was sure, did not ask if it was truly what she wanted. He should have, but he didn't—couldn't.

"It's the simplest thing in the world," he said, teasing his thumb over her again, more slowly, with a hint more pressure. "You fit *me* to *you* and we join."

"That's it?"

"Let's get through that much," Hadrian said, his thumb working all the while, "and then you may interrogate me further."

"Can you do this fitting business?"

"Not this time." He would not be wheedled on this point. Not, at least, for the next thirty seconds.

"Oh, very well." She reached under her skirts, easily, it seemed to Hadrian, and fished him into her hand. "You're sure this is how it works?"

"Positive, Avie love." Her expression was nearly a scowl of concentration, so intently was she focused on where their bodies would join. She brushed the head of his cock over the damp glory of her sex several times.

"Avis Seraphina Portmaine." He tried to sound stern, but her name came out as a desperate plea, and she smiled and seated him against the opening in her body.

"There, I think."

He gave a *minute* flex of his hips. "Absolutely there."

"Now what?"

He urged her down onto his chest and wrapped his arms around her. "Now you hold on to me, and we join."

She tucked her face into the crook of his neck, her body radiating a tension that hadn't been present a moment earlier.

"Or not." Hadrian let his arms fall away. "Perhaps you'd better do this." His cock was right at her door, the dampness and heat of her enveloping him, and he wanted nothing, *not one thing in all creation,* so much as to move.

"What do I do?"

"Think of it as fitting together the sections of your flute. You don't jam them together, though the instrument must be properly assembled if you're to make music with it. Assemble us, Avie, by moving." He patted her hip and waited, though God knew what daft analogy he might seize on next if the flute didn't make his point.

A bassoon perhaps, a clarinet, an haut boy, or—

She braced herself over him on her forearms, the scowl back, as if she were assembling her flute before a command performance at Carlton House and had misplaced her music. Her hips shifted enough to glove the head of his cock.

Just that much, and Hadrian was teased with a hot, wet paradise fitted exactly for him.

"Like that?" She moved again, then again, her undulations tentative—and tantalizing.

"Just like that, easily, as a breeze rocks a boat on a calm lake."

"It doesn't hurt exactly," she decided, "but this isn't like when you pleasured me."

"We're only getting started." He had to move or go mad—or he might go mad if he did move, gloriously mad. He flexed his hips shallowly, meeting her downward thrust.

"Merciful days. What was that?"

"A little resistance," Hadrian assured her. "We fit quite snugly." Magnificently, wonderfully, beautifully, *miraculously.*

"Is that bad?'

He wanted to thrust, and thrust and thrust, but now, especially now, he denied himself that pleasure.

"It's lovely." He folded up and nuzzled her breast through the fabric of her bodice. He nosed aside the dress, undid bows, then undid more bows, until her breasts were exposed to the summer air and to his hungry gaze. "Move again for me, Avie."

"I like it better when you move."

"Contrary female." He got his mouth on one of her nipples, and she gave up some of the tension infusing her spine. "You leave all the work to me, lazy baggage."

And slowly, slowly, he worked his way more deeply into her heat. "Tell me if I'm—"

Her grip in his hair was firm. "You're not. This is different."

"From?"

"Everything." She closed her eyes while he anchored his hands on her hips and ground his mental teeth in increasing arousal. "I like this much better, when you move, Hadrian."

Just like that, his frustration evaporated. She was coming alive as he penetrated her sweet heat, yielding to his invasion and catching the rhythm of it.

"Shall I kiss you, Avie?"

She shook her head, found his hand, and brought it to her breast. He plied her slowly, fondling, kneading, and then just when she opened her eyes to glare at him, he gave her the slight pressure on her nipple she'd been about to demand.

All the while, he eased his cock in and out of her body, slowly, in excruciatingly small increments, until she bit his earlobe.

"More, Hadrian. Now."

"This much more?" He drove deeper and with a hint of passion to his thrusts.

"More," she demanded. "I won't break, unless you insist on *dithering* and then I shall be the one to run screaming down the hill."

He treasured her frustration, her wonderful, glorious, *perfectly normal* frustration. "How do you know I'm not doing this perfectly?"

"Because you're not, not quite."

She fell silent, both relief and increasing wonder stealing into her expression as he intensified his efforts. He didn't have to ask if she preferred that, because she cuddled onto his chest and began to work her hips in a natural counterpoint to his.

"Oh…dear…Hadrian."

"Let go," he whispered, keeping a palm right on her backside to measure her rhythm. "Fly free, Avis. Let yourself soar."

"Ha-dri-an." She shook as her pleasure overcame her, and yet she let him take her higher and higher still, until she was moaning out her satisfaction right into the clear summer air, right into his own release. He tried to hold back, but Avie was coming and coming, her body gripping hard at his, forcing a pleasure on him too long missed and undeniable in its intensity.

"Holy everlasting powers," Hadrian panted. He gathered her close and rolled them, then caged her body with his before he'd even thought what being trapped beneath him might feel like for her. "Are you all right?"

"Hush." She patted his naked bottom, then stroked the same spot. "Give me a minute."

Hadrian wanted to give her the entire rest of his days. He was more sure of that than of anything else ever in his life. Bless the woman, he was close to tears, he was so proud of her, of them, of what she'd managed in the last few moments.

And he was appalled too, for he'd not protected her at the final moment, and marriage wasn't a possibility now, it was mandatory. Avie wouldn't like that. He hadn't planned it this way, but he simply hadn't known how it would be.

She clung to him, as if her feelings were equally riotous.

"Tell me you enjoyed that." Hadrian laid his cheek against hers and wanted to hold her close with all his strength. Forever.

He didn't look too closely at that impulse, for the cheek pressed to his was damp.

"Avie?" He pulled back and confirmed to his horror that she was crying. *Don't bungle this. Don't bungle this worse than you already have.*

"Love?" He brushed a thumb over that damp cheek. "Did I hurt you?"

"No." Her voice was firm despite the tears. "No, you did not. You *unhurt* me. I've never known anything as—Oh, *Hadrian.*" She held him to her, with her arms, and legs, even with her sex, and he waited, hoping she'd tell him *anything.*

"I'm,"—she eased her grip—"overwhelmed doesn't express it, not clearly. Touched? Pleased? I did this right, didn't I? That's not the best word, but you know what I mean? I'm *able.*"

"You most assuredly are." He reared back to frown at her, then realized what he'd said. "Able does not do justice to the passion and pleasure—" He fell silent a moment, for inspiration had befallen him.

"Promise me something, Avis Portmaine." He wrapped himself over her, threading his arms behind her neck and lowering himself so her face was cradled to his chest. "Promise me, if I tell you that was the loveliest, most tender, arousing, pleasurable experience I've had of its kind, you won't conclude you're a wanton jade, beneath contempt for your passions and undeserving of respect."

She nuzzled his nipple, and relief flooded Hadrian. Not sexual relief—he'd been wrung free of sexual tension only moments earlier—some other more profound relief, for her, for them both.

"I will not make those mistakes," she said. "Not yet."

He snuggled closer. "How could you be a wanton jade when you just gave me your virginity?"

* * *

"*I did what?*"

Avis had been relieved when Hadrian had tucked her face against his chest, relieved to be held so closely, and not subject to the scrutiny of his penetrating blue eyes. Now she wanted to see *him*, to see what manner of unkind, awkward jest he'd made.

"You heard me." He ran his nose along her jaw, incongruously relaxed and pleased with himself, while Avis's temper soared.

"Hadrian Bothwell, that is not possible." But then she stopped an inchoate rant, because all she knew for certain was that Collins had hurt her intimately. Nothing in her memories of that day remotely resembled the intimacy she'd just shared with Hadrian Bothwell.

"I know what I felt, Avie, and we shall discuss this. In detail."

"Not like this we aren't."

He'd slipped from her body, leaving Avis oddly bereft—bereft and mortified.

"Here you go." He levered up and off her, and before Avis could grab for her modesty, Hadrian pressed a handkerchief between her legs. He held up the little square of linen and dangled it before her eyes like some token of surrender.

"See?"

The handkerchief was again pressed gently to her sex, but not before Avis had seen several faint pink streaks crossing the linen.

Hadrian was still smiling, while Avie wanted to push him into the pond.

"That little resistance?" He repositioned his handkerchief once more. "Your virginity, my dear." He leaned down and kissed her mouth. "You gave it to me, Avie, not Collins."

"This cannot be. That,"—she waved in the general direction of the cloth and her privy parts—"must be from something of a female nature." Her face flamed at her own bluntness, and when she found the nerve to meet his gaze, Hadrian was regarding her curiously. He used the handkerchief on himself, then balled it up and tossed it on the grass. His manner held impatience, maybe even anger.

"Come here." His voice was a touch peremptory as he arranged her straddling his lap, then lay back, his arms around her. "Tell me what happened the day Collins attacked you and start at the beginning. Leave nothing out, and don't think to spare my sensibilities—or your own."

"This isn't necessary."

Except it was necessary. She'd never told this story, not to a journal, not to her sister, not to anybody. She'd tried to forget what she knew of that day, and that had only made the memories more tenacious.

Then too, after today, she did not expect to see much of Hadrian Bothwell. Perhaps he was the only person she *could* relate the story to.

His hands started a soothing, wandering caress to her back, her scalp, her neck, all the parts of her nobody ever touched—all the other parts—and something in Avis gave up. Hadrian would hold her for as long as it took to gather her courage, and he would listen to her no matter how miserable a tale she had to tell.

She was silent for long, long moments as those caresses sank into her bones, her heart and her mind. Hadrian wanted the story Avis had long tried to keep from herself, the one nobody wanted her to acknowledge, ever.

And he wanted her, for his wife—that boon she could not grant.

"The morning was beautiful as only spring can be here," she said softly. "Bright, clear, and cold, but not winter-cold, only spring-cold. For a number of reasons my mood wasn't sanguine. I was facing the female complaint in all its uncomfortable glory, and my mood was irritable and unsettled. In that situation, exercise can help. Alex probably picked up on my restlessness and suggested we go riding."

She fell silent again, mesmerized by the steady rhythm of Hadrian's hands, so warm, while her mind turned to a pervasively chilling memory.

"We wanted to race in your deer park," Avis said, and thank heavens, Hadrian seemed to grasp the nature of the indisposition she alluded to. He had been married, after all. "The park is level and free of rabbit holes. We knew that, because Harold kept the footing in good repair. Sometimes, I'd watch you race him."

"You never made it to the deer park," Hadrian pointed out, no pause in the movement of his hands.

"We decided to see if there'd been any foals first," Avis recalled, "so we detoured toward the mare's paddock, even though…" She faltered, and still he maintained his slow, easy caresses. "We detoured, even though Alex protested we should have brought a groom."

"One groom wouldn't have stopped a half-dozen drunken louts. So you were nearing the mare's paddock?"

She'd told herself the same thing. One groom against six young lordlings far gone with drink would have become another casualty of the day.

"We found a new foal." Avis's voice grew smaller. "Still wet, the mare was licking her colt as he steamed in the bright morning sun. I nearly cried, it was so wonderful—spring is like that, at least for me. Alex had dismounted, the better to see the foal, and needed the fence to climb back on. She managed, but Collins and his men had emerged from the trees by then, and I recall feeling even at that first moment a sense of doom, of dread. A sense I would never be happy again."

An accurate premonition.

"Alex was on her horse, and you were still mounted as well?"

Avis knew what Hadrian was about, guiding her back to her recitation with his questions, not allowing her to wallow in the emotions when he wanted the facts. She knew it, and was grateful for it.

Because twelve years later, the emotions still had the power to destroy her, and the facts still eluded an orderly assembly.

"We were both in the saddle," she said, "and like the polite fool I was, I didn't want to depart without offering a civil greeting. Hart was our neighbor and my intended, at least for the present. I owed him manners and hoped we might be cordial."

"You were innocent." Hadrian corrected her for the first time. "You and Alex were both innocent."

She took a slow breath. "There were six of them, though one galloped off as Collins grabbed my reins and another of his cronies took Alex's reins. I recall smelling liquor, even from several feet away, and Alex fought them with her whip. She was smarter than I."

"She wasn't engaged to anybody," Hadrian pointed out. "She wasn't concerned with maintaining civilities with a man she wanted to hoist from her future."

"I failed in that, failed to evict him from my future. Hart Collins has occupied some part of nearly every waking hour of my life since." She closed her eyes and focused on the sensations evoked by Hadrian's slow hands, by the warmth of his body beneath hers, by the powerful, steady beat of his heart next to her own.

"Alex fought with her whip." Hadrian repeated Avis's words. "And then?"

"Then they hauled us over to the cottage at the far end of the paddock," Avis said. "The daffodils were blooming, and Alex was still cursing the men. Collins pulled me off my horse and carried me bodily to the cottage, while his cronies called encouragement and one of them sang a bridal march."

"Where was Alex?"

Avis pressed her face to Hadrian's chest. "When she wouldn't stop yelling, one of them slapped her, and she yelled all the louder." Quiet ladylike, bookish Alex, bellowing her rage and fear.

"And then?"

"Collins set me on my feet long enough to backhand me. That blow woke me up, so to speak—confirmed that he was not intent on a simple prank—but Alex fell silent, as Collins directed that she be tossed into the cottage with us."

"What did she do next?"

"She was quiet," Avis said, her voice barely above a whisper, "but she looked at me, Hadrian, right in the eye, and she's my sister. I could tell she was planning something heroic, something dangerous. I tried to convey to her not to attempt anything rash, because drunk and rapacious men would not quibble at much."

"A sound assessment. Then what happened?"

"The cottage was musty, and like Collins's hand across my face, the unpleasant smell galvanized me, and I began to struggle. He laughed, and when Alex heard that laugh, I saw her courage falter. Collins enjoyed the pain and fear and debauchery. He told her to watch and be still as he tied my hands, or it would go worse for her when her turn came."

Avis drew in a breath, clearing her mind of that closed-in, stuffy cottage and replacing it with the fresh summer air and Hadrian's clean, spicy scent.

"Where were you when he tied your hands? Inside the cottage?"

"Inside, yes. He'd brought strong twine with him. I recalled seeing it tied to his saddle and wondering at it. With my hands tied before me, he dumped me on the edge of a table, like a sack of grain. There was no other furniture, not even a chair, which struck me as odd."

She'd forgotten that stray thought—why have a table without a chair?

"When I struggled to sit up, he got his hands around my throat and told Alex to watch that too. I tried to kick at him, tried to keep my legs together, but he wedged his body between my knees and pushed at my habit. He was prodigiously strong, and I could not get my breath."

In a sense, she still hadn't.

"Where was Alex?"

"By the door," Avis said. "I could see her, and she, God help her, could see me. The place was dim, but had a window, a single, small window, and I wanted to look at the window, at the way out, but I couldn't look away from my sister's face."

And still the rhythm of Hadrian's voice, his breathing, and his infernal questions remained calm and steady. "What was Collins doing?"

"He'd got his falls undone, ripped the buttons, I think, and outside, his friends all sang some jaunty college boy's song, in harmony."

"What did you see as you lay on that table, Avie?"

She'd seen the end of every good thing in her life, the end of a desire to live, even.

"I saw the horror in Alex's expression, and I knew she was being brutalized vicariously, and Collins was enjoying that too. When he put his hand around my throat, Alex started screaming, but he merely told her if she tried to interfere, he'd ensure I suffered the consequences."

And though Collins's brutality had been momentary, the retelling was aging Avis years and years, shriveling her to a string of ugly, miserable words.

True words, though.

"What happened then? What did Collins do?"

"He tore my habit and drawers, or cut them," Avis said. "Alex fell silent, and I recall hearing the sound of tearing fabric, even as my ears roared."

"Why were your ears roaring?"

"I couldn't breathe. He was choking me with one hand as he threatened my sister. He was touching me between my legs with his other hand, shoving his body against me."

He'd been everywhere at once, a foul, ranting miasma of inebriated male malevolence that still clouded her heart.

"And then?"

And then the first thread of courage had trickled through her, the first drop of rage. "I refused to faint," Avis said, her voice stronger. "I refused to leave my sister alone with him like that, but I *was* fainting, and then I heard another rip—my bodice—and he laughed again and said something about my breasts."

"Do you recall what he said?"

"I couldn't hear him at first." She rested her forehead against Hadrian's sternum. "He grabbed at me, at my breasts, and that meant I could breathe for a moment. He hurt me, bruised me, and the pain helped me not faint, but then I caught Alex's gaze. Hadrian, she had a knife."

Fenwick typically wore a knife, but not until that moment had Avis realized why the sight of it made her uneasy.

"You're sure?"

"She was younger than I, less of a useless lady, and she carried one in her riding boot. She was advancing on Collins, murder in her eyes, and I've never seen anything so frightening as my baby sister bent on taking a life."

"She did not kill him."

"No." Avis said it very softly, and for Alex's sake, Avis rejoiced in that answer. "No, she did not. As much as it pains me to know my sister saw me assaulted, at least she did not take a life."

"She escaped."

In some regards, Alexandra had escaped. In others, she'd sentenced herself to banishment, to the south and to spinsterhood.

"Collins sensed her movement. Right as he would have spotted her, I shook my head at her, and she must have read the desperation in my eyes. She did what I wanted her to do instead."

"Which was?"

"The latch on the cottage was old-fashioned, the simplest mechanism, but it worked on two sides of the door, two latches, really. We were locked in, but all it took was something slender inserted between the door and the jamb to lift the outside latch, and because we had brothers, Alex had the knack of it. She used her knife to lift the latch and pelted right into Collins's group of accomplices."

"What did Collins do?"

"Hit me again. And raped me."

* * *

Confession might be good for the soul, but it was hell for the hearts of all involved. Hadrian didn't have to be a former vicar to know that.

"Tell me exactly what happened, Avie."

Had Hadrian not been soothing himself tactilely with his hands on her naked body, not been reassuring himself that Avis was real and whole in his arms, he could not have asked that question. Her recitation battered his faith in a benevolent God, and how much more must it buffet her?

"I don't want to say the words."

She'd spare him those words, daft woman. Hadrian's hands stilled, and his courage damned near deserted him, until he recalled all the missteps, wantonness, and maliciousness attributed to Avis, and by the very people who ought to have shown her compassion.

"You need to say the words, love. I need to hear them, and you need to say them. You haven't said these words once in twelve years, and yet, within you, they're never entirely silent."

"Nobody wants to hear them. They're ugly." Her tone confirmed that she believed these words made *her* ugly, and hopeless, and eternally ashamed.

"What happened to you is ugly. You are glorious."

She was silent for a moment, as if weathering yet another blow. "I'll tell you this once, but then you must not ask it of me again."

Hadrian was demanding, not asking. "Tell me."

He resumed his caresses, his hands wandering over her face as well, mapping her features and trying desperately to fortify her with tenderness.

"He poked at me, between my legs, and as horrid as the entire situation was, because my belly had been aching, that made it even worse. I was on my back, on the table, and he stood between my legs, jabbing at me. I could hear him as if from a distance, and he was cursing me, telling me I was selfish, and stupid, and no man would want a great cow of a girl like me, and how was he to get sons on such a brittle, mewling stick, and it hurt as if he were stabbing at me blindly, Hadrian."

"How did he touch you?"

"Between my legs," she said, her breath hitching. "He jabbed at me even as he was cursing me, and he squeezed my breasts, one after the other, hard. I wanted to faint then. I wanted to die."

Why hadn't she wanted Hart Collins to die? Why had she never, ever allowed herself to wish for that? For Hadrian purely wanted to murder the bastard, slowly, after he'd subjected him to intimate, disfiguring violations—plural—before witnesses.

"What ended this?" To the extent that it had ended.

"Alex got away. She clambered onto a horse and made a dash for it, and she must have made it as far as the home wood before she was tossed. The men outside yelled for Collins to get the hell on his horse."

A man could hurt a woman intimately without entirely destroying her innocence, but Avie's recitation was not yet complete.

"Did Collins set his clothing to rights?"

"He couldn't, not properly." She rose up enough to peer down at him in puzzlement, her forearm pressing against his chest. "He'd torn off some buttons in his haste to sin, and he cursed vilely when he got my blood on his clothes."

Why would a man triumphant from despoiling his intended curse? "Did you see his member?"

"I did and I recall wanting to laugh, for it was the oddest-looking little dangle of flesh I'd ever seen. I'd spied on my brothers, of course, but never at such close range, and not for years. Then I realized I must be mad, to laugh at anything ever again, no matter how bitterly—and I did not care that I was mad. I also did not laugh."

She settled back down against him. "Gran Carruthers explained to me, years later, that a man will be stiff when he's in the act and soft immediately after."

Hadrian made silent promises to his beloved that in addition to inspiring her to passion, some day he'd inspire her to laughter—real laughter, the healing kind.

"Dangle of flesh, Avie?"

She buried her nose against his chest, blushing the blush of all blushes, judging by the heat next to Hadrian's skin. "Like a small boy. Not like you."

Hadrian shifted to kiss her temple, because Avis knew more than she grasped. "He had your blood on his clothes?"

"From when he'd tried to button up," Avis explained. "His fingers were bloody—I could smell the blood along with the spirits he reeked of—and it was like the musty smell, and his slaps, and all the other unpleasantness. The scent helped me not faint."

Unpleasantness.

"His fingers were bloody," Hadrian reiterated. "Think carefully, Avie. Was his cock bloody?"

He felt the shift in her, felt the first, piercing light of truth dawn, and then she began to cry.

"Not his—not that part," she got out. "You're saying he jabbed at me with his fingers, not his—only his damned infernal fingers."

"You were violated just the same," Hadrian said, and in a way, it was worse that Avie had suffered confusion as well as assault, though perhaps the courts wouldn't have termed such an attack. "Though excessive drink might have been responsible for the fact that he was unable to violate you with the part of him that could have got a child on you."

Or a terrible, fatal, disfiguring disease *and* a child.

First came a hitch of her shoulders, a crack in her emotional dam, and then she cried in silent, wracking sobs. Finally, she succumbed to the noisy, undignified tears of great grief.

Through it all, Hadrian held her and prayed that knowing the truth of what had happened—parsing through it deliberately, searching for facts and conclusions she'd not been strong enough or well informed enough to face alone—would contribute to her peace more profoundly than all the kindly silences she'd endured in the past twelve years.

"I must be heavy." Her voice was husky with tears.

"You are perfect." But when she levered off of him, Hadrian let her go—difficult as that was.

"We've tarried up here too long," Avis said, dragging the sleeves of her dress up over her arms. "I hope you can do something with my hair, Hadrian. I can't present myself looking like this."

Hadrian sat up, abruptly hating the dress, and hating worse Avis's prosaic tone of voice. "This changes everything, my dear."

"It changes nothing." Avis wiggled her bodice into order with alarming detachment. "I was a fallen woman this morning, I'm a fallen woman now, except that you've at least shown me what pleasure there is to be had in my lapse and helped me clarify a few details of my past. Have you seen my pocket comb?"

He passed it to her, trying to think around the frustration roaring through him.

"Avie, this hasn't been just a pleasant dalliance between a pair of sophisticated adults out to ease their mutual boredom. You offend me, God, and yourself if you imply that."

Avis set the comb to the side. "Perhaps I'll offend Him less do I finish dressing, for you seem disinclined to put yourself to rights."

Enough was enough. "Avis Portmaine, this role sits ill with you. I can understand that you're upset, and you deserve time to find your balance, but I took your virginity, and I will see the matter put to rights."

"The matter?" Her tone was curious, merely curious, but in her eyes, Hadrian saw something indecipherable and pained. "There is no *matter*, Hadrian. All the world thought me unchaste before this, now I am unchaste in truth. Reality has become consistent with perception. You'll have to do up my dress."

Fuck your dress.

"I wasn't Rue's first," Hadrian said through gritted teeth. "I'll be damned if the only woman to allow me to be her first will yawn and stroll down the hill without at least promising me she'll honor our betrothal. I don't care if you want a perpetual engagement, or you set a date five years hence, Avis. In some fashion, you will acknowledge that we belong to each other."

That little confession at least got her attention.

"I'm sorry, Hadrian," she said, her tone softening. "You made a betrothal announcement without my permission. I am under no obligation to—"

He assembled his attire, his movements jerky as he rooted among the clothes and blankets.

"What's this?" He held up a small piece of paper that certainly hadn't fallen from *his* pockets.

"That is mine!" Avis tried to snatch the note from him, but he had it in a firm grasp. The look on her face wasn't polite, or indifferent, or even sad. It was *desperate*, into the nearer reaches of unhinged.

He surrendered her property to her rather than endure the sight of her torment.

"I suspect whatever is in that note affects us both, Avie, as much as what happened on this blanket has affected us both. I'm asking you to share this burden with me."

The day was surpassingly beautiful, but Hadrian endured a taste of hell when Avis turned from him. As a vicar, he'd learned to deal in platitudes and appearances, and maybe a better gentleman than he would accede to whatever drove Avis now.

He could not accede, could not accommodate, could not *pretend*.

Perhaps Avis could no longer pretend, either. She put her face in her hands for a long moment, the picture of feminine torment.

"Avie, you've endured undeserved misery and injustice, year after year, and I cannot bear that you should endure it alone any longer." He reached toward her, but let his hand drop rather than inflict an unwelcome touch on her. "Avie, I am begging you. What is in that note?"

She raised her face from her hands, her expression blank and eerily reminiscent of the morning Hadrian had found her after Collins's assault.

"I had intended to betray you, you know," she said. "I'd trade on your affection for me, exorcise a demon or two, then set you free. I would use you. When you demanded a recounting from me, I should have refused, but I used you for that too."

Collins had used her. Hadrian could see her drawing the parallel. He brushed her hair back over her shoulder when he wanted to lash his arms around her.

"Collins was a selfish monster, my lady. You are hurting and overwhelmed, and you have every right to be furious, but you have used no one."

She smoothed the note flat against her skirt.

"I intended to use you, and for that I apologize. Despite my behavior this morning, I care for you very much, Hadrian Bothwell. Please recall, on some future night when you regret your public declaration bitterly, when you loathe the memory of this day, that I tried to spare you."

CHAPTER FOURTEEN

Avis passed Hadrian the bit of foolscap. She'd been to the sea as a child, stood in the frigid surf and been pounded by roaring, unstoppable waves, one after the other, and even the might of the ocean did not compare to the emotions swamping her now.

Relief was among them. Relief, to know the exact metes and bounds of Hart Collins's crime, and a towering satisfaction, to learn that he'd had to resort to an improvised and imperfect sort of violation. As consolations went, that ought not to have mattered, but to grasp exactly what had happened, to sort causes and effects, had unknotted all manner of anxieties.

Another wave slapped her with grief, for the ignorant girl she'd been, for the precious, tenacious friendship Hadrian offered, friendship she had trespassed on as far as she could stand to.

Shame swirled through her too, because she'd planned this assignation with cold calculation, the way a master of hounds assesses footing, distance, and speed when approaching an obstacle on horseback. She'd intended to use Hadrian's attentions to vault over some yawning emotional incompleteness, and then gallop on her way.

As Hart Collins had galloped off. The comparison nearly choked her.

Sheer mortification lurked beneath the surface too, because even Hadrian should not have to know the intimate details of what had transpired twelve years ago—more of the details.

And rage. She was well and truly ruined, had been for years, but the day's developments revealed to her a fraction of the joy and pleasure her ruination had denied her.

None of which was Hadrian Bothwell's fault.

She waited while Hadrian read the note, but being Hadrian, he had to read it aloud.

Tell Bothwell that marriage to the whore of Cumberland will make his family's title a laughingstock and Landover synonymous with debauchery and sin—assuming he survives the ordeal.

"Where did you find this?" His tone was clipped to within a hairsbreadth of murder.

"Can you at least put on some clothes while we discuss it?" At least cover up the bounty Avis would never plunder again?

She added a perverse gratitude to her list of emotions—gratitude that she'd plundered Hadrian's treasures once—for grief and gratitude were sides of the same coin.

"Help me," he said, holding up his shirt. "I've breeches somewhere in this mess."

Silently, they got him put to rights, and then Avis sat with her back to him so he could do up her hooks. She presumed further by using the pocket comb on his hair, but didn't ask Hadrian to tend to her similarly.

"Where did you find this note, Avie?" How stern he sounded, the wrath of God come to Cumberland.

"In my sitting room when we returned from church."

"You've carried that note around for two days?" The rest of the question hung in the crisp afternoon air: *Without telling me?*

"I've received other notes," she said, finger-combing her hair into three skeins. "I doubt it will be the last."

His brows knit, suggesting even the wrath of God was subject to puzzlement. "Is the handwriting the same as the others?"

Her hair was a right disaster. "I beg your pardon?"

"The handwriting on this one." Hadrian fussed with his cuff-links when Avis knew he wanted to bellow and shout and stomp about. "Was it the same as the others?"

"I don't—well, yes, the same as some of the others, as best I recall."

"You've a bloody collection?"

Bloody, from Hadrian Bothwell—though his word choice was apt. "Yes, Hadrian, I do. A collection going back years."

"Oh, Avie." The wrath and sternness went out of him, replaced by sorrow? Disappointment? Very likely, the emotional seas buffeted him too.

His arms came around her and he knelt up, folding his body over hers.

"You haven't said a word to your brothers, have you, or to Harold, or the magistrate?"

His embrace felt heavenly, but his protectiveness would be his undoing. "What is the point? Advertising these notes would only serve to further my shame."

He should have repaired to his side of the blanket, and then disappeared down the hillside. Hadrian was bright. The magnitude of the mess that was Avis's life would soon become apparent to him.

And yet, his arms were still around her, and the damned tears crowded Avis's throat again.

"Hadrian, I can't—You shouldn't feel as if…" A shudder passed through her, the result of tears that would not remain unshed.

"No more of this nonsense, Avie," Hadrian admonished as he lay back and drew her against his side. "No more bearing up heroically on your own, no more keeping secrets, no more soldiering on to protect everyone else's sensibilities. You have me now, and I will be damned if you'll push me away again."

Stubborn, awful, wonderful man. "But that note—"

"Threatens my life," Hadrian finished for her, proving he'd comprehended every vile word. "And obliterates your right to happiness as my wife. As a work of nastiness, it's brilliant. You will show me the others, and we'll find the culprit and lay information."

"Being nasty isn't a crime." They would not lay information.

"Threatening a man's life might be," Hadrian countered. "Publishing lies regarding a woman's good name surely is."

"They aren't lies. I'm not chaste, and nobody would have believed me had I insisted I was before today."

Hadrian gently shut her jaw with one finger. "That is a matter for another argument, Avie Portmaine. You will honor our betrothal now more than ever, for somebody means you harm in your own home. You need the protection my name can afford."

She pushed away from him and sat up, because next his hand would start up with those caresses, and Avis's skirts would soon be around her waist and her wits missing altogether.

"You are wrong, Hadrian. This note was delivered directly *after* you afforded me the protection of your name, as you put it. Engagement to you won't keep me safe. It will anger those who think I ought to retire to Blessings in permanent obscurity and you in harm's way."

Hadrian sat up too and scooted around behind her.

"Good. If they get angry enough, they'll do something obvious, and we'll know who threatens you. Hold still."

Avis wanted to argue with him, because this degree of zeal had likely sent countless good men into peril, and yet, his confidence fanned the small, uncertain flame of hope that even after twelve years, Avis had been unable to extinguish.

Hope that she could be free of the past.

Hope that her neighbors, people she'd grown up with, weren't as mean and judgmental as their behavior suggested they were.

Hope that Avis's family could someday be whole. Vim checked on her, Ben looked after Alex, and Ben and Vim occasionally crossed paths. Nonetheless, their strongest connection had become shared avoidance of the past—and each other.

And now her stubborn hope was complicated by a private, wonderful joy.

"I liked it." She spoke barely above a whisper, when Hadrian put the last pin in her hair and drew her back against his chest.

"Beg pardon?"

"You'll mess up my hair if you keep cuddling me like this."

"Then I'll tidy you up again. What did you like?"

Not a what, much more of a who.

Hadrian's embrace settled around her more comfortably. "You liked that part, did you? Liked making love with me?"

"Hush. I'm glad we did what we did today, Hadrian." She would concede that much.

"But you planned to have your way with me, then send me packing, engagement broken, hateful note in your pocket, and Bothwell none the wiser. It won't be like that, Avis."

"I can't put you at risk," she said, but she made no move to leave his embrace.

"I'm not at risk until we wed, if that note is to be believed, though as to that, I'd rather be married and have you under my roof at Landover, where the staff is loyal and would see to your safety. Furthermore, my lady, we'll study this wretched collection of yours and gain what insights we may."

We. How casually he yoked his fate to hers.

Avis shifted away, reaching for her boots. "The notes could be from anybody, or several people, or my own servants."

"It isn't anybody," Hadrian countered, grabbing her ankle and taking a boot from her hand. "You have the most delicate feet."

"Hadrian." Her reproof came out as exasperated endearment.

He slipped on her stocking, then her boot, lacing it up as he braced her foot on his thigh.

"Whoever wrote your note is educated. That handwriting is tidy, an example of careful penmanship, and your servants are not in the habit of using words like synonymous."

He put her second stocking and boot on with the same brisk efficiency.

"You're right." Why hadn't she reached those conclusions herself?

"If we read the whole of them, we might find more clues." He set her foot aside, after treating her calf to a bracing little squeeze. "You have to promise me something in absolute sincerity, or I will tell all the world what happened here today."

"You mustn't!"

The look he shot her would have quelled insurrections in the most unruly congregations.

"You would. You think you're keeping me safe by being my swain."

Hadrian brought her hand to his lips. "At last you speak reason. I am your swain, Avie. You are my damsel—in distress or otherwise."

He kept possession of her hand when Avis would have turned away.

"Besides, love, you liked it. Liked what we did together. Wouldn't you like to do it again? Under the stars, in a nice big fluffy bed, for hours and hours? Wouldn't you like for us to be lovers?"

* * *

Hadrian saw St. Just off shortly after breakfast, envious of a man who had family to the east, family in the Midlands, and yet more family all over the Home Counties. Rather than allow himself to brood on the departure of his friend, Hadrian forced himself to spend the day with his letters and ledgers, but was relieved when a footman ushered Fenwick into his library.

"Got your note," Fenwick said, peering around at Hadrian's desk. "Impersonating a productive landowner, are we?"

"I risk the wrath of a certain countess if I don't attend my correspondence. Thanks for coming. Shall you join me in some sustenance?"

"Sustenance is never a bad idea."

Hadrian poked his head into the corridor, gave orders to a footman, and turned back to the room to see Fenwick reading Hadrian's letter to Emmie St. Just.

"What the hell do you think you're doing?"

"Making sure you aren't playing Avie false." Fenwick set the letter down, casual as he pleased. "Does St. Just know you're writing to his wife?"

"In the first place, Ashton Fenwick, my correspondence is private, and in the second, he all but ordered me to assure his gravid wife that he fares well, lest she worry over him."

Fenwick set the note down and took a seat one instant before Hadrian would have smacked his fingers. "St. Just wants you writing to her so she won't worry about you."

"Regardless, it's none of your affair." If Fenwick would stick his nose into correspondence that was none of his business, would he also pen nasty notes to Avis?

Though Fen's attempt at spying had hardly been stealthy, and Fen was nearly as protective of Avis as Lily Prentiss was.

Fen crossed an ankle over one knee, the soul of nonchalance. "Apologies all around, but Avie is in a state about something and has been for a few days."

"How did you divine that?" *By reading her journal? By spying on her?*

"I had tea with her Sunday, as we usually do when we aren't together for the main meal of the day, and she was preoccupied. Then too, Lily has been glaring daggers at me, despite my allowing her to slap me at the last gathering."

"For dancing with her?"

"On general principles," Fenwick said. "Perhaps for *not* dancing with her. Some women express their finer feelings for a man in violence."

"You think Lily pines for you?" Hadrian hadn't considered this angle, but it fit, in a hopelessly juvenile way.

"Lily hates me." Fen was toweringly untroubled by Miss Prentiss's poor opinion of him. "She can't destroy me, but she knows I'll not raise a hand to her, so she wallops me from time to time. Something or someone has unbalanced the woman in some regard, though she seems to limit her displays of temper to me. Now, what did you haul me over the hill to discuss?"

"Do you recognize the handwriting?" Hadrian passed Avie's nasty note across his desk to Fen and watched his caller's face carefully.

"I don't, exactly." Fenwick held the note to his nose and sniffed it. "These are not my sentiments, but the penmanship looks ominously like my own."

"Like yours?"

"Give me a pen and a sheet of foolscap."

Hadrian complied, then watched over Fen's shoulder as he copied the note, word for word. Fenwick blew on the copy and sat back. "See?"

Hadrian set the original and the copy side by side. "The crosses on your t's slant up and these are downward. The loops on your p's and e's and so forth are narrower."

"Different day, different details, but that note is cowardly, mean and untrue. Shall you call me out?"

Somebody needed calling out.

"For reading my letter to Emmie St. Just, I should; but no, not for this note." Hadrian and Fen had worked together like dogs in the summer sun, shared many a drink, and a few meals, and while Fen might insult Hadrian to his face, Fen would not prey on a woman, not even on Lily, who deserved at least a verbal birching.

Fen's expression as he studied the note was impassive, almost as if he weren't surprised. "This is what's upsetting Avis?"

"Mostly." Hadrian considered resuming his seat behind the desk and chose the chair beside Fen instead. "I'm on her mind some too, I should hope, but this note has disconcerted her."

"It takes a lot to disconcert that woman, though this disconcerts *me*, for I don't know whose head to break in response."

"I share your dilemma." Hadrian went to the door to accept a tray from the footman. "Avis has had years to ponder the matter, and she won't even think of confronting those who wish her ill."

"Now, Bothwell,"—Fenwick's tone was patient—"do not tell me the lady has received similar notes in the past or I will have to turn her over my knee, and won't that be fun?"

Hadrian set the tray down on the desk, though dumping it over Fenwick's head had wicked appeal. "Avis is terrified, Fen. She didn't tell me about the note. I found it by accident and interrogated her."

"Spying on another's correspondence, Saint Hadrian? Perhaps you need to be turned over my knee."

Or perhaps he'd spill the teapot in Fen's lap. "Who is so angry at Avis they'd threaten my life if she married me?"

The levity in Fen's eyes was replaced by cold calculation. "That is a peculiar chain of reasoning. This person isn't necessarily angry at Avie, or she would have suffered attempts to harm her person."

"She hasn't?" Finding the answer to that question was part of the reason Hadrian had summoned Fen. Letters to Vim and Benjamin had been dispatched for the same purpose, though neither fellow was at a known location.

Fen's expression became grim, indeed. "You must interview the lady herself, for she might have hidden attempts at harm to her person—or not seen them for what they are. A passing bellyache can be attributed to bad fish, when in fact the culprit is poison, and so on."

"I must interview her? Just my hapless self? No half-savage, nosy, Highland steward to threaten spankings if she balks? And what do you mean Avie isn't the object of somebody's anger? Calling her the whore of Cumberland is hardly an endearment."

Fenwick reached for a sandwich, though how he could think about food when Avis could be in danger was a mystery.

"They are angry at her," Fen said, "but it occurs to me, and this is purely my barbarian imagination at work, the real object here is for Avie to suffer continued misery and isolation."

"Like a parasite doesn't seek to destroy its host." Hadrian poured them each a cup of strong tea. "A grim analogy, but you have a point. This person has had years to hurt Avie, and they've settled for cutting up her peace, while she remains in good bodily health."

Fenwick gestured with his sandwich. "Eat. Worrying requires sustenance, and that note is worth worrying over."

As was Avis's silence about the notes and its predecessors. "More barbarian wisdom?"

"My grandmother." Fen passed Hadrian a sandwich of chicken and cheddar on white bread, which should have appealed—but didn't. "Full-blooded Highland savage and a tough old boot. Have you seen the other notes?"

"Tomorrow. Avis asked for a day to gather her wits."

"She'd be safer married to you." Fenwick put a second sandwich on a plate, which he balanced on his knee with incongruous daintiness. "You could wrap her up in cotton wool here at Landover."

"Glad to know I have your blessing," Hadrian said, taking a bite of his sandwich, mostly so Fen wouldn't scold him. "Who would bear such a grudge against Avie that they'd employ a nasty trick like this?"

"Collins's staff?" Fenwick suggested. "They're local, and they have an interest in their employer's reputation."

"Good place to start. His accomplices would also be worth a look, though I never learned their names. Leaving notes around does strike me as a bullying tactic, and Collins was nothing if not a bully. I suppose we should look at Collins's mother too, though, and any woman who set her cap for the baron before Avie was engaged to him."

"A woman? We need look no further than darling Lily to recall that the ladies can have a nasty temper." Fenwick considered his second sandwich. "That widens the field of suspects considerably, though Collins's mother has every reason to be bitter. She's been without her darling boy's company for the past twelve years."

According to Harold, the baroness hadn't socialized much as a result. Some women would find that alone grounds for resentment.

"Avie hasn't let anyone know about the notes, so whoever is tormenting her has likely grown complacent over years of wreaking mischief. I'm determined to bring her detractor to justice sooner rather than later—twelve years is twelve years too long for Avie to suffer."

Fenwick saluted with his tea. ""There speaks a determined swain, but what of Avie?"

Hadrian ran a finger over the gilded rim of his tea cup and debated in what sense to reply to Fen's question.

"At least until recently, Avie has been determined to slink away." From the ill will stalking her, from marriage, from her right to a happy future. Hadrian hoped that her slinking days would soon be behind her.

Fenwick rose, sandwich in hand. Hadrian did not warn him about leaving crumbs on the carpet because Fen would leave no crumbs—he was that careful.

"So you must slay her dragons and climb her tower, else she won't marry you?"

"A chivalrous, poetic barbarian," Hadrian observed, "but yes. I suspect she won't marry me as long as she thinks I'm in danger if I take her to wife."

"She's sensible, and she wouldn't refuse you unless your safety meant a great deal to her."

A cheering thought, though Fen didn't look particularly cheerful. "How do you conclude that?"

"Think about it, Bothwell. She could marry you and put your life in jeopardy—if that note is to be believed—then sit back and enjoy being the chatelaine of Landover in Harold's absence. She'd be your viscountess in all but name, and if she were clever enough to catch a son of you, she'd be set for life."

"You're suggesting Avie wants me dead and let me find a note she'd planted herself? You should be writing horrid novels, Fenwick."

"I'm suggesting she'd give up a chance at all of that to keep you safe."

"She'd do the same for you."

Fenwick went to the door, speaking over his shoulder.

"Spanking is too tempting when I'm faced with such stubborn, pigheaded foolishness. I will make sure Avie is closely watched by such members of her staff as I trust, which is to say mostly myself, and I will report anything peculiar to you. She needs you, dunder-headed choir-boy-turned-swain that you are, and I will see you delivered to her. Finish your sandwich."

He swept out, leaving a ringing silence behind him.

Hadrian didn't finish his sandwich. He picked up the two versions of the note and compared them again.

They were very, very similar, indeed.

* * *

"You have been preoccupied ever since Mr. Bothwell announced your engagement," Lily observed, "and I don't think it's a joyous preoccupation." In the sunny confines of the little sitting room, Lily's gaze held concern, nigh constant concern.

"Engagements have negative associations for me," Avis said, which was the truth—a truth.

"My poor Avis." Lily knotted off her thread and snipped her needle free of her embroidery. "Are you sure Mr. Bothwell is the future you want?"

"Who can know what marriage to this or that man will mean?" Avis rose and paced to the windows, which Lily had closed while muttering about lazy chambermaids and chilly drafts. "I esteem Hadrian far more than I did my first fiancé, and I always have. He's a good man."

Honorable, kind, handsome, protective, *passionate*.

"He's still a man. He'll make certain demands on you, citing scripture to excuse his base urges." Lily's tone suggested those base urges had inadvertently been left off the list of deadly sins. "I know you aren't happy here, Avis, but I had hoped in some small way you'd be content. Still, Mr. Bothwell is in line to raise the Landover heir, and he could end up with the title. Then too, if you refuse his suit—"

Lily left off dissecting Avis's future to rummage in her work basket, leaving unsaid that if Avis rejected Hadrian's offer, more pity would come her way.

And more scorn.

"If I jilt Hadrian, I'll never have another offer, unless you count old Sully's flirting."

"Sully is influenced by Fenwick's poor example." Yet another deadly sin. "Insubordinate, that one."

"Don't start, Lily." Avis unfastened the window latch, because the day was brisk but not cold. "Fenwick is a superb steward, and he is my friend. I have enough on my mind without you feuding with him."

"I am sorry." Lily took one of Avis's shawls from the back of her chair and draped it around her own shoulders. "I should not let my distaste for that man burden you. If you marry Mr. Bothwell, we'll remove to Landover, and Mr. Fenwick's strutting, braying company will merely be that of an infrequent visitor, one calling on Mr. Bothwell."

The shawl was a soft peacock-green wool and went well with Lily's fair coloring, and yet, that was one of Avis's favorite shawls, and the room wasn't at all cool.

Something inside Avis shifted—another adjustment of the balance between fear and courage—at the sight of Lily appropriating that pretty shawl.

"You think I should marry Hadrian?"

"I should tell you yes." Lily rose to join Avis near the window. "I should tell you he's a decent enough fellow, he'll provide well, and you'll never want for anything. You might even be a viscountess someday."

Lily did not mention that Avis might be happy some day—happy *and loved*.

"But?"

"But I am your friend," Lily said, gaze on the back gardens, "and we've always been honest with each other. If you marry Mr. Bothwell, you'll exchange one set of problems for another. Your neighbors will still have their arrogant prejudices, but instead of managing a large estate, you'll be wife to the man running Landover, tolerated by the staff, perhaps even tolerated publicly for your spouse's sake."

Lily's sigh heaved cargoes of understanding about on a sea of regret. "That's not an improvement," she went on, "not when you have so much freedom and authority here, not when you will be consigned to the status of Mr. Bothwell's meek, adoring spouse if you marry him. We love you here, and I doubt Mr. Bothwell has expressed regard of a similar stature. He needs an heir for his brother, a lady to warm his bed, and you're the most easily available."

All true, but again, Lily had failed to note that Hadrian needed, and deserved, a lady to love him and those children he'd thus far been denied.

"What you say has some truth, Lily. Gratitude alone is a poor reason to marry."

"He at least appears to respect you," Lily said, adjusting her shawl—Avis's shawl. "Whatever you decide, I'll stand with you."

"And for that,"—Avis dredged up a smile—"I'll be grateful, but as I am expecting my intended to call, I had best put myself to rights."

"Shall I attend you?"

"No, thank you." Avis headed for the door at a brisk pace. "Though if you could have the footman take the tea tray and water the flower-pots and vases in here, I'd appreciate it. The roses look a little thirsty."

"Of course."

Avis resisted the temptation to hurl something breakable when she gained the privacy of her bedroom, for Lily did mean well.

Lily always meant well, and yet, when her advice included not only the usual laments regarding Avis's deportment and judgment, but also belittling of Hadrian Bothwell, Avis's temper flared. Lily had crossed a line, shifting from dispensing friendly caution, to dripping poison onto Avis's heart.

Something would have to be said, and soon. No company at all was better than the company of a companion determined to speak ill of such a decent and dear man.

Avis changed into an old dress with a high waist, a comfortable, gardening sort of dress that left her forearms bare and obviated the need for a corset. Hadrian might walk with her up to the pond—

But no.

She would allow no frolicking halfway up the hill where God and any of His creatures might see her with Hadrian. She could not think that way, could not contemplate leading Hadrian closer to the altar, even in his own mind.

For until the author of the notes was revealed, should Hadrian marry Avis, he might well end up dead.

* * *

"They have a biblical cast." Hadrian regarded the notes spread out across his estate desk as if he viewed a collection of adders, scorpions, and rats. "Lots of scriptural allusions."

"Like this one?" Avie plucked a note from the blotter. "'Easier for an honest strumpet to pass through the gates of heaven than for you to safely darken the doors of our church.'" She put it back and picked up another. "'A woman's good name is worth more than rubies, and her virtue more precious still.'"

She wasn't even reading the words—clumsy allusions to Matthew, chapter 19, verse 24, and Proverbs, chapter 31—she recited them from memory.

"Can you recall when you received that one?"

She set it down. "After Alexandra left for a post in the south."

One of the earliest, then. Upon her majority, Lady Alex had left Blessings, and thereafter somebody had begun harassing Avis by correspondence.

"And this one closely resembles the most recent note. I hate to ask this, Avie, but when did Fenwick come to work for you?"

Avis picked up the enormous ginger cat that had begun frequenting the library in the absence of Harold's great hound.

"I've never once heard Fen cite scripture." She ran her cheek over the top of the cat's head, and the beast began to purr. "He was on the estate before Alex went south. He made her nervous, but Vim vouched for him, and Ben found him trustworthy as well."

More bad news. "Nervous in what way?"

"She wasn't specific." Avis walked with the cat to the French doors, which had been thrown open to take advantage of the fresh air. "Most men make her nervous, and Fen is such a strapping specimen, he gave me pause at first."

Now, Fen flirted and danced with Avie and was markedly familiar with her.

"He's very protective of you. He either didn't know you'd been getting notes, or he did a convincing job of acting surprised to learn of it."

Which was exactly what Hadrian would have done, had he been the author of such scurrilous sentiments.

"I don't bruit it about." She set the cat down, and it strolled, tail high, through the French doors and into the gardens. "You think Fenwick is sending me hateful notes."

Avis was either keeping her own counsel in some significant fashion, or she was understandably distracted. Hadrian joined her at the French doors, just as the cat pounced into a bed of irises and disappeared from view.

"I don't want to think ill of your steward, but the handwriting is close, and your sister and your companion both took him into significant dislike."

While Hadrian's every instinct said Fen was a true friend to Avie.

"Alex didn't dislike him, exactly, but Lily can't abide him—says he's an ungodly barbarian."

And Fen, who was both shrewd and charming, actively antagonized the woman. "Have you ever asked her why?"

"I assume he flirted with her, and she took it amiss. Is there something you're not telling me?"

Fen's flirting was bothersome, but not bothersome enough to inspire hate, and Fen wouldn't force his attentions on any woman.

Much less Lily Prentiss. Though again, the name Prentiss sounded a bell of memory. Hadrian resolved to write to his former bishop, who had a prodigious recall of church gossip.

"I don't like to think Fenwick could mean you any harm at all," Hadrian said.

"But he understands what it is to be an outcast."

"And?"

Hadrian wanted to take Avie's hand in his, but before the open French windows, that would not do.

"And Fen might enjoy keeping you an outcast with him, enjoy tormenting you so you lean on him a little more, and marrying me will put an end to that."

"I will not cast aspersion on Fenwick, when so much aspersion has been cast on me, and Fen is one of few who's stood by me. Besides, what have I ever done to him that he'd cast stones like that?"

In her question, Hadrian heard the first hint that Avis was seriously considering that Ashton Fenwick, a man she considered her *friend*, had connived to keep her miserable.

Hadrian led her over to the sofa and drew her down beside him.

"Maybe his motives have little to do with you. Maybe some other lady, or ladies, scorned him because of his humble birth, and now you're a lady scorned by her neighbors."

"This is complicated," Avis said, letting her head rest of Hadrian's shoulder. "It just doesn't feel possible that Fen could be so unscrupulous and mean."

"I agree." Hadrian tucked an arm around her shoulders. "There's more, Avie."

"Something bad."

"St. Just and I went to church with you and Lily. Fen was supposed to join us, but instead went for a hack on St. Just's gelding."

"Fen is an indifferent congregant. He attends more to flirt than to worship, and he keeps in touch with his cousin."

"Who is his cousin?"

"Sara Bennett. You'd never know they were related. She's tiny and blond, and he's a dark giant, but she married a man built much like Ashton."

"You're falling asleep."

"Resting my eyes."

About damned time. "While we were at church, Fen could have planted that note."

"Fenwick would not plant a vile note, Hadrian, but it's easy enough to ask the lads if they saw him about on Sunday morning."

"Easy enough for me," Hadrian corrected her, then rose and scooped her up against his chest. "You shall go about your business, my dear, and not let this matter bother you, but first you shall rest, here, where you know you're safe."

He expected her to order him to put her down, wiggle about and make a fuss.

She slipped her arms around his neck.

"You will manage whatever mischief you're bent on, Hadrian Bothwell, without allowing a single footman to catch even a glimpse of your folly."

Of course, he did manage that much—the servants had been given their orders, after all—setting her on the bed in an airy, sunny guest room abovestairs, then taking a seat beside her.

"Hadrian Bothwell, this will not serve."

As fusses went, that was a pathetic effort.

"You aren't sleeping well," Hadrian observed as he turned her shoulders and undid the first of her myriad hooks. "Are you worried about this note?"

He brushed a kiss to the top of her spine.

"Don't do that, please. A seduction can go exactly nowhere, Hadrian."

Why did women's dresses have so infernally many hooks? "Nowhere at all? Or nowhere today, because you're beset by the female complaint?"

He'd been married, and that experience fortified him for certain discussions. He stole another kiss, and this time was rewarded with a sigh.

"Both," Avis said, as he pushed her dress off her shoulders. "What are you doing?"

"You can't sleep with your hair up. I'll rebraid it when you've had some rest." Which she apparently needed desperately. He sent his fingers questing for the pins securing her coronet, drawing each pin free until her braid hung down in a thick, dark rope and he could get a hand on her nape to massage tense, tired muscles.

"How often do you see the Baroness Collins, Avie?"

"Rarely. I see all of our neighbors rarely. That feels appallingly good."

"I do believe that was a compliment. When you see Collins's mother, does she acknowledge you?"

Avis stifled a yawn. "Oddly enough she is one of few who does. She called upon me shortly after I returned from Aunt Beulah's and apologized for what she termed 'the whole misunderstanding.' I don't know if Harold arranged it, or my brothers, but she seemed sincere."

Hadrian withdrew his hand, rose and unknotted his cravat.

"She might have done that to draw away suspicion, or perhaps Harold threatened dire retribution against Collins unless his mother observed the civilities. Do you mind if I open the windows?"

"I do not mind if you—Hadrian, what are you *doing?*"

CHAPTER FIFTEEN

Hadrian stopped halfway across the room and hung his coat over the back of a chair, then seated himself long enough to pull off his boots and stockings.

"A soft breeze from the gardens has appeal on such a day. The honeysuckle's in bloom so I thought I'd open a window."

Said with *such* an innocent expression. "I'm not referring to the window. You are disrobing."

He opened the window, and the breeze from the garden did indeed carry a sweet, flowery aroma.

"I don't intend you be the only one to rest," he said, unbuttoning his waistcoat.

"You can't be serious. The servants will talk." They'd proclaim Avis's wickedness from the rooftops.

Hadrian crossed to the bed and held out his wrist for Avis to undo his cuff-link. "Harold's staff is the soul of discretion, believe me, Avie."

They were Hadrian's staff now. Avis undid his second cuff-link, and then he was standing beside the bed, all the more virile and impressive for being shirtless indoors—this time.

"Hadrian, we can't. That is, I can't—" She *couldn't* stop looking, and her fingers nigh twitched with the need to touch him.

He stepped closer and drew her to her feet. "The dress goes, the chemise stays, if you insist."

When had polite, charming Hay Bothwell become a man who casually disrobed before a lady and gave her orders to do likewise?

"You presume on my privacy because you were married. You're used to this casual intimacy, but Hadrian, I am not." Though she could learn to like it very well—with him.

He knelt to slip off her boots, untie her garters, and peel down her stockings before drawing her dress over her head and unlacing her stays. "I will never knowingly violate *your* privacy, Avie, but then there is *our* privacy. Into bed with you."

She didn't immediately comply, not sure what he intended. All morning, he'd been intent on the notes, his mind whirling along, spotting patterns and details Avis hadn't seen. He'd been attentive over lunch, keeping the discussion to estate matters his prospective wife ought to find interesting, and then they'd taken a walk to inspect his gardens.

All the while, he'd been content to merely hold her hand.

She climbed onto the high, fluffy mattress, the bed dipping as Hadrian joined her. The sheets smelled of lavender and sunshine, the window admitted a soft breeze, and abruptly Avis's beleaguered sense of propriety was felled by sheer fatigue.

"I ought to kick you out of this bed." She settled on her side, facing that open window, away from him.

"Rue was a kicker," Hadrian replied, sliding an arm around Avis's middle. "She couldn't help it. She moved a great deal in sleep. I got so I could nap through anything."

Through several years of marriage, perhaps? "Do you miss her?"

"In a sense." Hadrian's fingers laced with hers against her midriff. "Ours was a peculiar union. It bore all the trappings of domestic bliss, but I don't think she was any happier than I was. Then she died, and my regret knew no bounds."

"Regret?" Though missing a late spouse "in a sense" implied that the spouse was also *not* missed in some way.

"For better or for worse, she was the wife I had, and rather than trouble myself to force some substance into our marriage, I let matters drift, as did she. Then came the accident. She lingered for ten days, though it was clear she was fading, and we came to a dreadful sort of peace."

"She was trampled by a runaway team?" Avis wanted to roll over, to see his face, because this topic had to be difficult, for all that Hadrian's body, aligned so closely with hers, radiated no tension.

"A damned beer wagon, in York. Somebody had the presence of mind to send for Harold, and he managed matters so I could sit with my wife until she slipped away. I don't think she suffered physically."

"How could she not?"

"Whatever injuries she sustained inside, they were of a nature that she could no longer move her legs. She felt nothing, not cold feet, not wrinkled bed covers, nothing below the waist. I'd initially resented her restlessness in bed, but that last week, I longed to see her toes twitch."

Avis considered this, considered the indignity to the lady, and understood, just a little, why Rue Bothwell might have gone peacefully to her death. Except that meant she'd peacefully left Hadrian to grieve, alone and likely bewildered at the swiftness of his wife's passing.

"You loved her."

His grip on her hand became more snug. "I did, and it's a relief to state that honestly. I wasn't in love with her, nor she with me, and had she not died, I doubt I would even have been able to say that much."

"I'm sorry for your loss, Hadrian. I was pleased to think you were happily married, to think you had somebody dedicated to sharing life with you."

She'd envied his wife ferociously, too. She could admit that now—to herself. "Go to sleep, love." He untangled their hands and slid an arm under her neck. "I'll wake you in time for tea."

"You'll stay with me?" Though he shouldn't, and she shouldn't ask him to.

"Of course, and yes, the door is locked. You're safe here, Avie. Please rest."

She drifted off, though Hadrian had divined something else Avis hadn't wanted to admit to herself: For years, she hadn't felt safe, not even under her own roof.

* * *

"He wants to know who Hart Collins's accomplices were." Harold passed the letter to Finch, who shared a tea tray with him on their sunny terrace, one of many small pleasures the summer afforded. "This could get ugly."

Finch scanned the letter.

"To hear you tell it, matters were quite ugly enough twelve years ago. What do you make of this Fenwick fellow? I met him on more than one occasion— tall, dark, rugged in a Highland sort of way?"

"Always flirting, aren't you?" Harold could tease, because Finch did flirt— but it was flirting only. "I like Fen and I respect him. I never once had a sense of anything untoward or devious from him, though he can be an unsettling man."

Finch set the letter aside, closed his eyes and turned his face up to the afternoon sun. "Coming from you, that says something. Unsettling in what way?"

"There are depths to him," Harold said, reaching for the teapot. Cook had a way with a fruit pastry and didn't begrudge anybody a serving at any time of day. "Some of those depths are troubled. Fen's orphaned and has a foot in two different cultures. I have the impression he isn't entirely accepted in either one. Leave me the raspberry tart, at least, would you?"

"I'll ring for more. You're getting positively gaunt, my dear."

"Putting on muscle. Keeping up with you has got me more fit." He poured them both tea while Finch licked lemon crème off his thumb with the artless appeal of the true sybarite. Finch had also put on muscle, and lost…sadness. He wrote regularly to his wife and children, who seemed to get on swimmingly without him, though Harold was considering having the lot of them to visit.

The summer sun, or true love, was making him daft.

"Eat," Finch advised, passing Harold the raspberry tart. "You'll need your strength."

"My strength?"

"It's officially summer, dear heart. If we set sail within a week, we'll have plenty of time to get to Cumberland and back here before fall."

"We will?" Harold bit into his tart and wondered if the Danes grew more flavorful raspberries, or if everything tasted better when shared with a loved one.

"You love those two, and you worry about them. The engagement is all well and good, but a nudge in the right direction is in order. We'll sail no later than Friday."

"Thursday. We'll sail on Thursday. Ring for more tarts, would you?"

* * *

"You're spending a lot of time at Landover," Lily observed as she rubbed at a patterned fruit knife with a flannel cloth.

Avis had declared it time to sort through the kitchen silver, because the day fast approached when she'd take up residence in the dower house. Hadrian wasn't in favor of the plan, because she'd be more isolated with a much smaller staff and only Lily to sound the alarm if something went amiss.

Assuming she didn't sack Lily first.

"I am engaged to the Landover heir," Avis replied mildly, though she'd told Hadrian engaged was all they would be unless they got to the bottom of the threatening notes. He'd kissed her, *patiently*, the wretch. "I had best acquaint myself with Hadrian's situation. Service for eight should be ample."

Lily sent her the most fleeting look, but Avie read both pity and the history fueling it: In their years together, Lily had never seen more than five others at the same table as Lady Avis Portmaine, and those five would be family, Fenwick, the local vicar and his wife, or Lily herself.

Where Avis might have felt shame and bewilderment even a few weeks ago, Lily's subtle dramatics now filled her with a satisfying sense of exasperation.

"You needn't look so woebegone, Lily. I do have some good news."

Lily held the fruit knife up to the sunlight streaming in the kitchen window. "We've little enough of that."

The shearing had been abundant, the hay harvest equally good, and both accomplished without a major injury. Was Lily truly so far above the realities of a country existence that she disregarded those blessings?

"I'm sending Fen down to Manchester to do some shopping."

"For?"

Avis waved a hand. "This house, my trousseau, some items Blessings needs. The hay is off, the crops are thriving, the foals, lambs and calves are on the ground, and it's a good time for him to be useful elsewhere. He's happy to go. He's bored watching the corn ripen and in need of diversion. I don't suppose you'd like to go with him?"

"Are you joking?" Lily resumed polishing the knife, though it was spotless and gleaming. "The last place I'd like to be is in that man's company."

"Any particular reason?" Avis kept the question casual, but it had plagued her ever since Hadrian had raised it.

"He's far too forward," Lily spat. "With you, me, everybody. The man's an ill-bred, godless, presuming offense to everything genteel and decent."

He offended none save Lily that Avis could see. "Do you protest too much, Lily? He's an exceedingly handsome ill-bred, presuming offense, as offenses go, and he works very hard. He'd provide well."

Fen was also not godless, though his piety was of the rustic variety.

"You do jest now." Lily set the fruit knife in the velvet-lined silver chest. "You're joking if you think I could consider matrimony with that man, if you think any woman should be so burdened."

"Is it Fen you detest," Avis pressed, for Lily had given her no real answer, "or holy matrimony?"

"Both, if you must know." Lily tied up the laces of the cloth covering to the silver chest, the trailing ends of her bow matching exactly for length. "Marriage is supposed to be for the protection of women, but married women die in childbed more than unmarried women."

"Because unmarried women aren't to be in childbed at all?"

Lily gave her a look that suggested she knew Avis had crossed a certain line willingly with Hadrian. She'd crossed it joyously, rapturously even.

"Can you be happy married to Mr. Bothwell?"

Yes—if Hadrian could be safe married to her. "One can't know these things until one is married. Were I to marry him, I think I'd be happy."

"You're sending Fenwick shopping for your trousseau, but you haven't set a date." Lily was asking if Avis had set a date with Hadrian, which was none of Lily's business.

"I'd like my brothers and sister to be at the wedding," Avis said, which was true enough. "Alex has recently changed positions and likely can't come north for a while."

"You're marrying the next thing to a title, Avis, *if* you marry. When Mr. Bothwell sends a polite note to your sister's employer, she'll be put on the first coach north."

Lily spoke with an odd authority, considering she'd never met Alex.

"Lady Alexandra has accepted employment in the home of a widower with two boys, and she wouldn't want to leave her charges so early into their getting acquainted."

"You're her only sister, and you're getting married—if you marry, but you don't seem convinced of that outcome yourself."

Another subtle question.

"I'm not." Avis filled the tea kettle from the oven well, set it on the hob and leaned back against the kitchen counter. "Hadrian is a good man and deserves so much better."

"You are the one who deserves better," Lily retorted. "When I think of you having to endure his attentions after what you've been through." She shuddered, eyes downcast, then raised her chin, all pretence of the genteel English rose banished. "You don't have to marry him, Avis. You don't."

"I know."

But she wanted to. More and more, she wanted to.

* * *

"This is for you." Fenwick tossed a scrap of paper onto Hadrian's desk.

Hadrian unrolled it carefully. "You've read it?"

"That's the odd part about affixing letters to little birds," Fenwick said, helping himself to a drink from the sideboard in Hadrian's library. "There's no address on the outside, no seal. One must read the contents to determine the intended recipient, and rather than have any old groom or footman read it, I insist the notes be brought to me with the seal intact."

Suggesting—testily—that Fen hadn't read the note itself.

"Benjamin Portmaine is concerned that Collins may be larking about in the south, but he doesn't know the man's whereabouts for certain," Hadrian murmured, setting the paper aside.

"If Benjamin can't find Collins, then Collins must truly be up to no good." Fen held up the decanter in invitation—quite the hospitable sort, was Fen.

Hadrian rose from his desk, the ramifications of Benjamin's note ruining an otherwise lovely summer day. "Just a tot will do."

Fen passed him two generous fingers. "You must keep a particularly close watch on Avis for the next few weeks. I'm sent off on a fool's errand, supposedly because we've finally reached that part of summer when brutal hard work isn't the order of every waking day."

"You're going somewhere?" Hadrian knew damned good and well what awaited Fen, and had argued long and hard with Avis about it when she'd awoken from hours of unbroken slumber. Hadrian took his drink to the French doors and tried to let the peace of the gardens fill his soul.

"I'm off to Manchester shopping for your bride." Hadrian heard Fenwick amble over to the table that held the family bible, which some helpful soul had once again left open to the Twenty-Third Psalm. "I'm to sell our cast-off furniture and otherwise absent myself from Lady Avie's side."

"Who else could she send?"

"Look at me, Bothwell."

Hadrian waited several heartbeats for form's sake, then swiveled his gaze from rose bushes slightly past their peak to the glower Fen turned on him.

"I myself showed you the similarity in the penmanship. I didn't send that note."

"I believe you. The evidence points to you, but my instincts rebel against such a conclusion." When it came to who was lying and who was telling the truth, a former vicar's instincts were to be trusted—mostly.

"So you're shuttling me offstage, keeping me from harm's way, but aren't you leaving Avis's pretty flank exposed?"

Hadrian was silent and Fen's eyes narrowed.

"For God's sake, you aren't setting a trap with Avis as bait?"

"She believes you innocent as well, but has it in her head that unless we solve this business of the notes, she must break our engagement. She sees that she's sending you beyond the reach of suspicion and does not accept that she's put herself closer to harm's way by doing so. I could not argue her from that position."

Fen tossed back whiskey that was likely older than he was. "God in heaven."

"Or Lucifer in hell," Hadrian rejoined. "Avie and I will make calls, attend services, and entertain our neighbors here at Landover, as if we're truly anticipating matrimony—which I surely am. If the culprit does not come forward, she will thank me kindly and try to send me on my way."

Hadrian had a creeping suspicion Avis would also send him on his way if her detractor were revealed.

"You'll allow this?"

A whiff of honeysuckle teased Hadrian's senses. "With Avis Portmaine, 'allow' doesn't signify. I would rather send her to Manchester with you than embark on this scheme, but she'll endure another twelve years of ostracism and vile notes unless something is done to resolve her situation."

"Preferably something violent and permanent." Fen held his glass under his nose, closing his eyes as if in prayer. "You think whoever is behind this will come after you, don't you?"

"The most serious threat in those notes is to my life, not hers, and then only in the event of our marriage. The more it looks like we're marrying, the more at risk I should be."

"Why not send me here to Landover?" Fen took a sip of his drink then swirled the remaining contents gently. "I could keep an eye on your saintly self and keep my distance from Avie."

Again, Hadrian was silent, and Fen's eyes went cool.

"Because you don't trust me after all," Fen concluded. "You don't want me to be guilty, but you aren't sure I'm innocent. A man can hardly prove he hasn't done something, unless he can discover who has done it."

Fen referred to the Scottish verdict, unique in the British systems of justice— insufficient evidence. Not enough evidence to convict—or to exonerate.

"Avie's safety has to come first," Hadrian said, but it tore at him to all but accuse Fen this way. Fen had likely been judged enough in his life, maybe even enough to create an unreasoning anger at his betters. Avis, however, had been adamant that Fen must be placed beyond suspicion.

"Because in your position, I might reach the same conclusions," Fen said, "I won't call you out, though you should not get me drunk for the nonce, lest my sentiments express themselves in closed fists applied enthusiastically to your vulnerable parts."

"For your restraint, I am grateful. Avis was insistent that you go, and she did not enlighten me as to her reasons. When do you leave?"

"First of the week, which assures it will be raining. Who are your other suspects?"

Was Fen's acquiescence too easy, and why did Avis insist on his absence?

"That's just it, we either accuse the entire shire, right down to the last gossiping goodwife, or we haven't any other suspects, particularly not with access to the Blessings manor house."

One dark eyebrow winged up. "Let me tell you something, Bothwell. Avis Portmaine could take my last groat, steal my first-born son, and slander me in the streets of London, and I'd still owe her."

"That is a dramatic sentiment." Sincere as well.

"But is it the truth?"

"Fen, if you can see another way, then stop pawing and posturing and share it with me. The handwriting is yours, the timing coincides with your tenure at Blessings, you're private about your past, and you have reason to resent a woman to the manor born."

That litany sounded damnably convincing, even to Hadrian's ears, but he went on, because Fen had made no rejoinder.

"Avis is convinced I can't turn this matter over to a magistrate without risking that you'll be charged. You're respected around here, and you wield a lot of authority. People take a certain glee when a man of stature falls low, and I doubt anyone would pass up the opportunity to drag Avie's name through yet another scandal. Sending you south is the best we can do for now."

"I don't want to see your dilemma, but the magistrate would likely agree with you. Don't expect me to thank you, though."

Hadrian pushed away from the door to consider the note gracing his desk.

Where in the bloody hell was Collins? Why didn't his mother socialize? Why didn't Fen volunteer a few details of his past when given the invitation?

"Sometimes strategic retreat is just that." Hadrian had retreated to Oxford twelve years ago, retreated to the church, retreated into a marriage devoid of passionate sentiment—while Avis had had nowhere she could safely retreat to.

"Will you marry Lady Avis?" Fen asked, setting an empty glass down hard on the sideboard.

"I'll damned sure try," Hadrian said, crumpling Benjamin's note. "It's more a question of whether Avie will marry me. Now, let me apprise you of a few details regarding this trip of yours."

* * *

"You needn't look so guilty." Fen checked the snugness of Handy's girth with a definite pull. "I know what this little sortie is about, Avie, and I'm willing to go."

Avis understood what Fen had left unsaid: Willing to go was not the same as happy to go.

He stepped back from his horse. "Don't look at me like that. Let's stroll in your garden and take our leave privately."

The stable yard was swarming with grooms, porters and footmen loading the last of the wagons bound for Manchester, so Avis accepted Fen's arm. From some window, Lily was likely watching and disapproving, about which Avis could no longer seem to care.

"You can trust Micah and Sam in the stables," Fen began, head lowered so he could speak near her ear. "In the house, I'd trust no one, and I do mean no one."

Avis kept her eyes front and her expression as bland. "Fen, I am sorry."

"And well you should be, sending me away when you need your allies around you, but your situation requires a resolution, else I'd put you over my knee for this folly. You're wise to appoint Bothwell your champion, but I cannot approve of toying with the man's affections, Avie."

How stern Fenwick sounded, how utterly serious.

"You encouraged me to dally with him, and now marriage to me could put Hadrian in danger."

"I encouraged you to dally, yes." Fen bent to snap off a white rose, but the blossom fell apart before he could bring it to his nose. "Dallying is good for morale, and you weren't inclined to take advantage of my generous nature, but *he's* not dallying, Avie. The poor sod loves you and probably has since boyhood."

"Poor sod?"

"Any man who's facing rejection from the woman he loves is a poor sod, so don't argue with me. Before I go, I will have your assurances that you'll take every precaution, listen to Bothwell, and trust no one save him, Micah and Sam."

"Not even Lily?" For Lily would tell Avis not to trust Fenwick.

"You already keep a certain distance from dear Lily, though I'm not sure why. She's honestly devoted to you."

Lily was devoted to finding fault, scolding, and keeping the internal scales tipped to the side of fear, probably as a result of a vicarage upbringing. Why had it taken Avis so long to see that?

"Devotion can be a burden. I'll miss you, Fen."

"Not as much as you think you will. Bothwell will see to that."

Was this jealousy? Teasing? Whatever it was, Avis didn't like it. "Hadrian is an old friend, and you are another old friend."

"Dear heart,"—Fen's smile turned piratical—"come here."

They were shielded by trees and foliage, so Avis stepped into his arms and let him embrace her. He knew how to hold a woman, knew how to comfort with bodily closeness and gentle strength, and that's exactly how he lured her in.

Without Avis quite knowing how, though, he was kissing her. A buss to each cheek, then her forehead, then softly settling his lips on hers.

He was skilled. Stealthy, easy with his overtures, and careful not to hold her too tightly. When his tongue touched her lips, though, Avis put an end to his nonsense.

"What in blazes do you think you're doing, Ashton Fenwick?" She stepped back and would have left his embrace, but he held her easily.

"Want to slap me?"

"Yes, in fact." Though she wouldn't slap him hard. This was Fen, and he was a friend, and she could make allowance for one kiss that apparently had some didactic purpose.

"You don't want to slap old Bothwell when he kisses you, do you?"

"Fen, that is private." Also true.

His embrace shifted, became less intimate without him moving. "Avie, you love him." His voice was quiet, his tone patient or...despairing.

"Hush." She should stomp away in high dudgeon. Instead, she hid her face against Fen's broad shoulder, breathing in horse and new hay.

"You want to slap me when my kiss is a little too friendly, but you want to shed your clothes and devour Bothwell when he kisses you. Am I right?"

"What I want doesn't matter." When had it ever?

"What you want, my dear, is all that matters," Fen said. "And you want him." He gathered her closer, as if he could will the words to settle in her brain, and then he kissed her cheek again. "Wish me safe journey, and don't get married without me on hand to instruct the groom and kiss the bride."

She kept her arm linked with his as they turned back to the stables.

"I know you are trying to make a point by kissing me like that, and I understand you mean well."

"But don't do it again." He patted her knuckles. "I won't and you're right: I overstepped to make my argument, and I will not do so again. I won't need to."

He said not another word to her, but parted from her at the mounting block, swung up on Handy and cantered off. Avis lowered herself onto the mounting block and watched the chaos of loading the wagons for long moments, letting the commotion swirl around her.

If Fenwick were smart, he'd keep right on going when he reached Manchester. More than anyone else, suspicion could all too easily fall on him. And yet, Fenwick had seen what Avis hadn't wanted to admit:

She loved Hadrian Bothwell.

CHAPTER SIXTEEN

The next weeks saw Avis drawn into a campaign to restore her standing in the community.

Hadrian went hacking along the bridle paths with her, added a call on the vicar, then escalated to calling on those most likely to receive her cordially—the widower barons who could talk hounds and horses with him, the tenants of both estates, the recent arrivals to the area who'd have no first-hand knowledge of Avis's past.

As they made one call after another, something in Avis relaxed, like the land eased out of the grip of winter into the benevolent embrace of the summer sun.

With Hadrian by her side, she was accepted as she hadn't been for twelve years. She still suffered nerves when they stood at somebody's front door, waiting for that eternity between knocking and being admitted, but Hadrian would merely smile at her, or tuck her hair behind her ear, or squeeze her hand, and the anxiety calmed.

While an entirely different uneasiness grew.

Hadrian was invariably polite, affectionate, and otherwise attentive, but he hadn't made love to her again, and Avis didn't know how to bring it up.

"Will you join me for tea?" Hadrian asked as the horses trotted up the long drive to Landover. "It's early yet, and we have plenty of time to walk you home."

"Let's picnic," Avie suggested. A picnic at least put them together on a blanket in private.

He slowed the horses to a walk. "Up at the pond?"

"I had somewhere else in mind."

"As my lady wishes." Within a half hour, they were walking through the back gardens, a hamper between them, a blanket on Hadrian's shoulder.

"Where are we going, Avie?"

The question of the hour, day, week, month and season. "To the mare's paddock."

His pace slowed. "I would not have chosen that spot, but I bow to your judgment." They set up under some trees, across the meadow from the crumbling remains of the cottage where Avis had been assaulted.

Not quite raped, not in the classic definition of the crime, but intimately assaulted.

The view was picturesque, as if the cottage were a folly or a ruin purposely designed to decorate that particular vista. Mares and foals napped, grazed, or swished at flies in the sun; harebells the same color as Hadrian's eyes grew along the pasture fence.

Avis yanked off her boots, then her garters and stockings, angry because the very landscape had been violated by Hart Collins and his crime.

"I'll burn it if you like," Hadrian said, wrestling with his own boots. "Burn it, bury the ashes, and plant a rowan tree or whatever you please."

"I would like that." Avis made up her mind as the words left her lips. "I would also like it if you made love with me, right here, right now."

The idea had percolated along the edge of her awareness every time she'd walked or ridden this direction with Hadrian over the past few weeks. She'd had no specific intentions when she'd asked Hadrian to escort her here, though a sort of tension had been coiling more and more tightly in her heart, in her spirit—and in her body.

"Such talk," Hadrian murmured, kneeling up and opening the hamper. "Perhaps I misheard you."

"Hadrian, was I so inept as all that?"

He went still, as if the bottom of the hamper had turned mysterious on him, then he sank back on his heels.

"I did not observe precautions last time, Avie. For the first time in my life, I *could* not. If you get a child of me, then your options are gone. I hope you understand that."

"I understand that the more time we spend together, the more you avoid me somehow. If currying favor with the neighbors is to cost me your affections, then the neighbors can go hang. You haven't even kissed me, haven't brushed my hair, haven't napped with me again."

And she was angry, *again*, to have to point this out to him, also bewildered, and maybe a bit proud of herself for forcing a confrontation.

More than a bit.

Hadrian's arms came around her. "Hush, Avie. The resumption of your social activities has taken a toll. I should have anticipated that."

She shoved him to his back and climbed over him. "I will not be hushed, not by you of all people. I miss you, Hadrian. Is that your point? Did you need to hear me say it?"

"It's gratifying," he admitted, drawing the backs of his fingers over her cheek, "but I wouldn't bring you misery for any price, Avie, except your own well-being. I miss you too."

And yet, he regarded her with a combination of wariness and affection, as if he'd happily endure more weeks of polite social calls.

So Avis kissed him. She poured her frustration and bewilderment into the kiss, and by degrees, Hadrian kissed her back. He came alive beneath her, his arms anchoring her to his chest, his kisses waxing hotter and his body—

He *had* missed her, as a man misses a woman he's made love with.

Avis subsided against his chest and inhaled his citrus and clove scent. "I want you, Hadrian. I want you, I want you here, I want you now."

Also everywhere and for always, which was a problem.

"Avie, this is complicated. I desire you until I'm nigh blind with it, but passion can bear fruit, and I won't trap you as Collins tried to."

Avis rolled to her back, so she was presented with the wide blue expanse of the Cumbrian summer sun.

"I hate your gentlemanly scruples, Hadrian Bothwell." Though she loved him, which was why becoming his wife would be complicated. "If the Baroness Collins is behind these notes, we cannot seek redress from her. Public opinion will be sympathetic to her, and perhaps it should be. You will be ostracized for marrying me, or pitied. The pity is worse, I can assure you. Worst of all would be if harm were to befall you—mortal harm."

Hadrian made no move to touch her, which was fortunate, because Avis was trying to *think*—without much success.

"I will be envied, if you marry me."

He believed that. The daft, lovely, dear, stubborn man believed that, and his belief warmed all the cramped, lonely, bewildered corners of Avis's heart.

"I *need*, Hadrian, to make a lovely memory with you here. My need is not rational, and it is certainly not convenient, but I won't apologize for it, either. I can understand that you seek to protect me from further scandal with your warnings and scruples, so let us compromise: If I conceive your child, I will marry you."

Because in that much, he was right, though Avis was right too, to insist on an opportunity to reclaim more of her past—more of her soul—from Hart Collins's grip.

As the foals capered and played in the summer sun, and the mares contentedly cropped the grass, Hadrian studied her. Avis saw all manner of emotions in his eyes: frustration, anger even, calculation, lust, affection, exasperation, and something warm and sweet and lost.

He sat up, and for an endless, unendurable moment, Avis thought he'd leave her on the blanket, doubly cursing a place in need of redemption.

"This is not wise." He yanked his stockings off and tossed them toward his boots. "You have me cornered. I will earn your ire do I refuse you, and I will earn your eternal resentment if our joining has consequences. This isn't how I wanted it to be."

* * *

Avie was nearly begging Hadrian for his favors, and his Avie should never have to beg, not for his attention, not for anything, and especially not here in this place, on another lovely day.

They'd been weeks at this business of calling on the neighbors, riding out together, and attending services together, but they'd not succeeded in provoking any notes, or any apparent increase in the gossip directed at Avis.

They had succeeded in straining Hadrian's self-discipline to the limit of his strength, though. He'd taken to nightly swims in the quarry pond, forcing himself to linger in its frigid depths until his limbs ached and his teeth chattered.

He took off his jacket and cravat, lay back on the blanket, and settled an arm around the woman he loved, for nothing less than love could result in the torment of longing he endured in her company.

"I'm proud of you, Avis Portmaine."

"You've barely started undressing. Why are you proud of me?"

"You can see to my clothes. A little effort for your pleasures isn't much to ask. I'm proud of you because not once in all these weeks of doing the pretty with me has your composure faltered. My composure, however, is jeopardized by your request."

His sanity, his heart, his *everything*, hung by a thread—probably a glimpse into the way Avis felt when one of these notes dropped into her quiet life, wreaking havoc from some unknown quarter.

She levered up to sit beside him. "If you're dithering, it won't do you any good, Hadrian, I have become a determined woman." Her hands went to his falls, while Hadrian laced his fingers behind his head and prayed for fortitude.

Also for erotic inspiration: If they were to indulge in a lapse in judgment, let it be the very best lapse he could give her.

She took a peculiar and charming approach, undoing his breeches and drawing forth his burgeoning erection. With his falls lying open and the summer breeze gracing him in unusual locations, she made an inspection of the rest of him: cuff-links, waistcoat, shirt, and every so often, she'd come back to his breeding organs for the occasional stroke or pat or caress.

"You are diabolical," Hadrian said when he was lying naked on his back. "I suppose you'll take another eternity to remove your own clothes?"

"I'll need your help with the hooks." She turned, swept her hair up off her nape, and presented that particularly vulnerable and fetching part of herself while Hadrian's cock leapt.

"You will pay for this," he warned as he sat up and started on her hooks. "A man can take only so much, Avie, and then he must retaliate."

"I live in hope." She sighed dramatically while Hadrian pushed her dress off her shoulders, trapping her arms.

"You can just stew in your hope, my lady." He set his lips to her spine and nibbled and teased and nuzzled his way south, then north, then out over her shoulder blades, to the juncture of her neck, her ears, and just about everywhere her warm, fragrant flesh was exposed.

"You're making love to my back," she whispered long moments later. "Not well done of you, when the rest of me feels so neglected."

She was teasing him. Saints be praised, Avis Portmaine was intimately teasing him, and he was proud of her all over again.

"We've time, Avie," he said softly, but he resumed undoing hooks, until the dress was pushed away and she was left in only her shift. Slowly, while she watched him, Hadrian undid one bow at a time until her jumps were discarded and her chemise was more off of her than on.

"I love how you look at me," Avis said, winnowing her fingers through his hair.

"How do I look at you?"

"Like I'm the answer to years of prayers."

He leaned forward to graze her mouth with his. Kissing her was the easiest thing in the world, as they sat nearly naked on their blanket in a little summer Eden.

He tried to hold back, to merely tease, and taste, and coax, but her tongue was bold, and she whimpered with wanting. Still, he would not be hurried, until the backs of her fingers brushed his cock.

"Not fair, Avie," he rasped. "One wants to savor such pleasure."

"Savor this." She put his hand on her breast and arched into his palm.

For two years, he'd been celibate, and for most of those two years, it hadn't been so difficult.

As an eighteen-year-old, he'd been one, eager, strutting, monument to perpetual arousal, but most of the pleasures he'd longed for then were yet to be experienced. Now, he knew what gratification could be, and how starved he'd become for pleasure.

For her.

He eased Avis to her back and settled his mouth over her nipple. He rode the rise and fall of her sigh as her hands cradled the back of his head in a slow, sweet caress that brought him closer to her.

"You like this?" He drew on her gently and used his tongue to heighten the sensations.

"I adore it, with you, Hadrian. I wish you had two mouths and four hands. I wish I had as many myself, so badly do I want to touch you everywhere."

"I'm in no hurry." He rolled to his back, though he'd never been in a bigger, harder hurry.

She sat up and surveyed him as he sprawled, trying for a credible impersonation of a happy, relaxed fellow—except for the erection arrowing up along his belly.

"You're in a peculiar mood," she said, stroking his shaft.

"We're taking our time. The ease of our pace now will pay off later. Trust me on this."

"I do trust you." She swirled her tongue around the head of his cock, then shifted down to her side, her head pillowed on his belly. "Just recall,"—another slow, hot, wet swipe—"this taking our time business was your idea."

He settled a hand in her hair and resigned himself to protracted torture, because he owed her this. He owed her any foray she wanted to make in the direction of sexual intimacy and confidence, even if it meant he embarrassed himself in ways that hadn't plagued him since his adolescence.

She undertook her explorations with a vengeance, alternately nibbling, caressing, and then suckling at him, until the urge to move his hips became imperative.

"Are you bored yet?" he asked.

Her grin said she wasn't fooled. She could *taste* his passion straining at the leash.

"Maybe soon."

"Maybe now," Hadrian growled, shifting to loom over her and join his mouth to hers. He pressed his cock against her hip—which brought not a scintilla of relief—then crouched over her, ready to exorcise any and all of her demons.

Her arms and legs vised around him, and her hips arched up in a slow, sinuous tease.

"Maybe five minutes ago," she growled back, and he laughed at her fierceness. He reached between them and feathered his thumb over the seat of her pleasure while she hissed out a breath.

"Now, Hadrian, please."

"Soon." He kissed her as he teased her, each moment of honest desire a small gesture of reparation for the twelve years she'd wandered alone in a wilderness of hurt. "Hadrian, *please.*"

He was inside her in one smooth, gloriously deep thrust. He paused, hilted in her damp heat, because the pleasure was sublime.

"Finally." She closed her eyes and laced her fingers through his. When he moved to withdraw, her ankles locked at the small of his back.

"I won't go far," he whispered, "and I'll come back, Avie, as often as you like."

He tormented them both with long minutes of slow, deep thrusts, resisting mightily the satisfaction threatening to swamp him. Avis was the embodiment of delight, giving and taking, taking and giving, her hands holding his in a grip both fierce and intimate.

"Hadrian…"

"I'm here, Avie. I'll catch you when you fly away."

"You too."

God, yes, *him too*. He sped up, and completion seized her. Her body fisted around him hard, repeatedly, until Hadrian was holding his own satisfaction at bay by sheer will, and then she eased around him in a voluptuous stretch.

"Damn you, Hadrian Bothwell." She sounded thoroughly pleased and licked at his throat as she squeezed his hands. "Damn you for leaving a lady unescorted."

"One doesn't want the dance to be over too soon." That hadn't come out as the teasing rejoinder he'd intended. She was owed twelve years of such dances, *at least*.

"I can still hear the music." She buried her face in his shoulder and held him, inside and out, until he began to move. From somewhere, he found the resolve to drive her over the edge yet again, and confound the luck if she wasn't just as appreciative of hard, fast loving as she was of the slow, languorous kind. If anything, her responses became more spontaneous the longer he was joined with her.

Hadrian took a moment to be still and let Avie recover. The sun was a pleasant heat on his shoulders, the meadow breeze cooled the hint of dampness at the small of his back, and bliss throbbed through him.

Here, where Avis had known such fear and pain, a good memory was taking root.

Proud of her was a monumental understatement.

"I cannot fathom," Avis said softly, "that such pleasure awaits all who speak their vows. It is incomprehensible."

"Talk later," he muttered, "love now." He surged up over her, taking her mouth and her body in one movement. He made a physical statement of mutual possession, and she merely sighed into his mouth and rocked her hips against his.

He drove her up in a slow, steady build of passion, his tempo increasing only gradually, until she was bowing into him, clinging to him, and panting against his neck.

"Hold on, Avie," he whispered.

"Can't."

"I want it to last."

"*Hadrian,* don't you—holy—"

Her whole body shook this time, and she didn't just whimper, she moaned, and keened, and bucked, and drove him right out of his mind and into the greatest depth of pleasure he'd ever endured. His body dissolved with the ecstasy of it, the bliss of it, until he was floating, breathless and suffused with joy, basking in the warmth and wonder of making love with Avie.

"Blessed beaming beloved saints." A sincere prayer on his part, in gratitude for having survived such an experience.

Avis turned her face to kiss his wrist, then rubbed her cheek against his knuckles.

He stayed awake, and he even managed to lift his weight away from the warmth and softness of her, the breeze tickling his belly.

"You'll get too much sun." She patted his backside, then stroked him gently, and Hadrian could feel that caress over all of his skin.

"Can't move."

She smiled against his hand and managed to draw the edge of the blanket over them, and that felt lovely too. For long, long moments, they remained thus, breathing in counterpoint, skin cooling, until Hadrian realized just being inside her was inspiration enough to rekindle his randy inclinations.

He needed something sweet, a dessert, after that last joining.

A slow, tender loving, because he could not bear to part from her after what had gone before. He came to regret his greed, because his first pleasure had been passionate, but this one, softer, more shared and less demanded, was the more loving.

The most loving.

* * *

"You labor under a misconception, my dear."

"I'm not laboring," Avis corrected the man blanketing her with his lovely, solid, *naked* weight. "I'm barely breathing, so thoroughly have you knocked my wits asunder."

Her heart too, for she could not have found what she sought in this meadow alone.

Hadrian nuzzled her neck and subsided against her. "It isn't always like this. For many, it's never like this. You will have expectations of me I'll never be able to fulfill."

She opened her eyes and tried to angle out from under him, the better to see his expression, but he cuddled her back into place, trapping her with his chin on her crown.

"You've had that much experience,"—she lipped at his earlobe—"that you can make such pronouncements?"

"I've had more than you, my lady, and as a vicar, one hears all manner of unhappy confessions and confidences."

"All manner?"

"You'd be surprised how many marriages that have only the faintest echo of love in them and no passion," Hadrian said, tone bleak.

Avis hated, *hated* that he'd been unhappy with Rue, at least in this regard. Bad enough she herself had lost so many years to self-consciousness and confusion. Hadrian had done nothing to deserve the same fate.

Hadrian kissed her ear, briskly, a call to focus. "Your mill wheel is creaking along at a great rate. Do you understand me, Avie? This wasn't a tumble for sport."

"Never that. Thank you, Hadrian."

"God above." He lifted up, and she missed even the weight of his chin resting at the top of her head. "You don't thank me for sharing pleasure such as this, Avie. Thanks are for chocolates, a game of cricket, or books one lends to friends."

Avis pushed his hair back from his face. "Don't get into a state, Hadrian. Your hair has grown longer."

"I'll cut it."

"You will not." She smoothed it back. "I love it long."

"What else do you love about me?" He closed the distance between them again, resting his cheek against hers. His question had been bold, and he was entitled to fortify himself for her response.

She stroked his nape, while the breeze set the meadow grass dancing a sunny hornpipe. "I would make you a list, but you've worn me out. I feel a nap coming on."

"Then I'll considerately keep my own list regarding present company for recitation at another time."

He allowed her an orderly retreat, but he'd made his point: She loved him, and he loved her. For her part, this loving encompassed both the infatuation of a wounded young girl and the mature appreciation of a woman who'd endured alone for too long. Her love included friendship, lust, and all manner of unruly hopes, but a fat measure of selflessness too.

She really and truly loved him, and he loved her back. How very, very delightful.

Also quite messy.

* * *

"I'm that happy to see you, Master Hay."

Cecily Carruthers beamed up at the young man on her front porch. This one had ever been a pretty lad, and such eyes! Harold was a handsome fellow too, of course, but the younger brother had a look about him that made a female— even a female as ancient as herself—sigh mightily.

"Lady Avis intended to join me today, but found herself indisposed," Master Hay replied. "She asked me to convey her regards."

"Shall I send you home with some tisanes, then?"

He looked a little uncomfortable, so she patted his arm. Young people had grown so proper in this present age. How easily their elders scandalized them.

"You needn't say more. Lady Avis wouldn't be lying abed for a simple cold."

"She did not give me particulars." Master Hay's smile was back in evidence, and Gran knew from that smile that the lady hadn't had to give him details. He was a noticing sort, always had been.

"Well, come sit a while." She latched on to a muscular arm and towed him into her cottage, forcing him to duck his head lest he bang it on the lintel.

"You're getting on well enough?" He'd caught her on a tidy day, not that the place was ever exactly messy, but Young Deal would forget to scrape his boots, and the grandchildren would get their muddy fingers on her drapes, and the cat might take a fancy to the harebells sitting in a blue crockery bowl on her table.

"I manage," she said, leading him to her kitchen table. "Young Deal looks in almost every day, and my Nancy's cottage lies just beyond the lea rig. What about you, Master Hay?"

"I'm in the company of a lovely lady. My day could not be better."

"Does Lady Avis buy that sack of goods?" She assembled the tea tray—the everyday, which matched well enough for a young bachelor calling on a tenant. "You've the look of a man with troubles, Master Hay." A handsome man, and he would stay handsome too, not grow saggy and whining like many others.

"Lady Avis warned me you were a hopeless baggage." He held her chair for her, as if she were some fine lady a quarter her present age.

"I am an old baggage, and you didn't stop by to hone your courting skills."

"I am calling on all the Landover tenants, but I do have a particular question for you."

"Let me get the tea steeping, and you'll be wanting some scones and butter." Because wouldn't those old biddies slurping tea and lady's pints down at The Snooty Fox be full of questions, when one of them saw Master Hay's fine horse tied to Gran's porch?

"If you made those scones, I'll have one."

Lovely boy. "You've heard from Master Hal?"

"He's thoroughly enjoying his summer on the water."

"Took that Lord James with him, didn't he?"

Her guest remained silent, probably torn between a younger brother's bewilderment and family loyalty.

"Don't begrudge your brother his choices," Gran said. "He's a good man."

"And a wonderful brother, but he's the one who suggested I put my questions to you."

She slid into a chair, but not before young Bothwell was on his feet, holding it for her again. "Sit, silly boy, and ask your questions."

"Your reputation is sadly understated," he murmured near her ear, but he subsided into his chair and let her serve him a flaky scone with clotted cream.

"What questions have you for an old woman who can barely see, hear or creak around?"

"Unless she's on the dance floor, reeling Fenwick under the table."

"Needs must. Young Fen knows how to turn a lady down the room, and there are those who think themselves too good for his company."

Gran's chair sported a thick cushion, the scones were fresh, and she had a young man captive in her parlor, proof that life yet held wonders and pleasure for an old woman with too many stockings to darn.

"I've announced my engagement to Lady Avis," Master Hay said, "but I have questions about the unfortunate incident in her past."

Now this was disappointing. Gran took a fortifying nibble of scone. "Put your questions to her. You know what befell her, and you know it wasn't her fault, not any of it."

Master Hay poured the tea and nudged a pink porcelain cup across the table. Old Deal had brought that cup back from Manchester as part of a matched pair back in '85, when the wool harvest had been quite good.

"I know the situation was not of Lady Avis's making. I know it better than most, but somebody delights in propounding the notion that Avis is wanton, fallen, and suffered no more than she deserved."

Protective was worlds better than nosy. Gran added sugar to her tea and took another nibble of a fine scone, if she did say so herself.

"I've heard the talk. Petty bitches, whispering behind their hands and averting their eyes. Worthless, the lot of 'em."

Master Hay had forgotten to pour himself any tea. Gran saw to the oversight.

"Who benefits from such talk, Gran?"

"A fair question. Not easy to answer. Any woman who thinks life has been unfair to her would feel superior to an earl's daughter plagued by scandal." At some point, every woman faced unfairness in life—as did most men, come to that.

"Was somebody else desirous of becoming Collins's baroness?"

"We've few enough titles locally that the list of his potential wives would have been short, and Lady Avis was the most reasonable choice. He could be charming, but most of the papas and mamas would see through that, even if the daughters didn't. Eat your scone, Master Hay."

He picked it up but didn't take a bite. "So maybe a young lady sought him, but wasn't seriously considered?"

"None that I can recall." Not that her recollection was perfect. "Young ladies are a vaporish lot, and they take odd notions." When he took a bite of scone, she put a second on his plate. Just watching a specimen like Hadrian Bothwell consume her cooking did her old heart good.

"This is the best scone I've eaten in ages. What do you recall of Collins's familiars?"

"A gormless lot. He was tossed out of one decent school after another, but always bringing his friends with him when he got sent down. Some of them weren't so bad, but it was clear they were sowing wild oats in Collins's company."

Gran had felt sympathy for the baroness, watching her son become more self-indulgent and disgraceful by the year. She still felt sympathy for the woman, who barely bestirred herself to come to services any more.

"Collins should have been at university when he assaulted Lady Avis."

Gran passed him the butter, made fresh that morning. "Collins would have been up in Edinburgh, drinking and wenching away the spring, while his poor mama thought he was at university."

"He attended in Edinburgh?"

"I don't know as he attended." Gran cast back, trying to recall details. "Young Deal claims the boy manufactured documents granting him admission, when no decent school would have him, and then off he went, his pockets full of spending money, while his poor mother thought he was gone for scholar."

"That presupposes a lot of planning on Collins's part." Now Master Hay added cream to his tea and stirred in the exact, same clockwise rhythm his father had used. Master Harold had the same habit, too.

"Collins was cunning," Gran said, mindful she referred to the baron in the past tense. "Like a slinking, predatory beast, and he could wind his mama around his finger."

"You are on good terms with the baroness?"

"You've been from home for too long, young man. Baroness Collins married a man no better than his son, and endured his foolishness until he broke his idiot neck racing a curricle in the rain. She's to be pitied, but no, I do not have a close acquaintance with her, but rather, with her abigail, who calls upon me for the same tisanes I'll be passing along to you, as well as headache powders and nerve tonics."

"I meant no offense, and you're right, I've been from home too long. Who might know the names of Collins's accomplices in crime?"

Old Deal had known them, just as he'd known each and every sheep in his flock, and when rain was coming despite a cloudless sky. Why did old age have to be so lonely?

"The baroness might recall those names," Gran said slowly. "Or her abigail. That lady never forgets anything to do with the Collins family."

She let him steer the conversation toward her grandchildren and great-grandchildren, the ripening crops, and Lady Avis's plan to take up residence in the dower house.

"Nonsense, that," Gran sniffed. "Avis Portmaine lets that flouncing companion of hers have far too much sway. You'll set that to rights when you marry, won't you? Married women don't need companions, not when they're married to the likes of you."

"Was that a compliment?"

Oh, such a smile he had. That smile had likely kept the pews full to bursting over in the West Riding.

"I state facts. I knew your parents, my lad, and while they had their differences, they were no more lonely than Lady Avis will be married to you."

"If we marry," he said, and Gran had raised too many children and grandchildren not to see the doubt in his eyes. "A lady can change her mind."

"She changed her mind before, you idiot, because she wanted to marry you, not Collins."

"I beg your pardon?"

She creaked to her feet, sparing him only a glance over her shoulder as she took the tea tray back to the counter. He was young and handsome now. Twelve years ago he'd been *very* young and handsome.

"I tended Lady Alex, you'll recall, because I'm the herbalist around here, and the physicians had done what little they could. Lady Alex told me."

"Told you exactly what?"

"Lady Avis had already informed her brothers she wouldn't go through with the engagement to Collins, because another had caught her eye."

He'd forgotten to stand, his pretty manners knocked aside by what was clearly new information. "You assume that other was my humble self?"

"I know it was," Gran said, scooping dried herbs from jars on the counter and into a cloth bag. "Lady Avis and Lady Alexandra were close, for they had no one else. Lady Avis told her younger sister you were a gentleman to your handsome bones, and why should she shackle herself to Collins when there was an honorable, intelligent, entirely lovely fellow such as you right next door?"

Odd, she could recall the words so clearly.

"That isn't the same as saying she wanted to marry me."

Gran had to measure the chamomile twice, then used a length of string to tie the bag closed. The bow wasn't as snug as it should be because her fingers ached.

Rain coming, most likely.

"After what Collins did to her, how was Lady Avis to contemplate marriage to anybody?" She passed him the sachet of herbs. "Make a brew of a half tea cup full of leaves to four cups of boiling water. Let it steep at least three minutes. You can add a little sugar or honey. This will help with female complaints."

"My thanks."

"You'll look after her?"

"I will do my damnedest." He rose and brushed a kiss to her wrinkled cheek—bless the lad. "And my thanks, Gran. If you recall anything more, you'll let me know?"

"Only if you'll dance with me at your wedding."

"I'll issue a decree, and every man in the shire will be required to stand up with you, should you ask it."

He would too. The Bothwells were men of their word.

"Best set a date, then, so I can send out my dance card. Wait until Fen is back from his wenching down in Manchester. He'll need to recover before he's up to my weight."

Master Hay looked a bit taken aback, as if he wasn't sure he'd heard a jest.

"I want to be just like you when I grow up." He gave her a careful hug and departed, leaving Gran to stare at her cooling tea, and wonder just how much the baroness would find convenient to recall about her son's cronies—for Master Hay would ask.

Sooner rather than later.

CHAPTER SEVENTEEN

"You will excuse us?" Hadrian's tone was polite, but his manner was not that of a man willing to dither over pleasantries.

And still, Lily looked to Avis for permission to leave her in company with her fiancé.

"Lily, if you'll give us a moment," Avis said, putting a sketch pad aside and passing Lily a sheaf of letters. "Perhaps you'd be good enough to have these posted for me?"

When Lily left, Hadrian closed the door behind her—a presumption for which Avis could have kissed him.

"If you marry me," he said, drawing Avis to her feet, "I'll ask that Miss Prentiss be turfed out."

He'd ask, he wouldn't insist. Bless the man.

"Because she knows you're bent on mischief?"

"I am not bent on mischief." He wrapped his arms around Avis from behind, which deprived her of the opportunity to read his gaze, but was a marvelous comfort. "The woman has a suspicious mind, and you're not some scatter-brained fifteen-year-old knotting your sheets so you can smoke Papa's pipes in the woodshed. How are you feeling?"

"Achy," Avis said, letting him have some of her weight. "It will pass."

"Even Rue let me do this," he murmured as he began slow, firm circles with his hand low on her belly. "She suffered badly, each and every month. Let's get you off your feet."

A knock on the door sounded as he settled her on one end of the sofa, but he gently pushed her shoulders down and answered it himself.

"Gran Carruthers sent you along some concoction for female troubles," he said as he set the tea tray down. "I had the kitchen brew it up, and you're to drink it with honey or sugar."

"You discussed my,"—she waved a hand—"with her?"

"I didn't have to." Hadrian fussed about with the tea tray, and the fragrance of chamomile and flowers wafted to Avis's nose. She knew this particular tisane, and even the scent of it brought relaxation.

Hadrian poured a cup, added a little sugar, then took a sip.

"It's not too bad," he pronounced. "I didn't discuss your indisposition. All I did was make your excuses, and she divined the nature of your discomfort. She thinks you should marry me, by the way."

Which opinion she'd offered with no prompting by her caller whatsoever, of course.

Hadrian passed Avis the cup, and like a jealous nanny, watched her drink. She didn't finish it all at once, but rather, settled the warm cup against her stomach.

"I really shouldn't marry you." She wanted to, but she spared them both that admission. "I've had another note."

He studied her for a long moment, hands on his hips, lips pursed in thought. When he sat down right beside her and put an arm around her shoulders, Avis fished a folded paper from her skirt pocket.

Had she expected him to stomp off, to tire of her problems, to blame her for the notes as she'd blamed herself? His arm around her shoulders, the tisane cooling in its cup, she accepted that he truly did love her.

God help him.

"The handwriting is the same as the others, and the paper a quarter sheet of foolscap," Avis said. "I don't care for the tone."

She cared very much for Hadrian's opinion of the situation, though.

"'A good woman can be the making of a man,'" Hadrian read. "'A bad woman can cost him everything.'" He folded the note up and slipped it into his waistcoat pocket. "This tells us a few things."

"Our plan is working," Avis said, taking another sip of her tisane. "We're mightily displeasing somebody." Who was hell-bent now on threatening Hadrian—a former vicar, for pity's sake, and the sole heir to Landover.

"But if the somebody who's displeased is supposed to be Ashton Fenwick, now he has to have accomplices," Hadrian said. "Your whole household knows he's reportedly larking away to the south, and they'd remark him stealing about, leaving notes in your sewing basket."

"The note was under my pillow, Hadrian."

Like a spider lurking among the linen. Avis had considered moving to a guest room, leaving the chamber she'd had since girlhood, her last sanctuary in her family's home.

"That location, under your very pillow, suggests a female accomplice. Your boudoir is hardly frequented by the footmen this time of year." He took her tea cup from her and wrapped her under his arm. "When did you find it?"

"This morning," Avis replied, leaning into him. "When I woke up, it wasn't there, but I went back to my room to get my flute after taking my walk and noticed my pillows weren't as I'd left them. The note was stashed among them."

"Were there footmen about?"

He was doing it again, being calm and methodical when Avis wanted to screech out indignation and exasperation. Did Gran have a tisane to restore a woman's sense of safety?

What had Hadrian asked?

"The footmen had not been in my room in some days. The weather hasn't been cool enough for fires at night, and I water my own flowers. The candles were fresh last night, and the lamps in my bedroom aren't trimmed or restocked by the footmen."

"So unless a footman were very crafty indeed, we're looking at a maid. Do any of them bear you particular animosity?"

His thumb stroked along the side of her neck, a soothing caress that anchored her to the discussion and to him.

"Of course some of the maids bear me ill will. Every one of them I've scolded for making sheep's eyes at the footmen, every one who has lingered too long among Vim's or Ben's things, every one who doesn't tend to her tasks unless the housekeeper is standing directly over her."

Good heavens, she sounded near tears—and she was.

"You do not have an easy time here, do you?"

"If you mean does my staff dote on me, no, they don't. They do what they're told, and when Ben or Vim are in residence, the staff dotes on them." As did Avis, so desperate was she for her brothers' company.

Hadrian was silent beside her, but his free hand was again making those slow circles low on her abdomen.

"I want you and Lily to remove to Landover."

"That will not serve, Hadrian," Avis said, letting her eyes drift closed. "Lily would not view herself as an adequate chaperone. Besides, if Fen can bribe somebody here at Blessings, he no doubt has spies at Landover."

"It isn't Fen. You know it isn't."

His confidence in Fen was reassuring. "What aren't you telling me?"

"I'm to pay a call on Lady Collins," Hadrian said. "I'd rather not delay it until you're feeling better."

"I'll feel better the day after tomorrow," Avis said, sitting up a bit.

"You go through *three days* of this every month?" How indignant he sounded, and over a simple fact of female biology.

"The discomfort is three days, the mess is longer."

"God in heaven. Rue was in bed for a day, sometimes not even that."

"It passes." And the important topic was not Avis's indisposition. "I'm struck by the fact that, again, the note threatens you, not me exactly."

"It does, but you are not to fret. The staff at Landover knows which side their bread is buttered on, and I will be careful."

"You'll tell me what transpires with the baroness?"

"I'll return tomorrow. You need your rest, and I'm loath to convey anything significant to you in writing."

"Prudent." When she would have risen, Hadrian leaned down and pressed a kiss to her mouth, a little show of possession, perhaps, but also comfort before he took his leave.

Avis was growing to depend on him, on his pragmatic willingness to solve her problems, be they female discomfort, threatening notes, or intimate demons in need of exorcism. A woman could come to rely on such treatment. A foolish woman who had no care for the man trying to protect her.

Lily rejoined Avis not five minutes later, and she was once again wearing Avis's green cashmere shawl.

"I've brewed one of Gran Carruthers's tisanes," Avis said, though in truth, Hadrian had ordered the kitchen to make it up. "Have a cup—it's very pleasant."

Lily appropriated the rocking chair to Avis's right and helped herself to a tea cake. "Half a cup will do, thank you. Mr. Bothwell didn't stay very long. I hope his regard for you isn't waning."

The usual concern laced Lily's tone, all bound up in sincerity and protectiveness.

"Your tea." Avis passed over a half cup.

"A bit more than that, please. These cakes are quite good. Is Mr. Bothwell pressing you for a date?"

Avis added a dollop more tea to the cup and passed it over again. "The cakes were made this morning. I'm glad you enjoy them." She rose and closed the door, because now, before she lost her nerve, she must speak more plainly than she had in all the years since Lily had joined the household.

"You forgot my sugar," Lily said, wrinkling her nose and setting the cup back on its saucer. "Or shall I try the honey?"

"Help yourself to whichever you prefer," Avis said, because Lily was playing some game, even in something so trivial as having Avis pour her tea.

And all the while, Lily oozed compassion, humility, and quiet sermons.

Avis resumed her seat as Lily stirred sugar into the half-empty cup.

"Lily, my affection for Mr. Bothwell and his for me have not wavered. If anything, my regard for him grows over time. If and when he and I marry, the services of a companion will not be required when I remove to his household. Your severance will be generous, and the character I write for you will be glowing."

This was right. This was a calm, reasonable decision made out of neither fear nor anger, and yet, it was a vital step toward putting the past in a proper perspective.

Lily said nothing for a long while. She sat with her tea cup poised before her, back straight, expression unreadable.

Whatever response Lily came up with—a scold, a sniffled acceptance, a small tantrum—it would not outweigh Avis's relief at having made the decision.

"Have you set a date then?" Lily's tone held the brittle cheer of somebody enduring a public betrayal, and yet, she'd managed to fire off a telling shot.

"A special license is a possibility," Avis said, rising. "Please take as long as you need to find another post, but as of this moment, you are free of any further obligations as my companion."

Avis headed for the door. Lily said nothing, but remained seated, a pillar of silence swathed in a green shawl Avis had once treasured, but now, never wanted to see again.

* * *

Two aspects of the Baroness Collins impressed Hadrian as he bowed over her hand. The first was her graciousness, apparent in her manners, her speech, her graceful movements. She was every inch the dignified lady, while he was surprised she'd even be at home to him.

The second feature he noticed was the sadness in her eyes. Parents watching a child slip away to a lingering illness bore this air of patient sorrow.He'd *known* sadness like that, when Rue had died, but it didn't still haunt him as Lady Collins appeared haunted, even as she smiled at him over a blue jasperware tea service that went nicely with her fair coloring.

"I'd heard you're doing the pretty in Harold's absence. Well done of you, Mr. Bothwell. Too few of us observe the civilities any more."

"I'm home to stay, and always glad to welcome a neighbor who comes calling."

She set her tea cup down carefully. "Harold extended the same olive branch. He and I left each other in peace."

Her voice held a guarded plea Hadrian couldn't afford to heed.

"I don't wish to disturb you," he began, but she stopped him with a shake of her head.

"I have my sources too, Mr. Bothwell. Hartley is back in the country, which bodes ill for him, because Benjamin Portmaine will put period to my son's existence does he learn of it."

"I don't think so." Hadrian could give her this much and hope she was willing to aid him in exchange. "Lady Avis and Lady Alex have enjoined their brothers from further vengeance. If Benjamin and Wilhelm have abided by their sisters' wishes all these years, only substantial provocation will deter them from that course now."

"Substantial provocation." She grimaced delicately, a woman who'd once been pretty, but whom care had rendered faded and fatigued. "That is my son, substantial provocation personified. You needn't spare me, Mr. Bothwell. Better than anyone, I know what Hartley is capable of."

Her sadness might be mostly for the execrable excuse for a man who was her son, but she was sensible enough to be sad for herself as well.

"I'm sorry." The words were out, from the long habit of a man who'd made his living dealing in sympathy and social conventions.

"I do not believe a single person has expressed to me that particular condolence." She picked up her tea cup and paused before taking a sip. "Lady Avis will thrive in your care."

Thus were Hadrian's condolences neatly tucked aside.

"*If* Lady Avis marries me. This is not a foregone conclusion."

The baroness rose, and Hadrian was struck again by the woman's inherent grace. How had the late baron merited the hand of such a lady, and how had she endured her marriage, if what Gran had said was true?

"What can I do to help, sir?" She faced him, arms crossed. "I called on Lady Avis after Hart used her so ill, offered her what consequence I had, but my visit seemed only to upset her and then she was off to her aunt's in the north. Harold's advice was to let sleeping dogs lie. Lady Avis seemed to be doing better, but then Lady Alex left up her majority, and matters have been difficult ever since."

"What does that mean?"

Lady Collins let her arms drop to her sides, the gesture calling attention to a complete lack of ornamentation about her attire. Not a watch pinned to her bodice, not a bracelet, not a ring.

Could any woman draw close to Hart Collins without suffering his rapaciousness?

"Lady Avis had put the incident behind her, or appeared to," the baroness said. "When she came home from the north, she attended services, guided her brother's domestic staff, and rode about the neighborhood, the same as any young lady of the manor might."

The incident. Hadrian wanted to up-end the tea service all over the faded Axminster carpet. "That changed?"

"After Lady Alexandra decamped, Lady Avis disappeared. I honestly see more of Lily Prentiss than I do Avis Portmaine."

"Lily calls on you?"

Lady Collins ran her hand over a cherry wood sideboard that sported not a single decanter, though a long scratch marred its surface.

"Miss Prentiss calls on my abigail. They have the same half-day, and the help can be more bound by convention than the titles, you know? Lily works for an earl's daughter, Tansy is employed by a baroness who is also an earl's daughter, albeit one aging in obscurity, so they must associate with each other rather than with the chambermaids."

"Working for the church, one grasped the hierarchies." Particularly a rural northern church, far from the plethora of titles sporting around in the south.

"I was surprised you chose the church." She resumed her place on the settee and poured another round of infernal damned tea. "Harold was relieved, though, and said as much."

"I am his heir. The military would not have been a prudent choice."

She peered into her tea cup, which sported a chip near the handle. "I thought you'd marry Lady Avis, all those years ago."

Some of Hadrian's ire dissipated, though he left his tea cooling on the tray.

"So did I." They shared a smile, two people at whom life had thrown unplanned challenges.

"Why are you really here, Mr. Bothwell? I appreciate the niceties, but if you've a point to your visit, you'd best get to it, for I won't be calling upon you."

To business, then.

"I am investigating what happened all those years ago between your son and Lady Avis. I've reason to think somebody is perpetuating awareness of that sad day, and doing so in a manner that casts Lady Avis in as poor a light as possible."

"My nephew once suggested the same thing."

"Your nephew?"

She apparently found that chipped blue tea cup fascinating. "He doesn't bruit it about. Ashton Fenwick is my late brother's child. He turned up here years ago, and while he avoids me now, he does keep an eye on his cousin, Sara Bennett, who is my younger sister's child."

Hadrian's meager serving of tea abruptly sat uneasily in his belly. "Fenwick never said a word about his connection to you." In all his years of service, Fenwick had never said a word, not to Harold, and Hadrian would bet, not to Avis.

"Would you, in his place?" She glanced to the window, where some small bird thumped and fluttered against the glass, as if sunshine and nectar had rendered it drunk and blind.

While Hadrian silently reeled.

Fenwick was Collins's *cousin*? A blood relation to the man who'd all but raped Avie? "What reason would Fenwick have for remaining silent about his relationship to you?"

"His antecedents are unfortunate," she said. "I acknowledge Ashton openly, but what can association do for either of us? Ashton could easily have been tarred with Hartley's brush, and my late husband never did a thing for my nephew beyond basic hospitality. Then too, Hart delighted in tormenting Ashton when they were younger."

"They associated?"

And God above, what would this knowledge do to Avis's fragile sense of safety?

The lady set her tea down untasted.

"They associated occasionally, as boys. Common he might be, but Ashton is more a gentleman than my son will ever be. Ashton traveled immediately after university, but then showed up in the area again some years ago."

"This leads me to my next question." Hadrian rose, though it was rude. The frantic bird would soon come to harm if nobody dissuaded it from attempting to fly through a pane it could not comprehend.

"Ask."

Hadrian opened the window—that was all it took—and the bird came to light on a bush several feet away. "Who was with Collins the day he assaulted Avis?"

"You'll file charges at this late hour?"

Charges were not out of the question, for premeditation in this case had involved accessories before the fact, a conspiracy even.

"I'd rather not, for her ladyship's sake," Hadrian answered honestly. "I want to deduce where the ill will and gossip regarding my intended are coming from, and put a stop to it."

"Fair enough, but other than a William Asterman, the son of an old friend, I'm not sure who was with Hart that day. Not all of his guests were party to that particular outing. He was forever bringing crowds of young fellows home with him when he was between terms or sent down. I put them in a guest wing, kept the maids out of sight, and made sure the firearms were locked up. Even his father grew impatient with his impromptu house parties. They were expensive in many regards."

"Where can I find this Asterman?"

"He was killed on the Peninsula. I will ask Tansy who else was about. She has the recall of an elephant and was in my employ at the time."

"I would appreciate it."

Hadrian offered the required parting platitudes, though he was frustrated with what he'd learned, and what he hadn't. He paused when Lady Collins had escorted him to the front door.

"If the baron intends to come north, will you tell me, my lady?"

"I hope Hart has learned a little discretion in twelve years. But yes, if he deigns to inform me he's coming this way, I will make sure you know. Lady Avis is owed that much, at least."

He wanted to leave, but common decency required that he ask one more question. "You'll be all right?"

She fell silent as a footman handed Hadrian his hat and gloves, then she took Hadrian's arm and walked out onto the front steps with him.

"You were raised without mother, sisters, or female relations of any kind. How is it you are such a gentleman?"

And how had her son turned out to be such a grease stain on the family escutcheon?

"Harold raised me to be what I am. You didn't answer my earlier question."

"I love my son, but I see his faults, Mr. Bothwell. If he sends word he's traveling north, I will give every maid under the age of forty leave, and remain with my relatives in Scotland until Hartley has resumed his wandering. Hartley is not welcome in my family's houses."

A snippet of Second Peter flitted through Hadrian's head, about a washed pig returning to its wallow, or—Proverbs 26—a dog returning to its vomit.

"I wish you safe journey, then, your ladyship. I cannot imagine the baron would set foot on English soil without assuring himself his birthright was in good repair."

Or stripped of all valuables.

"You will give my felicitations to Lady Avis on her upcoming nuptials?"

"If she sets a date, I'm sure she'd like you to attend the wedding breakfast."

He'd surprised her, but pleased her too—and when had this tired, lonely woman known any real pleasure?

"I would be honored, but likely decline."

"I understand." He bowed over her hand and took his leave, wondering how he would pass along the day's revelations to Avie, and if there was an innocent reason she hadn't yet heard from Fenwick.

* * *

"Who was responsible for tending to my room yesterday?" Avis asked her housekeeper.

"Really, Avis," Lily interjected, "you needn't concern yourself with such details. Mrs. Ellerby has the scheduling of the domestics quite in hand."

Across the tea tray, Mrs. Ellerby's shrewd gaze skipped from one lady to the other, while Avis mentally composed the character reference she'd send along with Lily.

"Mary Ellen and Angelina," Mrs. Ellerby said. "They are my upstairs maids, unless it's half-day or Sunday, and then one of the tweenies fills in."

"They would have swept the hearth, drawn the drapes, made the bed and so forth?"

"Aye, ma'am. Most days, they'll do a room together, so they can chat as they work."

"You'll send them to me later?"

Lily expelled a sigh, while the housekeeper murmured assent, rose, and excused herself from Avis's private parlor.

"Why you're taking this odd start is beyond me," Lily said, sorting through the tray of biscuits and tea cakes. "We'll determine the scheduling of the maids at the dower house when we remove there, which I hope will be soon. I cannot think of leaving you until that challenge has been met."

Avis could think of sending Lily away that very moment.

"I want no feuding among my help, Lily. Whoever I take to the dower house could be seen as making a come-down, and I don't want rebellion on my hands before I'm even settled in."

Lily popped the last chocolate biscuit into her mouth. "When will we move?"

"I don't know."

"This has to do with your so-called engagement, does it not?"

It had to do with twelve years of threats escalating to encompass harm to another who'd done nothing to deserve it. "My so-called engagement?"

"Your intended has barely been in evidence this week, Avis." She moved on to a ginger biscuit that would have gone nicely with Avis's second cup of tea. "I know you don't want to be seen as a jilt, but after all that calling on neighbors and trotting around, relations between you and Mr. Bothwell have decidedly cooled. I, for one, would not blame you if you sent Mr. Bothwell packing."

Avis had sent her siblings packing, Fen packing, and now Hadrian was to be banished. While Lily—whom Avis had formally dismissed—remained nibbling biscuits and swilling tea?

"I thought you liked Hadrian."

"I hardly know the man," Lily said, her expression shifting toward puzzlement, "and I have to wonder how well you know him, despite sharing a distant youth as neighbors. If he's neglecting you now that the banns are being cried, Avis, he's acting like a typical male, and he won't improve once you're married."

Avis set her tea cup down rather than dash the contents in Lily's face.

"That is a most unchristian, ungracious attitude to take toward a man who has done nothing—"

"Good morning, ladies." The object of their conversation stood at the door, smiling a welcome at them both. "I trust I am not intruding?"

"You are not." Avis went to him, not even blushing when he kissed her cheek.

How decidedly cool is that, Lily Prentiss? The sooner Lily was preparing some rich cit's daughter for the marriage mart, the better.

"Hadrian, please eat these scones before Lily and I consume them all."

He let her lead him by the hand to the settee.

"You're looking a little more the thing, my lady. Miss Prentiss, a pleasure as always." He offered a bow, Lily nodded, and went back to munching her ginger biscuit. With admirable skill, Hadrian engaged both women in small talk, keeping the discussion to inconsequential matters, until he asked Avis for a stroll in the gardens before the heat of the day set in.

When they were out of earshot of the house, Hadrian slid Avis's hand off his arm and threaded their fingers to lead her to a shaded bench.

"You're feeling better, Avie?"

"Physically." Avis sank down beside him and sat so their thighs touched. "I'm in a temper with dear Lily. I've told her that her tenure at Blessings has come to a close." They sat among blooming daisies, and the sun was lovely, and yet, Avis's mood would not lighten.

"I overheard more than I should have. She is ever protective of you, and that's not all bad."

"She's a bitter old woman in training. As a cautionary tale, she serves admirably."

Hadrian ranged an arm along the back of the bench, an invitation for Avis to cuddle up.

"You could not be like her if you tried, Avie. When you marry me, you can send her packing without a qualm."

"I haven't said I'll speak any vows with you, Hadrian Bothwell. Your very life might depend on my jilting a second fiancé." While Avis's happiness depended on becoming his wife.

He kissed her temple. "If you weren't such a stubborn, determined woman, the past twelve years would have ground you to dust and ashes."

What would those years have been like, if she'd spent them with a man who could see the benefits to be wrung from character traits others considered only flaws? A man who galloped headlong at problems rather than cowered before them?

"I fear for you, and I'm trying to be honest, Hadrian."

"Another fine quality, and in the same spirit, you need to know I called on Lady Collins, but have little to show for it."

Brave of him. Despite the morning sun, Avis felt a chill. "She turned you away?"

"She was all that was genuinely gracious, Avie. It was sad."

"She has a bereaved air." Another cautionary tale.

"She could not recall who all was with her son the day you were assaulted. Collins was in the habit of towing a gang about with him when he was between misdeeds at school. She'll consult with her lady's maid, who has perfect recall where her betters are concerned, and pass along whatever she finds."

The day you were assaulted. Hadrian's reference was neither casual nor apologetic. His words confirmed there had been such a day, while everyone else in Avis's life had assiduously, if silently, exhorted her to forget that.

"The baroness's abigail is Tansy Bilford. She's somewhat of a local legend for keeping journals of everything from snowfalls to first lambs. Her papa was known for the same propensity, and she's been with Lady Collins forever."

Hadrian fell silent, and Avis became aware of him physically—his citrus and clove scent, his heat, his sheer size on the bench right beside her.

"I've missed you," she said, squeezing his hand. The admission was slight, compared to the realization that when Hadrian was with her, she felt settled somehow, less anxious.

Less alone, God help her. He was a good companion in a way Lily had never been.

"I meant to get here before today," Hadrian said, reciprocating that gentle pressure on her fingers. "Without a steward of my own, I get pulled into estate matters at odd times. Have you made any progress determining who had access to your bedroom?"

"Lily and I were interrogating Mrs. Ellerby before you arrived. The two upstairs maids often work together, though, and unless they're colluding against me, they cancel each other out."

"Was that wise?"

"Was what wise?"

"Having that discussion with the housekeeper in Lily's hearing? You need to know I've written to my former bishop, inquiring into the situation that drove Lily's father from the pulpit."

Avis unlinked their hands, though she knew Hadrian's caution was well meant.

"Lily would eventually get wind that I'd questioned Mrs. Ellerby. I posed my queries as preparation for moving to the dower house, because I'll have to choose staff carefully."

He captured her hand again and brought her knuckles to his lips for a kiss.

"You'll move to the dower house, when we're in contemplation of marriage?"

She thought of little else besides his proposal, and his welfare. "I haven't set a date, and I'm not sure I will. I cannot abide that I'd put you in danger, not for anything."

"Your safety is my concern, and I had another reason for calling, besides the pressing need to assure myself you were well and thriving. Have you heard from Fen, Avis?"

"I have, in yesterday's post, and he included a sealed epistle to you, which struck me as odd in the extreme." She fished in her pocket and passed him a small folded and sealed document.

"Why odd?"

"Why not use the king's mail to correspond with you directly? I must assume he's keeping his communications private for a reason, but I can't fathom what it might be."

"Neither can I." Hadrian slit the seal with a penknife and glanced at the contents. "Well, then again..."

"What aren't you telling me, Hadrian? You know I would not disclose a confidence."

"So I have your confidence, but not your troth?" His tone was as close to bitter as she'd ever heard it.

"I hesitate to become your wife, not to hurt you, Hadrian, but because I am your friend and would see you spared more trouble."

"You're mistaken, but because you are my friend, and you will be my wife, you need to know Harold has run off with Lord James, eloped, as it were, and I've every reason to believe Harold and James are on their way here to assist in untangling our difficulties."

Of all the topics to intrude on their discussion, this one was almost humorous. "You're angry at Harold?"

"Scared for him," Hadrian said, sounding like an irritated papa. "He isn't safe here, though, not if he wants to spend much time with Finch. They are love-struck, to put it bluntly."

Blunt indeed, but hardly news to Avis. "They've been great friends for years. You don't like Lord James?"

Hadrian dropped his face to her shoulder, took a slow inhale, then rose and paced off a few steps, hands in his pockets.

"Relations between men are considered unnatural, felonious, sinful, and so forth, but I went to public school and university, Avie. Most men of privilege start their exploration of physical intimacies with other boys at school."

"Delicately put, but I wasn't asking about most men." Though Harold certainly qualified as a man of privilege, as did Lord James.

"Therein lies the rub, for which no theology treatise or bishop's sermon has an answer. Harold is my brother, my only family, and much like a father to me. It's at once simpler and more complicated when the question involves him."

Harold was also sailing back to England when Hadrian's welfare was imperiled. "More complicated how, Hadrian?"

"Right and wrong shouldn't depend on whether the act is committed by a schoolboy or a peer of the realm. If it's a sin, it's a sin."

"You aren't convinced it is."

"Not a great wrong, in any case, not when I see how Finch frets over Harold's happiness, and how Harold lights up when they're together. They genuinely love each other, and Finch provides Harold things I—things nobody else can. I left the church to heed Harold's summons, though I would have left the church anyway, if the alternative was to renounce my beloved only brother."

"That's the simpler part, isn't it?" She rose and threaded her arm through his. "You love your brother and want him to be happy, so you will learn to accept Lord James as Harold's friend, while you assume responsibility for Landover to free your brother from danger."

"Free him from having to choose between being loved and being safe. Have I shocked you? I know you care for Harold, but we've never overtly discussed this."

Having to choose between being loved and being safe. Hadrian had faced the same choice, and despite the threats contained in the recent notes, he'd chosen love.

Avis let that insight wash through her and leaned into the man who'd forsaken safety for her sake.

"One suspected some things about Harold, and I do not begrudge him his happiness any more than you do. Were you and I to marry—and I have not said we will—your brother and his friends would always be welcome in our home."

He held her then, a sudden fierce embrace she hadn't seen coming, and she realized how much he'd kept this anxiety from her. A man could be hanged for the kind of happiness Harold shared with his James, his title and lands stripped, his family ruined.

But Hadrian had only been worried for his brother.

Avis told herself again that Hadrian ought not to risk his safety by marrying her, but she clung to him as fiercely as he clung to her.

CHAPTER EIGHTEEN

The visiting resumed as August slid toward September, but with less of an air of expectation and exploration. To the best of Hadrian's ability, he comported himself as a man quietly enamored of his intended, and their deportment in public was exactly what would be expected of a prospective bride and groom.

Privately, however, Avis's behavior took on a silent desperation that tore at Hadrian's heart. She never went more than a few days without initiating lovemaking, usually when they stopped for tea after the day's social obligations.

Today was no different.

Avis set her plate down and turned a gaze on Hadrian that he'd come to dread.

"I've missed you, Hadrian."

He'd missed her too, though he hated to see her like this—needy, unsettled, yet somehow not emotionally present *to him* even as she sat across the tea service from him. He opened his arms, and she was straddling his lap, kissing him, devouring him with her mouth, and he could not hold his peace.

"Avie, stop."

"You said you wouldn't withhold favors." She started on his cravat. "You promised me that."

"I won't withhold anything from you." He put his hands on her shoulders, for once resenting her determination. "I *cannot* withhold anything from you, but for God's sake, let me lock the door."

Her hands fell away, and at least she blushed at her oversight. He did not assist her when she extricated herself from his lap. When had she'd grown so indifferent to the comforts of a wide, fluffy bed that she must come at him like this?

In bed, he could hold her, he could take his time, he could cherish her and shelter her in his arms while she slept. He wasn't even back across the room before she was embracing him again, running her mouth over his throat and jaw before fisting her hands in his hair and angling his head for her kiss.

"I love your hair like this," she muttered, "long enough to sink my hands—"

He turned her and backed her against his estate desk, feeling despair even as his body leapt at the contact with hers.

"Hadrian…I want…"

"I know what you want, but do you know *whom* you want, Avis? You've refused to choose a date for our wedding."

He covered her mouth with his, lest he hear again that she hadn't, in fact, agreed to marry him. The rational part of his mind looked down from the crown molding at a man too pathetic to protest when he was being used.

But used for what? Hadrian loved this woman, he wanted only to protect her and keep her safe, and what she wanted baffled him. He nursed the ache of that frustration like a precious flame on a cold, windy night, because the temptation to get Avis with child loomed with the allure of original sin.

He really should escort her to the stables, then immerse himself neck deep into the quarry pond until autumn arrived. What kept him in the room with her was the certain knowledge that she was no happier than he, that the entire situation had left her as miserable and desperate as she made him.

"We're visiting the Davises tomorrow, aren't we?" she asked, untying Hadrian's cravat. "After the drapes are hung in the dower house?"

"We must talk, Avis." Hadrian backed away, assisted her off the desk, and retied his cravat. When he was again presentable, he unlocked the door and led her to the sofa. "I've spoken with Vicar Chadwick, Avie."

"About?"

"*I* have set a date. I told him we'll be married the last Sunday of the month, in his church."

"You *set a date?* We haven't told anybody, haven't planned a wedding breakfast."

About which, neither of them cared. Hadrian had shocked Avis rather than pleased her.

"Everybody's welcome." Announcing the wedding date when there might not be a bride at the service seemed a detail.

"This is not wise, Hadrian. Before, I'd go months between notes. I've had three since we became engaged. I'm worried for you, though I've sensed you've grown weary of the entire business. Perhaps we should cry off."

"I've wearied," he agreed, kissing her knuckles, "of your unwillingness to admit we should be together. Of being used only to store up memories to warm your dotage, while your life passes you by. Of seeing you waste yourself on silly notions of what I deserve, when you care for me and I more than care for you."

"You care too much, Hadrian. You aren't thinking clearly. For weeks you've been trying to decipher from what quarter harm stalks us, and you have not succeeded. Perhaps we simply need to admit that even given more time—"

She had given twelve years of her life to fear and regret. He wanted to give her safety, love, children.

Himself.

"I won't argue with a lady." He *should not* argue with a lady. "Landover is under my control, and you would be safe here, from notes, from gossip, from everything but your own stubbornness. All well and good for you to consign yourself to misery, but you've decided I don't deserve to be happy, either."

"You don't know you'll be safe if I marry you," she said, while tears sheened her eyes, and she couldn't hold his gaze.

He used one index finger to lift a tear from her cheek and bring it to his lips. "You, my love, are lying to yourself. You tell yourself that your heart isn't breaking, that you'll be relieved when I no longer darken your door. That I'll be out of harm's way, and that matters more than being happy or loved. Oh, and this little business of passion beneath the wide Cumbrian sky was mere frolic and merriment. Why can't you trust that you will be safe as my wife, and I will be safe as your husband?"

He didn't slam the door when he went to summon a footman. He even escorted Avis to the stables and gave her a leg up onto her horse. When the groom walked a cob off to a discreet distance, Hadrian set a hand on Avis's boot.

"I haven't said I love you, because my sense is you would be burdened by such a declaration, but I am burdened by withholding my sentiments, Avie. I have known hurt in my life—"

He'd known disappointment, bewilderment, and heartache. Nobody arrived to the age of thirty, buried a spouse, sent his only brother to live in a distant land, and shepherded a congregation without knowing pain.

But this, this *cowering victimhood* Avis imposed on them both threatened to fell him. And yet, she had not ridden off, had not fled his declaration.

And had not precisely cried off—yet.

"I do love you," he said softly. "I love you, Avie Portmaine. I shall always love you, and the hell of it is, I would not change that for anything. Godspeed."

She kneed her horse away, but not before he saw that he'd once again made her cry. Before the lump in his own throat got the better of his composure, he marched back to the safety of his library, there to consider holy scripture, and unholy measures against those who quoted it to torment his lady.

* * *

"You've been closeted here ever since you returned from your calls with your intended," Harold observed.

Harald, rather, as this incarnation of Lord Landover sported a closely trimmed reddish beard, skin burnished by the northern sun, and blue eyes that sparkled in contrast to his complexion, as well as muscles common to those who spent their life in vigorous sport. He was altogether a more robust, happier creature than Harold Bothwell had ever been.

"My former intended," Hadrian replied. The habit of honesty between them was growing, apparently.

"I thought you said you'd set a date. She's broken it off?"

"Not in so many words." Hadrian rose from his desk—Harold's desk?—and came around to stare out the window at the long view toward Blessings.

"Then you're still engaged. Legally, it isn't a detail, Hay."

"You need me free to be engaged to somebody who can bear the Landover heir, I know."

"I need you free to be happy, but you've banished Fen, who might have taken on some of the stewarding for you, and you're spending too much time squiring Lady Avis about, when nobody would dare mistreat her in your presence."

"That wasn't the point."

"What was the point?" Harold regarded him with familiar patience, not reacting, not letting emotion pull him off balance. The sunburn and whiskers brought out the blue of his eyes wonderfully.

"I've missed you." Maybe honesty was a *bad* habit.

"I'm here now," Harold said slowly, "and I missed you too."

"A life of gay abandon roaming the seas with James wasn't adequate?"

"We're quite settled outside Copenhagen," Harold countered easily, "but no, it won't be enough, and James cares enough about me and is secure enough in my regard that we need not content ourselves with that. This visit was his idea."

A veritable doting uncle—or something—was James Finch. Hadrian tried to stir up resentment, but was too damned grateful to see his brother.

"James has already apologized for presuming on my welcome," Hadrian said tiredly. "My quarrel is not with you or your—with you or James. I was squiring Avie about in hopes of drawing out her detractor."

Also in hopes of winning her heart, but the flaming, roasting hell of it all was that Hadrian had the sense he'd done that, perhaps done that long ago.

"Have you been successful?"

"To some extent. She's received more notes, but only notes."

"This constitutes failure?"

"I've failed utterly." Hadrian's gaze swung back to the window and a view that could not have been prettier. Any morning now, frost would nip at the remaining flowers, and summer's brief hold on the land would be over. "My personal agenda for this social campaign was to woo my intended into a real engagement."

"She wasn't woo-able?"

"She's stuck in her cage. Fen was right."

"Whatever that means. Fen should show up soon, you know. Harvest is nearly upon us."

Hadrian turned to face this beloved stranger who was his brother. "He's on his way. I haven't succeeded in exonerating him, so he's another failed aspect of my campaign."

"A rather magnificent failure."

"You're not to flirt with him, Harold."

"Tell that to James." Harold's smile was indulgent, and not a smile Hadrian had seen on his brother previously—happily indulgent, and wasn't that just *delightful.* "If there are no nuptials in the offing, Finch and I had better prepare to hoist sail."

"Can you stay until the end of the month?"

"Of course."

Harold bussed his cheek, a display Hadrian could not have imagined his brother indulging in six months earlier, and left. The gesture was continental, and far more comforting than all the desperate kisses Hadrian had shared with his—

His un-intended.

Hadrian tormented himself for a week before finding the resolve to formally break the engagement, a week in which Fenwick sent word of his impending return, and Avis remained silent, while Harold sent worried looks to Finch, and Hadrian spent as much time on Caesar as he could.

He gave up the pretense of inspecting his land when he realized he was listening for the sound of a solo flute wherever he went. He could ride his property for twenty years without saying what needed to be said between him and Avis Portmaine. He'd just turned Caesar toward Blessings, his heart aching at the discussion to come, when Harold met him on the bridle path.

"I bear a message."

"From?" Please Almighty God, let it be from Avie.

"Lady Collins." Harold passed over a note, folded and sealed.

Hadrian scanned the contents, knowing it could not be good news. "She begs the favor of a call."

"Shall I come with you?"

"No, thank you." Hadrian tucked the note away. "The nature of the discussion will be uncomfortable, for her at least. I have a call to pay at Blessings when I'm done with Lady Collins, so don't wait tea on me."

"As you wish, but Hay? Don't do anything you'll regret. The call on Blessings can wait."

"Anything I'll regret?" Hadrian's smile was bleak. "You mean anything *more* I'll regret."

* * *

Hadrian changed his mind about the order of his calls because Blessing was on the way to the Collins's estate, and the task before him would not grow easier for being put off. Lily Prentiss joined him in Avie's pretty little parlor when he'd specifically asked to see the lady of the house.

"Lady Avis is indisposed," Lily said, her smile regretful. "Have you a message you'd have me give her?"

"No. No message. Is she ill?"

"Simply indisposed. I gather you and she have hit a rough patch?"

Her blue eyes held nothing but commiseration, and Hadrian wondered fleetingly if he'd misjudged the woman.

"Not a rough patch, exactly, but we do need to talk."

"You needn't say more." She patted his arm. "You're a good man, but she's not the lady for you. No one will judge you. You were eager to take a bride and do your duty to the succession, and they will unfortunately expect Lady Avis to cry off."

"I wasn't aware our engagement was over," Hadrian said evenly.

Lily withdrew her hand. "I didn't mean to offend, and of course I won't say anything until I hear it from Avis herself."

"See that you don't."

She regarded him evenly, despite his abrupt tone. "Blessed are they that mourn, Mr. Bothwell, for they shall be comforted."

Matthew, Hadrian mentally recited the reference, *chapter five, verse four.*

He took his leave of her, wondering if she'd intended that he be comforted by her words, or had she been assuring him that Avie would be comforted?

He pondered that conundrum all the way to Lady Collins's shabby little parlor, but when he heard what the baroness had to tell him, he was not comforted in the least—he was sufficiently alarmed to send Caesar back toward Blessings at a flat-out gallop.

* * *

"What on God's green earth are you doing here?" Lily Prentiss spat the question at Ashton Fenwick, who was exhausted, filthy, and thoroughly out of charity with life as he led his horse into the stable yard.

"I live here," he said, "I work here, and my friends are here. No doubt, you are peevish because you've been missing me, Lily."

"I have not given you leave—"

"Yes, I know, to use your name, to worship the ground you mince about on, to gaze longingly in your direction, or otherwise breathe the same air as you.

Fortunately, as a subject of our illustrious if mad monarch, I am privileged to breathe good English air nonetheless. You're blocking my way."

"No, Fenwick. It's you who's been blocking my way, and I've finally found the means to see that it stops."

Fen was not in the mood for her nonsense. The woman needed a good swiving, or perhaps a birching. Maybe Lily was the type to blend those two pleasures.

"You are being cryptic, my dear. How tiresome. I suppose next you will banish me from your kingdom with a magic spell, except it isn't your kingdom, is it, Lily love? The kingdom belongs to the Portmaines, among whom, greedy little dreams to the contrary, you do not number. Move aside."

"I'm warning you, Fenwick, you have insulted me for the last time. You can either take your leave now, or I'll see you charged, convicted and hanged, mark my words."

"Ah, finally, women have been given the headache of serving as magistrates." Fenwick handed his tired horse off to a groom. "We can expect failure to wipe our boots to soon number among punishable felonies. Please move."

She walloped him, as he'd intended, but it did nothing to reduce the feral glitter in her eyes.

"Lily Prentiss." Avis's voice cracked across the stable yard like a whip. "You are dismissed from your duties in my household, without a character, *this instant*."

* * *

Avis's voice had Hadrian shoving Caesar into a stall, for Fen knew not what manner of adversary he had in Lily.

"Lady Avis." Fenwick offered his employer a low bow and rubbed his jaw while eyeing Lily warily.

What in God's name was Avie doing in the stables now of all times?

"You don't mean that," Lily said, as she stood shaking in the stable doorway. "You can't mean that, Avis. You don't know what he's done. You don't know—"

"So tell her," Hadrian suggested, moving down the barn aisle and gesturing at the groom to get the hell away from the unfolding drama. "Tell her what you think Fenwick has done, Lily."

Fen did not turn at the sound of Hadrian's voice, suggesting he'd seen the wild light in Lily's eyes and knew better than to let down his guard.

"I'll tell her." Lily snatched Fen's knife from its sheath at his waist. "I'll tell her this miserable excuse for a man was one of those who abducted her and allowed her to be raped twelve years ago. He wasn't content to see her ruined, but he must perpetuate all manner of gossip about her, when he drinks at the local tavern, when he flirts with the ladies, when he works with the menfolk. He hates you, Avis, hates you and has betrayed your trust. You must see that."

"Put the knife down, Lily." Hadrian advanced on her steadily, willing to risk even the knife rather than allow Lily to turn her attention on Avis. "We'll hold accountable any who've wronged Lady Avis."

"He hasn't merely wronged her," Lily insisted, brandishing the knife in Fen's direction. "He's threatened her, in writing, for years, haven't you, Fenwick?"

"The knife," Hadrian urged quietly, holding out his hand. Lily's gaze flickered, from him to Avis, and in that moment, Hadrian charged her, snatching the knife, tossing it to the ground, and dragging the woman into his arms.

Out in the stable yard, Handy danced away, the groom barely hanging on to the reins, and silence fell, broken by the sound of Lily's tearful voice.

"That man isn't your friend," Lily said. "*I* am your friend, Avis. *I* am the one who has tried to protect you, the one who has kept you safe here at Blessings. They don't understand, they don't see you should be here *with me*, that this is where you belong. They're men, and they'll never understand."

"Lily." Hadrian kept his voice calm when he wanted to throttle the woman. "Give it up."

"I'll never give her up," Lily countered. "Avis belongs with me. She does. Blessings prospers when she heeds my guidance, and she's happy here with me."

"We know, Lily," Hadrian tried again, though Lily wasn't even struggling as he held her. "You wrote the notes, you spread the gossip, you undermined Avis's peace and well-being at every turn."

"I would never!"

"You learned of Fenwick's involvement from Tansy Bilford," Hadrian said, for Lady Collins's abigail had confirmed not only that Fen had been present twelve years ago, but also that Lily Prentiss had learned of it early in her tenure at Blessings. "What I want to know is, how did you know about the notes?"

Now Lily struggled against his hold. "She told—"

Avis shook her head slowly. "I never breathed a word of those notes to you. Not one word."

Proof beyond a reasonable doubt. Something went out of Lily, hope, hatred, a combination of the two. Hadrian could no longer stand to touch her. He passed Lily into Fen's grasp and crossed the stable yard to put an arm around Avis's shoulders.

"We'll need the magistrate," he said. "Lily's transgressions include threatening my life." A small transgression compared to the slander she'd spread about Avis.

"No magistrate," Avis murmured.

Fen knotted off a length of twine binding Lily's wrist, though she stood dazed and docile—for now.

"Lily isn't wrong," Fen said. "I committed chargeable offenses. I was there, just as she says I was, or there for much of it."

"I know, Fen," Avis said. "I've always known, and now is not the time."

Fen's eyes registered no less astonishment than Hadrian felt.

"I'll see Lily secured under guard in a guest room," Fen volunteered. "Bothwell, I am at your disposal."

And then Hadrian and Avis were alone, their arms around each other in the stable yard.

"How did you know?" Avis put the question to him even as she clung to him with gratifying ferocity.

"After I'd stopped here to speak with you earlier, I went to visit Lady Collins, who told me of Fen's involvement."

"You were here earlier?"

"I was, but Lily said you were indisposed and offered her condolences on the end of our engagement." *The bitch.*

"I'm not indisposed. She was growing quite bold. Doubtless she intended to put me in her debt by casting aspersion on Fen."

Avis had never needed a companion. She'd needed friends, and family, neighbors, and *Hadrian.*

"Lily quoted scripture at me, and then I recalled you telling me her father was clergy who'd left the church for a position in trade. There was a scandal there, Avie, something particularly unpleasant. My bishop wouldn't pass along many details about Prentiss's situation, but Prentiss didn't leave the church voluntarily. He was defrocked."

"The scripture is how you knew Lily was my enemy?"

A good old biblical term—enemy. Hadrian's guts churned to think how badly Avis's trust in her companion had been abused.

"All of your notes had a biblical cast to them," he said, "and all the worst gossip about you was from the women. You'd told me Lily socialized more than you did. Lady Collins had questioned her maid, who remarked Lily's willingness to spread veiled contumely regarding you, and further commented that Lily was very interested to learn Fenwick had been among Collins's cronies."

Avis was a substantial woman, but in his arms, she felt frail, as if the first chilly autumn breeze might blow her away.

"You weren't surprised by Tansy's recitation, were you, Hadrian?"

"I was disappointed." Hadrian eased back. "When I saw Lady Collins earlier, she told me Fen was Collins's cousin. I withheld that information because I didn't regard it as relevant, and I did not want to upset you."

While Avis had withheld the same information, likely to protect Fen—and Hadrian.

"I knew Fen was among Collins's familiars the day I was assaulted, but I didn't want you judging him for crimes he did not commit."

"Excuse me." Fen stood on the path leading to the gardens, looking uncertain and weary. "Lily is behind a locked door, guarded by two men I trust, but did I just hear you both say you knew of my involvement with Avis's assault, and my relation to Collins, and neither one of you accused me of further wrongdoing?"

"There was no further wrongdoing," Avis said, facing him. "Alex noted your resemblance to the young man who galloped off from the group as we approached the cottage. I don't know if she recognized you, but I did."

"I told them all I was going to keep watch," Fen said, expression miserable. "I hadn't even gone to university at that point. They were older than I, bigger than I was, holding their liquor better than I could, and capable of taking my life if I thwarted them."

He kicked at his knife, glinting in the dirt of the stable yard, then went on speaking. "In hindsight, I've often wished they had taken my life. I went to find help, Avie, but we were in the middle of a great, sprawling wood, and I got turned around, and there was no help. There was no help at all, so I went galloping back to the scene, claiming we were about to be discovered, but I was too late. I was too bloody late."

He raised closed eyes to the heavens. "I am so sorry."

Confession was the worst trial for all concerned.

"So you've atoned," Hadrian said, "by keeping her safe ever since."

"Not ever since. I ran back to Scotland to attend university, but couldn't run from the memory of what was done to Avis and to Lady Alexandra. I came back and put myself in service here. I did not think I was recognized—I'd gained height and muscle—or I would not have made Avis or Lady Alex look on my face."

Avis left Hadrian's side and went to her friend. "You must not blame yourself. You must not." She wrapped her arms around him and held him, while Fen buried his face against her hair.

"I'm sorry, Avie, I'm just so damned—"

"Hush."

They clung to each other for long, long moments, while Hadrian mourned for twelve wasted years.

And was not comforted.

CHAPTER NINETEEN

Fen might have been crying. Avis wasn't sure and didn't want to know if he was. She kept her arms around him, hurting for her younger self, for Alexandra, and now for Fenwick, who'd banished himself to Blessings because as a boy, he'd failed a challenge many men would never have attempted.

"Ashton Fenwick, you must know I do not blame you. Sixteen is young, and Collins's family would not have held him accountable for harm befalling you."

They hadn't held Collins accountable for the harm Avis and Alex had suffered.

Fen eased out of Avis's embrace. "I don't deserve your understanding, Avis Portmaine, but I'm grateful for it. Vim and Benjamin didn't know who they were hiring, or they'd have likely turned me over to the magistrate."

"So you took a great risk to remain at Blessings. God knows what Lily might have got up to had you not been on hand to keep her in check. I see no need to inform my brothers of your connection to Collins."

He was puzzled by this forbearance, clearly, but Avis did not have time to explain to him that forgiveness was one of few powers left to a crime victim. Hadrian had disappeared into the stables, and it was to Hadrian that Avis owed the greater debt.

"Go up to the house, Fen. Get something to eat, and tell the maids to pack up Lily's effects."

"Shall I send for the magistrate?"

A clip-clop of hooves coming up the barn aisle distracted Avis from answering. Hadrian drew Caesar to a halt as the horse emerged from the gloom of the barn into the quiet of the stable yard.

"I must discuss potential charges with Hadrian, for Lily threatened my happiness, but she might have taken Hadrian's life."

Something silently passed between the men, an entire discussion that Avis could only guess at—about responsibility, friendship, and trust.

"Bothwell, get off your horse," Fen said, "the lady wants a word with you."

"Go, Fen," Avis said, shoving at his shoulder. "I want a word with Hadrian *in private*." She wanted much more than a word, too.

But what did Hadrian want?

He swung off his horse and looped the reins around the hitching post. "I am at your service, Lady Avis, for I want a word with you too."

So grave. Did he want a word of parting, because Avis had kept Fen's identity from him? Because Lily had been found out and her scheme finally foiled? Because Avis had not agreed to his choice of wedding date?

"Walk me up to the pond," Avis said, for if she was to beg, let it be in a place that had wonderful memories for them both.

Hadrian bellowed for a groom to see to his horse, then winged his arm at Avis. She grabbed for his hand instead and kept hold of it until they'd reached the still silver mirror of the quarry pond.

"The blankets are still here," Avis said, surprised to see the hamper tucked in the shade of the rowan.

Hadrian dropped her hand and marched over the tree. "Did you think they wouldn't be?"

She'd thought exactly that. She'd assumed that when she'd balked at his proffer of a wedding date, Hadrian had quit the marital field.

"Cooler weather's coming,' she said as Hadrian snapped the blankets out over the grass. "Summers here are brief, and winters fierce."

"And you've been denied twelve summers of trysts by the pond, twelve winters of cuddling with a husband before a cozy fire. What will you do to redress that larceny?"

"What will I do with Lily?" For Avis couldn't read Hadrian's mood, couldn't even establish the topic of their conversation. Desperation welled at his clipped tone, a fear that now, now when she needed Hadrian more than ever, he'd decide that his objective had been achieved—or could be abandoned.

"What I'd like to see befall Lily," he said from across the spread blankets, "and what a former churchman's scruples suggest should be her fate, I leave as conundrum for you to resolve. I doubt she is entirely sane and thus cannot endorse summoning the magistrate."

"I don't care what happens to Lily. I don't even want to talk about her." Not now, especially. "Will you sit with me, Hadrian?"

He looked out over the pond, an expanse of cool silver that would soon be edged with ice. "I'd rather lie with you."

He'd muttered. Avis couldn't be sure exactly what he'd said. "I beg your pardon?"

"I would rather lie with you," he said, dropping to the blankets, and wrenching off a boot. "I would rather make passionate love to you, raise a family with you, and ensure that Landover continues to prosper for several more generations at least. You will please join me on these blankets *this instant.*"

Avis nearly fainted onto the blanket, for polite, dear, considerate Hadrian Bothwell, former vicar of St. Michael's of the Sword, was working up to a proper rant.

"You are not withdrawing your proposal?"

He tossed his second boot to the edge of the blanket. "I won't allow you to send me on my way, Avis Portmaine. Nobody's threatening anybody now, unless you consider holy matrimony a threat."

He started on her boots next, a man very intent on his task.

"You don't need to marry me to keep me safe, Hadrian, and I do not consider holy matrimony a threat."

"Wait until our sons use the portrait gallery to practice their archery," he said, reaching beneath Avis's skirts to loosen her garters. His touch was far from loverlike, but he was certainly getting the job done.

"We're to have sons, plural?"

He paused, Avis's stockings in his hand, and gave her a look that should have set the nearby pond to boiling. "Winters in Cumberland are long and cold, Harold needs his heirs, and I need you, Avie."

Avie, he'd called her *Avie.*

"How could you possibly need me? I let that vile woman keep me cowering and alone at Blessings for years, let her convince me I deserved all the talk she kept circulating about me. I want to slap her, Hadrian, to see her pilloried as she pilloried me, and have her whipped at the cart's tail all the way to London."

Now, now when Avis needed to keep her wits about her, tears welled, and words fled.

"Avie, don't cry. You cannot cry now, when I'm trying to confirm a date for our wedding. I forbid it, and I'm begging you, woman—"

He kissed her, soundly, deeply, passionately, and Avis kissed him back, until they were sprawled on the blankets, Hadrian's jacket tossed in the direction of his boots, his cravat hanging from the lowest branch of the rowan like a white flag of surrender.

He lifted his mouth away from hers and remained crouching over her. "You're entitled to be angry, Avis. Furious and hurt and raging, all of it. You're not entitled to send me away again. I won't politely accommodate your wishes this time. I can no longer be that sort of gentleman if its means I lose you."

This Hadrian didn't propose out of duty or loneliness, and Avis had no intention of sending him on his way.

"Twelve years ago, I was young and confused, Hadrian. I know what and who I want now, I know who I am. You can set any date you like, but promise me, you'll never leave me."

He gave her that promise, with words, with kisses, and with intimacies as brilliant as the Cumbrian sunshine, until darkness fell, and they wandered down the hill, arm in arm, a date set, and names picked out for the first several of their children.

* * *

"Mrs. Ellerby has declared herself in love with you, and you've been overheard singing to Handy," Hadrian informed Fenwick. "A barely recognizable baritone rendering of 'Green Grow the Rashes,' though why you'd inflict such sentiments on a gelding, I do not know."

"I'm that pleased to have escorted Lily Prentiss back to her mother's household," Fen said, ambling along a path that wound through golden birches, "and Handy has a fine ear."

Handy had a fine owner, whom Hadrian was about to enlist in some mischief. "Has Avis left to pay her call on Gran Carruthers?"

"Am I your spy, Bothwell, to report Lady Avis's comings and goings to her fiancé? In another week, Avis will be coming and going from Landover, unless you bungle badly."

Perhaps Handy had a prescient owner as well. "I was rather hoping we could do some spying together. I've been thinking about correspondence, notes, and Lily Prentiss. Will you sit with me for a moment?"

Fen wasn't wearing his knife, and he wasn't wearing a smile either. "Bothwell, I don't know what you have in mind, but if it's something Avis should know about, then I will not for any reason—"

Hadrian took a seat on the same bench he'd occupied when he'd overheard vicious gossip about Avie. "Cease bleating, Fen. I'm not going behind Avis's back, but I've been thinking."

Fen sat beside him, making the bench creak. "You're soon to be a new husband. Thinking isn't what Avis will need from you for a good while."

"Jealous?"

Fen crossed long legs at the ankle. "Brutally. If you hurt or offend Avis in any way, I will hunt you down and sing all my Scottish ballads to you in public."

"I'll take the best care of her, Fen, and do my utmost to make her happy." For in the ways that mattered, Fenwick was the one relinquishing Avie into Hadrian's arms.

"See that you do. Now what has troubled your febrile imagination?"

"I wrote to Avie when I was off to Oxford all those years ago. What happened to that letter?"

The breeze stirred the leaves twittering on the birches, a current of not quite cool air laden with the scent of dying undergrowth.

"Lily was not on hand to steal any letters twelve years ago," Fen said. "Avis wasn't on hand either. She told me she was off to her Aunt's for some time with Lady Alex immediately following Collins's assault."

"I sent my first letters to her here at Blessings. Let's say they went astray, or Vim held them for her and forgot about them—or perhaps they passed those letters to Lily. What I want to know, though, is what happened to the letter I sent *less than seven years ago*, before I married Rue?"

Fen uncrossed his ankles and sat up. "You think because Lily Prentiss dealt in notes, she might also have been tampering with correspondence?"

Hadrian knew it, the way he'd known, two minutes into a sermon on marriage, which of his flock had been straying.

"I want my letters, Fen. Lily Prentiss was sly, conniving and not quite rational, and she coveted everything Avis was owed, everything Avis was. It makes sense Ben or Vim would might have given her the early letters to pass along to Avis at an appropriate moment, but what of the most recent one? I want your help searching Lily's quarters."

Fen stood, and shadows cast by the birches danced over his features, giving his countenance a fey, whimsical quality. "I knew there was a reason I didn't allow Avie to burn all of Lily's effects. Come along, Bothwell, lest the footmen find your maudlin prose and read it to the maids."

Hadrian rose and fell in step beside Fen, whose pace was brisk indeed.

"Do I take it you haven't inventoried Lily's effects yet yourself?"

"Not successfully."

Ah, well. "Two heads are better than one," Hadrian said, "though one appreciates loyalty and initiative in one's friends."

Fen paused, his hand on the door to a side entrance. "Good to know, Bothwell. One appreciates a tolerant nature as well."

"You can't help it that your singing voice is abominable. Get moving."

* * *

Avis had spent half the morning reading and rereading two of Hadrian's letters, which Lily—may she end her days scrubbing chamberpots in her mother's pokey little cottage—had secreted in her sewing basket.

"Come along, my dear, or we'll be late." A tanned, bearded, and smiling version of Harold, Viscount Landover, waited in the doorway to Avis's private parlor. "Hadrian will suffer apoplexies if I deliver you to the church even one minute past the appointed hour."

Avis rose, for she did not want to be even one second late. "Will I do, Harold?" She turned for him, enjoying the swish and sway of a soft green dress she'd been saving for a special occasion.

"You are a vision, a happy one, I think."

"I am happy, and by the end of the day, I expect to be happier."

Avis took his arm, and let him escort her to his coach. She wished her siblings might have attended the wedding, but in their absence—Alexandra's letter was late this month for some reason—Harold was the nearest thing she had to family.

Then too, delaying the wedding another few weeks to allow her siblings to travel to Blessings had no appeal whatsoever.

"Are you nervous, Avis?"

"Of course, not. People get married all the time. A small ceremony on a pretty morning shouldn't be an occasion for nerves."

"Very sensible of you." Harold looked so much like Hadrian when he smiled.

"If Fenwick were here, he'd threaten to turn you over his knee for smirking like that, Harold Bothwell."

"Fenwick is at the church, ensuring a certain brother of mine is present for this small ceremony."

Hadrian would be at the church, of that, Avis had no doubt. Twelve years ago, he'd written to Avis not to ask for her hand, but to ask her permission to wait for her until she was ready to hear a proposal of marriage.

Seven years ago, he'd written again, to ask if there were any hope of paying her his addresses, for she'd remained dear to him, and was daily in his prayers. Avis had needed those prayers desperately, and would thank Hadrian for them after the ceremony.

"That is not the look of a woman anticipating holy matrimony with her adored swain," Harold said. "Shall I turn the coach around?"

"Don't you dare, Harold. I was thinking that if Lily's sole transgression were to steal a certain letter Hadrian wrote to me seven years ago, I'd still wish Lily to the Antipodes."

"And rightly so, but I can assure you, East Bogmore is a worse fate than the Antipodes. I made inquires, Avis, and neither Mr. Prentiss nor his wife is possessed of a sweet temper. Lily will step and fetch for both of them as well as for her mother's older sisters, and have the cold pity of the entire parish."

"Fitting, considering how lavishly she pitied me." That pity would devastate Lily, and was probably the most arduous penance that could be inflicted on her.

The carriage slowed, and despite Avis's brave lies to Harold, butterflies leapt in her middle. The ceremony would be very quiet, and yet, it would be at the church. Avis had avoided the church and nearly all gatherings with her neighbors for years.

"Courage," Harold said as the coachman halted the team. "Hadrian is arse over teakettle for you, and he has paid many, many calls this week in anticipation of your nuptials."

This was news to Avis, who'd assumed Hadrian had spent his time overseeing the harvest, enjoying the final days of Harold's visit, and readying Landover to receive the next lady of the manor.

"I would have paid those calls with him, Harold," Avis said, though she would not have enjoyed them.

"There's something you need to know, Avis, something I'm sure Hadrian plans to tell you after the ceremony, so please contrive to be surprised when you hear this news."

Harold's gaze reflected no merriment, but they were at the church, so surely his news could not be entirely bad.

"Tell me," she said, "for in less than a minute, I intend to dash up that church aisle and become Mrs. Hadrian Bothwell."

"Benjamin sent a pigeon with the news that Hart Collins has died in a riding accident. Lady Alex was apparently in the vicinity at the time, though Ben has yet to provide the details. Alex is fine, Ben is fine. You will be fine too."

He climbed out of the coach, while Avis anticipated some sense of relief, some change, *something* as a result of Collins's departure from the earthly realm.

All she felt was impatience, and a burning urgency to speak her vows. Hart Collins could indeed, well and truly, finally, be laid to rest. She would be grateful for that realization just as soon as she was married to Hadrian, and had celebrated the blessings of the wedded state at length and enthusiastically.

Avis climbed out of the carriage, into a church yard as crowded with vehicles as it might have been on Easter morning.

"Harold, what are all of these coaches doing here?"

"I haven't a clue," Harold said, leading her up the steps to the church doorway. "Hadrian's inside, Avis, his heart in his throat, his gaze glued to the doors he hopes you'll come through any moment. Fen's ready to drag you up the aisle if you don't go willingly, and James and I will abet him."

Harold was smiling. He was also in deadly earnest. Avis put her gloved hand on his arm and two liveried footmen swung the doors wide.

A moment later Avis approached the altar and saw Hadrian, her friend, her fiancé, her lover, her every wish, dream, and hope come true. He stood at the altar beside a smiling Fenwick, his hand extended to her for all to see. Flute music filled her ears, soaring and sweet, while the entire congregation rose in a show of respect and goodwill.

Hadrian had done this—filled the church with nearly every soul in the shire, some of whom Avis barely knew, but each of whom she'd be happy to get to know in the churchyard, at the assemblies, at market, and as Landover's lady.

No bride ever received a more precious or appreciated wedding gift from her groom. When Hadrian kissed his wife shortly thereafter, the applause shook the rafters of the little church.

Ashton Justician Bothwell was born exactly eight and a half months after the wedding, and his christening was attended by his family's Danish contingent, the entire shire, and his godfather, the newly belted Earl of Kilkenney.

He was soon blessed with siblings a-plenty, not a one of whom showed a vocation for the church, and all of whom—including his sisters—had a sorry tendency to practice their archery in the Landover portrait gallery.

THE END

To my dear Readers,

I hope you enjoyed Hadrian and Avie's story, because I certainly had fun writing it. I'm sure you noticed that Fenwick teased us in that last scene by acquiring an earldom. Ever since Hadrian's book first came out, I've been asking Fenwick, "What's with that earldom, you? Spill the old beans so I can write the book, please."

I got *the eyebrow* in response, until earlier this year. I'm happy to say that Fenwick's story, **Ashton: Lord of Truth**, will be on sale as of September 20, 2016 (September 9, if you download the ebook from my website store). Fenwick has been chafing under the burden of a title for three long years, and has accepted that it's time he found a countess and tended to the succession.

He doesn't want much, just true love and mutual, unending devotion. In Matilda Bryce he finds trouble, secrets, and kisses worth stealing—and true love, too, of course. I've included an excerpt below.

In October, I'm putting out a novella duet, **The Virtues of Christmas**, which features two Regency holiday stories, one for Michael Brenner and Henrietta Whitlow, a second for advice columnist Patience Friendly and her stubborn Grinch of a publisher, Douglas MacHugh.

If the name MacHugh rings a bell, that's because we met a fellow named Hamish MacHugh in **The Captive**. Hamish, if you'll recall, is big, Scottish, and has a wary respect for the ladies. He crosses paths with Miss Megan Windham, and soon lands on his kilted backside—literally and figuratively. **The Trouble With Dukes** hits the shelves December 20, 2016, and is the first in the Windham Brides series.

To stay up to date with all of my releases, signings, and sales, you can sign up for my newsletter, like my Facebook page, or follow me on Twitter. I love to hear from my readers, so please don't be shy.

Happy reading!
Grace Burrowes

ASHTON: LORD OF TRUTH

A bump-and-jostle of the criminal variety introduced Ashton Fenwick to his temporary salvation.

Fortunately, she was neither the little thief who so deftly dipped a hand into his pocket, nor the buxom decoy who feigned awkwardly colliding with him immediately thereafter while the real pickpocket quietly dodged off into the Haymarket crowd.

Or tried to.

Ashton was exhausted from traveling hundreds of miles on horseback, and had barely noticed the thief's touch amid the sights, noise, and stink of London's bustling streets. In the instant after the bump, and before the jostle part of the proceedings—a game girl, from the looks of her paint and pallor—Ashton realized how London had welcomed him.

"Stop the wee lad in the cap!" he bellowed. "He's nicked my purse!"

Five yards down the walkway, a woman darted into the path of the fleeing thief and faced off with him. A housewife from the looks of her. Plain brown cloak, simple straw hat, serviceable leather gloves rather than the cotton or lace variety.

Ashton had an abiding respect for the British housewife. If the nation had a backbone, she was it, not her yeoman or shopkeeping husband, whose primary purpose was keeping brewers in business and the wife in childbed.

The lady was nimble and sharp-eyed. When the child dodged left, so did she, and she never took her gaze off the miscreant.

"Give it up, Helen. You chose the wrong mark." A hint of the north graced the woman's inflection, also a hint of the finishing school. A lovely combination.

The child gazed up, though the woman was diminutive, then small shoulders squared. "You needn't take on, Mrs. Bryce. I dint nick 'is purse."

"You didn't steal my purse," Ashton said, letting the thief's accomplice scurry away, "because I know better than to keep it where it can be stolen, but you got my lucky handkerchief."

"Hit's just a bleedin' 'ankerchief," the girl shot back. "Take it." She withdrew Ashton's bit of silk from inside her grubby coat, the white square a stark contrast to her dirty little fingers.

A crowd had gathered, because Londoners did not believe in allowing anybody privacy if a moment portended the smallest bit of drama. Some people looked affronted, but most appeared entertained by the thought of the authorities hauling the girl away.

"Helen, what have I told you about stealing?" Mrs. Bryce asked.

Helen's hands went to skinny hips clad in boy's trousers. "What 'ave I told you about starvin', Mrs. B? Me and Sissy don't care for it. 'E don't need 'is lucky piece as much as me and Sissy do."

Somebody in the crowd mentioned sending for a patroller from nearby Bow Street, and if one of those worthies arrived, the child's fate would be sealed.

"We won't settle this here," Ashton said, taking the thief by one slender wrist. "Let's repair to the Goose and have a civilized discussion."

The girl's eyes filled not with fear, but with utter terror. Ashton was big, male, and he was proposing to take the child away from the safety of public scrutiny. Well, she should be terrified.

"Mrs. Bryce," Ashton went on, "if you'd accompany us, I'd appreciate it. Ashton Fenwick, at your service."

"Matilda Bryce." She sketched a curtsey. "Come peacefully, Helen. Unless you want to find yourself being examined by the magistrate tomorrow morning."

The child was obviously inventorying options, looking for a moment to wrench free of Ashton's grasp. As many spectators as had gathered, somebody would snabble her, and she'd be in Newgate by this time tomorrow.

"If you'd join us for a pint and plate, Mrs. Bryce," Ashton said, "I'd be obliged. I realize a lady doesn't dine with strangers, but the circumstances are—"

"She's a landlady," Helen said, stuffing Ashton's treasure back inside her jacket. "Down around the corner, on Pastry Lane. Was once a bakery there. I could use a bite to eat."

The child could use a year of good meals, for starters. Ashton hoped the thought of hot food would tempt the girl from more reckless choices, but he kept a snug hold of her wrist nonetheless.

"Helen offered to return your goods, sir," Mrs. Bryce said. "Can't you let it go at that?"

"Perhaps," Ashton said. "But the longer we stand here debating, the more likely the authorities are to come along and take the child off to the halls of justice."

"Move, Helen." Mrs. Bryce seized the girl by the other wrist and started off in the direction of the nearest pub. "If the law gets hold of you, it's transportation or worse. Heaven knows what will become of your Sissy then."

Mention of the sister wilted the last of the child's resistance, and Ashton was soon crossing the street while more or less holding hands with a small, grubby female.

Who still had his lucky handkerchief.

The Goose was a respectable establishment, and because the theater custom was in general a cut above London's meanest denizens, the food might be better than passable. Ashton bought steak, potatoes, and a small pint for each of the ladies.

For himself, brandy. He was in London, prepared to take up residence at no less establishment than the Albany apartments. Titled lords ready to embark on the joys of the social Season drank brandy, or so Ewan claimed.

Besides, Ashton was hoarding his whisky for emergencies and celebrations, which this was not.

"Now," he said, when the child had shoveled down an adult portion of food in mere minutes. "You, Miss Helen, need to work on your technique if you're intent on a life of crime. Would you like some cobbler?"

Her eyes grew round while Mrs. Bryce wiped the child's chin with a linen serviette. "Don't encourage her. She'll end up on the gallows at the rate she's going. Do you want her death on your conscience?"

"Do you want her starvation on yours?"

Over the empty plate, the child's gaze bounced between the adults on either side of the table. "About that cobbler?"

Ashton reached into the girl's coat and withdrew his handkerchief, then passed it to Mrs. Bryce. "Wait here, child, if you want your cobbler."

He went to the bar, placed an order for three cobblers, and kept his back to the tables while the kitchen fetched the food.

When they'd chosen their table, Mrs. Bryce had taken off her hat and gloves. Her hair was an unusual color, as if she'd used henna to put a reddish tint in blond hair, which made no sense. Few women would choose red hair over blond, but then, Ashton was in the south. Everything from the sunshine to the scent of the streets was different.

"Your cobbler, sir," said the publican, putting a sack before Ashton. "We expect return of the plates in a day, if you please. Mrs. Bryce is always very good about that."

The barkeeper was short, graying, and solid—not fat. His blue apron was clean and free of mending.

"Mrs. Bryce patronizes your establishment often?"

"We're neighbors, across the alley and down a street, and her tenants frequently send out for their meals. She always sees to it we get our wares back. Haven't seen her in a bit, or had an order from her lately. Please give her my regards."

"She runs a good establishment?" Ashton asked.

"We hear nothing but compliments from her tenants. The place is very clean, very quiet, if you know what I mean. A widow can't be too careful. She keeps out the rabble, which isn't always a matter of who has coin, is it?"

Ashton had a very particular fondness for widows of discernment.

"True enough," he said, putting a few coins on the bar and gathering up the cobblers. "My thanks for a good meal."

A hearty meal. Not the refined delicacies Ashton had been expected to subsist on from the earldom's fussy Italian chef.

Mrs. Bryce was dissuading Helen from licking an empty plate when Ashton rejoined the ladies.

"I have here three cobblers," he said, setting the sack in the middle of the table. "I'm too full to enjoy my portion. Perhaps Helen's sister would like it?"

Fine gray eyes studied him from across the table. Mrs. Bryce's gaze was both direct and guarded, which made sense if she'd lost her husband. Widows were as vulnerable as the next woman, and yet, they had more freedom than any other class of female in Britain.

"Sissy loves her sweets," Helen said, kicking her legs against the bench. "I'm right fond of a treat myself."

Ashton slid onto the bench. "I'm fond of young ladies who take responsibility for their actions."

Helen shot Mrs. Bryce a puzzled glance.

"He means, you stole his handkerchief, and now we must decide what's to be done." Mrs. Bryce folded up Ashton's handkerchief and passed it to him.

Ashton set the cloth beside the cobblers. "What would you do, Helen, if somebody had stolen your lucky piece?"

"Ain't got a lucky piece. If I had a lucky piece, maybe I wouldn't be stealin' for me supper."

Ashton snatched off the girl's cap, and ratty blond braids tumbled down.

The child ducked her head as if braids were a mark of shame. "Gimme back me 'at, you!"

"How do you feel right now?"

"I'm that mad at you," Helen shot back. "You 'ad no right, and now everybody will know I'm a girl."

Ashton passed over the hat. Helen jammed it back on her head and stuffed both braids into her cap before folding her arms across her skinny chest.

"I gave you back your hat. All better?"

"You know it ain't. Damned Treacher saw me without me cap. Now I'll have to cut me hair again and stay out of his middens for weeks."

Mrs. Bryce watched this exchange, looking as if she was suppressing a smile. She had a full mouth, good bones, and a sunrise-on-summer-clouds complexion worthy of any countess. She was that puzzling creature, the woman who didn't know she was attractive.

Or perhaps—more puzzling still—she didn't care that she was attractive.

"So, wee Helen," Ashton said, setting the empty plates out of the girl's reach. "You've returned my handkerchief, and I've returned your cap. You still disrupted my day, gave me a bad start as I arrived in your fair city, and have inconvenienced Mrs. Bryce, who I gather is something of a friend. How will you make it right?"

The child scrunched up her nose and ceased kicking the bench. "I don't have anything to give you. You could thrash me."

From her perspective, that was preferable to being turned over to the authorities. Mrs. Bryce was no longer smiling, though.

"Then I'd have a smarting hand," Ashton said, "and more delay from my appointed rounds, because you would require a good deal of thrashing. Fortunately for us both, you are a lady, and a gentleman never raises his voice or his hand to a lady."

Now the looks Helen aimed at Mrs. Bryce were worried, as if Ashton had started babbling in tongues or speaking treason.

"Your papa wasn't a gentleman," Mrs. Bryce said gently. "We mustn't speak ill of the dead, but Mr. Fenwick is telling you the truth. Gentlemen are to protect ladies, not beat them. In theory."

"I don't know what a theory is, ma'am. Can I 'ave my cobbler yet?"

"May I," Mrs. Bryce replied. "I think Mr. Fenwick expects an apology, Helen, and you owe him one."

"I'm sorry I nicked your lucky piece. If I'd known it was a lucky piece, and not just fancy linen, I might not 'ave nicked it. Next time, keep your purse in your right-hand pocket, and nobody will be stealin' your lucky piece."

Helen clearly didn't realize this earnest advice was in no way helpful.

The comforts of the Albany awaited, and those comforts had been sufficient for ducal heirs, nabobs, and Byron himself. Once Ashton stepped over the threshold of that establishment, he declared himself the Earl of Kilkenney in new and irrevocable ways.

He'd rather be enjoying a plain meal at the Goose, and getting lessons in street sense from a half-pint thief.

"As it happens, I'm glad you didn't get my purse, because I'm newly arrived to London this very day, and to be penniless in London, as you know, is a precarious existence."

"Perilous," Mrs. Bryce translated. "Dangerous."

"Not if you know who your mates are and are quick on your feet," Helen said—more misguided instruction. She was a female without protection or means. Odds were, sooner or later, the London streets would be the death of her.

"You have nonetheless taken up a good deal of my time when my day was already too busy," Ashton said. "I need to establish myself at suitable lodgings. I need to hire a tiger for my conveyance. I need to get my bearings in anticipation of taking up responsibilities for the social Season."

Not only a busy day, but also a damned depressing one.

"You need a home," Mrs. Bryce said, and she wasn't translating for Helen. "Or a temporary address to serve as your home."

Her gaze turned appraising, though not in any intimate sense. The tilt of her head said she was evaluating Ashton as a lodger, not a lover. A novel experience for him, and a bit unnerving.

His attire was that of the stable master he'd been for years before he'd become afflicted with a title. Decent, if plain, riding jacket. Good quality, though his sleeve had been mended at the elbow. His linen was unstarched but clean enough for a man who'd been traveling, and a gold watch chain winked across his middle.

"What is your business in London, Mr. Fenwick?" Mrs. Bryce asked.

He was here for one purpose—to find a woman willing to be his countess. She'd have to comport herself like a faithful wife until at least two healthy male children had appeared. Not a complicated assignment, and the lady's compensation would be a lifetime of ease and a title.

Ashton had had three years to reconcile himself to such an arrangement, three years during which he'd tried to find the compromise—the woman he could adore *and* marry, who might adore him a little bit too—but she hadn't presented herself.

Though three wee nieces had arrived.

"My excursion to the capital is primarily social," Ashton said. "I'm renewing acquaintances with a few friends and tending to business while the weather is fair. I'll return north in the summer."

And be damned glad to do so. According to Ewan, house parties followed the social Season, and rather than hunting grouse, Ashton could pass his summer with further rounds of countess hunting.

He could take up that apartment at the Albany some other day. Next week would do.

Or the week after.

A voice in Ashton's head said he was putting off the inevitable, retreating when he ought to be marching forward. Another voice said Mrs. Bryce would not consider offering a strange man lodgings unless she needed a lodger desperately.

"As it happens," Mrs. Bryce said, "I have an apartment available. A sitting room and bedroom, with antechamber, and kitchen privileges. Breakfast, tea, and candles are included, and your rooms will be cleaned twice weekly, Tuesday and Friday. Bad behavior or excessive noise is grounds for eviction, and if you sing or play a musical instrument, you will do so only at decent hours. Coal is extra, payable by the week."

"Mrs. Bryce makes the best porridge," Helen added. "She puts cream on it if it's too hot."

Don't put off what must be done. Don't shirk your duty.

"What is your direction?" Ashton asked.

"Pastry Lane is around the corner and halfway down the street," Mrs. Bryce said. "The rooms are quiet, clean, and unpretentious, but suitable for entertaining such callers as a gentleman might properly have."

No game girls, in other words.

"There's a garden," Helen offered. "Big enough for Mrs. Bryce's herbs, but not big enough for a dog. She has a cat."

Mrs. Bryce also, apparently, had something of a champion in Helen.

The child was skinny, but not starving. When truly deprived of food for a long period, the body lost the ability to handle a meal of steak and potatoes washed down by a small pint of ale. Helen's diet might be spare and irregular, but Mrs. Bryce's porridge figured on the menu often enough to keep body and soul together.

"I like cats," Ashton said. "What about a mews?"

"No mews, I'm afraid," Mrs. Bryce said, brushing a hand over the handkerchief on the table. "If you need a mews, I can suggest Mrs. Grimbly, off of Bow Street, though you must provide your own groom."

The fingers stroking over Ashton's handkerchief were slightly red, the back of Mrs. Bryce's hand freckled. No rings, and a pale scar ran from wrist to thumb.

Not the hands of a countess, though, to Ashton, beautiful in their way.

"I can stable my horses elsewhere," Ashton said. "My brother is more familiar with London than I am and recommended an establishment he and his friends use. What do you charge?"

She named a figure, neither cheap nor exorbitant, though her focus on the handkerchief had become fixed. The cuff of her cloak was fraying, her straw hat was the lowliest millinery short of Helen's battered cap.

Mrs. Bryce was in need of coin, while Ashton was in need of peace and quiet. The social Season hadn't yet begun, and a week or two of reconnaissance was simply the act of a prudent man—or a reluctant earl.

"Mrs. Bryce bakes her own bread," Helen said. "And she serves it with *butter and jam.*"

"May we start with a two-week lease?" Ashton asked. "I am new to London, and a trial period makes sense for all parties."

"That will be acceptable, though I'll want the rent for both weeks in advance with an allowance for coal."

Ashton extended his hand across the table. "Mrs. Bryce, we have a bargain."

Order your copy of Ashton: Lord of Truth!

CPSIA information can be obtained
at www.ICGtesting.com
Printed in the USA
LVHW041154301222
736164LV00004B/102

9 781941 419083